COURT OF CLAWS
BRIAR BOLEYN

Cover Design by Artscandare Book Cover Design

Developmental Editing by Rachel Bunner, Rachel's Top Edits

Proofreading by The Marginatrix

Flourish Art by Polina K, Emmie Norfolk, Gordon Johnson (GDJ)

ACKNOWLEDGEMENTS

To my ARC readers who are named and renamed in the pages of this book. Thank you for allowing me the creative freedom to make characters in your honor, human and Bearkin alike!

To the sisters of the world who read with us and share our delight in magic and fantasy.

Leslie Morgan @theoriginal_b00k_nerd
Isra K, @chaiwithbooks
Kelly P. And Lady Shinron @kale_dragon
Shelbe Heckman @shelbe_reads
Phyllica Williams @phyllica_catherine
Jenal Hall @jenalreads
Mya Wall @bookishmya
A'Dailya Bontemps @bookedagoodtime
Tuva Wiggen Mo @tuvareads
Molly Dunn, @mollyolecule
Rebekah Winter, @thank.thegods.for.smut
Ashley Stevenson, @ashstevensonisreading
Rebecca Stevens, @fueledbybooksandespresso
Meghal Patel, @bookish.apothecary
Holly Bretanus, @acourtofthornsandholly
Kelly Hammond, @picklespublishing
Nicole Merkx @Koowl_
Shannon Isom @shannonl0vesbooks
Rachel Bunner, @rachels.top.edits

Sonya J., @redsonya_loves_to_read
Taylor, @taylorcorelibrary
Elika Z., @elleandherlibrary

Find me on Instagram or contact me via email to join my ARC Team!
author@briarboleyn.com

CONTENT & TRIGGER WARNINGS

Blood of a Fae is a dark fantasy romance series that deals with topics which some readers may understandably find triggering.

A trigger and content warnings list may be found at the end of the book.

Please keep in mind that the content warnings list will spoil certain plot elements. Avoid reading the trigger warnings list if you do not have any triggers and do not wish to know specific details about the plot in advance.

JOIN MY NEWSLETTER

CONTENTS

PRONUNCIATION GUIDE

Aercanum: AIR-kay-num

Agravaine Emrys: Ag-ra-VAYN EM-ris

Ambrilith: AM-bri-lith

Atropa: uh-TROH-puh

Avriel: AV-ree-el

Bearkin: BEAR-kin

Brasad: BRAH-sad

Breena: BREE-nuh

Cerunnos: Ser-UHN-os

Devina: DEH-vee-nuh

Ector Prennell: EK-tor Pren-ELL

Eleusia: EL-oo-see-uh

Enid: EE-nid

Erion: EH-ree-on

Eskira: es-KEER-ah

Ettarde: eh-TAHRD

Exmoor: EX-moor

Fenrir: FEN-reer

Florian Emrys: FLOH-ree-an EM-ris

Galahad Prennell: GAL-uh-had Pren-ELL

Gawain: GA-wayn

Gelert: GEL-ert

Glatisants: GLAH-tis-ants

Gorlois: GOR-lwah

Halyna: Ha-LEE-nuh

Hawl: HALL

Haya: HI-uh

Idrisane: ID-ri-zayn

Javer: JAH-ver

Kairos Draven Venator: KAI-ros DRA-ven Veh-NAH-tohr

Kastra: KAS-truh

Kaye: KAY

Khor'a'val: KOR-a-VAL

Khor: KOR

Khorva: KOR-vuh

Lancelet de Troyes: LAN-suh-let deh TROYZ

Laverna: la-VER-na

Lucius Venator: LOO-shus Veh-NAH-tohr

Lyonesse: LEE-oh-ness

Lyrastra: LIE-rah-struh

Malkah: MAL-kah

Marzanna: mar-ZAH-nuh

Meridium: MEH-ri-dee-um

Myntra: MIN-truh

Nedola: NED-o-la

Nerov: NEH-rov

Noctasia: nok-TAY-zhuh

Nodori: no-DOH-ree

Numenos: NOO-meh-nos

Odelna: o-DEL-nuh

Orcades: OR-kay-deez

Orin's Horn: OR-inz HORN

Pelleas: Pel-LEE-us

Pendrath: PEN-drath

Perun: PER-uhn

Rhea: RAY-uh

Rheged: RAY-ghed

Rychel: RYE-chel

Selwyn: SEL-win

Sephone Venator: se-FOHN-ee

Siabra: SHAY-bruh

Sorega: soh-RAY-guh

Tabar: TAY-bar

Taina: TIE-nuh

Ulpheas: UHL-fee-us

Ursidaur: UR-si-dor

Uther: OO-thur

Valtain: val-TAYN

Varis: VAR-is

Vela: VAY-luh

Verdantail: ver-DAN-tail

Vesper: VES-per

Vespera: ves-PAIR-uh

Ygraine: Ee-GRAYN

Zephrae: ZEF-ray

Zorya: ZOHR-ee-uh

BOOK I

PROLOGUE

*M*eridium, *Valtain*

The air was filled with screaming and wailing.

Covering one ear with her free hand in a fruitless effort to drown out the sound, the woman hurried across the courtyard.

In her arms, the child she held whimpered softly and burrowed his face more tightly against his mother's shoulder.

"Shhh, shhh," she murmured. "You're safe now. Everything will be all right." Brushing her hand over her son's back gently, she tried to reassure him with her touch.

The words had to be true. Anything else was unthinkable.

Her eyes scanned quickly, constantly.

There!

Along one stone wall of the courtyard was a row of arched passageways leading to other rooms in the complex. The woman hurried over to one, the child still pressed tightly to her chest.

They were just in time. As she stepped into the shadowy passage, an eruption of screams filled the courtyard from the way they had just come.

The boy began to tremble. His mother wrapped her arms tightly around him. "Shhh, shhh," she reminded him.

Her eyes were furtive and desperate as she made her way further into the passage.

There was a scrambling sound from outside the entrance.

A group of small figures streamed past. Running over the ground on all fours like animals. Chasing something. Someone.

More screaming. Then pleas. Words the woman could pick out but didn't want to.

A ripping and tearing sound joined the screams.

She felt herself begin to tremble as hard as the boy.

Her hand touched a latch. She inhaled sharply. "There." She moved her hand and an opening in the stone wall appeared. Stepping in quickly, she closed the stone panel behind her, pressing until she heard the click of the latch.

At last, there was quiet. Inside the cool, stone room all was dark and still.

The woman fumbled her free hand along the wall. Light burst up from a torch, filling the small room with pinpricks of dust.

She sank to her knees, cradling the boy against her, and leaned back against the cold stone wall.

"Where are we?" The boy's weak voice suggested he did not much care but had asked the question more from habit than anything.

His eyes were dull and glazed, his skin a pale sickly shade of gray. While his mother's shaking had subsided, the boy had not stopped trembling since he had started.

The woman did not notice. She merely clasped the child closer to her body.

"A storage room," she murmured. "I was here once before, with my father as a child. He was in charge of overseeing the celebration." She looked around the room slowly. "They stored wine here then."

The child leaned his cheek against his mother's chest, his own rising and falling weakly.

The woman caressed the boy's hair.

"Sleep now, my love. You are safe here. With me." She kissed his brow and only then did she seem surprised.

"You are so cold, my darling." She looked down at the boy's face. "You told me you had not eaten or drunk anything since we arrived at the festival."

The little boy did not answer. His eyes were half-closed.

His mother gave a frantic shake, her grip harder than it would normally have been. The child's eyes opened slowly.

"I forgot," he said hollowly. "I forgot about the tea. I had a sip of Ashlyn's tea. Just a sip."

"A sip." The woman's face was ashen. "Perhaps it will not matter."

Perhaps this strange plague was not from food or drink at all, she thought to herself. If it was, how was it that none of the adults had been affected?

Only children. All of their children.

Some had dropped, withering away in their parents' arms, their lives vanishing as swiftly as dew from the petals of a flower in the morning sun.

Others had turned sickly. Life seemed to go out of them. And then...

The woman shuddered and looked down at her son again.

His breathing had become a rattle. His lips were dry and parted.

"My love." The words were a plea. "No." She shook her head, the tears already falling. "No, no."

The boy's eyes closed slowly. His body was limp in her arms. She pressed her face to the child's head, breathing in the scent of his hair, his skin, holding him close to her breast as she had since he was an infant.

She had always protected him. How could she have failed him today?

The boy's breathing was slowing.

His mother let out a keening wail. "Not my child. Not my boy."

But already the child was motionless in her arms and she knew.

A sob broke from her lips. First one, then another.

Time passed. When she finally lifted her head, her face was red and tear-streaked and the torch had burned low.

She stared dully across the room, noticing for the first time what she had not been attentive enough to observe in her haste and panic.

A large stone archway lay on the far side of the chamber, grand and imposing, its smooth gray stone weathered but enduring. It stretched high up to the ceiling, covered in layers of cobwebs and dust.

Sheets that had once been white trailed over it. The coverings may once have hidden it completely but now they had fallen away and hung in tatters blowing in an unseen breeze like ghostly shrouds.

The woman stared at the arch. A silent sentinel watching her from the darkness, its former grandeur muted by years of neglect.

A choked whimper escaped her lips. She moved, as if to rise and step towards the archway, then seemed to remember the boy's body in her arms. She looked down at the pale face, the frozen features, and a fresh wave of sobs wracked her frame.

Bending her head low, she cradled the boy, rocking him for the last time, then gently laid him on the floor and took a tentative step towards the arch.

A gurgling sound filled the room behind her, as if from a throat filled with water.

The woman paused, her face a mask of horror.

The child was stirring where he lay on the floor. His lips were parting.

It defied belief. It defied hope.

The woman's eyes widened, fresh tears streaming down her cheeks. "No, no. Not this. Spare him, Vela, spare him, I beg of you."

But the gods were silent as the boy's eyes slowly re-opened.

CHAPTER 1

The dream was so real I was shaking. My mind was still full of the image of the fae woman sitting alone in the dark, holding her dead child's body, then feeling that same small body begin to stir once more—but this time with a horrible and unnatural life.

I felt weak and confused. My body still overcome simply from the effort of processing an entirely fictional experience.

I forced my mind back to the last thing I remembered before the dream.

There was only blackness. An empty space I knew should be filled with rich detail.

Panic started to seize me. Where was I? What was this?

My eyes remained closed as I drew a quick breath, then moved my hands to clutch at the sheets on the bed in which I lay.

But my hands would not move.

Voices began to fill my ears. They were coming from close by.

"This? This is what everyone is talking about?" A woman's voice. She sounded outraged.

"Indeed. I admit I don't see what all the fuss is about. Plain creature, isn't she?" A man's voice. Bored and blasé.

My eyelids flickered, once, twice, closed. For a moment, I felt a start of terror, afraid they were not going to open at all.

I willed them open. Slowly they lifted. The effort took more time than it should have. The light was blinding at first.

"Yet he brought this fae bitch back." The woman again. Harsh and accusing. She sounded very near me.

"Look at the little thing. Pale as snow. Eyes fluttering like a moth." The man. It sounded as if he were standing over me. "Typical Valtain." He gave a derisive snort.

They were talking about me. That much was clear. I was finding it difficult to care, however. They were only a small part of all that was disorienting.

Where was I? I knew I was lying down. And that was about it.

I felt horribly exposed. Was I even clothed?

I tried to move my head, but was held in place. I could only blink slowly.

The woman answered the question for me. I felt a hand touch my chest lightly and something was flicked off. A blanket or sheet. How far had she pulled it down?

I felt a swell of fury go through me and cursed my frozen limbs. Why couldn't I move this time? Was I dead?

It was a stupid thought and yet suddenly I felt afraid I was trapped in some underworld where cruel strangers stood over my body, examining me and poking fun. Surely it was not far off from the truth of what was happening.

I screamed silently at my muscles to move, my limbs to raise. Nothing happened.

"Ah, I thought so." The woman was amused. "Look at this, would you?"

Footsteps came closer on my right side.

"Why the girl has already been marked. And not by him, it seems." The man sounded cruelly delighted. "A name. Florian? What the fuck is a Florian? Some man she let bed her, I suppose."

I felt a wave of shame wash over me. So the scars had not faded as much as I had hoped. That bastard's name was still legible upon my flesh.

Florian's lasting legacy.

Well, he would have no other. I had made very certain of that.

"Perhaps it isn't a man's name but a woman's."

"Only a man would mark a woman like that," the man said. "Men don't want other men touching their things. She's been used before, clearly." I could practically see the sneer on his face. "I bet she liked it, too."

"Secondhand fae bitch," the woman spat, leaning down over me. "Yet he returned with *her*. Why? Why her? She is not even Siabra."

The fury in her voice made me rejoice. She might insult me all she liked, but evidently my presence alone was enough to infuriate her. And this was a woman I could tell I would delight in infuriating with every opportunity. If only I could spit in her eye and tell her so to her face.

My vision was coming into focus as my eyes became accustomed to the light. I blinked and the woman's face began to take shape.

Narrow bright black eyes. Sharp, angular cheekbones. Glossy black hair that hung long around her shoulders. She had every claim to beauty from the little I could see.

"To rub her in your face, I suppose. And it's working all too well, isn't it?" The man gave a lazy yawn. "She's waking up. We should leave. Come on. Even you know better than to push him too far."

"Shall I leave her in this state or release her?" the woman pondered.

Rage flashed like a bright light. *She* had done this to me? This woman was the reason I was frozen like this?

How I had had enough of being someone's plaything. A toy to be molded and shaped, forced into poses and positions. I had told myself no one would ever do such a thing to me again. Yet here I was.

Silently I swore revenge. Yet at the same time, I marveled at her power. She held me in place without even lifting a hand. How? How had she done it? What sort of magic did these people possess?

I recalled the word she had used. Siabra. Someone else had used the same word, not very long ago. A violet-haired woman who had spat it like a curse.

Siabra. They were that and I was not. I was something else to them. Something different enough or strange enough to poke fun of.

"Oh, I rather think the latter, don't you?" the man drawled. "Much more fun that way. Perhaps she'll even wet herself before he comes back."

"You did say he was across the palace?" the woman demanded. "In that case, we have plenty of time. Perhaps I'll do some further... redecorating."

A world of horrific possibilities opened in my mind.

"Yes, but I still think we should..."

There was a slamming sound. Like two heavy double doors crashing open, shoved hard by someone who didn't give a damn about cracking the walls. Even without being able to move my limbs, my heart gave a jolt.

Heavy footsteps paced towards us.

"Shit," I heard the man mutter nervously. "Fucking shit."

Evidently made of sterner stuff than her companion, the woman said nothing.

"Release her. Now." The newcomer's voice was deep, furious, and all-too-familiar.

My heart gave a painful lurch.

Draven.

Yes. I knew him. The tenseness of my body had eased imperceptibly at the sound of his voice. He was familiar. Everything in me said I could trust him.

"Release her now, Lyrastra. You will not like what will happen if I must ask you again."

Instantly I felt my body relax. I flexed my fingers and with relief felt them connect with cool fabric.

I raised my arm, felt it wobble, but managed to touch a hand to my chest.

With relief, I found I was clothed. I wore a thin shift of some kind. A sheet was draped across my body. I fumbled, pulling it higher over my chest.

Then I tried to sit up. This was a conversation I very much wished to participate in.

But the strain was too much. When I tried to prop my elbow up, even that much effort left me trembling.

I gritted my teeth and tried once more. This time I managed to push myself a few inches back in the bed. Enough for me to lift my head a little higher on the pillow on which it lay.

Enough for me to see those around me.

Turning my head slowly, I took in my surroundings.

I was in a bedchamber, as I had already surmised.

The room was incredibly opulent.

It was not hyperbole to say the decor dripped with gold.

Every surface gleamed with the bright yellow stuff, from the polished four-poster bed to the burnished walls made of patterned gold panels. Even the floors ran with the lustrous metal. Black and white marble stone that looked as if pure gold had been poured over it and then swirled into beautiful designs.

High above our heads, a large chandelier illuminated the room, gold and dripping with green jewels. The light had been dimmed–perhaps out of courtesy as I slept. Now it cast long shadows on the floor below.

Half-way across the room, Draven stood in the shadows. He had yet to step into the light.

The woman who he had called Lyrastra was near the bed, a few feet to my left.

She stood very still, her face contorted in stubborn anger. Even as my hate for her mounted, I couldn't help but acknowledge her loveliness. Lyrastra was tall and willowy, with long, lithe limbs. Dark hair cascaded down her back like a waterfall of silk. She wore a dress of scarlet silk, its edges trimmed with gold, and overtop that a long, flowing cape of shimmering burgundy hung around her shoulders, fastened at the neck with a clasp of gold. Narrow sandal straps studded with tiny rubies wound up her ankles, showcasing her long perfectly-formed legs.

Despite her wealth of beauty, there was an ice to her that betrayed her cruel streak. She held herself with a haughty, imperious air. There was evidently no doubt in her mind that she was above *me* in all ways.

But the real question was why did she bear me such malice in the first place?

No, I reminded myself. The real question is where the hell are you?

I opened my mouth to ask just that, but then I caught sight of the look on Draven's face and decided perhaps I could wait just a few more minutes.

"What the fuck are you two doing in here?"

He sounded furious. He looked furious. I felt a sense of glee growing. Good. These two were in for a treat. Let the wrath of Kairos Draven be unleashed upon them.

But even I wasn't prepared for what came next.

Draven stepped into the light. My mouth may have fallen open.

He looked the same as he always had... and yet entirely different.

As always, he was a vision of masculine beauty. But then, I was used to that part of things. Wasn't I?

His piercing green eyes glowed in the light of the golden chandelier. The thin silver ring he always wore in his left ear was there, contrasting against his rich bronzed skin. The upper part of his body was encased in armor, made of a shining black metal. Fitted black pants hugged the muscles of his thighs and his lean legs, as he moved purposely and deliberately towards the bed. Towards me.

But it was his horns that had really caught my attention. Small horns of black bone that jutted out from his forehead.

My memory might have been a hazy jumble, but I was fairly certain I would have remembered the horns.

Not to mention the distinctive points of his ears which mirrored my own.

Horns and points.

No, it wasn't possible.

I felt dizzy as I stared at the horns. They hinted at something primal and untamed lurking just below the surface. Something I couldn't deny I'd always suspected was there.

But this? Horns and points. No. It wasn't possible. It just... Wasn't.

Kairos Draven was fucking fae.

And not just any kind of fae. He was the very kind I'd seen portrayed on the wall of the Temple of the Three. The kind I'd whined to Draven about worrying I'd turn out to be.

He'd told me not to worry. That I showed no sign of sprouting horns or claws.

I felt choked laughter crowd my throat. Well, he'd certainly have known, wouldn't he?

Somehow, I managed to keep my shit together as Draven crossed over to the bed. For a moment his eyes darted left then right between my two brazen visitors.

He seemed to come to a decision and crossed towards the man.

"Ulpheas. You miserable spineless creeping toad. I asked you a question."

Ulpheas, was it? Ulpheas had a lean build with narrow shoulders and a narrow waist. He was tall, but not as tall as Draven. He was not as handsome either, though he was not an unattractive man. Something about him reminded me of a bright, preening bird. His hair was a honey-blond, styled in a fashionable cut that seemed artfully tousled. His clothes were even more ornate than his female companion's. I watched as he blinked blue eyes tinged by heavy dark blonde lashes up at Draven, and was opening his mouth to speak when he lost his chance.

Draven's hand wrapped around Ulpheas's throat and lifted him into the air with ease.

A choked sound emerged.

"You dared to come in here. To bring *her* here. As if you had any right to step foot in this room."

A choking came again. I thought Ulpheas might have been trying to say "sorry" but if so, he was far too late.

Draven dropped Ulpheas to the floor with a thud.

"I saw her raise her blanket back up over herself when I came in. Which one of you dared to touch her? Speak up."

I felt a twinge of annoyance. I appreciated what Draven was trying to do, but I had a name, didn't I? I could speak for myself and tell him who had done it.

But clearly Draven didn't want that. Or he didn't care to hear from me.

For a moment, there was silence and I wondered if Ulpheas and Lyrastra would each blame the other. Or perhaps deny the accusation altogether.

"I did." Lyrastra didn't sound particularly apologetic. She was practically purring. "And why, might I ask, does your precious prize have another man's name carved into her chest, my esteemed lord?"

"No." Draven's voice was cold.

"No?"

"No. You may not ask. You may go. Now. Before I really lose my temper, Lyrastra. You will not like it if I do." He pointed at where Ulpheas was rising from the floor. "By rights that should have been you. Don't think I don't know that."

Lyrastra smiled slowly. "Come now, we are family. Besides, you would never harm a woman."

"I would never harm a *defenseless* woman. There is a significant distinction." Draven tilted his head slightly towards the door. "Now get out. If I ever catch either of you anywhere near this suite again, my response will be harsh and swift. Consider this a restrained warning courtesy of my recent return."

Lyrastra seemed in no hurry to go. Instead, she turned her head slowly to look down at me.

I gasped as I got my first good look at her eyes. Mesmerizing and reptilian. They were the eyes of a snake. The iris was divided into thin, vertical slits of gold, yellow, and iridescent purple. With a flash, her pupils dilated and contracted, revealing a dark obsidian hue that contrasted with the vivid colors of the iris.

"Valtain whore." The words were spat so quietly I didn't think anyone but me had heard.

She turned away, her long slender limbs carrying her towards the door with a serpentine grace.

When the door had closed firmly behind my two unwanted guests, Draven approached me. "Are you all right? Can you move? Did they hurt you?"

"That woman is your *family*?" I was appalled. Even more appalling was the way the words would hardly emerge from my lips at all. My voice was dry and raspy. Just how long had I been asleep? "How exactly are you related?"

"She's my sister-in-law," Draven said shortly. "Are you hungry?" He moved towards a door across the room I hadn't noticed before.

"Wait," I said sharply. "Stop." I willed strength into my arms, then pushed myself up into a sitting position with everything I had. "Don't you dare walk away. Where the fuck am I? What is this place? What's happened to me?"

His pace slowed, almost begrudgingly.

Turning back towards me, something like hesitation crossed his handsome face. Was he afraid? Afraid to speak to me? Why?

"I know you, I remember you," I assured him quickly. "I remember almost everything." At least, I thought I did. "We went into the ruins... But then..." I trailed off. "It must have been last night. Or the night before."

Draven's eyes narrowed. "You can't remember anything after that?"

"I..." I bit my lip, feeling frustrated. "No, I remember. We entered the ruins. There were harpies."

He waited expectantly. "Yes. And then?"

"And then..." I blew out my lip. "We set up camp."

Draven's face softened slightly. "Who set up the camp? Who was with us? Besides you and me. Do you remember?"

He wanted me to remember. For some reason that alone was a relief. He hadn't... Well, done something to me. Like Lyrastra had. If I couldn't recall some things, it had nothing to do with him.

I wracked my brain. "You. Me. The horses."

A faint look of amusement crossed his face. "Yes, there were horses. You'll be happy to know Haya is safe and stabled. Who else? Think, Morgan." His voice was much gentler than it had been with Lyrastra and Ulpheas.

I hesitated. "A... child?"

"Good. A girl. Yes." He paused. "Odelna was her name."

"Was?" I said sharply. "Is she...?"

"She's safe," he assured me quickly, but an odd look had come over his face.

And then with a surge, like water breaking through a dam, I remembered.

"Oh gods..." I whispered. "Lancelet. Lancelet was there."

Draven ran a hand over his face. "Yes. She was with us, too."

My breathing quickened. "I remember. I remember now. She was dragged away by those... by those fucking things. Those fucking monsters. Those... those children."

Pain crossed his face. "The children. Yes."

I flung back the blanket that covered me and forced myself to sit up. Every muscle in my body shrieked in protest. I could feel myself starting to tremble again. "We have to go back. We have to go back for her, Draven. Did you just... did you just leave her there? How could you?" Panic was rising in me.

"Morgan, lie down. You have to understand. About Lancelet..."

"No, no," I said, shaking my head furiously. "Don't you dare say it. Don't you dare. She was still alive. She might still be alive. We have to go back. We have to go *now*."

Draven lifted a hand slowly. For a moment I thought he was going to push back a lock of his raven-black hair. Instead he reached out towards me and gently pushed against the center of my chest just above my ribs.

I fell back against the bed as if struck by a strong wind.

He withdrew his hand. It had been the lightest and briefest of touches.

And yet the moment he touched me, I felt lightheaded and strange. My heart was beating too fast. My skin felt hot where he had touched it. I shook my head, trying to shake off the sensation.

For a split second, I caught a similar perplexed expression on Draven's face. Then it smoothed into inscrutability.

"You can't even sit up," he observed. "But you want to stage a rescue."

"Yes, I want to stage a fucking rescue," I exclaimed, struggling to regain my upright position. "The real question is why don't you?"

He held my gaze steadily. "Because I already have, Morgan."

I was speechless for a moment. Then, "What's that supposed to mean? What are you talking about?" I glanced at his forehead. "And while we're at it, when are you going to tell me where the fuck I am and since when have you had horns on your head?"

My cheeks felt hot. With embarrassment or anger, I wasn't sure. But something wasn't right. That much was abundantly clear. Something was very, very wrong. And I needed to figure out what.

Draven clasped his hands and looked down at them. I felt a wave of sick apprehension. He didn't want to meet my eyes. That couldn't be good.

He sighed. "All fair questions. But Lancelet first, yes?"

"Fine," I snapped. "Give me whatever bullshit excuse you want to make and then let's go back there and find her."

I didn't want to ask how far back "there" was. I was afraid I wasn't going to like the answer very much.

Draven didn't rise to my bait. "She's gone, Morgan. But I know you aren't going to believe me. Still, you're going to have to trust me." He glanced at me and caught me shaking my head stubbornly. "Fuck. How do I explain everything?"

"Start at the beginning," I suggested pointedly. "What did you do when she was dragged away?"

He looked at me quizzically. "Maybe we should start with what *you* did. What exactly do you remember?"

"What I did..." I started. Then I stopped. What had I done? "I..."

I must have looked confused.

Draven cleared his throat awkwardly. "Vesper. Do you remember Vesper?"

"Of course, I remember Vesper. He... I..." I stopped. "He made me leave you. Leave her. He dragged me away."

I watched Draven's face harden. "I thought he was saving you. He had seemed so infatuated. What a fucking fool I was."

A bitter laugh rang from my lips. "What a fucking fool *you* were? What about me? I was the one kissing the treacherous fuck."

"And he turned out to be different than you had thought, I take it? What did you learn about him?" Draven asked carefully.

I could see what he was trying to do. Or trying not to do, I should say. He was trying not to rub it in. That he'd been right. That I'd moved to fast. Trusted too quickly.

And then been wrong. Dead wrong.

"He's dead," I said hollowly. "Does it matter?"

Draven met my eyes. "I know, Morgan. I saw the pile of ashes."

Bile rose in my stomach as I remembered. Oh yes, I had killed Vesper. I had done more than that. I had fucking incinerated the man.

"He betrayed me. He tried to kill me." I wasn't sure if I was offering the words in my defense or as a horrid boast of some sort.

Besides, there was so much more to it than that. Vesper had already stabbed me. He hadn't seemed particularly eager to finish me off though. I might have let him take the sword and leave. Then crawled away. Maybe I would even have made it.

But Vesper hadn't been satisfied with just taking the sword and wounding me.

He'd wanted to lie in wait for Draven and the others.

Odelna, a voice in my head whispered. Draven and Odelna. There were no others. Even then, you knew that, didn't you? But you couldn't let him hurt Draven. You had to do everything you could to stop him. Everything, no matter what it was. No matter what the cost.

Shut up, I told myself. Lancelet might have been following behind. Anything had been possible then.

And now?

I could feel Draven's eyes on me. "You turned him to ashes, Morgan. How exactly were you able to do that?"

I met his green gaze then averted my head. "I don't want to talk about it."

He shrugged. "Fine. So, Vesper tried to kill you and instead you killed him. But he'd almost succeeded."

I understood. "You found me. Was I...?" Did I even want to know?

"You were barely breathing."

I gave a short laugh. "I'm surprised I was at all."

I saw a tumult of emotions cross his face. Fury, regret, and something else. "What matters is that you're here now. You're alive."

"But Lancelet's not," I retorted. "Or so you claim. Wherever here is."

I felt dizzy with rage and grief and panic. I felt dizzy with not knowing which of those feelings I should give precedence to. I didn't want it to be grief or panic. So I went with rage.

Pushing myself higher up in the bed, I hid my trembling hands beneath the sheet. "Now tell me where she is. Tell me where my friend is, Draven. Or so help me, by the Three I will..."

I nearly said "blast this room to smithereens," but stopped myself just in time. Draven had never witnessed my magic. And the Three knew I didn't think I could access it that easily. The thought of what I had done to Vesper was still fresh in my mind. Did I really want to make an empty threat when I had no intention of ever using magic again if I could help it?

I clenched my jaw. "Don't make me fucking pull those horns off."

Draven surprised me by giving a low chuckle. "They're more firmly attached than they might look."

I didn't smile back. "Fascinating. And yet to me they seem to have appeared almost as if by magic. Care to explain?"

Draven looked away. "Let's finish discussing Lancelet first. You said you wanted to know."

"Fine."

"I told you before that she was gone. When Vesper left with you, I tried to get to her. She was under attack, as you witnessed. But I was too late. Those... things... dragged her into a passageway. I was shielding Odelna."

I shifted uncomfortably in the bed. That I remembered. I had left him with a small child unable to defend herself and now I was berating him for failing to save my friend, too.

"When I was finished, I searched for her but she was gone. There were too many of them for me to take Odelna farther into the passage." He met my gaze. "I left her. I left Lancelet. I let her be dragged away. Don't think I don't know that. The blame lies with me."

I felt my cheeks flood with shame. The blame was not his alone and we both knew that. "I left her, too."

"You did what I told you to do," he said. "Do you remember?"

I remembered. I remembered the expression on his face from across the room as he had realized he couldn't save us all. Couldn't come to *me* without leaving a child to die, let alone get to Lancelet.

I didn't think I would ever forget it.

And yet... he *had* saved me. Because here I was.

He had said he would find me. And he had.

Now I studied his face and what I saw surprised me. Grief. If it wasn't for me, then it must be for... Shit. He believed what he was telling me.

"I couldn't get to her. I had to get Odelna away safely. We were responsible for her. I had to find you. I thought maybe with you and Vesper, we could go back and try to..." He shook his head. "Well, that didn't quite work out. I found you bleeding out on the floor. I managed to get you back here. Get you to a healer. And you've been recovering ever since."

I wanted so badly to ask where "here" was. But I didn't want to stop the flow of his words.

"I went back the very next day, Morgan. And I didn't go alone. I took people with me. We scoured that place. Every inch of it. We went into every passageway."

My heart began to hammer. "And? What did you find?"

"What did we find when we went back? Many more of those creatures. We put them down, whenever we came across one."

Creatures. Monsters. Things. Someone's child. Children.

"But we found no trace of Lancelet." He turned his head and looked at me. There was sorrow in his emerald eyes. "I had hoped I could at least bring her body back to you. But in the end, we couldn't even do that much."

I swallowed hard. "No. She couldn't have just disappeared."

"She didn't just disappear. Don't make me say the words, Morgan. Please. You know what must have happened to her."

Bile rose in my throat again.

Eaten. He meant she had been eaten. Every piece of her had been torn apart. Flesh shredded. Bones chewed. I thought of the room Vesper had led me through, with the floor littered with gnawed-on bones.

Would I have recognized Lancelet from merely her bones?

"No." The word came out as a whimper. I didn't trust myself to say more. I didn't want to cry. I wouldn't. Still, I felt hot tears fill my eyes.

"I've lost friends, too. It never seems real." Draven's face was weary. "You asked where you are. I know I owe you an explanation."

I could only manage a nod.

"I took you home. To my home." He hesitated. "To my court, I suppose I should say. You're in the heart of the Siabra Empire. In the city of Noctasia, in the kingdom of Sorega."

I felt a rushing in my ears. None of the names were making any sense.

Draven hesitated again. Longer this time. "On the continent of Myntra."

The rushing grew louder.

"I beg your pardon." My eyes were still wet but the tears were now forgotten. "I must have misheard you. Did you say...continent?"

Draven nodded slowly.

"We're not on Eskira? We're... somewhere else?"

He nodded again and I wanted to punch him.

"What the fuck have you done?" I exploded. "How could you have taken me to another fucking continent? You fucking liar! You claimed to have searched for Lancelet? How? How was that possible?"

"You already know how. There are ways. To travel vast distances."

I stared. "You used an archway?"

"Something like that. I brought you back here. Then I traveled back. That same day. As soon as I knew you were... stable. That wasn't a lie."

I felt slightly remorseful for calling him a liar, but only slightly.

"You've kidnapped me!" I caught his expression. "And don't you dare say that's nothing new," I said furiously. "You know this is different. Before we weren't on an entirely different continent!"

"But you still considered yourself abducted?"

"You weren't really abducting me," I admitted. "Not then. But this! Yes! Take me the fuck back! Now!"

Draven's jaw locked. "I can't do that. Not yet at least."

"What the hell do you mean you can't take me back yet. I have to go back. Kaye is all alone. Lancelet's family... I have to tell them. And as for Arthur..." He could have burned Camelot to the ground by now for all I knew.

Draven held up a hand. I wondered when in the history of trying to calm someone down that had ever managed to work. "I know. I know you're upset. You have every right to be upset. But I can't take you back."

"Like hell you can't," I shouted. "You have the power to take me from one continent to another. You can take me right back again if you wanted to!"

He shook his head stubbornly.

"You could take me back," I translated. "But you don't *want* to. Why?"

He said nothing.

"Fine. I'll walk back." I started to struggle out of the bed.

"You're weak as a kitten. And besides, there's an ocean between Eskira and Myntra. Don't you know your geography?"

The Kastra Sea. I remembered it. Suddenly I hated the fucking thing for existing.

"Most people in Pendrath are only vaguely aware that Myntra even exists," I snapped. "As someone who claimed to be a native to Eskira, shouldn't *you* know that? Fine. There's an ocean. I suppose I'll have to charter a fucking boat. After I walk to the coast."

"It's a perilous journey."

"And my other option is what? You really think I'm going to stay here? With you?" I demanded, my voice beginning to shake.

"You really have no other choice." His voice had turned icy. "There are things I must do here. And when they're done, I'll take you back home."

I stared. "And how long will these things take to complete? Hours? Days?"

"A few months perhaps." He had the grace to look chagrined.

"Months! I don't have months! Kaye needs me now. You heard what Lancelet told us about the state of Pendrath. Things are in chaos."

He gave me a hard look. "And you think things are bound to improve when you return to your brother the king without the sword?"

"The sword..." I had almost forgotten the fucking sword. Excalibur. "Fuck."

A woman's face flashed before my eyes. A fae woman of surpassing beauty with magnificent violet eyes and a wild tangle of silver and amethyst hair.

"She took it," I said hoarsely.

Orcades had stood over me. Held the sword in her hands. She had seemed to pity me for a moment. Then she had said...

"She knew you. She knew you were Siabra," I blurted out. "She said she would spill your blood with Excalibur."

Then she had left me there to die. Very pretty, but not the nicest full-blooded fae I had ever hoped to meet.

"Who did? Who knew?" Draven asked.

"No! No questions from you until you answer more of mine," I said.

Draven's eyes narrowed. "I've been answering them all. I'm being nothing but forthright with you."

I snorted. "Sure you are. Says the man who kidnapped me and brought me across an entire fucking ocean without even asking me first."

"You were in no state to be asked. What part of 'almost dead' are you having trouble understanding?" He sounded as if he were losing his temper again. We both were. Good. I didn't care how angry he was getting. This was turning out to be the worst day of my life. And considering one particular night in a dark and rainy stable, that was saying something.

"Perhaps you should have found me a healer on Eskira then, instead of bringing me to... whatever the hell this place is." I waved a hand at the gorgeous surroundings.

"You're in a palace. In the Court of Umbral Flames. Where the best healers in all of Aercanum reside. But you wanted me to what? Find you a healer right there in those deserted ruins where we might have been attacked at any instant? Or take you all the way back to Cerunnos? You would have died by then."

I clenched my jaw. "What's with the horns? You lied to me."

"I did no such thing. I said I wasn't worried about *you* sprouting any."

"Semantics. You're no better than Vesper was. You were a liar the entire time."

"Don't forget a killer, too. And what? You expected me to be a man of honor? Like your precious Sir Ector?"

The mention of Sir Ector stopped me cold. He had treated Lancelet and I like daughters. He would be heartbroken to hear what had happened. So would Galahad.

"Don't you dare say his name. He's better than you in every way. But yes, it's true. Laugh all you want, but I had almost started to have hope."

Draven raised one brow. "Hope?"

"Hope that you were better than I had thought you were. Hope that you might have a shred of honor. Hope that you cared about... About people other than yourself." I stopped myself just in time. I had nearly said "about me."

The look Draven gave me was almost reproachful. "I did everything I could. I did what I thought was right."

"Yet you hid who you were from me the entire time. How? Tell me that much at least. How did you do it?"

He shrugged. "That's easy. A glamor. I had it done when I left the court. I wasn't hiding from you, specifically, Morgan. Don't flatter yourself." The words stung me. "I was hiding who I was from everyone on Eskira. You really think your brother knew the truth?"

"Why hide?" I demanded. "Why go to all the trouble? What *are* the Siabra, anyhow?"

"A good question, for another day. And a long story."

"Another day?" I was incredulous. "You brought me home with you and you don't think I deserve to know who the hell you really are? Who your people are?"

"I'll tell you everything. Just not all at once. You need to rest." He paused. "Another thing. Don't leave this suite. For now."

"Oh, so now I'm officially your prisoner, am I? At least it's refreshing to finally have you say it."

Draven rolled his eyes. "You're not my prisoner. Do you think prisoners have rooms this luxurious? This is my personal suite."

"Your personal..." Should I have been flattered, I wondered? I thought back to Lyrastra and Ulpheas's quaint little visit. "Your sister-in-law. Lyrastra?"

"What about her?"

"She wasn't pleased to find me here. Not at all."

"So what?" Draven said dismissively. "It's none of her concern."

"So she called me your 'prize.' Your 'whore.' What do you make of that?"

The lines of his face became flinty. "She called you that?"

I nodded. "They seemed to think I was some sort of... I don't know. Captive. Like your spoils of war or a trophy you found in Valtain or something. Why would they think that?"

"Some Siabra hate the Valtain fae," Draven replied.

"But you *are* fae. Aren't you?"

"We split with the Valtain, long ago. We don't think of ourselves that way anymore. We're Siabra."

I thought of the mosaics Merlin had shown me in the temple. All this time, I had thought the other side of the wall simply depicted a darker side of the fae. But it hadn't shown the same fae at all. It showed Draven's people. The Siabra. With their horns. With their snake eyes.

Yet the room I was in wasn't a dark cavern but the most lavish of royal apartments. There was clearly more to the Siabra than what the mosaics suggested. And if I was stuck here—not that I planned to be for long—then I was going to discover the truth of what they really were.

"Lyrastra and Ulpheas and the others... they don't know much about you. Or where you really come from. I would prefer that it stay that way," Draven continued.

"You mean they don't know I'm a half-fae, half-human princess you've kidnapped from Pendrath, a kingdom at war with all of its neighbors?" I clarified.

"Something like that. They don't really give a damn what's going on in Eskira though. So if you're expecting sympathy from those two, you won't find it. They won't care that you're a princess either. Human royalty is... well, next to meaningless to them."

I wasn't going to let his bluntness sting me again. "I see. Well, I wasn't about to run up and down the hall screaming that I was a lost princess in need of saving, don't worry."

I could save myself, thank you very fucking much.

"How reassuring." He shocked me with a brief and glorious grin, but I refused to return it.

"No, I think I'll just leave," I continued, deciding to test the waters. "You know, walk out the door. Unless you plan to try to restrain me." I couldn't help it. I thought of our conversation long ago in the forest when he offhandedly mentioned women asking him to gag them in bed and felt a betraying heat suffuse my cheeks.

"Is that an invitation?" Draven said lightly, his green eyes flickering over me briefly.

He rose from the bed and crossed over to a large floor-to-ceiling window in the corner and looked out. "You're welcome to try. But if you're simply fishing for information, then yes, there's a barrier on the door for now. I hope to remove it soon. As I've said, you're not a prisoner. It's to protect you more than anything."

A barrier spell, he meant. And Lyrastra had magicked me into stillness. Who were these Siabra that they used magic with such ease? Had the Valtain fae been the same? It was strange to consider using it for small things after my own magic had so far been only blunt and destructive.

"But considering where we are... Well, good luck finding your way out."

I glared at him as he pushed open the window. A draft of warm air wafted into the room.

Unable to help my curiosity, I slid over to the edge of the bed and lowered my feet to the floor. The first touch of my bare feet on the cool solid marble left me dizzy. I stood in place for a moment until the lightheadedness had mostly passed, then took one excruciating step at a time. All of the strength seemed to have left my body and I had none in reserve.

Draven stood gazing out the window, waiting patiently as I made my way to his side. He didn't even glance over at me, though I knew he was aware of my painstaking progress.

Only when my foot slipped on the marble and I stumbled did his arm shoot out.

Before I could stop him, his hand was on my waist, steadying me. I could feel the warmth of his skin through the fabric of my shift. I glanced down at myself and was chagrined to realize just how thin the material was. The outline of my breasts was easily discernible. Crossing my arms, I lifted my head quickly and hoped he hadn't noticed.

"What is this?" I took one last step to bring myself up beside him.

His hand stayed steady on my hip, holding me upright. Part of me wanted to demand he remove it. But the truth was, I felt as if I might keel over at any moment and was doing my best not to clutch at his sleeve for extra support.

How humiliating.

I followed Draven's gaze, out through the glass doors and as I did, I sucked in my breath. A balcony jutted out in front of us, carved from shining black rock. Obsidian perhaps. The rock's surface sparkled with carved glyphs and sigils that reminded me of the markings along each of my arms. It was easy to see why the balcony had been literally covered in such protective magic. A palpable heat radiated through the air and beyond...

I took a step forward, then another. Draven moved with me, his hand still vaguely protective on my hip.

A whiff of sulfur. A whisper of smoke.

And below the balcony's edge, a jaw-dropping vista unfurled.

Lava cascaded down a mountain's rugged slopes, painting the landscape with liquid fire in a molten ballet of destruction and creation. Streams of melted rock glistened and glowed, casting brilliant hues of red, orange, and yellow as they flowed over the ground.

A rumbling sound cracked through the air, filling my ears with the sound of the earth's very heartbeat.

I took another step forward. The heat was scorching and yet I could sense that this was the limit of the volcano's power. It could not reach beyond the edge of the balcony. We were safe where we stood. The entire palace was enveloped in protective magic.

I looked higher up to where the air was filled with sparks and embers bursting forth from the mountainous rock, filling the sky with a mesmerizing display.

And then my eyes widened and a shiver ran down my spine.

The sky? There was no sky at all.

I had raised my eyes expecting to see clear blue or cloudy gray, only to be met with a dark vastness. But a darkness unlike any night sky I had ever seen.

We were deep within the embrace of Aercanum itself.

We were below ground. The palace was subterranean.

CHAPTER 2

High above us, a ceiling mimicked the starry heavens. Luminescent streaks embedded within the stony sky shimmered and twinkled, casting a soft radiance that contrasted with the harsh red light of the volcano. Constellations of crystal, unfamiliar yet captivating, graced the faux firmament.

As I stared out before me, I was filled with wonder, awe, and something very different. An inkling of terror.

"Where are we?"

"I've already told you. We're in the Court of..."

"Umbral Flames," I finished, now with true understanding. "And these are the flames."

The hint of a smile played on his beautifully curved lips.

"Don't you fucking dare smile at me," I snapped. "What kind of a people would build a palace *below ground*?"

"Paranoid people," he quipped. "My ancestors liked the idea of being hidden and sheltered below Aercanum's surface. And they had the power to bring their dream to life."

The Siabra must be powerful indeed. Well, that went without saying. Draven had already been an intimidating man. And that was when I simply believed he was a royal guard. Assassin turned royal guard turned abductor.

Now he was something even more powerful.

Did I *want* to know the extent of his true powers?

"It's..." I stared out at the vista again. "Incredible. And terrifying," I added.

"Terrifying?" Draven looked amused. "Why?"

"Because that's an active volcano and we're... what? Miles below the surface of the actual continent?" Even just saying the words sent claustrophobic shivers through me. I looked up nervously. "What if the entire thing just... collapsed?"

Draven chuckled. The sound sent a fluttering sensation through my stomach that I quickly suppressed. "It won't. This palace has been here for thousands of years. It's practically indestructible. These walls have never been breached. Do you know how much magic went into building this place?"

I studied him closely. "Here I thought you were simply an expensive hired blade. Who are you exactly?"

He scratched his chin. "It's... complicated."

"But you're someone important? Aren't you?" I challenged. "Lyrastra and Ulpheas called you their lord."

Draven shifted uncomfortably, his hand dropping away. "Because I am. I'm their prince."

I gaped. "So you'll be what? King of all of this some day?"

"Not necessarily. I told you, it's complicated."

"Well, maybe you can at least uncomplicate for me why they think I'm your prize captive and whore." I was starting to lose my temper again.

Draven looked distinctly uneasy. This was not good.

"I brought you back here because it was the best place to go in a hurry. I couldn't take you back to Pendrath. Especially not without that sword."

"Forgive me for not thanking you," I said, my voice dripping with sarcasm.

He ignored me. "But there are dangers here, too. As I've said, many Siabra harbor animosity towards the Valtain. They would harm you if they could."

"So you've saved me by bringing me somewhere everyone wants to kill me?" I rolled my eyes. "Wonderful plan."

"I brought you here because there was nowhere else I could bring you that was any better. You must trust me on that."

"I don't have trust you on anything," I said bluntly. "What aren't you telling me?"

His jaw tightened. "To keep you safe, I needed everyone to accept that you were under my protection. There had to be no doubt in their minds."

I raised my eyebrows. "So just tell them to leave your nice half-fae friend alone. Tell them I'm even not from Valtain. I'm from Pendrath. Simple, right? After all, you're their prince."

He shook his head. "It doesn't work that way here. The Siabra... We have our own culture. Our own rules."

"So instead, you told them I was what...? Your captive? A captive you keep in your personal suite?" My eyes widened. "Oh no."

Draven took a step away from me and leaned against the doorframe of the balcony. He folded his arms over his broad chest in a gesture that radiated stubbornness and was all too familiar.

"They've assumed you're my captive. I haven't claimed that."

"Oh, ho! How very magnanimous of you! To neither confirm nor deny. In the meantime, there's a barrier on the door to keep your deadly friends out and me inside." I clenched my jaw. "She called me your whore, Draven."

"I know," he said, hurriedly. Was it my imagination or was there a faint hint of pink in those gold-bronzed cheeks? I had never seen Draven blush before. "But of course, you aren't. You're no such thing. I'm sorry that word was used against you. It's not one I would ever use towards a woman."

I held his gaze. "What did you tell them I was?"

"My consort. In a sense."

My jaw dropped. "Your...consort? What the hell does that mean? They think we're what...? Married?"

My heart was pounding in my chest.

"No, no," Draven said quickly. "Not married."

My eyes narrowed suspiciously. "Then what? You said 'in a sense.' In what sense?"

Draven cleared his throat. "In Siabra culture, those of royal blood may designate a person who is not their official spouse as their... Well, as their..."

The blood drained from my face. "Your *mistress*? They think I'm your fucking mistress. Is that it?"

He nodded. A little too quickly. "That's the closest term, yes. The position is nothing like the crude word Lyrastra used. You are not a whore."

"Well, I know that," I erupted. "And you know that. But does your entire court of Siabra know that?"

"They know that I've brought home a mysterious and beautiful fae woman who is clearly of Valtain origin based on her unmistakable appearance, and that I've decleared her to be my official mistress. Under my protection and part of my house, now and for all time," Draven said quietly.

I was not going to let him distract me with the fact that he'd just called me beautiful. Absolutely not. "And if it were true," I said quietly. "It might almost be romantic. But it's not. It's a lie."

He ran his hands through his thick black hair. It was long, nearly chin-length now, and getting longer. "I know that. It's not... an ideal situation. I'm not claiming that it is. But this was the best way I could think of to protect you."

"You took me halfway around the world, to a place where I can't even see the sun... Forgive me if 'for now and all time' seems like it has a distinctly ominous ring to it."

"Actually, the palace has some chambers that receive sunlight. If you like, I'll take you to..."

"That's not the fucking point, Draven," I interrupted, though I was a little impressed. "And you know it. You took me further than I thought was possible. Far from Kaye. Far from the people who I need to protect. Did you ever think about that? And now you say you won't take me back. Meanwhile, your friends are creeping into this bedchamber, immobilizing me and insulting me—"

"They aren't my friends," he interrupted.

"Your fellow Siabra then. Your sister-in-law! And however noble this position of royal mistress supposedly is, there is clearly some dispute over just how noble or else Lyrastra wouldn't have just called me a 'whore'!"

"You're right," Draven said, his voice even.

I stared. "I am?"

"You are, yes. Some will never see the position as anything but a demeaning one. I can't change that. I acted quickly. I did what I did to try to shield you. I couldn't shield you completely and for that, I am truly sorry. But for now, we are stuck like this. Bound together. Whether we like it or not."

"Not. Decidedly not," I said. "Unbind us."

He looked out over the volcanic vista, his face clouded. "I can't. I must remain here until I've dealt with certain things. And you must remain where I am. I can't take you back to Pendrath. I can't ask anyone else to take you. For one, I don't trust that your sociopathic brother wouldn't kill you simply for coming back empty-handed..."

"Oh, please don't pretend you're any better than Arthur is," I said with disdain.

"You really think I'm the same as he is?" Draven sounded stung.

"Well, at least in Camelot, no one ever called me a whore and I wasn't forced to become some man's mistress. I would have joined the temple. I would have had an honorable role."

"If Arthur had ever let you join the temple in the first place. You're naiver than I gave you credit for if you really believe he would have let you go and become the new High Priestess. He would never have let his own sister hold that much power."

I suddenly remembered Vesper's words. His claim that Draven was supposed to kill me in the end.

Well, he had been wrong about that. Draven had certainly had the chance. But he hadn't taken it.

Then my own words rang out in my mind. What had I told Vesper about Draven? That Vesper was wrong about him.

He's nothing like you, I had said. He's a thousand times better.

I looked at Draven and felt a deep sadness that I was loathe to show.

"I hate you," I said slowly and distinctly. "I think I really hate you now. You believe you're a better man than Arthur? You claim to have saved me, but I'm still locked in a prison. You say you'll take me home but first you'll see to your own interests. And besides, I don't believe you have any intention of returning me. You'll use me for your own ends, won't you? Whatever those are. That's your real plan."

Draven's face was impassive. "That's not true. But I'm sorry you feel that way. This isn't how I want things. I swear it. I had no other choice."

I took a step towards him. "If you think I'm going to fall into line and become your fucking royal mistress in actuality, then you have another thing coming."

"I would never have expected that. The thought of an unwilling woman... It's a horror to me. You should know me better than that by now." He seemed to realize his mistake.

"I thought I did," I said softly, my eyes locked on him. "I was wrong."

I pointed to the door. "Now get the hell out of my room."

He hesitated, then nodded slowly. "I'll leave."

"Good." Secretly, I was surprised it had been so easy. Then my stomach growled and I wondered where I was going to find some food. Well, one thing at a time. "Go then."

He started towards the door. "Unfortunately, I'll have to return come nightfall."

My mouth fell open. "Excuse me? What the hell is that supposed to mean? You just said..."

"I know what I said," he assured me. "You won't like this, but we're sharing this room. If you're trapped with me, well, then I'm trapped with you, too, Morgan."

"What. Do. You. Mean." My jaw felt so tight I was surprised I could get the words out at all.

"I mean we need to be convincing. The court must believe that this is real, even if you and I know that it isn't." He touched his hand to the door. "I'll be returning here every night to sleep. And only sleep. We'll share a bed to keep up appearances."

He hesitated, then his lips twitched. "After all..."

I wanted to punch the hint of the smirk from his handsome horned face. I looked back at the bed. There was a table beside it with a large, expensive-looking porcelain vase. "No. Don't say it. I'm warning you."

"After all," he finished, ignoring me and opening the door. "It's not like it's going to be the first time."

By the time I managed to reach the table, he had already closed the door.

CHAPTER 3

I sat back down on the edge of the bed, my head reeling.

On the plus side, I was no longer traveling through an eerie ancient forest having to camp out each night in a tiny tent.

On the downside, I was trapped in a palace with a horned man who had told everyone I was basically his bed toy.

Oh, and I wasn't allowed to leave my room.

I glanced across the bedchamber at a door in the wall to my left, near the paneled-windows that led onto the balcony. There was another door on the opposite wall.

Rooms. I wasn't allowed to leave my rooms. I supposed I should explore them and see just what my prison consisted of.

I started to push myself up, then paused.

No, that wasn't the worst part. It wasn't even close to the worst part.

The worst part was Lancelet.

My friend. My friend was gone.

Draven obviously believed she was dead. I couldn't see how he would have any reason to lie. Surely, even he wouldn't be that cruel. He had claimed he'd searched for her. And not just him but his people, whatever that was supposed to mean. They had found no trace.

Lancelet had died, in horrible pain, frightened and alone. While I was whisked away by Vesper.

She had probably died thinking I had abandoned her willingly. That I had been too much of a coward to return and fight for her.

Hot tears stung my eyes. I lifted my chin. No, I wasn't going to indulge in a good cry. Even though it was very tempting to throw myself back down on the bed and bury my head in the pillows as I sobbed.

I would not give myself the luxury of tears. Not when I had the greatest luxury of all: Being alive.

I was in a palace, while Lancelet no longer breathed.

If the worst thing I had to face was escaping from the Siabra and not feral cannibal children who had turned into monsters a hundred years before I'd even been born, then I had no right to complain.

I stood up carefully and started to look around me more closely.

Well, the bed was certainly a masterpiece. The immense four-poster structure was adorned with cascading heaps of soft, shimmering fabrics. Gold-carved columns stretched up towards the ceiling at each of the bed corners, covered by a canopy of billowing silks. The mattress was huge. Easily large enough to fit four adults.

At least there would be plenty of room for Draven... If he actually dared to come back. I had to hope he was joking. Had to.

Because if he thought I'd hold back from attacking him in his sleep, he had another thing coming.

I had been restrained when I had been on the mission to find Excalibur. I'd *had* to be. I needed him.

But now? I was seething and he was the closest thing to a punching bag I had.

The far wall near the door was covered with a long row of tall, golden-edged mirrors. I prowled towards them, suddenly nervous to see my own reflection.

Just how long had I been in that bed for? I had assumed a day or two. But had it been longer?

An image of a pale girl draped in a thin gossamer shift came into view and my breath hitched in my throat. Everything that had once been so familiar was gone. Or that was how it felt. The girl looking back at me seemed like a stranger. Her frame was so delicate.

I touched my fingers to my arms, tracing the intricate markings that were imprinted there in glowing silver. They cast a silvery radiance upon my gold-tinged skin.

My hair was a mess of knots. But at least it was somewhat familiar. No longer crone-gray, it was a distinctive silver shade that reminded me a little of Orcades' purple and silver tresses. The strands of liquid metal luster mirrored the glow of the markings on my arms.

I stepped away from the mirror and walked to the nearest door, the one by the balcony and pushed it open.

A sitting room beckoned, replete with plush velvet armchairs and chaise lounges, upholstered in deep emerald and plum tones. The furniture was arranged in an inviting ring around an enormous stone hearth, where a fire crackled invitingly. Dark wood bookshelves lined the walls, filled with beautiful leatherbound tomes. I caught sight of gilded lettering on the spines in numerous languages, not all ones I recognized. A gleaming mahogany desk stood in a nook beneath a row of stained-glass windows that overlooked the volcanic spectacle outside. Quills, inkwells, and thick paper and scrolls covered its surface in an orderly arrangement.

On the far wall in roughly the same position as the last one was another door. I crossed over and stepped into a marble-floored foyer with a soaring ceiling, topped by another exquisite crystal chandelier. Three doors led off the chamber.

I pushed against the first one, but it wouldn't budge. Frowning, I tried again. Nothing.

It must lead out into the main hallway, I concluded, and thus be locked like the one in the bedchamber. At least, for me, anyway. Draven had appeared to have no trouble passing through the wards.

I tried the next door and discovered a bathing chamber fit for Zorya herself. A huge marble tub with gold faucets sat below a beautiful picture window overlooking the fiery landscape. The walls were tiled in vibrant shades of green and blue, with gold gilding between each one. A vanity cabinet covered with a spread of perfumed oils, toiletries, and scented candles rested nearby. I caught a whiff of a familiar scent.

Sandalwood. Draven's trademark.

I closed the door firmly and went on to the next one.

A spacious dining area lay inside, featuring a large polished table inlaid with mother-of-pearl and trimmed with gold filigree. Delicate porcelain dishware decorated in intricate patterns rested upon a silk table runner, accompanied by crystal goblets and gold eating instruments.

On the opposite wall behind the table lay another door. Noises were coming from beyond it.

My heart thumped. I had assumed I was alone in the suite.

There was a clattering sound and then a bang, as if someone had dropped a hot pan.

Curiously, I pushed the door open a few inches and peered inside.

Gleaming copper pots and pans hung along a brick wall over a large cooking area. Reams of dried herbs, fruits, and spices hung from the ceiling on vines of twine, filling the kitchen with color and fragrance. The scent of cooking food infused the air, tantalizing my starving stomach and drawing out a low rumble.

The clattering sound of metal on metal came again and my eyes darted to the far side of the room... where a huge brown bear stood, hunched over a counter, tearing something to shreds.

I gulped. The bear was covered in thick, coarse fur and stood taller than Draven by at least another head.

As I watched, it took another swipe at whatever was on the counter. I started to slowly close the door, preparing to run through the dining room, back to the bedroom... and then what? I hadn't been left with any weapons as far as I could remember. I gnashed my teeth in frustration. What sort of a fae court had a bear in one of the kitchens? Or was this Draven's idea of a joke?

Or worse... Had one of his friends, perhaps his lovely sister-in-law, put the bear in here, hoping for a worst-case scenario?

Now a clunking noise was coming from the counter. The bear let out a low growl and made another swiping motion with its paw.

I froze. The bear's paw was holding a large knife, chopping with impressive dexterity.

In my shock, I must have let go of the door and it slammed shut with a squeak of the hinges and a bang, smacking me in the face. I let out a yelp of pain, clutching my hand to my face.

The clunking noise stopped.

"Who's there?" the bear growled.

That was not possible. Bears did not speak.

And palaces were usually built above ground not below, I reminded myself. And people—even fae—usually did not have horns growing from their heads or the eyes of snakes.

Steeling myself, I pushed open the door again and peeked through the crack.

The bear was looking right at me.

I gulped.

"Yes?" the bear said coolly. There was still a faint growl to its tone. Perhaps that was always the way with bears.

It was tempting to just come right out and say "What the hell are you?" But I suspected this would be considered unforgiveable decorum. Even to a bear.

"H-hello," I managed. "I'm Morgan." Morgan, you know, the official royal mistress of your bloody prince. I decided to leave that part out.

"I know," the bear said, with a decidedly grumpy tone. "Lady Morgan, so we've been told."

I decided I'd take it. I'd had enough of being a princess anyhow.

"And?" Did bears have eyebrows to raise? If so, this bear was raising theirs.

I stood up a little straighter. This bear had an attitude. Well, I could relate to that. "I'm also starving. I won't get in your way, but do you think I could come in and try to find something to eat?"

The bear looked at me from behind expressive large brown eyes, full of surprising wisdom and depth.

"Well, come in then," the bear said gruffly.

With fascination, I realized the bear might be female. Still, it was hard to say for certain.

I pushed the door open wider and took a tentative step into the room. "It's an honor to meet you...?"

There was silence for a moment as the bear looked at me. For a moment I wondered if they were going to tell me to get lost after all. Or eat me.

"Hawl," the bear said finally. "What do you want to eat?"

"Hawl. Pleased to meet you, Hawl. I'm ready to eat just about anything. An apple, an entire loaf of bread. I'll take whatever is easiest and get out of your way."

Hawl examined me from behind fur-rimmed dark eyes. "There are pastries on the tray there. Be careful, they're probably still hot." The bear nodded towards a copper tray on a large wooden table in the center of the room.

I stepped towards the tray and picked up a pastry. The aroma was overpowering. Apple and cheese and cinnamon. My knees felt weak as I opened my mouth and took a large bite. Immediately I let out a faint moan.

"I told you they were hot," Hawl said, a little crossly. "Silly little creature."

I groaned again, but not from pain. The pastry was hot but it hadn't burned my mouth. The texture was light, flaky, and buttery. A mixture of sweetness and tartness filled my mouth as I tasted the filling in the center.

"Good," I managed to mumble between mouthfuls as I crammed more pastry in as fast as I could. "Very good."

I swallowed and tried to get a hold of myself. "This is delicious. Thank you."

It was difficult to tell from the bear's features but I thought Hawl seemed pleased.

Sure enough. "Hmph," they grunted.

I couldn't stand the curiosity anymore. "I beg your pardon if this is rude, but there are no creatures like you where I come from. May I ask... what are you?"

Hawl gave a snort. "Not many in these parts either. We're called Ursidaur. Some call us Bearkins."

I was fairly sure Kaye still had a stuffed bear named Bearkin that he liked to sleep with sometimes. I decided not to volunteer this information.

"How fascinating," I said, as politely as I could. "And are there many Ursidaur in the Umbral Flames court?"

Hawl made a sound that might have been a laugh or a growl. "You're looking at the only one."

"Do you like living here?" I asked cautiously, wondering how much information Hawl might be willing to share.

Another ambiguous grunt. "It's all right."

"And do you usually cook for the prince?"

This time Hawl did seem amused. "Does having a bear cook for you bother you?"

"No, not at all," I said in surprise.

"Good. Because I was the only one willing."

"Oh. I see. Because I'm not Siabra, you mean?"

Hawl gave a snort. "Something like that."

For an instant, I wondered if Draven could possibly be the reason. Were the other Siabra...afraid of him?

"Someone's knocking."

I quirked my eyebrows. "Hmm?"

"Someone is knocking," Hawl said again, more impatiently this time. "In the foyer. Someone is at the door. Probably looking for you."

"I don't hear anything," I replied.

"Humans," Hawl muttered. "Well, they're there whether you hear them or not. Ursidaur have exceptional hearing."

"That makes sense," I said, grabbing another pastry. "I'll go and see who it is. It was very nice to meet you."

But the Bearkin was already turning back to the counter and picking up their knife again.

"I really doubt Draven would knock," I muttered to myself as I strode back through the dining room. "Knock the door down, yes. Knock politely, no."

I reached the foyer. Sure enough, there was a tapping sound. It was coming from the door I hadn't been able to open.

I marched over. It wasn't as if I could unlock it for whoever was out there on the other side.

"Yes?" I called, feeling more than a little ridiculous. "Who is it?"

The door opened.

Two people stood outside in a hallway. A young man and a woman. I could immediately tell they were Siabra.

Their coloring was different from the part-fae I was used to seeing back in Eskira. In fact, looking at them and thinking of Draven, I was beginning to realize how easily I stood out. If the Valtain fae were known for their enchanting beauty and vibrancy of hair and skin, then the Siabra were a contrast, yes. But by no means an unattractive one. Indeed, the more Siabra I saw, the more I realized the temple depiction had not done them justice. Their appearance was more wild, more untamed. Their coloring more earthy rather than vivid. No less beautiful. But beautiful in a stark and even fiercer way.

"Good day, Lady Morgan," the young man chirped cheerfully. "We're your new bodyguards."

"My what?" I stared at them as the young man gave me a winsome smile. He reminded me of Galahad immediately though he was clearly a few years older, with a slender, more athletic frame and darker skin. The young man radiated a warm and friendly demeanor. I studied his attire. He wore a forest green doublet adorned with embroidered leaves and paired with dark russet trousers. Soft-looking moss-colored slippers covered delicate cloven-shaped hooved feet, like those of a deer.

The woman next to him was more severe in appearance. She possessed a warrior's build with broad shoulders and a muscular physique. Her gruff expression contrasted sharply with the young man's. Her dark skin was a rich, radiant brown. She possessed fine, delicate features but her face was lined with scars, some fresh, some old and faded. Her hair was long and styled into many small braids, all swept back and twisted into a heavy knot that seemed both practical and elegant. Two formidable-looking blades were strapped to her back. The hilts were wrapped in worn leather, suggesting the weapons were regularly used in actual combat and not simply there to look impressive.

I snuck a look at her feet. They were as ordinary as mine. Evidently not all Siabra had distinctly animalistic-features like Draven and her companion.

I envied her those blades. If only I had one to put beneath my pillow.

The warrior woman's eyes were razor-sharp and penetrating as she stared back at me.

I looked back and forth between them, then furrowed my brow. "Are you...?"

"Brother and sister? Yes." The young man beamed. "I'm Crescent di Rhondan and this is Odessa."

Odessa di Rhondan gave a tight nod.

I frowned. "Bodyguards? Whose idea was that? I suppose I don't need to ask."

"The prince mentioned there was already a breach on the barriers protecting your suite. Odessa and I have had those repaired and we'll be putting guards in rotation outside here in the hall," Crescent said pleasantly.

"Repaired them? You mean you can do magic? What kind?"

Crescent shrugged modestly. "I can, yes, but wards are not my area of expertise. We called for a member of the prince's court who specializes in barrier magic to repair what had been tampered with."

"How do we know they'll actually work the next time Lyrastra or her friends want to get in?" I asked, not feeling particularly reassured. "They didn't the first time."

Crescent hesitated. "True. I believe the one who erected the barriers in the first place is going to be..."

"They'll be dealt with," Odessa said bluntly, speaking up for the first time. "They screwed up and we've let them know it."

Crescent nodded his agreement. "I wouldn't have put it quite like that, but yes, we're using someone else now. Someone well-trusted by Prince Draven. I'm sure you'll meet him soon. And, as I've said, there will be guards in the halls as well from now on."

I stepped forward, peering down the hallway. The decor was different out here. The hall was a black marble with a few white swirls. The walls were a deep lush green broken up here and there by the presence of tall gold columns that stretched floor to ceiling.

I could see no windows and no doors. At least, nothing obvious. Perhaps the doors blended in with the walls so subtly I couldn't pick them out.

"Ah, yes, guards." I nodded. "To keep me in and others out. Forgive me if I don't celebrate."

I tilted my head. "But if I do have bodyguards assigned to me now, then I suppose that means you can protect me as I explore the palace."

I was suddenly wildly enthusiastic to get out of the suite of rooms. Then I remembered what I was wearing and looked down, letting out a curse. "Just let me find something else to wear and we can..."

"I'm sorry, my lady, but we're not permitted to take you anywhere at the moment. We simply wanted to introduce ourselves." Crescent's face was apologetic. "At least, for today. Perhaps another time we might be permitted..."

"I'm not allowed out at all?" I interrupted. "Not even with *guards*? He said that, didn't he? And did he tell you what I am to him? Who I am?"

I suddenly wondered if I should be keeping my mouth shut, but it was too late.

Crescent looked started for a moment. "He did. Of course, the prince explained your position, Lady Morgan."

I scowled. "And?"

"And it is an honor to serve the Prince's Paramour." Crescent gave a small bow. "We will guard you with our lives, my lady."

"Paramour?" I exclaimed. "I'm not Draven's paramour, I'm his captive. And as such, I would appreciate being let out. I'm not a prisoner, am I? Did he say I was?"

Crescent looked distinctly uncomfortable.

I felt only slightly guilty. None of this was his fault. But he seemed like he might be something of a pushover. Perhaps if I pushed hard enough, he'd get out of my way and let me out the door.

"No, but he..." Crescent began.

Odessa stepped forward, blocking her brother slightly. She crossed her arms over her chest drawing my attention to the unique armor she wore. Made from black and red leather, the breastplate was shaped perfectly to her body and laced up like a corset. Her arms were bare and the top of the breastplate wove up over her shoulders, tying behind her neck with straps like a halter. In Camelot, the style of armor might have been impractical. But then, from what I had already seen of the volcano outside, the kingdom of Sorega had a much warmer climate.

"You'll have to take this up with the prince," Odessa said bluntly. "Prince Kairos said you stay put for now. So you stay put."

I glared at her. She stared back sternly. I couldn't help but feel angry—with her more than her brother, as she had not even attempted to mince her words.

Worse, I felt the familiar sensation of tears pricking at my eyes. I didn't want to be here, arguing with two strangers about whether I deserved to be let out of my room. I wanted to go home. I wanted to see Kaye. I needed to tell Lancelet's family she wouldn't be coming home.

I lifted my chin so Odessa wouldn't see my eyes glisten. "Fine. Then go and get your prince. I want to speak with him."

Odessa and Crescent exchanged a glance. "We can't do that."

"Why not?" I demanded. "He's told you I'm his paramour, hasn't he? That implies a measure of care for me, does it not? Yet he has restrained me in these rooms as if I were a child. Or worse. A prisoner. That does not seem particularly respectful or caring to me."

"I'm sure the prince loves you very much, Lady Morgan," Crescent said gently. "We are confident he has done this only for your protection."

It took everything I had not to burst out in maniacal laughter. Crescent was so sweetly sincere that I had no wish to offend him, but he thought Draven *loved* me? He couldn't have been more wrong.

"I'm sure when the prince is finished meeting with his mother, he'll return to you soon," Crescent finished.

My eyebrows shot up as Odessa elbowed her brother sharply in the ribs with a frown. "His mother? He's gone to meet with his mother?"

If Draven had a mother, then she must be the queen. Was she the ruler of the Siabra Empire? Was that why Draven was still only a prince?

Crescent rubbed the spot his sister had hit him, but otherwise seemed intent on ignoring the rebuff. "Yes. Prince Kairos's return has caused quite the stir, you know. The Queen Regent had nearly given up hope of ever seeing her son again."

"Just how long was Prince Kairos gone exactly?" I asked curiously.

The siblings exchanged another look.

Good. That meant I was asking the right questions.

"More than twenty years. He left when his brother...Oof." Another elbow to the ribs had been delivered mercilessly by Odessa.

"She probably knows most of this already, Odessa," Crescent protested, rubbing his torso.

I lifted a hand and began to study my fingernails. Surprisingly they were clean. "Oh, I do," I said, striving for the appearance of perfect innocence. "Draven... I mean, Prince

Kairos... used to speak of his dear mother all of the time. But his brother. I find I can't recall much about him."

There was silence. An awkward silence. I raised my head finally to see Crescent biting his lip.

"What?"

"Prince Kairos's brother is... dead."

"Did he pass while Draven was away?" I felt a pang of guilt, but needed to know more. "That's very sad."

Crescent was shaking his head. "No. Not while he was away. You really don't remember him speaking of this?"

"I must have been distracted. You know how things get... between lovers." I tried not to vomit as I spoke the word. "He used to tell tales of his family so very often though."

I fluttered my eyelashes and tried to look as stupid as possible. It was such a turnaround though that I didn't expect either of them to fall for it. Indeed, Odessa was practically rolling her eyes.

"Prince Kairos killed his brother, my lady," Crescent said quietly. "It is a hard thing to forget."

A shiver crossed my skin.

"He killed him?" I whispered.

"Which is why it's so odd you should say he mentioned his 'dear mother,'" Odessa piped up. "When the queen was the one who banished him for treason."

I gulped. "Banished? Treason?"

She ignored me and whirled around to face her brother instead. "You have a very big mouth. If you've finally finished spilling secrets to this woman you hardly know, we should go." Odessa glanced back at me, her eyes cold. "For all we know, she could be a..."

"A what?" I demanded. My eyes widened. "A spy? Is that what you were going to say? You think I'm a spy for Valtain?"

Odessa scowled and tossed her head with its heavy crown of braids, in a gesture both annoyed yet also graceful.

"You think the prince would bring a fae girl who was secretly a spy home to meet his mother? I suppose that tells me more about what you think of your prince than it does anything else," I said flippantly.

"We trust Prince Kairos," Odessa snapped. "We are loyal to the Umbral Throne and the true Venator heir."

"True heir? Does that mean there's another?"

"Don't answer that," Odessa commanded her brother. To me, "We are shutting the door now. If you have more questions, you may take them up with the prince when he returns to you."

The look in her eyes and the little sniff she gave with her nose told me what she really thought of me. She might not have stooped to using the crude word Lyrastra had, but Prince's Paramour or not, she clearly saw me as little more than Draven's unwise indulgence.

My cheeks flared with heat and I opened my mouth to argue but it was too late. The door had already closed in my face.

CHAPTER 4

W hen the door to the bedchamber opened later that evening, I was ready and
waiting.

I sprang up from my chair as Prince Kairos Draven, who I was now silently referring
to as "morally gray asshole," entered the room.

I had spent the afternoon and early evening hours alone. Hawl had disappeared. But
before they did, they had been kind enough to leave out platters of freshly-prepared food.
I had gorged myself on a salad of fruit and tender greens, fruit tarts, and a rich creamy dish
of seafood and rice.

After which I had spent roughly two hours pacing back and forth across the rooms of
my suite, endeavoring to get some exercise and help my body to strengthen itself again.

Finally, I had given up, exhausted, and begun to explore the nooks and crannies of the
rooms in which I was trapped.

In the bedchamber, I opened a wardrobe to find a set of clothes that seemed to have
been made for a woman close to my size. Decadent gowns, soft robes, sleeping sets, and
even what looked like a riding habit hung neatly side by side.

I chose a simple pair of short pants and a sleeveless tunic that looked like they would be
comfortable to sleep in. The clothes were loose-fitting and draped softly against my body.
The lavender fabric felt like a whisper against my skin. Silver lacework trimmed the edges
of the tunic, adding a small touch of luxury.

Feeling self-conscious about wearing what were essentially sleeping garments around
Draven, I added a long black velvet robe for modesty then pulled it around myself and sat
down in an oversized armchair near the bed with a stack of books perched beside me and
prepared to wait.

Some of the books were quite heavy. I hadn't decided yet whether I would be lobbing the stack at Draven if he opened the door. Besides, I was growing tired and questioned how good my aim would be at that time of the night.

Things had been simpler when we had been on the road. I would change in my tent, then fall asleep. Sometimes I would listen to Draven's soft snoring. It hadn't kept me awake. If anything, it had lulled me back to sleep. It was... comforting to know he was there. Near enough to hear me if I called out.

Then the others had joined us. First Vesper. Then Lancelet. Then Odelna. And everything had changed after that.

An hour or so later, I had nearly fallen asleep in my chair.

Beside me a book about the creation of the subterranean palace, the seat of the Court of Umbral Flames, lay open and discarded. I had read enough of the first few chapters to confirm that the kingdom of Sorega was not entirely underground though its ruling court was. Cities lay just over our head on the surface of the continent. Specifically, the capital city Noctasia could be found directly above the volcanic royal palace, an extension of the royal court in many ways. It seemed that the Siabra transported themselves to the surface with relative ease by accessing something called stitching. With stitching, one could go from the city to the palace and back again easily in the span of just a few minutes.

But when the door opened, I was on my feet in an instant, thoughts of sleep quickly forgotten.

"How was your visit with your mommy?" I asked sweetly, placing my hands on my hips.

Draven seemed startled by the question. He seemed much more fatigued than when he had left that afternoon. The dark stubble that usually lined his jaw was thicker and darker than usual. He already had a hand up to rub wearily at his forehead.

For a moment, I thought of what Crescent had told me—that Draven's brother was dead, that Draven had been banished and absent from court for twenty long years.

My entire lifespan, in fact.

Then my pity vanished. This man had slain his own brother. He had been banished for good reason—for treason.

"Why did you kill your own brother? Were you planning on telling me that anytime soon? And why would you bring me back to a court you had been *banished* from? It doesn't exactly seem like a safe place for either of us."

Draven had gone very still. "Crescent was here, I take it? Did you like him? He's a useful fellow. His sister is deadly with those blades. But he can be something of a chatterbox."

"Do I like him?" I seethed. "I certainly like that he's a chatterbox. But he's just another jailer, isn't he? They wouldn't let me leave these rooms."

"On my orders," Draven said quietly. "For your own safety."

"So you keep saying. And now you're back here, to do what exactly?"

"To sleep. I'm tired. Aren't you?"

He moved towards the side of the bed and started unfastening his jacket. My heart pounded. He was really going to do this. He really planned to sleep in the same room, no, the same bed as me.

His presence was undeniable. Perhaps that was why it had been so easy to accept that he was a prince. He commanded attention, even now, while simply undressing. Waves of black hair framed his face, drawing my gaze to his strong nose and chiseled cheekbones.

Evidently he had changed to meet his mother.

He was clothed in regal darkness, in clothes more luxurious than any I had seen him wear before. Trousers of black fabric, expertly tailored to his muscular legs, with just a hint of a subtle sheen. His shirt was a midnight-black silk and overtop he wore a jacket tailored to perfection, gleaming with silver threads embroidered in the pattern of vines. Ornate delicately engraved silver buttons traced its front while a high collar touched the golden bronze skin of his neck.

As I watched, he finished unbuttoning the jacket and tossed it onto a nearby chair, then set his hands to the silver belt at his waist.

"Stop," I protested, my cheeks heating. "What the hell are you doing?"

He paused and looked at me quizzically as if I were the one acting strange. "Getting ready for bed. I've already eaten. Have you?"

"You only think to ask me that now?" I muttered.

His lips formed a small smile. "I wasn't trying to starve you. I sent Hawl to prepare some food. Did you encounter..."

He paused as if suddenly realizing that perhaps he should have warned me there would be a bear... creature... in the kitchen.

"Hawl was delightful," I conceded, refusing to admit they had given me a bit of a fright at first.

"So you have eaten? Good. Are you tired?"

"What the hell is this, Draven?" I exploded. "We're simply changing our bedtime routine? From setting up camp and crawling into my tent, now you want me to crawl into bed with you?"

His beautiful lips quirked. "Something like that." He gestured to the bed. "Twice as big as your tent, if not more, wouldn't you say?"

I shot him a death glare, then eyed the bed. The morally gray asshole was right. The huge canopy bed was at least twice as big as the small tent that had held me, my bed roll, and not much else. The little tent I had slept in from the time we had left Camelot up until...

Up until the ruins of Meridium.

"Which side would you like?"

"What?" My head whipped towards him.

"Left or right? There are tables on each side, if you need a place for your books." He gestured to the pile of books I had left near the armchair.

"Those?" I snapped. "Those are weapons. A hard enough blow and I could kill you in your sleep."

His lips twitched. "Knowledge is always a weapon in the right hands."

"I knew you'd say that," I muttered, lifting the largest tome and hoisting it one hand. Then, "I'm not going to get cozy with you. Left, right, never. This isn't happening."

He sat down on the side of the bed–the left side, the one I hadn't already been sleeping on earlier in the day–and started pulling off shiny steel-toed black boots.

"I don't think I've made things as clear as I should have, Morgan," he said, his deep voice almost conversational. "You can choose to think of me as your enemy all you like, but I'm going to protect you whether you like it or not."

"Not," I snarled.

"Whatever you prefer. But you *are* under my protection. And for now, you are fairly safe. My court believes you are my..." He cleared his throat.

"Paramour?" I offered sourly.

"The Prince's Paramour is the formal title, yes," he acknowledged. "Mistress. Consort. I can use whichever word you find less..."

"Demeaning? Humiliating? Revolting?" I offered.

He grinned and eyed the pile of books I had near me. "Were all of those books thesauruses by chance?"

"No," I said, with gritted teeth. "Some were geography texts. I'm learning your terrain so I can spy on you and then return with Arthur's army."

Draven made a choking sound. "Spy on..." Then he chuckled. "Let me guess. Odessa?"

"I don't know what about me she finds more disgusting. That I'm supposedly your lover–" The word stuck in my throat for a moment, then passed over my lips for the second time that day, strangely not in an altogether unpleasant way. "Or that you've taken a Valtain spy to your bed."

"Fae-human spy," Draven corrected. "Though I doubt anyone truly thinks I've stolen you from..." He stopped.

"Oh, please, do go on," I encouraged. "What were you about to say?"

He ran his hands through his dark hair, leaving it tousled in a way I might have almost found endearing were he another, less despicable man, and then sighed. "There are a great many things you ought to know and I know I ought to tell you them. But we don't have time to go through them all tonight. Now where was I before I got sidetracked?"

"Your court. The one you ran away from for twenty years. Just how old are you anyway?"

Draven's face turned rueful. "A hundred and fifty or so, give or take a few years. I'm a child compared to most of the Siabra."

I stared at him. "A child? You're the oldest child I've ever met. That's... I thought you were a few years older than me. Maybe five or ten." Not fifty or a hundred.

"I left this court not only because I had to," Draven said. "But because I wanted to. You should understand that."

"So why did you return?"

"Partly to protect you."

I made a sound of disbelief. "And partly to...?"

"To take back what was rightfully mine. To make some changes. And to offer the court something in turn."

"Care to elaborate on those cryptic statements? By what was rightfully yours, I assume you mean the throne?"

"I do, but it's not as easy to attain as it is in Pendrath."

"What do you mean?" I was curious despite myself. "You're a prince, aren't you?"

"Your brother was given the throne. He didn't have to fight for it, did he?"

"Of course not. He inherited it, lawfully..." I trailed off. "Well, he inherited it."

By rights, the throne of Pendrath was meant to be mine. I was the eldest child of Uther Pendragon. But my fae blood had marked me as unfit in my father's eyes. And so he had disinherited me and raised up his bastard son by another woman to sit on the Rose Court throne.

I had not fought for the seat. I had meekly stepped aside. I had always believed there was no other choice.

And now? I was done with being meek. I still had no use for thrones.

Draven gave a wide catlike yawn. "Look, I'll tell you more soon. I promise. But in the meantime, one of the reasons you can't leave this room is because you're not exactly... receptive to playing the part you need to play."

I gaped at him. "You mean because I don't want to pretend to be your fucking paramour, you're locking me in here?"

"I wouldn't have phrased it quite like that, but yes. Essentially. You can't leave this suite until you understand who the court expects you to be. And until I can trust you to pretend—for both our sakes."

I lifted one of the books. But then I thought of the damage it might do if I threw it. To the book, not to Draven. I had my respect for the written word to consider.

"I think it's a good thing I had Hawl put all the sharp knives away," Draven said, watching me. I couldn't tell if he was jesting or not.

I bared my teeth. "Lucky for you. How exactly do you want me to act? I suppose I should follow you like a puppy begging for your caress."

"Not quite so desperate as a puppy," Draven managed to say with a straight face. "But public displays of affection—while the nobles of the court will act as if they despise such lowborn conduct—would be very convincing."

"So, what? I'm supposed to... kiss you or something? In public?" I twisted my lips to show my revulsion at the prospect, but the truth was my heart was thumping against my breastbone and my eyes had gone straight to Draven's full perfectly shaped lips.

"Perhaps nothing quite so affectionate, but subtle touches here and there, to show we don't despise one another. I can lead the way, if you'll permit it. Small signs of public affection would go a long way to cementing your place here. We need to be convincing." He looked at me then shook his head. "You need to pretend you don't hate me quite so much, Morgan. Do you think you might be able to do that?"

I took a step towards him just as he stood up. Mercifully, he had not yet removed his belt or trousers. I had distracted him from that.

"Let's get one thing straight. If you dare to try to show me any *public affection*," I hissed. "I'll murder you in your sleep. I may be weaponless, but I'm not entirely defenseless."

Draven studied me for a moment, then lifted his shirt over his head. With a swift motion it was flung onto the same chair as the jacket.

Then he stood before me, half-naked. His smooth, bronzed chest was bare save for a cluster of curling dark hairs that started at the top and then gradually narrowed into a tapering trail that stretched between his ribs and down past his navel all the way to...

I forced my eyes up and realized he was gazing back at me, his green eyes measured and discerning.

"I know you're not defenseless, Morgan," Draven said quietly. "I saw the ashes. Remember?"

I swallowed, not sure whether he meant the words as a compliment or a rebuke. Was he saying he was actually... frightened by me? Or possessed a healthy respect for whatever he thought I could do?

It was a start.

"Now, I'm going to sleep," he said abruptly. "It's been a long day. I would suggest you do the same. This is the first day you've been out of bed in a week. Your body is still recovering." He started to pull back the coverlet. "And before you tell me to go sleep on the floor or the couch in the other room–no. The answer is no. There are servants who might enter to tend these rooms. While I trust most of them, they'll need to see every indication that we're a..."

"Happy, normal couple?" I supplied, pushing my lips up into a false smile.

Draven smirked. "Never normal. That would be dull. A couple, however–yes. They need to see the bed has been slept in by both of us. See our hairs on the pillow. Smell our mingled scents on the sheets."

"Just how trusted are these servants if they're going to smell our sheets?" I demanded, my cheeks flushing at the thought of our "mingled scents."

Draven grimaced. "Good point. They won't try to kill you, that's about all I can guarantee. But spy for someone else in the court?" He shrugged.

I stared back at him. "The servants here would do that?"

"Yours wouldn't?" he said coolly.

I thought of the Rose Court. "Point taken."

He started to lay down, then sat back up and clapped his hands. Instantly, the chandelier over our head dimmed to a small point of soft light.

"Fine," I snapped, seeing that this was going to happen tonight whether I liked it or not.

I knew I could physically try to remove him from the bed... I also knew I'd fail. Still, it might be fun. If I were in better condition.

I could use magic, a voice in my head suggested.

But a picture of Draven turning to ash filled my vision quicker than I could imagine and my stomach churned.

No. Never. I wasn't going to do that. Possibly not ever again.

I had killed Vesper. I had killed Florian. I had killed those men who had attacked us in Nethervale.

I had killed the monstrous children in Meridium.

But the killing had to end. I had to end it.

Draven might be able to embrace this much bloodshed, but I wasn't sure I had the stomach for more of it.

Still, he didn't have to know that.

"Fine. You can sleep here for one night. We can figure something else out in the morning."

"Fine." His voice was already beginning to slur with fatigue. "Whatever you say... Princess."

If he had said "Paramour" I would definitely have thrown a book. Respect for the written word or not.

I stood there in the gentle glow of the room with my hands on my hips as he closed his eyes.

It was as if he didn't even care that I was there. Gradually, his body relaxed. A peaceful calm washed over his handsome features. One hand rested lightly on his bare chest. I watched that hand for quite a while, standing there alone in the dark as he slept.

CHAPTER 5

In the morning, I woke up ready to demand that Draven tell me why he had murdered his own brother, but when I sat up in the bed, rubbing the sleep from my eyes, I realized I wouldn't be getting answers to my questions anytime soon.

Draven was already gone.

It felt as though we had passed some bizarre sort of test.

We had slept in the same bed and... I hadn't killed him. Yet.

And thank the Three, we hadn't touched. I had stayed far over on my side and he on his.

That was a good thing. Wasn't it? So why did I feel strangely bereft by his absence?

Probably because he was the only person I knew in this foreign land, I reminded myself. One could grow used to anything. Even one's own abductor. Stranger things had happened.

Yet now all my former fury was returning. He had left me again. Gone out to do important things and left me to stew here with books and...

And a bathtub.

A very large bathtub.

I hopped out of the bed and practically ran to the bathing chamber where I turned on the taps. Lifting some of the small bottles on the table to my nose, I selected a perfumed oil that smelled of rose, sandalwood, and pine and dumped it in, trying not to think about why I had chosen that particular fragrance.

The air filled with steam and soon I was stepping naked into the deep marble tub. My eyes almost rolled back in my head with pleasure as the hot water covered my skin and relaxed my sore muscles.

After scrubbing myself and washing my hair with a slippery herbal substance that left it smelling wonderful and relatively tangle-free, I emerged from the tub and wrapped myself in a large fluffy towel then walked back to my room.

As I entered, I stopped cold.

Someone was already in there. A woman was bent over the bed, making it up. I wondered if she had already sniffed it while I'd been in the bathing chamber.

She must have been one of the servants Draven had mentioned.

"Good morning." There was a coolness to my voice. After all, she had not even asked my permission to enter. "May I help you?"

"Name is Breena. Been attending the prince and his household since he was a boy," the woman announced, without turning her back. "I've taken care of ladies, too. The finest in the court. Nothing you have that I haven't seen already. Laid out some clothes for you on the bench over there."

I opened my mouth to say I had already found clothes in the wardrobe, then glanced over at the bench she had indicated.

A row of new outfits lay spread out. Each one was prettier than the next.

I closed my mouth. "Thank you. They look very nice."

I watched her finish tidying the bed and was about to ask how long she planned to be in the bedroom.

"You can take an outfit into the sitting room and wait for me there. I won't be long."

"Wait for you?" I asked, perplexed.

"I'll do your hair, of course." Only then did she glance back at me. Breena was a petite, plump woman with rosy cheeks and delicate, furry ears. Over a dress that reminded me of the uniforms that servants wore back in the Rose Court, she wore a crisp white apron adorned with green and gold embroidery. She reminded me of an industrious mouse.

A clever, nimble mouse who may or may not be "trustworthy," I reminded myself.

Breena bit her lip. "So it's true. A Valtain fae girl." She shook her head. "Well, at least you're a girl."

I frowned. "I'm half-human, actually. Would you have minded a boy? Is there a rule against that sort of thing here?" I thought of Galahad and then I couldn't help but think of Lancelet.

"No rule, nothing like that. I meant I was grateful you were..." She gestured with her hand. "A person. Someone. Anyone."

"Anyone?" Understanding dawned on me. "You mean the prince hasn't brought home anyone before?"

Breena snorted. "I should think not. The queen is already having a fit and it's been more than twenty years since..." She trailed off, leaving the sentence unfinished. I assumed she was about to reference the banishment I wasn't supposed to know about.

"And yet... I'm still here," I said cautiously.

"Hmm," was all Breena said.

I took it that meant "for now."

I noticed a tall screen off in one corner. Going over to the bench, I selected an outfit and then stepped behind the screen.

"Prince Kairos is one hundred and fifty years old or so, correct?" I called through the screen to Breena. "I'm surprised he never married."

I bit my lip, wondering if she would take the bait.

Sure enough. "He was supposed to," the servant muttered. "Still should. Not too late. She's still not wed, is she? Might still make a powerful match. But the other? No, I won't speak of that. You ask him, if you wish. That's for him to tell, not me."

That was not particularly informative.

I popped out from behind the screen and went to look in one of the mirrors. A tunic of pale blue muslin that hit my leg mid-thigh had been paired with fitted trousers of a sturdy material in a dove gray. Around my waist I had cinched a woven leather belt decorated with small blue stones I thought might be sapphires. The belt made my waist look narrower than it was. The blue and the gray complemented the silver of my hair, which hung wet and stringy around my shoulders.

Breena marched over, towel in hand, pushed me into a chair before the mirror and began to dry my hair.

"So the prince has never had a... mistress?" I asked carefully. Truthfully, I wasn't sure how much I really wanted to know about Draven's past love life.

"Oh, he's had women. His fair share, aplenty. The ladies have always flocked to him, haven't they? Only to be rejected politely more times than naught. Men, too, for that matter. He favors the women though. Known him since he was a boy, haven't I? I can tell you that much. He's choosy though, very choosy." She was watching me in the mirror, her eyes hawkish.

"He is certainly a... very striking man," I ventured, trying to sound grateful for having been selected as Draven's paramour. It took considerable effort.

What I'd said was true, at least. But I wasn't going to go overboard with my flattery lest it get back to Draven and go to his head.

"Very handsome. And intelligent, too. And such a commanding air about him," Breena agreed. "He'll make an excellent emperor."

"Emperor?" I asked. "But I thought there was a queen..."

"Queen Regent," Breena corrected. "Not empress. Queen Sephone rules until a true ruler can be found. That was supposed to be Draven's elder brother, but..." She made a clucking sound and moved off to find a brush.

"But he died," I finished quietly, trying to conjure up the proper respectful tone. "That must have been..."

"Shattering, that's what it was," Breena snapped. "It shattered this kingdom into a million pieces and I don't think we've ever been the same." Breena sighed and began to work on my hair, plaiting it and weaving it into a loose elegant braid that reminded me of a fish's tail.

"Because Prince Kairos committed fratricide, you mean," I suggested, keeping my voice carefully neutral.

Breena scowled. "He did what he did. There are some who would call it that. And others who would call it something else entirely."

My eyebrows went up. "What do you mean? Draven–Prince Kairos, I mean–*did* kill his brother, didn't he?"

"I won't argue with that. But there's some killing that can be justified and some that cannot. Prince Kairos, well, he's always had a softer heart than most in this court."

A soft heart? Were we talking about the same Draven? What could possibly be "soft" about killing your own sibling?

Then I thought of Odelna. Draven had insisted on sheltering the child, on bringing her with us. He had protected her. Protected me.

But not Lancelet. He wasn't strong enough, fast enough... good enough... not for that.

With a shock, I realized I blamed him more than I did myself.

How unfair was that. I was Lancelet's friend. I was the one who had left all three of them behind. If anyone was more to blame it was me.

But I had assumed Draven would always be able to do anything I needed him to. Protect me, protect anyone. And I had to give him credit. He had tried.

With a pang, I realized he probably knew I blamed him. And he hadn't shirked the blame. He had accepted it as if it were his due.

Perhaps Breena was right. There was a very slight chance that Draven would make a good king. Or emperor.

Then I set my face stonily. Or perhaps he would if he didn't keep women locked up in his bedchamber against their will.

"There," Breena said with a tone of satisfaction. "You look rather pretty." She looked over my shoulder at my reflection in the mirror and patted my shoulders. "I suppose there is no accounting for taste. Draven has always had an eccentric streak. It runs in the family."

"Does it?" It was rather a backhanded compliment but I wasn't about to complain. I doubted Breena dished out many compliments in general.

"You've dressed me up and done my hair. Does that mean I'm going somewhere? Is Prince Kairos expecting me?" I asked hopefully.

Breena's face turned sympathetic. "I'm afraid not. I just thought you should look nice for when he came back."

I bit my tongue and resisted saying I was not here to simply look pretty for a man. Not that Draven didn't succeed in looking fairly pretty himself... basically all of the time.

"Thank you," I managed. "I suppose I'll go and read for a while then."

And plot Draven's downfall and my imminent escape, even if I had to climb out a window.

Though the windows seemed to be an off-putting escape avenue, I thought desolately. I suspected the wards that kept the volcanic heat and ash and smoke out only went a little ways out from the castle. If I managed to climb out over the balcony, I would probably find myself quickly roasted alive.

Breena nodded, her mind evidently already elsewhere. "I'll tidy up here, then be out of your way. I understand that creature Hawl is seeing to your meals."

That creature? So Hawl was not necessarily accepted among the other servants? If Hawl even *was* a servant. I wasn't sure what Hawl was exactly.

"Yes, they—he—she—is an excellent cook," I stumbled.

"I believe the Bearkin is a female. Not that you can tell one way or the other. Not that the creature seems to care one way or the other what they are, or perhaps they would put on clothes like a decent person," Breena tutted with annoyance.

"Not a fan of the Bearkin then," I murmured beneath my breath.

I moved into the dining area where I found the kitchen empty but a pot of steaming tea and a plate of cooked eggs, herbed biscuits and fruit waiting for me on the counter.

I poured myself a cup and filled a plate, then returned to the sitting room and began to read about the construction of the palace.

A few minutes later, I heard Breena depart.

Eventually the details of palace construction became tedious and I skipped ahead to the next chapter which discussed the demographic makeup of the kingdom of Sorega in relation to the rest of Myntra.

While the fae of Valtain had dominated southern Eskira at one time—until their sudden departure for who-knew-where, the Siabra seemed to rule the entire continent of Myntra. The Court of the Umbral Flame was their seat of power, but there were smaller Siabra courts all over Myntra, ruled over by the higher ranks of the nobility. Sorega contained the most prominent and the greatest number of Siabra, but other races inhabited Myntra, including–I was shocked to read–humans.

Indeed, the city which lay above us–Noctasia–was something of a cosmopolitan mosaic, where people from all over the continent traveled and converged for everything from festivals to marketplaces to royal ceremonies and processions.

I put down my book for a moment and stared out the windows across from me where a burst of liquid flame drew my attention. Everything about Draven's court was strange...yet also familiar. I might have been back in my room in the castle in Camelot, reading a book from my shelf. Except here, I felt...

I cursed silently as I found the word I was looking for.

But it was true. I felt *safer* here than I did in Camelot, despite what I might have said to Draven and despite how unsafe Draven seemed to believe I truly was.

Here, I was with him at least. Back in Camelot, who would have even a hope in hell of protecting me from Arthur's wrath when I returned without the sword?

Would my brother believe I had stolen it?

My thoughts were cut off by a tapping sound. At first, I thought Breena had returned and this time was doing me the courtesy of knocking.

But the tapping sound wasn't coming from the bedroom exterior door or even from the foyer beyond the sitting room. It was much closer.

I looked over next to the hearth and the large wooden bookcases lining the walls on either side of it. The tapping continued. I walked over to the hearth carefully, even going so far as to peer into the stone recess. Nothing. I walked past the bookshelves and over to a full-length mirror on the adjacent wall. The tapping grew louder.

And then I gasped. The mirror was opening very slowly, inch by inch, revealing a gaping dark space behind it and... a boy.

The boy grinned up at me cockily from where he sat on a ledge behind the mirrored door.

"Hello there."

"Hello," I replied.

"Care to explore the palace?" The boy could not have been more than twelve. His eyes sparkled with mischief. His skin was smooth and sun-kissed with a warmth reminiscent of golden spices, while his shiny jet-black hair had been cropped unevenly as if he had been trying to escape the haircut while it was being given.

The boy's messy hair reminded me immediately of Kaye and my heart gave a painful little lurch.

"I thought I wasn't allowed out."

The boy snickered. "Do you like following the rules? I don't."

"Not really," I admitted. "Especially not this one."

The boy's face broke into a playful smile, revealing a row of pearly white teeth.

"Then let's go," he suggested. He reached out a hand and I willingly took it, climbing up onto the ledge and peering past him with interest.

"What is this place?" I inquired.

The boy shrugged. "A tunnel. They're all over the palace. But hardly any are used. And no one dares to use these ones, because..." He grinned at me. "No one would risk Prince Kairos's wrath."

"No one but you?" I pointed out. I refused to think of just how wrathful Draven would be if I snuck out through this mirror.

Well, it would serve him right. Perhaps when he returned he would finally realize that he could not keep me locked up like some princess in a story. Funnily enough I could not remember reading about famous mistresses locked up in a story. At least, none that had happy endings.

"Pull it closed behind you," the boy said, pointing to the latch.

I did as instructed as the boy snapped his fingers and lights bloomed along the walls revealing a narrow passage that increased in height a few meters down. Good. I would be able to stand up.

I crawled behind the boy until I could safely stand, then looked about me. "How did you do that?"

I pointed to the lights that glowed from small sconces along the walls.

"What? This?" The boy grinned and snapped his fingers again and we were thrown into darkness.

"Very funny."

A snapping of fingers and the lights returned.

"It's magic," the boy said, with a wink.

"Yes, I figured as much but what sort? And do all Siabra have it?"

"Oh, I'm not Siabra." The boy lifted his hair from over his ears and pointed at rounded ears as he walked down the passage. "I'm human."

I stared. "How... is that possible?"

"Ever since the curse, the humans here have sometimes been born with magic."

"The curse?"

"Something to do with the Siabra. They can't have kids, you know."

"They can't?" I thought for a minute. "That doesn't quite make sense. They must have or they wouldn't exist."

The child seemed surprised, then thoughtful. "Oh, well, I guess they used to be able to. But they can't now. But their magic, it had to go somewhere, right? So it went into human kids instead. At least, it does sometimes."

"So you're human but you were born with magic," I summarized.

The boy's explanation didn't quite make sense. I was sure he was leaving parts out by accident. Or perhaps because he didn't know the full story. Surely Draven's people were able to have children. But I had read that the fae only had children rarely, perhaps because they were so long-lived. Maybe it was something like that. There wasn't the same cultural imperative to procreate like there was with short-lived humans who needed to produce a legacy more quickly.

"What's your name, anyhow?" I asked the boy.

"Beks. And you're the Prince's Paramour." He grinned.

"You are *not* going to call me that," I exclaimed. "That's a title, not my name. You can call me Morgan."

"Morgan? Okay, Morgan. Walk faster. You want to get there today, right?"

"Get where exactly? Where are we going?" I said, as I quickened my pace.

The boy gave a careless shrug. "We could go anywhere. The menagerie. The gardens. The temple. The library."

"A menagerie? That sounds interesting."

"There are animals there from across Myntra. And even some from across the ocean," Beks boasted.

"Impressive," I murmured. "The library might also be nice..."

"Or I could take you to *him*," Beks suggested, with a roguish look.

"Him? To Draven you mean?" I raised a brow. "You know where he is? Right now?"

Beks nodded enthusiastically. "He's training. I watch them all the time now that it's started."

"Now that what's started?" I asked with frustration.

Beks shook his head at me in amazement. "Don't you know anything?"

"Apparently not," I said crossly.

There were so many things I was missing. Draven hadn't just left me in that room. He had left me utterly in the dark. Now I wondered again why.

"Your paramour is a prince, yes?" Beks said.

"So they tell me," I muttered. Paramour. Ha!

"And if he were the eldest prince, he would be emperor now. Since his father is dead. But he is the second eldest. And his brother is dead," Beks explained.

"But since his brother is dead and he's a prince, shouldn't he be on the throne now?" I asked, genuinely puzzled. "That's how it works everywhere else."

"Maybe where you're from. But he killed his brother. His mother had to banish him, then she became queen."

"Queen Regent. And yet she let him back in," I pointed out. "He's here now and doesn't seem banished to me."

"He was banished for ten years," Beks clarified. "He was gone much longer. He left before I was born."

That much was plainly obvious. Beks was nowhere near twenty. I hid a grin.

"But everyone would talk about him. The Prince of Claws. The Lost Prince. They would wonder why he hadn't returned. His mother missed him," Beks said. He sounded almost forlorn. Though nothing anyone else had said had given me the impression the Queen Regent was a particularly doting parent.

"So banished wasn't really banished forever? Just for a little while?" A humiliating punishment but hardly what one might expect for killing the heir to the throne. Elsewhere, Draven might have been simply executed.

The Siabra certainly had their own way of doing things.

Beks nodded seriously. "After ten years passed, then fifteen, then twenty, well, no one thought he was coming back. But then he did. And he brought you." Beks beamed and suddenly I wondered if he saw the whole thing as somewhat romantic. The lost prince returning with me on his arm.

"Ah, yes," I said weakly. "He did. His mother must be... very happy?"

"I'm not sure," Beks said, tilting his head consideringly. "She's the queen. I suppose so. But anyhow, Prince Kairos can't just have the throne. If it had been left vacant for twenty-five years, the next in line would have had the right to take it. The prince's cousin, Avriel."

"But now the prince is back, so...?"

"So Prince Kairos can claim it, but he'll have to win it." Beks beamed. "It's like a game."

I was skeptical. "A game? How is it played?"

"I'll show you," Beks said. "Just follow me. We can see the menagerie another day."

I followed obediently behind him as we wove our way through the narrow passageway. The lights followed us as we walked, sconces lighting up one by one a few meters ahead, then darkening behind us after a few moments. It was a very useful trick. I wondered if I could learn it or if it was the sort of magic you had to have been born with. After all, Crescent had said he couldn't create wards but he could do other things.

I might have been able to burn people to death with my bare hands but that didn't seem particularly useful in day-to-day situations. Nor something I planned to brag about to little Beks.

The walls around us were a damp brick. The floor was dusty stone, with trickling pools of water in some places. I was reminded of the passageway out of the castle in Camelot that I had taken to join the hunters and to go for clandestine nighttime walks.

I might have been an entire continent away, but the nature of secret passageways in castles had not fundamentally changed. They were not luxurious. They had been built for stealth and practicality.

Now my eyes caught sight of discreet, strategically placed peepholes along the walls. Some were relatively close together. These must have looked into living apartments like my own. Others were few and far between. I surmised that meant they looked into larger public areas like ballrooms or the menagerie Beks had mentioned. Some were small, hardly larger than an eye. Small footstools had been placed at some of them. I guessed Beks had done so, being too short to reach the holes otherwise. Still other peepholes were more like tiny windows.

As we passed one of these, I paused to flick aside the hanging brass cover and peered out at a bustling courtyard with a beautiful garden covered by a glass dome.

We walked further along and came to an alcove, furnished with hanging tapestries and a long low leather bench. Whoever had used these tunnels–whoever still did, I reminded myself, for surely Beks could not be the only one who knew of them—had apparently had the thoughtfulness to build in sitting areas where spies might come for a time of respite.

"What were these passages used for?" I asked Beks.

"Spying mostly, I suppose. The last emperor would keep spies who would watch his enemies through some of these. But I've heard the royal family used them to get around the palace, too."

"What do you mean?"

"So that they could travel without having their movements watched all of the time. Emperor Lucius used them to visit one of his mistresses in secret." Beks glanced back at me, as if seeing the connection. "Or so I've heard. She was the wife of one of his enemies."

One of his mistresses? I assumed this was Draven's father. Lovely.

"I suspect you hear a very great deal," I muttered. "If you spend much of your time playing in these passages."

I caught a guilty look on Beks' face. "What?"

"Oh, nothing. Come on, we're almost there."

"Where is there?" I asked, but Beks just moved faster ahead of me.

I jogged along behind him until finally he came to a halt.

"This one has two holes. So we both can look. Go further down and you can look from the other one." He pointed a little way ahead to where I caught a gleam of brass.

Wherever we were about to spy on, the room must have been large indeed to warrant multiple peepholes.

I walked ahead to the little window, then carefully moved aside the brass plate.

We were looking down over a training room.

The room was colossal. Easily the size of two of the Great Halls of the castle in Camelot, or more. The ceiling was the highest I had ever seen within a building.

Roughly divided into sections, the room catered to different styles of combat. In one corner, a large space had been devoted to a towering climbing wall. Taking advantage of the vaulted ceiling, a rocky rugged surface allowed participants to test their agility and endurance. Suspended ropes, precarious pillars, and swinging objects made up another obstacle course nearby.

In another corner, rows of archery targets lined the wall. I watched as a tall, muscular brown-haired man let his bow loose and an arrow sliced through the air, hitting one of the targets with a sharp "thunk."

Across from the archery station, racks of gleaming swords and axes sat alongside rows of wickedly curved daggers, next to a dueling ring where two men were fighting.

My heart sped up. Draven!

His opponent possessed flaming red hair and owl-like brown speckled eyes. He was a little broader than Draven was, thicker in the neck and shoulders. But Draven was meeting him, blow for blow, with seeming effortlessness. He moved with his familiar catlike grace, but at a greater speed than I had ever seen. Had he been holding back before?

Then another familiar figure caught my eye across the room. A lithe, dark-haired woman. Even from here I could see that her eyes were a striking serpentine blend of purple, yellow, and gold.

Lyrastra was moving solo through a meticulously choreographed fighting routine, her every motion a mesmerizing dance. Nearby, a man I assumed was a trainer called out a suggestion. She ignored him and kept on with her routine, her slender figure undulating and weaving, each step calculated and deliberate.

Slowly, I began to understand the sort of game Beks had in mind. Some sort of a physical competition for the throne. I wondered just what exactly was involved.

A sharp cry broke through my thoughts. I looked across the training room at a sparring area with a padded floor surrounded by ropes where a man and a woman were engaged in hand-to-hand combat.

The man was tawny-haired and handsome, with a lithe, well-toned physique. He moved with an impressive, effortless grace I had only seen before in Draven, muscles flexing and rippling below the surface of his amber skin. Glistening gold scales flowed up his sinewy forearms extending up to his broad shoulders.

His partner was small and petite with blonde hair pulled back in a bun. She wore light sparring armor that showcased her delicate but strong frame. But the thing that stood out the most was the golden tiger-like tail that extended from her lower-back. It swayed with a feline grace as she danced over the padded floor around the scaled man and seemed to give her an advantage in agility and balance.

"Stop dancing, Pearl, and fight me," the man yelled, his voice ringing out across the training room.

I was shocked. He sounded truly annoyed, as if he had grown impatient with his smaller partner's technique of avoidance. But if I were Pearl, I would be dancing around, too. The man had an attractive allure, but there was something about him that frightened me. The look in his eyes said he was not playing games. That he wanted to win at any cost.

Pearl was lightning quick. I watched as she moved swiftly behind him and landed a punch in the man's torso, then was off like a shot towards the other side of the ring.

The man scowled nastily. "You can't run forever, stupid little cat."

Sure enough, the next time Pearl tried the same move, the scaled man waited until the blow had almost landed–this time on his opposite side–then a muscular arm shot out.

Pearl gave a yelp as she was pulled forward, then thrown face down onto the floor.

Before I could even blink, the man had his foot to her neck and was crowing loudly.

I wasn't the only one who had been watching the spectacle. Draven and the red-haired man he had been dueling had slowly approached the sparring ring and now stood a few feet away.

"She's fast, I'll give her that," the scaled man called over to Draven, his face still stretched in a wide grin. "But not fast enough."

Lyrastra had stopped her practice, I noticed. She was standing very still, watching the proceedings.

"You caught the cat," said the man Draven had been fighting. "Well done, Avriel. Is that what you wanted to hear?"

Avriel? This must be the cousin Beks had mentioned. So this man was part of Draven's family? I stayed very still, listening.

"I don't need your approval, Gawain," Avriel said with a sneer. He moved his foot, grinding it ever so slightly against Pearl's neck and she let out a cry before going silent. "I only need you to step aside."

I winced. With that much weight on her neck, I wondered that she could cry out at all.

"Pearl's in this now, Avriel, just like you are," Draven said evenly. "Now let her go. The trials haven't even begun yet. She deserves a chance like everyone."

"Not officially, no. But the same rules apply," Avriel replied. "Training incidents are an accepted part of the challenge. If little Pearl didn't understand that, she shouldn't have come here today." He nodded at the man he had called Gawain. "He's not even a contender, but he understands. Don't you Gawain? You're only here to train the prince but if I had gotten you under my foot today, would you be whimpering like Pearl? Or would you face your death like a Siabra?" He glanced across at Draven, a grin spreading over his face. "Don't look so petulant, cousin. What can you do, after all?"

Lyrastra was still watching from the corner. Her trainer had stopped what he was doing and was observing, too. The entire training arena seemed focused on Avriel and his foot resting precariously on Pearl's neck.

"Do?" Draven crossed his arms over his chest. His only tell that he was truly worried.

"Nothing," Avriel supplied. "You can do nothing. Because this match has already been won. And I'll be doing us both a favor if I eliminate her before the challenge even starts..."

Draven moved slightly forward. My breath caught in my throat.

Avriel's foot shifted.

"No," Draven shouted sharply. He moved forward with lightning speed crossing into the sparring ring like a flash.

But it was too late. The sound of crunching bones filled the air.

Avriel lifted his foot. But Pearl did not rise.

I glanced at Lyrastra. Her face had gone pale. Her hands were curled into tight fists.

"...when I take pathetic little Pearl out of the running for us all," Avriel finished slowly, with a small smile. "She was never going to get very far, you know. What does it matter if she died now or later? Either way she'd have been dead. Either way you'd have been too late."

"She might have withdrawn before the ceremony," Gawain said. "And you know that, Avriel."

Avriel shrugged. "Perhaps. She was a persistent little bitch, Pearl was. She might have kept at it. Been a thorn in your side. No need to thank me, Kairos."

Draven said nothing. Instead, he simply turned away.

I watched as he seemed to notice Lyrastra for the first time. Their eyes met. Draven went very still.

Then he began to walk back in the direction of the dueling ring. Gawain was not far behind.

"Of course, if it was the sweet little morsel I hear you have hidden away in your rooms, then I'd have taken my time with her. Do you hear me, Draven? I'd have turned that little Valtain bitch over, spread her nice and wide and..."

I would never know how Avriel planned to finish that sentence. For however it had begun, Draven finished it.

With a flash of impossible agility, he vaulted into the sparring ring, springing through the air and landing on his feet in front of the scaled man.

In an instant, his hands became a whirlwind of rapid blows, each strike delivered with catlike grace. Avriel tried to muster a defense but it was pointless. Draven's strikes landed seamlessly, outmatching his cousin's every move.

Blood flew through the air like droplets of water, landing on the padded mats as Avriel's face quickly became a raw canvas of brutality.

One final blow and Avriel went sprawling on the ground, blood trickling from his split lip, his chin stained with crimson.

Only then did Draven step away.

"I could kill you now, Avriel," I heard him say quietly. "But what difference does it make if you die now or later? Either way, you'll be dead."

And then he walked away.

I stood back from the hole in the wall, my whole body trembling.

This was a game? The game Draven had to play to gain the throne?

I turned to my right to where Beks had backed away from his own peephole.

"You said it was a game," I said accusingly. "That? That wasn't a game. That was life and death."

Beks' eyes were wide. "Pearl... That's never happened before. They fight hard, but... But Avriel. Well, Avriel..." His voice trailed off.

I felt sick as I thought about poor Pearl's body lying there on the mat.

That was the man who might wind up the ruler of all of these people?

Not if Draven had anything to do with it.

Suddenly I started to understand what might have been important enough to come back for–besides supposedly protecting me, as Draven had claimed.

"I'd like to go back to my room now," I said. "I think I can find the way on my own."

"I'll come with you," Beks said quickly. Clearly, he didn't want to stay either. "Just in case."

I nodded and let him lead the way back down the passage.

"I guess that's why they call it the Killing Throne," Beks mumbled as he walked along the dusty stone corridor, his little back hunched in a way I found heartbreaking. I wished he hadn't had to see any of what we had just seen.

The only comfort I could take from it was that he had also witnessed his future emperor defending the weak.

I paused. "Excuse me?"

"The Killing Throne. That's what they call it. The real name for the Umbral Throne," Beks elaborated.

The Killing Throne. My heart sank. And soon Draven would be seated upon it.

CHAPTER 6

T hat night I found myself within a chilling tableau.

I lay upon a cold stone floor. A boy kneeled over me. His face was pallid and his eyes were strange.

I opened my mouth to ask him what was wrong, just as he lowered his face to my stomach and sank sharp teeth into my skin.

As I cried out with pain, I realized the boy was not alone. Other children crowded around me. Each one was more nightmarish in appearance than the next. Their eyes were devoid of life and yet an insatiable hunger lingered in their vacant stares.

Their gnarled hands clawed at me, tearing into my skin, as a cacophony of distorted cries and guttural moans filled the air, further intensifying my sense of terrible dread.

Piece by piece, they consumed me.

I felt each bite. Each pull of flesh torn from my bones.

The putrid stench of decay hovered around me. Was it the scent of my own devoured body or the macabre children who held me captive in this hellish torment?

Wave after wave of agony washed over me until I could bear no more. I opened my mouth and to my horror felt a breeze of air from a hole in my cheek.

Into the void, I screamed and screamed.

I woke in a cold sweat, gasping for breath, my lips still parted to form a scream.

"Morgan." The voice was deep and commanding. "It's all right. You're safe. It was only a dream."

I tried to focus, my breathing ragged. "It's dark. Where are they? Where are they? We have to get out. They're coming."

"They aren't here, Morgan." The deep voice became soothing and hushed. "It's just us. You're safe now. What did you see?"

I let out a choked sob. "Lancelet. *I* was Lancelet. I could feel their teeth ripping into me. They were..."

Frantically I raised my hands to my face. Touched my cheeks. I was whole. Complete. Alive.

I didn't deserve to be.

"I shouldn't be here. I don't deserve to be here." I let the truth tumble out. "I don't deserve to be alive. Not when I left her."

There was silence. So he didn't disagree.

Then strong hands grasped my wrists, pulling my hands away from my face.

"You know that's false. If anyone is to blame, it's me. Blame me, Morgan. There was nothing you could have done."

I didn't try to pull away. "You don't deserve my blame. I have been blaming you because it was easier than the truth. When really, I'm the one who left her." The words flooded out. "I *let* Vesper drag me away. I was a coward. I saved my own skin. No one else's. At least you saved Odelna. And me. You saved me."

Silence again.

I realized I had just admitted Draven had saved me. Like it or not. "I didn't deserve saving," I said. "You should have saved her instead. You should have looked for Lancelet. Not me. Why didn't you look for her instead..."

I knew I was being unreasonable. I didn't care. There was nothing reasonable or rational about the loss I felt. It was a pain in my heart I didn't think would ever go away.

I could hear the desperation in my voice. The grief. My cheeks were already wet. Now fresh tears flowed down my face. I didn't bother to hide them or wipe them away this time. No one ever wanted to cry. But sometimes you got to a point where the tears just couldn't be held back.

He let out a frustrated growl. "You... I..."

A light glowed from on the bedstand. My eyes slowly focused. In the soft embrace of the lamp's glow, the small black horns upon Draven's forehead reminded me he was from a world not my own. His green eyes were stormy and turbulent, a blend of sorrow and simmering fury.

"What do you want me to say, Morgan? I'm sorry. I will always be sorry for not being able to save her. I hardly knew her, but I could see her worth. She was a good friend to you, I know that."

"She was the best," I choked out. "The dearest."

"But you," he continued, ignoring me. "I will *never* apologize for saving you. I will never fucking regret coming for you. And I would do it again in a heartbeat. So don't ask me to say sorry. Don't expect me to. And don't you ever, ever fucking say you didn't deserve to be saved again, do you hear me? Listen to me clearly, you are worthy. You deserved saving. You deserved much more." A dark look came over his face. "So much more than I've given you."

I was shocked by the torrent of words. More than shocked. I was moved. I tried to hide it. "You don't owe me anything. Some freedom maybe. I'm probably entitled to that."

He gave a wry chuckle.

He was still holding me by the wrists. He seemed to realize it, too. I watched as he stared down at my hands. But instead of letting go, he started to make small motions along my skin with his thumbs, slowly and gently tracing soothing circles over the silver symbols that crossed my arms. After a few moments, he slid his thumbs down my wrists to my hands, opening them gently. His fingers moved across my skin, fingertips dancing along the contours of my palms, tracing the paths of each lifeline. Each stroke was deliberate, each stroke a caress.

I felt disoriented. Disarmed. What was this? A nighttime truce between two warring parties?

I could break it. Yank my hands away. Speak rough words that would drive him away–well, to his side of the bed at least.

But something in me was stopping me.

Something about his touch on my skin felt more right than anything I had ever felt before.

He wouldn't meet my eyes as he worked. His gaze remained lowered, his eyes fixed on my hands, his jaw locked stubbornly.

I tried to stay silent as my body awakened under his touch, relaxing and softening, the warmth returning to my limbs after the chill horror of the dream. Eventually the pleasure was too much to bear. As his fingertips dipped into the hollows of my palms and massaged gently, I let out a little moan of gratification.

Draven froze.

"I'm sorry..." I started to say, embarrassed.

He raised his head and looked at me. His eyes were blazing in a way I had never seen before. Not with sorrow or fury now, but with something very much like desire.

Heat suffused my cheeks, flooding down my chest, filling every part of me with red hot fire.

Before I could stop him, he leaned his head forward, dipping his lips down towards me. The Three help me, but I didn't move a muscle. Didn't cower. Didn't back away.

"We should go to sleep." He released my hands and slid back, rising from where he had been seated on my side of the bed. "I just got back. You were screaming when I came in."

I looked at him in confusion. He was already crossing over to his side of the bed.

Suddenly the distance from my side to his seemed too great.

I watched in silence as he stripped off his jacket, shirt, and boots, then started unbuckling his trousers.

He glanced up at me as he slid the belt from its loops. But I wouldn't look away.

The merest hint of a smile lurked at the corners of his lips as he dropped the belt on the floor.

I tried not to react as he slowly unfastened the buttons of his trousers one by one, then slid them off his long muscular legs.

His body glistened with a faint sheen of perspiration. Had he just returned from the training room? Had he been there all this time?

I thought of what he had done to Avriel. The brutality he had so easily displayed.

Still, my own strange desire was not abated. If anything, it was heightened.

Black undergarments clung to his form, accentuating his physique and leaving little to my imagination.

I felt as if I were spying again. Seeing something which I had no right to see.

And yet, were we not sharing his bedchamber? I hadn't asked Draven to take off his clothes.

No, I was merely an innocent bystander enjoying the view. And refusing to look modestly away.

Was there really anything so very wrong with that?

He slid under the coverlet and turned onto his side, his back to me.

I tried not to let out a sigh of disappointment.

With as much aplomb as I could muster, I leaned back against the pillows, my heart racing, my skin afire.

Had Kairos Draven almost kissed me?

Had it just all been an elaborate practice run for when I was finally allowed out of this chamber and he had to pretend I was really his lover? That was probably it. And then he had gotten cold feet. Perhaps the idea of kissing me was too disgusting to bear. Even as a pretense.

That thought was enough to drench the flames from my skin. I pulled the coverlet up under my chin and turned over to face the bed table beside me.

"Morgan?" Draven's voice was soft and sleepy.

"Mmm?"

"If you have another nightmare, just remember... I'm right here. Nothing can happen to you. You're safe."

Safety was an illusion and he of all people must know that.

But I understood what he was trying to do.

Still, I said nothing. Just closed my eyes and tried to force a sleep I did not want to return.

To sleep was to dream. I had begun to fear my dreams.

CHAPTER 7

"For fuck's sake! You have got to be kidding me!"

There was no one to shout at so I gave myself permission to erupt.

Draven was gone again. He had crept out with the stealth of a cat in the night.

Our brief truce was forgotten. Reckless fury filled me.

I rifled through the clothes Breena had stowed on shelves in the wardrobe, pulling out a flowing sleeveless dress of diaphanous panels of fiery oranges and reds. Flickering flames danced along the hemlines, embroidered in red and gold thread. Yanking open a drawer, I added slender spiraling cuffs of gold to each of my upper arms, before cinching a braided gold sash around my waist.

Two could play this game.

I strode to the sitting room and found the place where Beks had pushed open the door from the inside, sliding my fingers over the mirror beside the bookcases.

Ten minutes later I stood back, panting and frustrated. It was no use. Surely there must be a way to open the panel from the outside. But if there was, I couldn't find it.

I thought briefly of stretching out my hands and simply melting the mirror way.

That method lacked subtly. I didn't necessarily wish to scream where I had gone to Draven. Perhaps he knew about the access passage in the sitting room, but perhaps he didn't.

Imagining him wracking his brain trying to decipher where I had disappeared to was a much more satisfying mental picture.

Just as I was considering testing the limits of the balcony wards to their full extent, the mirrored door pushed open.

"Took your sweet time coming back, didn't you?" I said, a little testily.

Beks looked surprised. "I wasn't sure if you would... Well, after yesterday." The boy looked uncomfortable.

"Oh. That. I had almost forgotten." It was true. "Right."

I stepped into the recess as Beks backed away. "Well, thank you for coming to check. I need to get out of here."

"Happy to help," Beks said graciously. "Whatever the Prince's Paramour desires, Beks of Noctasia is here to serve."

"Noctasia?" I said, choosing to ignore the other thing. "You're from the city above?"

"Of course. Few humans live in the palace." Beks was already running ahead. "Where would you like to go today? Wait, I think I know a place. Something different from yesterday. Very different."

"Different from yesterday would be good," I muttered, following behind.

We walked for about fifteen minutes, this time taking a new route off a fork in the path, before Beks began to slow his pace.

"We don't just have to watch today," the boy explained with a familiar twinkle in his dark eyes. "There are more doors, like the one you just came through."

He flicked at something in the wall beside him and I heard a creaking sound. A tall rectangular panel was opening, large enough for us each to fit through.

"Go ahead," he encouraged. "Push it open. I already checked. It's empty. There's a ceremony in the city today. Everyone is there."

I wasn't sure exactly what that meant, but I did as he said. Pushing the panel all of the way open, I stepped down a low ledge onto the floor cautiously, then looked around me in awe.

We were in an incredibly beautiful space. Some sort of a temple from the look of it. Two majestic rotundas, separated by a low rise of stairs, stood on either side of me.

Domed ceilings stretched over top each rotunda, their graceful curves creating a sense of boundless space and light. Delicate gold inlays decorated the interior of each dome, while spectacular painted friezes depicting exotic creatures and scatterings of arcane symbols covered the upper walls.

Slender fluted columns lined the perimeter of the temple's rotundas, their capitals covered with carvings of leaves and foliage that unfolded like a bouquet.

Along the walls, ornate censers swung from delicate gold chains, releasing fragrant incense into the air. I caught a whiff of cedar, rich and woody, and jasmine, sweet and intoxicating.

I walked slowly into the rotunda to my right. Brilliantly colored stained-glass windows covered the curving ceiling interspersed with panels of gold. The colorful glass filtered the muted volcanic light that found its way through. Rays of rainbow light danced across the white marble floor.

My wonder was mixed with an odd sense of premonition as I crossed to the center of the rotunda.

A ring of large, exquisitely crafted paintings adorned high-arched shaped gilded frames embedded in the ancient stone walls. Each one featured a picturesque landscape scene. There were twelve in all. I supposed they showcased various locations across the continent of Myntra.

I stepped up to the first one, peering into a vividly-painted serene sylvan realm where towering trees swayed in harmony with a gentle breeze. Another revealed a vista overlooking swirling mists and jagged cliffs. I turned from one to the other, taking in seascapes, mountainous terrain, and soft swelling hills and valleys. One painting almost reminded me of Pendrath. It showcased rolling hills leading into rich green forests, with a city in the far distance that almost resembled Camelot.

Struck with a pang of homesickness, I was just stepping closer to take a better look when a voice called out from behind me.

"I had not taken you for a devout woman, Lady Morgan."

I turned to see Crescent and Odessa di Rhondan entering the temple through a large stone doorway. The official entrance.

"I wouldn't call myself one necessarily." My voice carried easily, echoing across the marble and stone.

From the corner of my eye, I caught sight of Beks. He was scuttling under a long stone bench with the speed of a spider. Putting a finger to his lips, he winked. I understood.

"Must one be devout to enjoy these paintings?" I asked, as Crescent reached me. I saw him exchange a glance with his sister. Then Odessa turned around and marched back to the doorway they had come in, her two blades crossed over her muscular back.

Apparently, Crescent was on Morgan-duty today.

"Well, not these ones, no." Crescent grinned and I couldn't help smiling back a little. While Odessa put my back up, there was something easy to like about Crescent. It was too bad he had been assigned to me as a duty. We might have been friends.

"But those in the other rotunda—" He gestured for me to follow, then led the way out past the hidden gold-paneled door that Beks and I had come in through and up the small dividing steps into the second rotunda. This one had a black marble floor and instead of landscape paintings in gilded frames, there were silver arched frames that depicted...

"Is that Zorya?" I exclaimed, stepping in for a closer inspection.

Long fair hair cascaded down a beautiful pale-faced woman's back as she stood in front of a golden boat. In the distance high on a mountaintop lay a spectacular palace.

"The Palace of the Sun," Crescent pointed out. In legend, Zorya resided in the Palace of the Sun where she opened the gate for the sun's rays each morning.

I walked past another painting that depicted a young woman with sharp, knowing features that belied her youth. She was dressed in a black gown. Strands of ebony and silver hair fell around her shoulders. There was a gleaming curved blade strapped to her back and her hands were cupped in front of her. They were filled to the brim with bones.

"I believe you call her Marzanna," Crescent offered.

I nodded slowly. "But I've never seen her like this before."

In Pendrath, the goddesses were always depicted in sculpted stone. I had never imagined them in full color. The paintings made them seem so lifelike. So real.

"Devina!" I exclaimed as I passed to the next image. There was no mistaking the goddess of the hunt.

And yet, this was a new Devina entirely.

The goddess depicted by this artist was a tall woman with nutbrown hair and violet eyes. She wore the familiar leather armor she was often depicted wearing in Pendrathian art, with a spear in one hand. There was a floral wreath around her head, full of bright pink and purple buds. And there the similarities seemed to end.

Horns poked through the floral crown, just like Draven's. Only smaller, more delicate and deer-like. The hand that held the spear was human, but in Devina's left hand she held a bouquet of vibrant feathers and her fingers ended in talons not tips.

The goddess wore a pretty homespun dress, the kind of embroidered gown a peasant girl might wear to a country fair. But the dress ended mid-thigh and from there down, Devina sprouted slender furred legs that ended in delicate pointed hooves.

The most surprising thing to me—and the thing that would surely have disturbed my brother Arthur the most—was how natural it seemed.

This Devina was as beautiful as the one back home. Of course, she had horns and claws and hooves. Why should that surprise me? She was the goddess of nature and everything wild, was she not?

"She's Siabra? Your Devina is Siabra?" I asked Crescent.

"She's fae," he said simply. "Why wouldn't she look like us?"

I walked to the next painting.

Crescent followed quietly behind, his leather boots padding softly on the marble floor.

A tall and robust man stared down at me from behind fierce, cold eyes. A long beard tinged with gray reached down to his chest. On the man's head sat a helmet carved with lightning bolts. He wore a suit of gold and silver armor. Overtop the armor a cape of brilliant red flowed majestically around his shoulders. In one hand he gripped a round shield, emblazoned with the symbol of an oak tree. And in his other hand...

I gasped.

The man held Excalibur. I would have recognized the blade anywhere. The dark metal blade had been unsheathed as if in preparation for imminent war. I recognized the etchings that covered the blade, patterns of leaves and thorns like those surrounding a rose.

"Perun," Crescent said from behind me. "Perhaps you've heard of him?"

All I could do was nod.

"But he is not the only one to hold the sword," Crescent noted, almost conversationally. He indicated the next two paintings where a noble-looking man and woman were represented, with something none of the other paintings had contained–a shared background which stretched from one to the other.

A stunning woman with honey beige skin filled the first frame. Tall and slender, her shining black hair was loose around her shoulders and on her head she wore a crown of willow branches and roses. With shock, I saw that her eyes were like Lyrastra's, beautiful, narrow, and snakelike with turquoise and purple shades. As I looked more closely, I realized she was scaled like Avriel, too. Pale gold scales wound down her left cheek and stretched down her neck disappearing below the neckline of the pure white gown she wore.

In her hands she held Excalibur, stretched out like an offering, resting lightly on her palms. But in contrast to the naked blade the fierce-looking man held aloft, here Excalibur was sheathed. The hilt of the sword glimmered with a silver hue, vines winding around the grip. At the top of the pommel I spotted the brilliant carved ruby rose.

A shiver went through me as I remembered touching that sparkling ruby gem, moments before Orcades prison disappeared around me and I broke through the surface of the water holding Excalibur above me... as Vesper ran to the edge of the lake.

"Vela," Crescent explained. "And next to her, Khor. Legend says she was the first of the fae."

I turned to him. "And Khor?"

Crescent's dark-skinned face turned thoughtful. "Some say he was human. Some accounts claim fae. What do you think?"

I turned to the painting of Khor.

Khor was golden-haired and dark of skin, and he was laughing. I had never thought of a god or goddess laughing before. Vela seemed to be in on the joke, I realized, for a small smile was playing on her lips, too. Or perhaps they were simply happy to be together, I thought, as I took in the shared backdrop the painter had given them. A breathtaking vista of a volcano spewing lava as it sat on the edge of a majestic sapphire ocean.

The golden-haired god was decked in a silver breastplate with a white tunic beneath, and he was stretching out a hand to his consort in the painting beside him, as he sat proud and upright on...

"An exmoor!" I exclaimed with delight.

Khor was riding a huge ivory-hued cat, its eyes bright and cunning. The cat wore armor similar to its rider. A massive breastplate of silver covered its chest and on its back was a curved saddle of resplendent gold.

"I understand that you've seen one in the flesh," Crescent commented, his brown eyes dancing. "The very one our prince brought back."

I stared at him. "Draven... Your prince brought the exmoor back?"

Crescent nodded. "He's been trying to train her ever since. Perhaps we might go and have a look together one day." He flushed slightly. "With the prince's approval, of course."

I frowned darkly. "Of course. Only with my liege's approval."

I turned back to face the paintings. Further down the curving row were more figures, many of them with brilliant-hued skin and vibrant shades of hair.

"So many fae in your pantheon," I murmured. Whereas in Pendrath, the gods were always depicted as human. Now that I had seen the paintings, I had to admit it made more sense in some ways for them to have been fae.

"I thought you would appreciate the artistry. The temple is sadly out of favor with most of the Siabra nowadays."

"Why?" I asked curiously. He was right. The place was empty except for ourselves. Back in Camelot, the Temple of the Three was a constant hub of activity, always filled with worshippers from the city and all around Pendrath.

"We used to revere them," Crescent replied. "But ever since our split with the Valtain, not so much."

I stared stupidly. "But... What does one have to do with the other? Do the Siabra not believe in respecting the gods?"

For someone who didn't even consider herself all that religious, I was oddly offended by this.

Crescent shrugged. "Depending on who you speak to these days, the Siabra may not even consider the gods divine at all."

My eyes must have widened for he laughed. "Most Siabra no longer care, Lady Morgan. They believe the gods and goddesses are part of our past, not our future. Some have decided that is a question best left for scholars. As for whether we still respect them... In a sense, we do. Some we still celebrate for their great deeds. Others we fear for their terrible ones."

"Like Perun, you mean? Did he not bring down Vela herself?"

Crescent tilted his head. "Did he? Some of our stories say it was the other way around."

"Is that why they both hold Excalibur?" I challenged. "You can't have it both ways. Who was the victor?"

Crescent crossed his arms over his chest and looked contemplative. "I have heard it said that Perun and Vela have lived many times before. And in some lifetimes, Perun triumphs. In others, Vela. It is a cycle that goes on and on. Spanning countless millennia."

I gaped. "I have never heard anything so..." I was about to say "far-fetched." Or perhaps "sacrilegious."

But Crescent's face had turned pensive and almost sad. He was looking back at Vela and Khor with a wistful expression. "Of course, who knows if the cycle will continue," he murmured. "With all that has happened..."

"What do you mean?"

He glanced at me. "Oh, I meant the curse."

I tried to speak lightly. "The Siabra curse? Of course. The prince has spoken of it, but I fear the details escape me now."

"It is his very reason for being. I am not surprised he has spoken of it to you," Crescent said. "Everything you see around you has changed because of it, discernible or not. Our lives are static. Frozen. We live without knowing if we will go on. It is a terrible way to exist. The Siabra have fundamentally been altered because of it."

I had no idea what he was talking about, but all I said was, "Because of this dreadful curse, yes."

"Of course, the prince has seen the damage the curse has brought first hand. More than anyone. Why, it nearly brought down the royal house."

I was on precarious ground, but fortune favored the bold they said. I had to risk it. "You mean because of what happened to his brother?"

Crescent nodded. "The Crown Prince Tabar was very different from his younger brother, Prince Kairos. Some said that was why he would make an excellent successor to his father, the Emperor Lucius Venator. They shared the same ruthlessness of spirit." He grimaced. "Others would say it was that ruthlessness that got us into this mess of being cursed in the first place. The price of our own cruelty."

He met my eyes. "Still others claim the emperor acted alone, brutally, irresponsibly. And doomed us all."

Emperor Lucius. Draven's father.

I held my breath, then took a risk. "By 'dooming us all,' I presume you mean when he doomed the fae children of Valtain first."

Crescent's face became pained. "That act of war–some would say of cowardly treachery against our own kin–has haunted us for one hundred and fifty years. Not an extraordinarily long time by fae standards of time, but not insignificant by any means either."

I put a hand against the stone wall to steady myself, hoping Crescent wouldn't notice how pale I'd turned.

The fae children. The fae children who Draven had claimed all died at the hands of a brutal enemy who had unleashed a terrible plague.

The brutal enemy? It was Draven's own people.

His words rang in my mind...

"From the smallest babe in arms to children as old as your brother Kaye, they sickened and they died. They died swiftly, here, in this place. And then the fae took their children's bodies and left Valtain."

But the children had *not* died. At least, not all of them. They had lingered, somehow, some way, continuing to exist as horrible twisted versions of themselves.

Did Crescent realize this? Did he know the children had not actually all died? Did he realize how much fucking *worse* things really were?

What sort of monsters were these Siabra? I felt a wave of revulsion as I understood where I stood, in the temple of a people who spurned the gods and whose emperor had destroyed the lives of so many innocent babes. Of course, the Siabra had chosen to ignore the gods. How could they offer up prayers after what they had done?

But Crescent's face was so sorrowful, so full of regret.

"Perhaps the Siabra deserved everything they got." I couldn't keep the malicious edge out of my tone. "Have you ever wondered that?"

"Many times," Crescent admitted swiftly. "I'm sure the prince has, too. What the old emperor did... Well, he acted without mercy. If he had known the price would be his own lineage, would he have done differently? I am sure he would. But we cannot change the past. We can only regret it and live with its consequences."

He met my eyes. "I saw the children in Meridium, Lady Morgan. I was a member of the party the prince took back with him to search for your friend. The young knight-in-training from Camelot."

I was stunned. "You! You were there?"

He nodded. "You were insensible at the time. Too weak to know what the prince was doing. But as soon as the prince knew you were safe in the palace, he called his people to him. Odessa and I were honored to be asked to join the rescue effort." I watched as he swallowed hard. "Though as it turned out, there was to be no rescue. I am so sorry. What we saw, what we learned... It haunts me still. I know the whispers have filled the court."

"Good," I said viciously. "What the Siabra did to those children haunts me, too."

Crescent's expression turned quizzical. "And yet your allegiance is to the prince. It seems strange that you should be able to balance the crimes of the Siabra with your love for him, but I suppose that is the incredible power of love."

I bit my tongue. Hard.

"Why did Kairos kill Tabar?" I asked bluntly, setting aside subtly for one day. "Why did he kill his own brother?"

Crescent seemed surprised. "Why, to save Lyrastra, of course. And because of what Tabar had done to Prince Kairos's..."

"Thank you, Crescent," a deep voice called across the rotunda. "That will be all for now."

I looked to see Draven standing in the doorway of the temple. He was a commanding presence, tall and arrogant, arms crossed firmly over his broad chest, a familiar scowl on his lips. Cloaked in regal black, he wore a tunic accented with leather shoulder patches and high sturdy boots. Had he been working in the training arena today? Perhaps taking a turn on that treacherous climbing wall?

Behind him stood Odessa, looking superior and smug.

Next to her was a tall thin man with a pallid complexion. His face was framed by a meticulously groomed pointed black beard. Piercing eyes as dark as the midnight sky held my own with a relentless calculating gaze. At first, I thought the man was wearing a long cloak of onyx and gold. Then I realized the cloak was in fact wings. They folded behind his back, magnificent but ominous, like the wings of a predatory bird. I watched as the man stepped into the room.

"Where is he?" the man said curtly. "I can smell him."

Without waiting for a reply, the bearded man raised one arm.

I gasped as a powerful force swept the room.

There was a shrieking sound and Beks slid out from under the bench where he had been hiding, his small body rolling across the floor like a ball and then rising into the air at least five feet off the ground.

"Stop," I cried, running forward. "Stop that at once. Put him down!"

The bearded man had the gall to look surprised. He ignored me.

"She is right," Draven snarled, stepping forward. "Lower him at once, Javer. He is your pupil, not your toy. Treat him with respect or I will have him reassigned to someone who will, regardless of what the Queen Regent has told you."

Javer's face flashed with anger but he did as he had been told. Lowering his hand, Beks crashed to the floor with a cry.

I ran to him, crouching down to help him rise. The boy was rubbing his shoulder gingerly.

"My master," he whispered, smiling weakly. "I've been sneaking away from our lessons. Now you see why I..."

"Silence," Javer commanded. "You will follow me. Now. You have missed days of instruction because of this foolish truancy. You will make them up immediately."

Beks looked at me helplessly and shrugged.

To my fury, Draven said nothing more, only stepped aside so that Javer and the boy could pass.

When they were gone, Draven glanced between Crescent and me. His face was stony. "I take it I interrupted a history lesson."

"Crescent was just bringing me up to date on a few details I had forgotten," I replied sweetly. "How kind of you to bring the prince here to me, Odessa. How thoughtful."

Odessa's jaw clenched ever so slightly but she said nothing.

"I will deal with this," Draven said, raising a hand to his brow as if he were weary. "You two may go. Thank you, Odessa."

"Yes, thank you, Odessa, for caring so very much about my whereabouts. I thought you were a warrior but I see I have mistaken you. You are simply a paid snitch," I snapped.

"That's enough," Draven said sharply. "She did what she was told to do."

I turned to him, seething. "Yes, and she should not have been told to do it in the first place. Just as I should not have been confined to that suite. I am not a problem for you to *deal with*."

"You're right," he said. "I have been a fool. I'm sorry."

My jaw may have dropped if I had not made a point of holding onto it.

"You're... sorry?" I managed. "And just what do you plan to do to remedy things?"

"I can't remedy everything," Draven replied, causing me to scowl. "But perhaps I can at least grant you more freedom, once you understand."

"Help me to understand then, Draven. You promised me answers when I awoke that first day, but you have given me none."

He nodded. "I'll try."

I watched as he clasped his hands behind his back and approached the painting of Vela.

"Crescent told me about the curse," I said. "I know everything now."

"Everything?"

"I know the Siabra were the ones who did that to the fae children."

"We are fae, too. Do not forget it," Draven said softly, without turning around.

"Two sides. Split asunder. The fae that remained in Valtain and the fae who left for Myntra and called themselves Siabra," I surmised. "But what split them?"

Draven turned to face me. "Can you not guess?"

I thought of the wall in the Temple of the Three. "Appearances? Could it really be so trite?"

"Claws and feathers. Hooves and horns." Draven's expression was sardonic. "There was a time not so long ago when you were terrified of displaying such features yourself."

"That was..." I stopped. "That is true. But now I see people around me who bear them and I can look at you without flinching. There is a strangeness to the differences, yes, but also beauty, too." I wondered if I was saying too much.

"I agree. And yet, such things became the basis for cracks in the unity of the fae. Oh, it was a pretext at first. Nothing more. Bitter feuds were exacerbated by it though. Houses that had once merged our features began to specifically breed them out through careful marriage alliances. Two groups slowly emerged. More different and more divided. There were the fae you see traces of in Eskira. The fae you have in your very own blood. The Valtain."

"Brilliant colors of hair. Beautiful shades of skin. At least, I have always thought so." I touched my hair self-consciously. My silver strands were muted, but I would take them over the former dull gray any day.

He nodded. "Because you are not your dimwitted, narrow-minded, rainbow-hating brother."

"Your powers must have differed, too?" I calculated. "Was that part of it?"

Draven shrugged. "The Valtain fae tend towards the elemental more than we do. But it was all an excuse for enmity and war. Just as with humans. When humans fight, do you even have the excuse of varying appearances? You all look the same to us."

I opened and closed my mouth again, then thought for a moment. "Historically, humans have fought wars based on even more subtle, stupid differences, it's true."

"What matters is there was a war. The Siabra had left Valtain and yet they couldn't let matters go. The Valtain fae felt much the same. Across two continents, they spread seeds of hate."

"Until the seeds of hate fell upon their children," I finished.

He nodded. "My father chose to do something unspeakable. He thought it would put an end to things once and for all." I supposed it had in a terrible, terrible way. "I would not have done the same."

"But your brother would have?" I guessed. "And that was why you killed him? And... something to do with Lyrastra? He was going to hurt her? Why?"

"No. That was much later. Lyrastra was his wife. Tabar believed she had failed him."

I had forgotten Lyrastra was his sister-in-law. She had been married to a man who already seemed unspeakably vile to me. "How? How could she have failed him?"

For a moment, I thought he would not answer.

Then, "Simply because she did not bear him a living child."

I stared without comprehension. "And so, he what...? Was going to kill her for that? Is that the kind of thing your people usually do? Murder their spouses for failure to be fertile?"

Monsters. The word echoed in my head. Monstrous.

"At times, in the past, yes. We are not a gentle people, Morgan. We have always had our own rules. You may find they differ from the ones you are used to considerably. Please notice I do not say that is a good thing, nor that we are better than you are."

I was beginning to understand the other things Crescent had said.

"You can't have children," I said slowly. "That is the curse that was put upon you."

Draven nodded. "Very rarely. And when a child is born, it rarely lives past its first year."

"And yet your brother would have punished his wife for failing to bear him an heir?" I suddenly felt more sympathy for Lyrastra than I had thought possible.

"She had delivered ten stillborn children uncomplaining," Draven said softly. "And she would have gone to her death, silent and still uncomplaining."

Silent and uncomplaining did not sound like the Lyrastra I knew, but I said nothing. I believed him.

"And yet now she hates you? Even though you saved her life and were banished in the process?"

A dark look flickered over Draven's face. "It's complicated. As the crown prince and heir to the empire, Tabar had the right to do as he saw fit. Even if it meant killing his wife and taking another. By robbing Lyrastra of her death, I robbed her of an honorable way out of an impossible situation."

I stared speechless. "But she still *has* her life. She owes you everything. And despite all that, she can't show you an ounce of gratitude?"

Draven grimaced. "Gratitude... I'm not sure Lyrastra has that in her nature. But no, she was not grateful. At least, not at the time. You see, like all of us, she had become used to the way things were done, wrong and backwards though it may seem to you and me now. When I killed her husband, she believed she had lost all dignity. Nor can she ever remarry for under Siabran law, a man or woman mated to a prince of the royal blood can never take another. I doomed her to loneliness."

"That's ridiculous," I said at last. "All of it. That she should have to suffer if she wished to marry, but also that you doomed her to loneliness. She can still have lovers, friends. If she is childless, well, so is everyone else around her. She's not alone in her plight. She might find other things to occupy her time than anger. Other hobbies and pursuits."

Draven's lips twitched ever so slightly. "I believe she has found something to occupy her of late, yes."

I thought of how I had seen Lyrastra in the training arena.

"You mean the competition?" I said before I could stop myself. "This game or whatever you Siabra call it. To win the Killing Throne."

Draven's eyes narrowed but he didn't dispute it. "The Umbral Throne, yes."

"Whatever," I muttered.

"The Blood Rise, it's called. Some call it the Bloodbath. Most simply call it a competition, as you have."

"And it's what exactly? A fight to the death?"

"Something like that. For Lyrastra, it's a way up to the position she always thought would one day be hers."

"Empress, you mean. What about for you?" I met his eyes directly. "You're going to die for the Umbral Throne?"

"No, I plan to live for it," he said bluntly. His tone was so resolute I felt my heart quicken. It was so easy to believe him when he spoke like that. "I plan to win the competition, attain the throne, and start putting this empire to rights."

"Is that even possible at this point?" I asked sourly.

He smiled slightly. "Things can't get much worse. A hundred and fifty years may seem like lifetimes to mortals and only a drop in the bucket to most Siabra, but regardless it was enough time for our culture to be significantly altered. My father's legacy. Imagine a people doomed to childlessness, Morgan. Imagine what that does to them. Whether we choose to remain childless ourselves or to have children, the fact remains that a society exists for its children. We live knowing they are our future. Without children... well, there is no such future."

"Even for such a long-lived people?" I was skeptical. But then, I still was only vague on how long a fae like Draven would live. Hundreds of years? Millennia?

"Even for us. A hopelessness fell upon the Siabra as soon as the curse took effect." His face turned grim. "It has led us to equally dark paths."

"Worse than turning children into undead monsters?"

"Perhaps not worse, but similarly evil," he said softly. "Think of stolen human children. Stolen human brides–and husbands, too. Used and discarded when they failed to be enough or to succeed."

"To succeed..." I stared. "You mean..."

Draven's face filled with distaste. "There are some Siabra who refused to accept the curse. They would try to breed human women, even though almost all such pregnancies ended in death for the mother."

"And stolen children?"

"Stolen and treated as pets until they reached old age. Taken from their true homes and families to soothe the aching loneliness of some in this court."

I swallowed. "Is Beks... one such child?"

"Beks?" Draven shook his head. "No, he was orphaned, I believe. He shows rare talent and so my mother decreed he be assigned to a court mage who would hone his abilities. Javer is unpalatable, I know, but he is exceptionally skilled."

"Levitating people into the air?" I said harshly. "How can you allow Javer to teach a child after that?"

"I'll see to it that what you witnessed does not occur again. But Javer is a strict teacher. I doubt that part of his approach will change. And there is no one else," Draven said directly. "Beks is a shielder. They are extremely rare. His value to the court is incalculable. Unfortunately, Javer is the only one who possesses the same abilities and is willing to teach him. Leaving Beks on the streets of Noctasia, letting his abilities go to waste. It wasn't an option. In time, he'll have a valuable role at court. A role previously unthought of for a human."

"For a human," I repeated. I shook my head. "Perhaps the curse has been a good thing. Have you ever thought of that? The Siabra don't seem particularly redeemable."

"Perhaps." Draven's eyes were stubborn. "But there is good in us, too, despite what you may feel. I must believe that."

"Who put the curse on the Siabra? Who exactly and how?" I demanded.

"How is the unknown. It was a dark, powerful magic. As for who, the High King of the Valtain placed the curse, as far as we know. Gorlois was his name. Is his name, I suppose I should say, for he's still alive as far as we know. His royal house claims descendance from the original fae."

"And where is he now? Where are they all?"

"Biding their time and waiting somewhere, I suppose," Draven said. "Admittedly, we haven't been eager to pursue them. But Valtain was simply one of their territories. The king's favorite seat of power, but one which he abandoned. Out of principle or pique, I was never quite sure."

I thought of Draven's age. He must have been a child when it all happened. A mere babe in arms.

"You mean this will all start up again? The entire war? Or else what? They'll just wait until all the Siabra have died off and then come home?"

Draven shrugged. "Who can say. But in the meantime, under my rule there will be changes. We must leave this dark path and find another."

"If you make it to the end of the competition. If you become emperor."

"If I do, it will benefit not just my people, but yours, Morgan. Do you not see that?"

I stared at him. "What are you saying?"

He shook his head in frustration. "Why do you think I am doing this? Keeping you here until the end of the competition?"

"I've asked myself that more times than I can count," I said, my eyes blazing. "Why don't you explain your brilliant logic to me?"

"As soon as I have redeemed myself in the eyes of the court and survived the trials, become emperor, all of Myntra's resources will be at your disposal as well."

"What do you mean?" I said slowly. "I think you mean they'll be yours and solely yours."

"My power will be yours," he insisted. "There is no way the Queen Regent would offer to help end a war on another continent, especially a human war. But with me on the throne? We'll return to Pendrath and we'll end your brother's foolish war. You'll set things right in Eskira."

Hope bloomed in my heart. "And Kaye... Kaye will be king." I looked at Draven. "You'd do all that for me?"

"I want to help my people," he said directly. "To protect them above all else, even from themselves. I want to repair the past–foolish though that dream may be, I *will* pursue it as emperor. I have no wish to wage any more meaningless wars. I have no lust for endless slaughter between mortals or fae versus fae as my father and brother did. I wish for change. I wish for peace. Not only here in Myntra, but in Eskira, too. And ending Arthur's war?" He gave a modest shrug. "I believe it will be a fairly simple thing for us to do."

Us. It was a fine word. A tempting word. I desperately wanted to believe him. He made sharing power with me sound so simple. As if power wasn't fought for and bled over all of the time.

"Perhaps not as simple as you think. Who is Orcades?"

He blinked. "Orcades?"

"She was under that lake. A fae woman from Valtain. She was trapped in the place I found Excalibur. She took it from me and I think..." I took a deep breath. "I think she planned to give it to Arthur."

Draven looked thoughtful. "To your brother? Would he even be able to wield such a tool, I wonder?"

"He certainly believed he'd find a use for it. Who was she? Do you know?" I remembered the long list of titles she had spewed. Not all but some. "She called herself Slayer of the Siabra. When she found out you were there, she did not seem pleased."

Draven's eyebrows went up. "She saw me?"

"Heard you, more like. Or sensed you somehow. I don't know exactly, I was busy lying on the floor in a pool of my own blood at the time."

Draven looked amused more than anything. "Slayer of the Siabra. She would brag about that. What would Orcades want with a mere mortal king?"

"You know her? Personally?"

"As you might imagine, she's much older than me, so no, we've never met. But I know of her, yes. And I suppose she knew my father. She was the Valtain's greatest warrior. Gorlois's firm right-hand. She's one of the High King's daughters."

I quirked a brow. "And yet she was imprisoned in a lake."

"Surrounded by priceless treasure and invaluable magical artifacts, yes," Draven agreed.

"Why the hell would he put her down there?" I had an odd idea. "Was she being stored just like the treasure?"

Draven shrugged. I'd somehow expected that. "More likely punished for something. What matters is you got her out. Not too grateful though, was she?"

I thought for a moment. "She didn't run me through with Excalibur, at least."

"Just left you there to die and took it herself instead?" Draven grinned. "And you call me a monster."

I swatted at him, not sure at that moment whether I truly wanted to wound him or not. He jumped back with a laugh.

The sound was... pleasant. I couldn't remember the last time I had heard him laugh so freely.

I eyed him speculatively. "So, a truce?"

"I would like that, yes." A look of hesitation crossed his face.

"What is it?"

"I cannot undo naming you my paramour—nor would I, for your sake. Not yet. If you are to roam the palace freely and go where you will, you must agree to abide by that term."

"Play the submissive little lover and you'll let me out of my cage?" I bared my teeth. "Fine. If that's the way you like them."

"Like what?"

"Your women." I glared, refusing to allow my mind to imagine Draven with any woman. Even a submissive one. Especially a submissive one. Especially a submissive one who asked nicely to be gagged.

He smirked in a way that sent my heart suddenly flying. "I don't like submissive women. Surely your presence in my bed is the clearest indication of that."

I refused to be baited. Or tempted. I wasn't sure which he was going for in that moment. "Just because you've brought home a rogue princess who won't do your bidding doesn't mean you actually like her." I tried not to sound tongue-tied. "Her. Me."

Draven looked amused. "You. But I do."

"You do what?"

"I do like you, Morgan. Why the hell would I have saved you otherwise?" He began striding out of the temple. "There's something about you. You've got... grit."

I stared after him. Grit? I had *grit*?

I decided I was not going to say thank you for that compliment. If that was even what it was.

"I want something else from you," I called after him.

He turned back to me swiftly and I caught my breath.

The volcanic light streaming through the stained-glass windows above us had landed perfectly on his golden-bronze skin, bringing it to a glow. Tall and broad-shouldered, he cut a striking figure, emanating an air of effortless strength and power.

What had Breena said?

That he would make a fine emperor?

Certainly a fine-looking one.

His green eyes gleamed as they met my own. "You request a favor, my sweet?"

"Yes, my love," I said, tossing my head as arrogantly as I could manage and trying to channel Lyrastra. "I want a trainer."

"A trainer? In what?" Draven seemed amused. He wasn't refusing.

I paused. "In what?"

"Well, it seems to me there are a few things you could request training in. Weapons and fighting, certainly. But also..." His eyes dropped to my bare arms, covered with silver markings. "Magic. How to use it. How to control it."

I clenched my jaw. "Politely, I decline. Weapons, yes. And sparring. I want to get back into shape."

He hesitated briefly, then nodded. "Very well. I'll set up something. With the very best of our warriors."

That sounded promising.

I followed as he led the way out of the room.

CHAPTER 8

T hat night I dreamt of war.

    I sat upon a horse on the peak of a hill at the edge of a forest.

Down below me, a village burned. The smoke was blowing eastward, leaving my view clear.

A ring of soldiers on horseback surrounded the village. Others stood nearby with swords already drawn. I watched as they went from house to house, lighting each one on fire and dragging the people out. Men were put to the sword. Women fared worse.

I watched as they neared the village's small temple. The shrieking and wailing of women filled the air. A group of girls–acolytes most likely–were pulled forward, their dresses torn. A boy ran forward to try to tug a girl away. A soldier made a swift movement with his arm and an ax flew through the air. The boy fell, the ax embedded in his skull.

The girl screamed and screamed.

Fire lit the sky. The killing went on.

It was all senseless.

I sat on my mount, trembling.

This was a victory. I was meant to take the news of it to the king. Pendrath was triumphing over the enemy scourge in Tintagel.

But to call this a triumph was a perversion. How could this be victory when such brutality was used against defenseless peasants and priestess girls?

Torches were thrown onto the small thatched roof of the temple and it erupted in flames.

Lastly, I watched as a pyre was erected in the center of the village. The king had decreed that Tintagel would be made an example of for daring to join Lyonesse in such defiant rebellion. Rebellion of what, I now wondered? We were not Tintagel's masters. Were they not a free kingdom?

Of course, the worst would be saved for traitorous Rheged. Rheged who had dared to withdraw its support after swearing it.

If we ever managed to get that far. I had my own doubts.

The girls in white robes were dragged to the pyre.

Mumbling a prayer to the Three, I turned my mount away, my stomach churning, the smoke hoarse in my throat.

Setting my course to the northeast, I began to skirt carefully around the village and through the rocky hills that led to the coast.

I would not be returning to Camelot.

Let them call me a deserter. Let them hunt me and hang me.

I rode for Brightwind and the court of King Mark.

I woke up heaving and retching, the smoke from the burning village still stinging my eyes and tasting bitter in my throat.

Leaning over the side of the bed, I managed to reach for a wastebasket just in time.

Vaguely I felt the bed shift. Draven was still there.

"What the hell?" I heard him mutter. The bed moved again. He must have been getting up.

I clutched the basket tighter to my chest, hardly able to believe I was back in the palace.

The dream. It had been so real. My horse. The smoke. The darkness. The terror.

"I have to go back," I mumbled. "I have to stop it."

Draven's hand touched my shoulder. "Was it something you ate? Shall I call a healer?"

I met his gaze, still too numb to care that he was staring at me over a bucket of my own puke.

"I have to go back," I said, enunciating more clearly. "They're at war. I saw it. Arthur... It's horrible. He's destroying everything in his path. Killing innocent people. Children. Priestesses."

"You had a nightmare," Draven said. He tucked a strand of my hair behind my ear with the rare gentleness that had always shocked me. But this time, I wouldn't be brushed aside.

"It was real," I said stubbornly. "I've been having dreams. I don't know how it happened but I could see it all as clear as day. I was on horseback, overlooking a village as it was..." I gulped. "Completely wiped out. They killed everyone. There was a pyre set up. For the girls from the temple." I felt tears pricking the corners of my eyes and blinked rapidly. "They did it because their king had told them to, Draven. *This*. This is how my brother is waging his war."

"Are you really surprised if that is the case?" Draven asked quietly. "You know better than anyone what's lurked in him all of this time. For many men, war is simply an excuse for unrestrained evil with few consequences."

"Surprised, no. What's *unacceptable*, however, is that my people are there and I am here. Trapped here with you. Because of you," I tried to keep my voice level, but it was difficult. "This is unbearable. I have to go home. I have to do something."

"You will return. And when you do, you'll have my army at your back. Nothing will stand in your way."

I shook my head. "No. I know what we talked about but it's not enough. It's not soon enough. We must go now. Unseat Arthur, raise Kaye up."

I saw his eyebrows go up. "Kaye?"

"Of course, Kaye!"

He looked back at me levelly. "Some would say there is a woman who has a stronger claim to the throne."

My jaw dropped. "I don't want it. Do you really think that's what this is about?"

"Kaye won't want it either, Morgan."

He was right.

"No, but he'll accept it and he'll help me stop all of this. Don't tell me your plan is to try to raise me up in some foolish gesture to place an ally on the throne of Pendrath. Is that your plan?"

Draven made a dismissive sound. "I have no need of allies in Pendrath. But when you return to stop your elder brother, I want your victory to be sweeping and decisive. Right now, you would return alone, Morgan. I cannot leave my people–as much as I may wish to go with you."

My mouth felt dry. He wanted to go with me?

He sighed and ran a hand over his face. "Moreover, and though I know you don't wish to hear this said again... It was a dream, Morgan. A dream, and nothing more. Take comfort in that."

He rose to his feet. "I have to go. I slept later than I should have. We will discuss this again soon. In the meantime, there is someone coming to fetch you to bring you to training. As you requested."

"Training?" My heart leaped, even though I knew it was such a minor thing to be pleased over in the grand scheme of things. Still, I needed my body to be strong and capable when I confronted Arthur and his army. Who knew what I would need to do? I had recovered from the wounds Vesper had given me, but my endurance had not.

And I'd admit, part of me was curious about what sort of things the Siabra warriors here might be able to teach me.

Draven was dressing swiftly. I glanced back at the bed. Strange. My pillow was nearly next to his, in the space in the center of the bed that was normally empty.

I felt a moment's unease. Had I been sleeping closer to my enemy than I had realized? And how often did that happen without my even noticing?

Draven was buckling his belt. "Don't overdo it today. I need you tonight."

I gulped. "You what?"

"We'll be attending a ceremony to officially open the competition. There will be rites, of a sort. All of the contestants will be present." He looked over at me and cleared his throat. "Breena will be coming to help you dress. I've taken the liberty of choosing a gown. I hope you'll find it acceptable."

"This is the start of our truce then?" Freedom for compliance. I shrugged. "As long as the gown covers my..."

"It will cover those blasted marks," Draven said shortly. "If you'll permit, I'd like someone to take another look at them. Perhaps Javer could..."

"He's a healer, too? No. Absolutely not. That man is not touching me. Over my dead body. You saw how he treated Beks!"

"Not a healer, no. But a court mage of not inconsiderable skill. His specialties lie with shielding and levitation, as you got a glimpse of. But..." He paused as if he knew I was going to reject whatever he said. "He's a member of my court. A loyal one. I trust him."

Did that mean Javer was no longer part of the Queen Regent's court? Or loyal to her?

"I'd rather Crescent do it than Javer," I said stubbornly. "Or better yet, why don't you forget about them altogether?"

"Forget?"

"Yes! It's my body, isn't it? If anyone should be bothered to see Florian's fucking name carved into my skin it should be me."

Draven looked thoughtful. "And? Does it? Bother you?"

"Look at me, Draven. I chose none of this." I held up my marked arms, then tugged at the neck of my tunic to give him a good glimpse of the letters written above my breasts. Written with a dagger I would never forget the sight of. "But it is all part of who I am now."

"Scars of battle." Draven shook his head, his expression wry. "You're right. I didn't understand. You fought that fucker and you won. In a sense, his name is a sign of your victory. You're still standing. While he..." He trailed off.

"Is lying in an unmarked grave? Or at the bottom of a lake?" I guessed.

Draven grinned. "He's exactly where he deserves to be. It was a pleasure to take care of him for you. An honor. What you did with that earring..." He whistled then brought a finger to his lips in a sign of admiration.

"It wasn't as if I planned it." I vividly remembered the spurt of blood as I'd shoved the rose stem into Florian's exposed neck.

Draven's grin fell away. "No. Of course, not. But I find it heartening that such violence is in you."

I stared at him uncomprehendingly. "Why the hell would you find it heartening? Shouldn't you be more worried I'll stab you with an earring?"

His lips twitched. "And yet strangely, I'm not. As for why? Because you'll need it, Morgan. In this place? Maybe more than ever."

He strode to the door, then hesitated. "Well, good-bye then. Have a nice day."

This was awkward.

"Just go," I snapped. "We don't have to pretend with each other in here at least."

Something between a scowl and a smirk crossed his face. And then he was gone.

Had I been too harsh?

I decided I shouldn't care.

Rising from the bed, I disposed of the contents of the wastebasket, then freshened up in the bathing room.

By the time the knock came on my door, I was clothed, fed, and had been sitting reading for a quarter of an hour, growing more and more impatient.

I hurried to the door, waiting for it to open.

"Oh. It's you." My lips twisted in dislike. "You're my escort?"

"You would prefer my brother, I know." Odessa's voice was curt and clipped. "Come. Follow me."

"Your brother... or pretty much anyone else," I muttered as I hurried after her.

Clearly there would be no apologies. I certainly had no plans of offering one.

Odessa's back was squared as she marched down the hall ahead of me. Her sepia braids had been woven into a crown around her head today.

I stole a look at her armor. The fusion of red and black leather was even more stunning today. A new scarlet cuirass laced up her back, flawlessly molded to her form.

Her armor was so pretty while she herself was so... prickly.

I focused on where we were walking. We were passing through vast swathes of the palace. I had become used to the narrow passages Beks had brought me through. Now we were out in the open, moving through broad marbled corridors and passing other Siabra who stared at me with undisguised curiosity.

I wondered if they all knew who I was.

After a little while, we reached a secluded corner of the palace at the end of a long hall. Odessa stepped forward and pushed open a heavy wooden door.

My eyes widened as I peered in. A training ground, yes. But not like the one Beks and I had spied on. And one like nothing I had ever seen before. It was as much a garden—no, a forest—as it was a sparring arena. Enclosed within sturdy walls draped with vines and plants, an open courtyard stretched before us, smooth cobblestones glistening under the warm volcanic light that reached us through a glass-domed ceiling overhead. Towering trees stood in each corner, like sentinels overseeing the proceedings.

The air was warm and humid, like a hothouse back in Camelot. Along the stone walls a shimmering, glowing moss grew in great quantities, providing even more natural light.

At the center of the training ground, a grand pavilion draped in red and black canvas beckoned. I spotted weapons racks inside, filled with an impressive array of swords, spears, shields, and other tools, some the likes of which I had never seen before. The collection was impressive and I wondered who was responsible for it.

Around us, the air was filled with the familiar peals of clashing weapons. Shouts of glee and frustration echoed across the courtyard. I felt myself grinning in expectation. Oh, I had missed this.

It took me a moment and then I realized something.

All of the warriors in this training area were female.

"What is this?" I demanded of Odessa. "Do women not train with the men in this court? Are we segregated?"

She scoffed. "Not at all. There are men who would love to train in Steelhaven. I simply don't permit it. I wanted a place of my own."

"You don't permit..." A terrible realization was growing. "Oh, no."

Odessa's face broke into a wide grin. "Oh, yes."

"Oh, no," I said through clenched teeth. "You are not my new trainer."

"Don't you want the best?" Odessa asked. "Because that's what the prince is giving you. The best. Steelhaven is my creation. And these women you see around you? They're the best you could hope to go up against. Better than most men. For generations, the court has cultivated various factions of trained warriors. You're looking at an elite force–the Steelmaidens. And you're lucky to even be looking."

There was the smugness again.

I rolled my eyes. "Of course, I am."

Odessa crossed her arms over her chest. "Please don't tell me you're one of those women who believes men are always the superior warriors. Or that only a man can truly challenge you in a sparring ring."

Her words stung. "Of course not! My best friend is..." I stopped. "She was... an incredible knight. She would have been."

Odessa's face softened slightly. "The girl we tried to save?"

I nodded. "And back in Camelot, Dame Halyna was one of the best knights I've ever seen. She trained the squires."

I wondered if she was still training. Perhaps Dame Halyna was on the frontlines now, leading Arthur's soldiers. I thought of her helping to burn villages to the ground and tasted ash in my mouth. No. She would never participate in something like that.

Not even under coercion or threat of her life? I pushed the thought back. Now was not the time.

"Well, then, I don't see a problem," Odessa said with a shrug. "You don't have to *like* the people you train with. Sometimes it's even better if you don't."

I thought of Draven. "Yes, but..."

"Fresh meat. Excellent. I claim first dibs, Odessa." A woman approached us, her lips curled into a rapacious smile.

My eyes narrowed. "Lyrastra."

"Greetings, Prince's Paramour," she said with a laugh. "Are you really here to train? I admit, I could hardly believe it when Odessa told us. Isn't the Prince's Paramour supposed to laze about in bed all day, wearing scanty garments, and waiting for her man to return?"

The mental image made me want to vomit. At least, it did until I inspected it more closely.

Cursing my vivid imagination, I tightened my jaw. "That sounds incredible dull. Not my cup of tea."

Lyrastra eyed me with incredulity. "So we're supposed to believe you've done this before? That you can hold your own in a fight?"

"I can do more than dance around by myself looking pretty, if that's what you're asking," I snapped, thinking of the nimble routine I had seen her going through in the competition training arena the other day.

Confusion crossed Lyrastra's face briefly, then her familiar arrogant veneer returned. "Fight me then. I promise, there won't be any dancing."

"Excellent," I said coolly. "Sounds like a good match. I'm in."

Odessa stepped forward, frowning. "I have no issue with this. But there will be no use of magic. Lyrastra, you are already well aware of the rules."

"Of course, I am," Lyrastra said, smiling sweetly. "Your ring, your rules, Odessa."

"Let's get started then." I gestured to the weapons rack. "I don't have my own gear. I take it this is communal?"

Odessa nodded. "Suit up and choose a weapon." She glanced at Lyrastra. "Swords to start."

That was a bit of a relief to hear. I didn't want to admit it, but I was out of shape. Swords were familiar at least.

Secretly, I hoped this didn't end with Lyrastra wiping the floor with my ass.

"Swords?" Lyrastra looked disappointed. "Daggers would be more fun."

Odessa snorted. "Save it for another day. Lady Morgan was on the brink of death not long ago. I remind you of that, Lyrastra, because I doubt you would endear yourself greatly to the prince if we don't bring her back in one piece today."

I glared at Odessa. "I don't need you to coddle me. I can set my own limits."

She frowned. "Fine. Get to it then." She stomped off towards a wooden enclosure where two young women were fighting with spears.

"I'll be waiting over there," Lyrastra said, pointing to an empty ring. "Eagerly." She waggled her fingers then stalked away.

"Wonderful," I muttered.

I went into the pavilion and located training armor in my size. Stepping into a changing room, I quickly pulled it on. There were training swords on the rack. I assumed Lyrastra had her own.

My hands were already sweaty as I lifted a small round wooden shield from another rack. Why did I have a bad feeling about this?

Perhaps because I had no business going up against someone like Lyrastra so soon after getting back on my feet. She had been training hard for the competition, while I? Like it or not, she was partly right—I really had just been lying in bed.

I recalled what she had done to me that first day when I had woken up and a burning rage went through me.

On second thought, perhaps this was perfect timing. Draven wasn't around to hold either of us back today, and Odessa seemed to have given up trying.

I marched over to where she stood waiting for me and closed the wooden gate behind me.

"Let's do this," I said shortly.

The air seemed to crackle with anticipation as we gripped our swords tightly.

Then, blades clashed. Sparks flew.

Lyrastra fought well. She was swift and sure, spinning her blade with aggression and arrogance, immediately seeking to undermine my confidence.

She also enjoyed penning me in. I found myself trapped against first one side of the ring, then the other, each time getting away only by dropping to a tumble and rolling past her.

Lyrastra sneered as I stood up the second time, brushing dust off. "Don't mind getting down in the dirt, do you, Lady Morgan? I'm sure our prince appreciates that about you. Men often do."

I choked back the first retort that had come to mind and reminded myself that I couldn't deny being Draven's lover—no matter how much I might long to.

There were other things I could have said now that I knew more about Lyrastra and her history. But they were too cruel. Though I doubted she would have held herself back for my sake were our positions reversed.

I set myself against her firmly instead, attacking with everything I had.

It wasn't enough. I could feel that already. I was panting. Sweat was dripping from my brow.

Meanwhile Lyrastra looked fresh as a flower.

She was faster than me. Perhaps even stronger than me, at least for now.

I wasn't sure I could beat her, I acknowledged to myself. But that didn't mean I was going to just give up.

I'd realized I was taller than her by a fair measure and, when I was at my best, I suspected I was heavier and more muscular, too. She was slender and lithe, but that could work against her.

I threw myself up against her, smashing my shield into hers and hoping I was right about being a little heavier.

She looked a little startled as she hit the fence, but quickly regained her equilibrium. "Oooh, feisty, Paramour."

"Shut up," I grunted. "Shut your mouth and fight me. Stop holding back."

Her eyes widened then narrowed as if she took in the implication. I felt a little smug. So she wasn't holding back. This was all she had.

In that case, maybe I actually stood a chance.

I caught a crafty smile on Lyrastra's lips just as I parried and thrust my sword, and then with a swift motion her leg hooked through mine, throwing me off balance.

I smashed to the mat with a cry of outrage, my elbow hitting the ground hard. I cringed. There would be a nasty bruise there later. Hopefully Draven's gown came with a wrap or a shawl.

It was a blatant act of cheating, but if Lyrastra wanted to play dirty I wasn't going to tattle or complain and have her think me weak.

But it wasn't entirely up to me.

"Hey!" I turned my head at the angry yell to see Odessa marching over. "I told you to keep it clean, Lyrastra. Do that again and you won't be welcome here for a week."

Lyrastra's lips thinned but she said nothing, simply nodded.

I jumped up, readying myself to resume. Lyrastra gave me a sly smile that told me she was convinced she could get away with much more than a little leg twist.

I was hardly back on my feet when she lunged at me. Raising my shield as fast as I could, I managed to deflect the blow. With a resounding thud, the arm I had just landed on took the brunt of the impact. I forced myself not to wince.

Now Lyrastra was panting. Good.

"Whore," she spat, leaning forward towards me, her serpentine eyes gleaming. "You have no right to be here. None at all. In this ring with me or in the prince's bed."

Despite myself, some of her words surprised me. "You like to throw that word around a lot. For a woman so much older than me, you have a shockingly narrow vocabulary. Don't tell me you care about who the prince gives his favors to, Lyrastra. Can it be? Are you actually... jealous?"

I couldn't help it. Once I'd started, the words kept spilling out.

"First the elder brother, now the younger?" I whistled, blatantly trying to provoke her. "Does it drive you mad to think of me there, in your prince's bed, waiting for him to come to me? Perhaps you wish you could switch our places?"

I pressed sharply forward, unleashing a flurry of rapid strikes. Lyrastra responded with swift parries, maneuvering and repositioning.

But she wasn't quite quick enough. For a moment, I had her. Pushed up against the wooden fence, I leaned over her as she licked her lips.

"But he doesn't want you, Lyrastra," I whispered cruelly. "Does he? He wants me. And you can't handle it, can you? You're pathetic. I thought the Siabra had a sense of pride. But look at you, you're just a jealous, cheating..." I wasn't sure exactly how I planned to end that sentence, so I was almost glad when she interrupted.

"Shut up," Lyrastra roared, her gold and purple eyes filling with fury.

With a lightning-fast thrust, she caught me off-guard, piercing my defenses and grazing my arm with her sword before I could block.

I jumped backwards, sidestepping and narrowly evading a second attack.

"You have no idea," Lyrastra snarled. "No idea who you're dealing with. But perhaps it's time I gave you a taste."

And with that, she dropped her shield and reached a hand forward towards me.

A shadowy serpent slithered forth from her fingertips.

My eyes widened. I took a step back, then another, as the serpentine entity slid to the mat.

Before I could even open my mouth, it was upon me, coiling around my legs, constricting my movement. I reached my hands down, desperately trying to untangle the creature but instead, the serpent stretched and slipped around my hands, binding me still tighter.

The snake's grip was painful. I could feel the circulation in my wrists being cut off. I clenched my teeth.

This was the moment. I could reach for my own powers. See if they would come for me.

I could turn this serpent to ash and send Lyrastra up in a fiery blaze.

But as I looked up at her, at the hate and anger in her face, I knew I wasn't going to do that. And my own anger began to dissolve.

I sighed. "All right, Lyrastra. You've won. Cheated, but won. Is that what you want to hear? I yield. Let me go."

But in response the snake's grip simply became tighter. I let out a cry of pain.

"Let her go, Lyrastra!" Odessa leaped over the rail, her eyes flashing with anger. "Release Lady Morgan and then get out. I warned you not to pull a stunt like this. Did you think I was joking?"

Lyrastra's eyes flickered briefly to Odessa then back to me. "We're not through," she hissed, her voice just loud enough for me to hear. "Next time we're alone, you and I, you're dead."

The serpent vanished as if it had never been.

It had been impressive conjuring. But all I really cared about was getting the feeling back in my legs.

Shakily, I stood up and leaned against the fence.

Odessa watched as Lyrastra leapt over the side of the fence and disappeared out the courtyard entrance. "You really put her back up."

I scowled. Was I going to be blamed for this? "Wasn't exactly hard to do. I didn't even have to try."

"You'd be surprised. With the others, she's usually quite restrained. She's a good teacher to the younger girls."

A good teacher? Lyrastra?

"She really doesn't like you," Odessa said, looking at me.

That was a massive understatement considering the threat I'd just received.

"I'm still not exactly sure why," I admitted. "She seemed to hate me even before she met me."

"She pinned you to your bed at your first meeting. So I've heard." Odessa seemed to be considering something. "She has some reason to dislike you. More than you may know."

"There are many things I wish I knew, Odessa. But no one seems to see fit to tell me any of them." I thought of Crescent. "Well, hardly anyone."

Odessa pursed her lips. "Her husband was killed. Prince Tabar. You know this?"

"By Kairos, yes. To save Lyrastra's life."

Odessa nodded. "A life she did not particularly want anymore."

"Yes, yes, she was doomed to loneliness. Spare me." I rolled my eyes. "We all have hard lives. We all have our own sob stories." Ten stillborn children, Draven had said. "Still, Lyrastra seems to have endured... a great deal," I conceded.

Odessa looked a little gratified by the acknowledgement. "She did. And she had one small hope, too. With her husband's death, there was one possibility still within reach."

"And what was that?"

"Remarriage. To a powerful man. One who was much more worthy of her."

"I thought the mates of princes or princesses could never remarry," I observed.

"They cannot remarry outside of the royal family," Odessa corrected. Her eyes met mine. "There was–is–one prince still left."

My eyebrows shot up. "She wanted to marry Prince Kairos? Her husband's brother?"

I had been striking out blindly when I accused Lyrastra of jealousy. But had my jabs landed better than I could have hoped?

"It may not be common where you are from, but within Siabra culture there is nothing shameful in the idea of a man marrying his dead brother's wife. Indeed, it is seen as an honorable gesture to many."

"But... brothers." I wrinkled my nose.

Odessa looked as if she wished to say more, then she shook her head. "There is still more you do not know. But it is not my place. The proving ground is not meant to be a gossip hall. But when you look at Lyrastra next, I would ask that you look at her and see not just her enmity towards you but her lost hopes. She hates you, yes, because she truly believed she had a chance. To marry a man more honorable than her husband had ever been."

A chance of happiness? Was that what she thought I had stolen from her? Would Draven have made her happy? Did he know that was what she had wanted?

"And to be empress," I reminded Odessa. "Don't forget that important part." I paused. "And did she? Have a chance?"

Odessa studied me in silence for a moment. "I don't think so."

She started to turn away. "The question might more accurately be phrased as 'Does she?' Why don't you ask him yourself?"

CHAPTER 9

D^{oes she?}

The words rang in my mind.

Ask him myself? I scoffed at the idea.

But I also felt shaken. Would Draven really consider marrying his sister-in-law? Now? Could a Siabra emperor have a consort and a paramour?

More importantly, why the hell did I care?

Perhaps Draven was already planning to marry. After all, why bother to inform me? What was between us was merely a sham, wasn't it?

But Lyrastra claimed she wanted to kill me. Wouldn't that mean anything to him? He swore he wanted to protect me.

Not if he already cared for her, a small voice in my head said. He had already saved Lyrastra's life by killing his own brother. Even though doing so meant his loss of his direct place in line to the Umbral throne and his banishment, albeit temporary.

What sort of a man would do all of that for a woman he *didn't* love? Perhaps that was the better question.

But then he had extended his own banishment. Stayed away from the Court of Umbral Flames for twenty years.

Why would he do that if he could have returned and claimed Lyrastra's hand much sooner?

I ground my teeth as I walked down the hall, Crescent not far behind.

Who knew how Draven's mind worked? Did I really want to know?

"We're passing the menagerie, if you'd like a peek," Crescent observed from behind me.

He had been unusually quiet since he'd met me outside of Steelhaven. I'd assumed he'd picked up on my mood and was trying to give me space, which I appreciated.

"Oh?" I glanced to the right where the corridor had opened up onto an octagonal courtyard. At the far side were large brass gates leading into another area where the sounds of animals could be heard.

I shrugged. "I suppose I'll have a quick glance. If you don't think anyone will mind."

Crescent smiled. "You're the Prince's Paramour," he reminded me. "You don't need anyone's permission to explore the palace."

That wasn't exactly true. Or at least, it hadn't been until today. But I decided not to remind him of my previous confinement.

Walking up to the gates, I gave them a push and one slowly squealed open.

I stepped inside with Crescent close behind and looked around curiously. The Royal Menagerie was part hothouse, part zoo. The air was warm and humid, with large plants and vines covering the walls and leading up to another glass dome like the one that covered Steelhaven. A ring of cages stretched before me.

I walked slowly over to the first one and heard a gentle chiming. Peering through the bars, I let out a gasp of delight. A graceful bird with dazzling wings fluttered on a branch. As the creature met my eyes, it lifted its wings, revealing feathers as kaleidoscopic and colorful as stained glass. As the bird flapped its wings they emitted a tinkling sound, sweet and airy like a chorus of bells.

"An ambrilith," Crescent said. "They're native to Myntra."

"Beautiful," I murmured. I nodded my head at the ambrilith, in an instinctive gesture, and to my surprise the bird lowered its own head in response.

"They're keenly intelligent," Crescent explained. "A shame to keep her locked in here."

I looked at him with surprise. "Why are they kept here?"

"For the queen's amusement mostly. The menagerie has always been an indulgence of the royal family. Though I know Prince Kairos finds it distasteful."

"Oh, he doesn't like the idea of keeping wild creatures contained, does he?" I murmured ironically.

I stepped up to the next stall where two small deerlike creatures stood side-by-side. They had emerald-green fur and long, curling antlers. As I watched, one lifted a dainty hoof, then raised its head and let out a melodic haunting call.

"Verdantail," Crescent offered. "They're considered a delicacy."

"Don't you mean 'delicate'?" I corrected him.

He paused. "No."

I curled my lip. "Oh."

"The last emperor had a special predilection for verdantail, but the queen does not seem inclined to..." Crescent paused as if trying to find the right words.

"To eat these ones?" I supplied. "I'm sure they're very grateful."

I walked past the verdantails then stopped abruptly. "Oh!"

In the dimly lit far corner of the menagerie cage, a colossal feline sat hunched.

Cloaked in a velvety coat of obsidian, the creature's fur was accented with bold, golden stripes. But the once sleek and lustrous fur was matted and unkempt, the dark black and gold stripes dulled by neglect. Its once powerful limbs seemed weary, and as it shifted its weight slightly, the exmoor's movements seemed to lack the grace and agility I had taken as its hallmark.

Familiar amber eyes glowed with intelligence, but also held an unmistakable glint of anger and bitterness.

"I don't understand," I said, taking in the forlorn beast's faded magnificence. "This isn't. This can't be..."

"This isn't the exmoor you brought back," Crescent said hastily. "That one is being trained by the prince in another area of the palace. At least, he's working on it. I understand exmoors are very challenging to train."

"So this one is...?"

"This one has been in the menagerie for, oh, since shortly after the prince was banished. One of the nobles brought him back after an expedition to a far region of Myntra."

Crescent watched my face as I studied the exmoor. The sight of the obviously neglected feline sitting huddled in the shadows tugged at something in my heart.

"His name is Nightclaw," Crescent said helpfully. "Prince Kairos has named the female Sunstrike."

"He's a dangerous beast," a voice barked. I heard a thumping sound and turned to see a grizzled older man approaching. He held a heavy wooden cane in one hand, which he was using to hit the ground. "Make no mistake. He'd take your head off soon as look at you."

I glanced at the exmoor. As the man had approached thumping his cane, the creature had seemed to shrink further back into the shadows.

"Really?" I said, my voice cold. "I've encountered exmoor before. This one doesn't look very dangerous to me. Simply neglected."

"This is Master Rodrick, the menagerie keeper," Crescent said quietly.

"I tried to mate him with the female the prince brought back," Master Rodrick growled. "Unsuccessfully. He shows no interest in breeding. Useless lump of a creature."

My eyes passed over the grizzled menagerie keeper coldly. "Hardly surprising considering how dejected he looks. When was the last time he was allowed to roam freely?"

"Roam freely?" Master Rodrick scowled. "The last time I let him out of that cage without a muzzle, he took a chunk off my leg." He lifted a trouser leg and gestured to a scarred welt. "He can die in there as far as I'm concerned. Miserable beast."

"How many exmoor are there in Myntra?" I asked bluntly.

"Only the two now as far as I know," Crescent answered quickly.

"He's right," Master Rodrick conceded. "The one the prince brought back from Eskira and this one. No one knows how it found its way over here. Of course, there was a time they were common. Native to Myntra they once were."

"Well, then. Considering there are only two in your entire kingdom, I'd have thought you'd be putting this one to better use," I pointed out.

"The Prince's Paramour makes a good point, doesn't she?" Crescent said, tilting his head to one side. "Why, the prince himself plans on using the female as a battle mount if all goes well."

"A foolhardy plan," Master Rodrick grumbled. "I've said as much."

"Yes, you and Prince Kairos have never gotten on well, have you?" Crescent murmured. He raised his voice a little. "Nevertheless, I believe there is historical precedent for it. "Why, Hawl was telling me the other day..."

"Hawl?" The menagerie keeper glowered at Crescent. "The bloody Bearkin? You talk to that...thing?"

For a man who was supposed to be a caregiver to animals, Master Rodrick did not seem to be a particularly enthusiastic admirer of the rich plethora of beings in Arcaenum.

"Why, yes. They're a wealth of information, I've found, as Hawl spends a great deal of time in the library," Crescent answered. "In any case, Hawl mentioned that exmoors used to make up an entire contingent in the Siabran army–similar to the cavalry. This must have been when they were still native to Myntra and no longer only found in Eskira."

"Fascinating." My eyes were on the exmoor. Nightclaw surveyed me with a keen awareness. I could tell the creature was listening to every word we said. From behind his formidable jaws, sharp fangs gleamed, reminding me of the feline's predatory prowess. Even now, there was a beauty to the exmoor's dulled features, the delicate curve of his ears, the pointed whiskers.

As I watched, a low growl rolled from the exmoor's throat. To me it seemed as if it were a rumbling lament of discontent and frustration.

The creature was trapped. Trapped as I had recently been.

The beast drew a breath and abruptly I saw how labored the effort was as its chest rose and fell.

"It's a proud and noble creature with incredible intelligence and look at what you've done to it." I was unable to contain myself any longer. I crossed my arms over my chest. "Open the cage."

"What? Absolutely not," Master Rodrick retorted.

Crescent cleared his throat. "You would refuse a command from the Prince's Paramour?"

"The Prince's Paramour is a bloody fool of a woman if she thinks that creature won't rip her throat out the second I open that cage," Master Rodrick said angrily.

"It might rip *your* throat out, Rodrick," I said softly, meeting the keeper's gaze. "But I don't think Crescent or I have anything to worry about." I glanced at the exmoor. "Do we, Nightclaw?"

"Now she's talking to the thing," Rodrick muttered. "Spare me from foolish women."

"You'll keep a civil tongue in your mouth when you speak to the Prince's Paramour, Rodrick," Crescent said with surprising sharpness.

Rodrick ground his teeth and glared at me. "I won't do it. The beast deserves to die in that cell."

"He won't be dying in there," I said crisply. "But you might, if you don't open the gate. Or do I have to summon the prince?"

Or melt the bars of the cage to molten metal. That was... tempting.

But I thought the threat of summoning Draven would be enough. And I wasn't wrong.

Master Rodrick narrowed his eyes. "I've warned her. You heard me, Crescent. Her blood be on your hands if the creature slays her. Do you hear me?"

"Yes, yes, we all hear you," Crescent said soothingly. "You're simply doing what the Prince's Paramour has instructed. I am your witness to that."

"Open it," I commanded again. "I don't want him spending another day in that horrible cage."

Master Rodrick stared. "You're not planning to put him back in again? Just where do you plan to keep him? There's no way this beast can be housed in the royal stables. Why, he'd eat the horses. He's untamable. Unmanageable. Completely savage. I tell you, I won't be responsible for this idiocy."

Despite my best efforts to ignore his hyperbole, Master Rodrick' negativity was starting to get to me a little.

"I..." I paused. "We'll put him..." I had absolutely no idea. I hardly knew the palace at all. But I meant what I said. "He'll be put somewhere I can begin training him immediately."

If Draven could do it, so could I.

"I'd hoped you'd say that," Crescent murmured quietly from behind me. He raised his voice, "We'll take him to the Shadow Gardens. No one uses them anymore. The Prince's Paramour may keep him there, safely contained, and Nightclaw will have much more room to prowl."

Rodrick grunted in derision. "The Shadow Gardens. Fine. Good luck finding him in there again."

He fished for a key on his belt and began unlocking the cage. "I don't wish to be present for this."

I rolled my eyes. "I can only imagine why not."

Rodrick glared, then began pulling open the gate. He positioned himself so that he was secured behind the gate and the wall–the spineless man.

Nightclaw was rising to his feet. I watched as the exmoor took a slow step forward, then another.

"You heard all of that, didn't you?" I said encouragingly, meeting the feline's amber eyes. "We're not going to hurt you." I glanced at Rodrick. "No one is going to hurt you again," I promised. "You've been mistreated. Neglected. I understand. But your new life begins now. Today. With me. Will you come with me? Will you follow?"

I looked quickly at Crescent who seemed to understand.

"You follow me, and the exmoor..." He shrugged easily. "Well, hopefully he'll follow us both. Yes?"

The exmoor was reaching the doorway of his cage. As he made to pass the old menagerie keeper, the creature paused then let out a long, low growl and bared his fangs.

I watched in amusement as Rodrick shrank back, pulling the gate of the cage more tightly against his body as a shield.

The exmoor shot the keeper a look of disdainful loathing, then padded towards me.

I looked at the feline's back, the matted fur–and beneath that, telltale signs of old injury.

"You beat this creature, didn't you?" I accused Rodrick. "No wonder he hates you. You beat him with that cane. Over and over, until you thought his spirits were broken. But you were a fool if you thought a man like you could ever break a creature like him."

Rodrick glared. "Get him out of here. Go if you're going."

"I should let him at you," I said, staring at where he cowered pathetically behind the cage door. "It's the least you deserve. Tell me, did he take the chunk out of your leg before or after you struck him?"

Rodrick eyes narrowed but he said nothing.

"I'll be telling the prince about this," I said shortly.

It was one thing not to tattle on Lyrastra. This was quite another.

Crescent said nothing, simply led the way out through the courtyard.

I followed him.

And to my great gratification and not a little glee, Nightclaw followed us both.

CHAPTER 10

I t had been a long day and I suspected it would be a long evening.

When I entered my room, Breena was already there, scurrying about busily.

"Where have you been? You're late! We must get you ready at once." Then her eyes widened. "Oh, by Blessed Vela, what have they done to you?"

I glanced down at myself. I supposed I was more bruised and battered than when I had left. Lyrastra's attack on my legs had left me leaning more heavily on my right side, almost limping. I inhaled, taking what I hoped was a subtle whiff and my nostrils flickered.

Distinctly exmoor-ish.

It wasn't an unpleasant smell. An animal, earthy tone. I rather liked it.

But I could see Breena's lips curling from here. "Good Khor, have you been in the stables all day? Did a horse tread on you? What did they have you doing? Mucking out stalls?"

"Something like that," I said cautiously. "I was at Steelhaven earlier."

"Steelhaven!" Breena looked furious. "I suppose this was *his* doing."

"It was mine. I wanted a trainer. I'm used to having physical training." I cleared my throat. "Odessa claims to be the best."

"That Odessa di Rhondan and that brother of hers," Breena grumbled. "Supposed to be keeping you safe, the two of them, and yet you come back here looking like you've been trampled by beasts."

Thankfully there had been no trampling. Only a great deal of curious stares from Siabra nobles and servants as Crescent and I had led Nightclaw through the palace halls until we finally reached the Shadow Gardens.

Located on the fringes of the palace, the gardens lay within a huge stone quadrangle. An arched arcade wall provided a high border, encompassing a secluded space more wild than park-like with dense foliage, rough dirt paths, and hidden clearings.

"This should be enough room for him," Crescent said quietly as we entered. "At least, for now."

"For now," I echoed. Then I glanced at him. "For now?"

"You do plan to train him, don't you?"

"Well, I hope so." In truth, I had absolutely no idea what such training would involve. "All I knew was that I had to get him out of that place."

Crescent nodded. "This is a good start."

"How will he feed? I assume he's used to having meals brought to him." I glanced with chagrin at Nightclaw, as if worried I might offend him. "And not hunting."

Not like Sunstrike, the female exmoor Draven had brought back.

"I'll arrange all of that. But later, perhaps he might like to try to hunt for himself. We could see about bringing him to the surface, perhaps taking him out to the royal hunting park if the prince agrees. You might even be able to keep him there."

I looked at Nightclaw who was observing us both as we spoke rather than racing off into the gardens.

"It's almost as if he can understand us, isn't it?" I said softly. "His eyes are so intelligent."

Crescent nodded. "No wonder the prince brought back the female. Such nobility and strength."

"He's surprisingly..." I searched for the right word.

"Compliant?" Crescent grimaced. "I suspect that's because of Rodrick. But underneath, you see what I see, don't you?"

I met Nightclaw's amber eyes. "An indomitable force to be reckoned with?"

I stepped towards the massive feline. "You can go now. Go on and explore." I kept my voice soft. "I'll be back to visit you here soon. Don't... Don't run away? Okay?"

I nearly added, "Please don't run out into the palace and eat any of the nobles" but decided Nightclaw was intelligent enough not to have to be told.

Besides, they probably tasted terrible.

Now, back in the suite, with Breena, I wondered how Nightclaw was faring.

Breena was touching my hair, tutting softly to herself. I looked past her at where she had been laying out things and let out a gasp.

"Is that my gown?"

A dress was hanging on the door of the wardrobe. A dress like nothing I had ever seen before.

Crafted from a sheer, opalescent fabric, the gown was the very embodiment of beauty. With a breathtaking palette of emerald greens and sapphire blues, I was reminded of moonlit forests and tranquil waters. The bodice was a deep shade of ocean blue. Silver threadwork, evocative of starlit vines, intertwined along the high halter-style neckline, while from the waist down, the gown cascaded in layers of flowing, gossamer-thin fabrics.

Green chiffon, soft as a summer breeze, lent the skirt an ethereal elegance, falling and draping in asymmetrical layers, each one decorated with delicate silver beadwork. While there was a more solid piece of fabric down the center of the skirt, the overall translucency of the material would also allow the wearer's bare hips and legs to be glimpsed with every step.

The gown was sleeveless and backless. Slender shimmering silver straps crisscrossed over the back of the dress, adding to its sensuous allure.

The last time I had worn anything like this had been at the Rose Court ball to welcome the delegation from Lyonesse.

That night...had not gone as planned.

A sense of trepidation filled me as I stared at the dress.

"It is a little scanty," Breena admitted, from beside me as she followed my gaze. "But a beautiful gown. The prince has excellent taste. I believe he'll be wearing shades to match."

Perfect. We were going to *match*.

"Now, you need a bath before I can dress you and see to your hair," Breena announced.

Practically shoving me across the room, she hurried me into the bathing chamber and left me in peace for fifteen minutes before pounding on the door and insisting I speed things along.

Soon, I was seated before her in front of a mirrored vanity in the bedroom, watching as she dried and brushed my hair, then began to expertly wind it into soft curls and tendrils. Delicate pieces of mother-of-pearl blossoms hung with tiny crystals were woven together and placed atop my head like an ornate crown. They caught the light of the chandelier overhead and accentuated my silver halo of hair.

By the time Breena was through with my hair and had helped me step into the gown, fastening it carefully behind my neck, I was dazed. Looking into the full-length mirror on the wall, I hardly recognized myself.

"Is all of this really necessary?" I managed to say. "A crown seems a little... overboard."

Breena waved a hand. "It's hardly a crown. Most of the nobles will have some sort of headdress far more excessive than yours."

She studied my reflection. "You look very pretty. I hope the prince will be pleased."

I did a half-twirl and the gossamer fabric swirled around my hips. The crystals in my hair gleamed, mirroring the eddies of markings up and down my arms.

I was more than pretty. I was unrecognizable.

I also felt half-naked.

The bodice of the dress was modest enough, but the rest of me felt precariously close to unclothed. As if I were covered in feathers and not a gown at all.

Breena had covered the bruise on my elbow with a light dusting of powder. Nevertheless, I was just about to ask for a shawl when the door to the bedchamber swung open.

Draven stood in the doorframe. I could see there were others waiting behind him. I spotted Crescent, Odessa, and yes, even Hawl.

Apparently, we would be arriving at the opening ceremony with a full contingent.

Draven was looking me up and down. I tried to discern approval or disappointment in his face, but all I saw was the stern set of his lips.

Breena had been right though. We were dressed to match.

His attire was a fusion of strength and simplicity, of masculinity and pure elegance. Clad in a sleeveless tunic of rich midnight black, his bronzed neck rose above a high, round-edged collar. Adorned with an intricate silver motif of interlaced horns, the tunic parted midway, showing off his chest and accentuating the sculpted lines of his form. A gasp escaped me as I beheld the cascading tendrils of dark, curling hair caressing the contours of his chest.

A wide belt of dark leather cinched his waist. A large leather sheath trimmed with silver accents was strapped to his belt. Strictly ceremonial, I assumed.

Just above his horns, a gold diadem rested on his brow, a slender half-moon band of polished gold that reminded me that Kairos Draven was most certainly a Siabra prince.

He looked wicked and handsome and fine.

And I was to be on his arm. A prize fit for an emperor.

I felt like a fraud. Breena had made me up, but underneath I was just the same. Bruised and grimy and smelling faintly of wild beasts.

I felt light-headed and nervous as I approached Draven.

"This is it," he said almost gruffly. "Once we leave this room together, you must understand your place, Morgan."

"By your side, my prince," I said smoothly.

He nodded and I thought he looked a little pleased, as if he hadn't expected me to know my line so easily.

"Exactly. But more than that..." He hesitated.

"What is it?"

"We both must change once we set foot outside the walls of this room. You may not like the man I become, but I assure you, there is no other choice. Do your best to watch where I lead, follow as best as you can."

I nodded. "I'll try."

He was hesitating again. "I know none of this was your idea. You did not consent to being named Paramour. But once we leave here together, I would have your word to bind you. To know you understand that what we do, we do to protect you."

Now it was my turn to hesitate. Then I nodded, briefly. "I do. I understand."

He looked relieved. "Good. Then let's go."

I followed him into the hall.

We walked in silence, down gilded marble halls, empty now save for our little group.

I glanced behind me at where Crescent and Odessa walked side by side. Hawl and the red-haired man who Draven had been sparring with the other day came behind them. Trailing behind came Javer, and after him, to my surprise, followed Beks.

We moved through the labyrinthine palace complex until we reached a set of grand doors. A row of guards in black and gold polished armor stood on either side.

"Most of the nobles and contestants are already inside," Draven murmured to me.

"Fashionably late, are we?" I murmured back.

He smiled slightly and placed his hand on the small of my back. "Now it begins."

Two guards stepped forward and pushed open the double doors.

A rush of sound spilled out.

A throne room of dark and glorious splendor stood before us, filled with people.

Along the walls to the right and left were tiered rows of seats, mostly filled by what looked like hundreds of Siabran nobility—their gazes all firmly fixated on us.

In the center of the room was a lower space, like the middle of an arena. On the far side of the room, directly across from the doors, stood a raised platform of gleaming gold on which two thrones sat. One was smaller, draped in rich black and deep purple velvet.

A woman was seated upon the smaller throne, swathed in a blue silk dress. The bodice of her gown was made of fine, delicate lace spun to look like cobwebs. Around her graceful neck, an onyx and silver necklace hung in the form of a raven, its crimson eyes gleaming like droplets of blood. Her ruby red hair was woven with black and silver ribbons and glistened with moonstones, and overtop it rested a high crown of twisted gold and silver metal, embedded with diamonds.

This was Draven's mother. The Queen Regent Sephone. She was beautiful and enigmatic. Had I expected anything less?

She smiled slightly as Draven walked us slowly into the room. Was the smile for her son? Or for us both?

Beside the queen lay what I presumed was the Umbral Throne. Carved from dark volcanic rock and encrusted with red rubies and other gems, the throne looked off-putting and deadly. Sharp, razor-looking protrusions bordered the edges of the throne and made me wonder how comfortable it would be to sit in.

Draven's touch on my back intensified as he led the way into the room and towards an empty row of black silk cushioned seats that seemed to have been reserved for us.

Stepping back, he let the group around us enter the row first, each one slowly taking their place.

Javer ushered Beks to a pair of seats hurriedly, as if afraid his protégé might make some embarrassing misstep.

Hawl awkwardly stepped into the row after them, their massive furred body completely filling the space.

There was a tittering from around us, as if the crowd found Hawl's very presence an amusement. The Ursidaur ignored them all, taking a seat with surprising grace. I felt a swell of pride.

Gawain, the large-framed red-haired man, sat down beside Hawl. Crescent was seated next. Then Odessa.

And then... Only one seat remained.

I started forward, assuming Draven's place must be elsewhere. Perhaps on the dais beside his mother.

A firm hand on my hip stopped me.

"Wait," Draven murmured.

He stepped in front of me and claimed the seat, then gestured.

For a moment I was frozen. Incredulously I stared at the seat he was offering to me.

His lap.

He thought I was going to sit on his fucking *lap*.

My lips were parting. I was going to tell him this was not right. Sound started to come out.

And then Draven's strong hand grasped mine and gave a ruthless tug, whirling me towards him as if we were following the steps of some ancient dance, and I was sinking down onto him, my hips colliding with his chest, my ass resting on the firm hard lines of his thighs.

His hands snaked around my waist, holding me possessively against him.

While his lips... His lips went straight to my neck, nuzzling my skin as if I were a delicacy to be sampled.

I couldn't help it. I gasped.

"Play nice, Morgan," he whispered against the sensitive skin of my neck. "Easy now."

"Easy" was what you said to a fucking horse. Next thing you knew he would be calling me "good girl," too.

My cheeks blazed. Everyone was looking at us. Watching Draven touch and caress me as if I were his pet.

I caught the eyes of a woman across the throne room, bright blue and lascivious. She smiled and licked her lips, then turned to whisper something to the man beside her. He grinned appreciatively.

What kind of people were these Siabra exactly? Were they getting off on this?

"Do they all know who I am?" I hissed.

Draven lifted his lips to look up at me. "Who you are?"

"Who do these people all think I am, Draven? Your paramour, yes. But do they think I accepted the role willingly? Or do they think you brought me here as some kind of captive?"

A hint of amusement came over his face and then was gone, leaving his handsome features smooth. "A little of both, I suppose."

My skin felt hot. Not only from anger, though I was disinclined to admit it.

"Do they care if this... this thing... we're supposed to be in, is even consensual?"

Draven's green eyes turned world-weary. "Most won't care. I'm sure some are decidedly hoping it's not."

"What a wonderful people," I muttered.

So this was my role. The Prince's Paramour. The prince's Valtain prize, more like it—at least to some. And evidently Draven believed it was in our best interests not to correct those misimpressions but to drive them along.

As if in answer, he ran a hand over the curve of my waist, down over my hip and along the swell of my thigh. I gave a sharp intake of breath.

"Hush," he murmured. "Things are about to begin."

The Queen Regent was rising slowly to her feet below. I watched as she stood, slender and graceful, clasping her hands before her.

"My son has seen fit to grace us with his presence," she said, her crystalline voice carrying through the hall. "And so, we may now begin."

There was a smattering of laughter and applause that quickly died away.

I looked around as the Queen Regent began her speech, down the row, past Hawl, where a small hand had popped out and was waving enthusiastically.

A larger hand clapped down on the small one, smacking it away. I watched as Javer leaned slightly forward with a frown, muttering darkly to his apprentice.

But Beks continued to grin down the row at me, kicking his childish legs out gleefully to kick the seat in front of him.

What was he even doing here? I supposed the apprentice of a court mage had a more prominent role than I had realized. That, or Javer simply didn't trust Beks to be out of his sight for a moment.

I gave a small snicker, my eyes continuing to roam. They lighted upon Crescent, who was looking marvelously elegant in a tailored taupe and mossy green silk jacket and fitted pants. Then my eyes widened. Crescent's hand was locked through Gawain's.

I watched as the large, red-haired man turned to smile softly at his companion and gave his hand a small squeeze.

"They're mates," Draven murmured very quietly in my ear. "Their daughter, Taina, is at home with her nurse."

"Daughter?"

I felt Draven nod ever so slightly. "A human child. She was orphaned in Noctasia. Gawain found her and they decided to take her in. They've raised her together from the time she was an infant."

The idea that Crescent would make a fantastic father was hardly surprising to me. But the idea of the two men's bond being so public and official was something else. In Camelot, liaisons with men or women had been commonplace enough—at least before

Arthur's recent restrictions. No one had frowned on it. Camelot was even proud of being more liberal than elsewhere in Pendrath. But while Lancelet may have taken as many female lovers as she liked and chosen to never marry, there was no formal process that I was aware of to officialize a bond between two men or two women.

Perhaps in the future, under a different monarch—one such as Kaye—there would be, I told myself.

For the first time I thought of Galahad and wondered, truly wondered, at his decision to cut romantic love from his life by joining the temple. Had he done so because he was really certain it was the right life for him? Or because he saw no better path because Pendrath had never provided him one?

"We stand witness to a clash of destinies," the Queen Regent was saying below. "The path to the Umbral Throne is paved with harsh sacrifice, stained with blood, but above it all one contender shall triumph." She held up her hands. "Those brave souls who dare to enter this crucible of fate, come forward."

Draven shifted, sliding me off his lap, and bringing us both to a standing position.

He moved without haste, his hands never leaving my body, touching me almost lazily, as if the entire ceremony or the entire night for that matter was some sort of elaborate foreplay and not the kick-off for a deadly competition.

We stood with our bodies pressed together for a moment. His hands wrapped around my hips, his hot breath on my face.

Vaguely, I was aware that every eye in the room was upon us.

Then, "I'll be back soon," he murmured, his lips nearly touching mine, and was gone.

I took his seat, stretching out my arms and resting them along each armrest. Every inch of me was warring with myself.

Part of me was furious with how Draven was treating me.

Part of me was furious for liking it.

Part of me knew he had tried to warn me—though not as explicitly as he might have done.

And another part of me was simply undeniably curious about all of the pomp and spectacle of the Siabra court.

I focused on this last and watched as a dozen candidates, all strong and radiant men and women, made their way down to the floor before the dais below where for the first time I noticed the long stone slab table in the middle.

There was Lyrastra. She was the first to reach the bottom steps and to stand before the throne near the edge of one side of the table. With her jet-black hair and serpentine eyes, she was a manifestation of striking beauty and cool confidence. Her tall, willowy figure was garbed in a gleaming green silk dress that reminded me of the precise color of Draven's eyes.

As Draven reached the bottom and stood directly across from his sister-in-law, I wondered if Lyrastra had worn the shade on purpose. They made a striking couple, standing so near to one another.

I spotted tawny-haired Avriel, looking sickeningly arrogant as he took up a place right next to Draven, almost too close for comfort. He lifted his chin in greeting to his cousin, then Lyrastra, and then, to my surprise, met the Queen Regent's eyes and gave a cocky smile.

The queen returned it with a small smile of her own.

Was Avriel a favorite of the queen? Shouldn't Draven have been his mother's favorite of all the candidates, if anyone?

I thought of Draven's complicated family dynamics. Murdering his elder brother must have made the relationship between him and his mother somewhat strained.

Slowly, the Queen Regent stepped down from the dais and came to stand before the stone table and the twelve contestants.

A simple chalice that seemed to be made of a plain dark wood had appeared on the table before her and now she lifted this up.

"Let the chalice be their witness," she decreed, her voice carrying upwards. "Let the verdict be swift."

"And merciless," those in the seats all around me finished, as if saying the words by rote.

I shivered.

Without another word, Sephone passed the cup to Lyrastra.

For a moment, Lyrastra held the chalice in her hands, staring into it. Then she lifted it to her lips and took a deep sip.

When she lowered the chalice, I thought her hands were shaking a little, but I couldn't be sure.

She looked across the table at Draven, then held out the cup.

Draven took it and did not hesitate. He lifted it to his mouth and sipped.

The chalice was passed to the contender standing next to Lyrastra. She was a small, agile-looking young woman with long, curling blonde hair and delicate horns that furled away from her temples. She reminded me a little of Pearl, the girl Avriel had killed in the training room.

Odessa leaned towards me. "Rhea. She's a distant cousin to Lyrastra."

I nodded, surprised that Odessa was being considerate enough to tell me the contestants' names.

Rhea lifted the chalice daintily to her pretty lips and took a small sip. A moment passed and she smiled, then carefully held out the cup to Avriel.

"Treacherous bastard," Odessa muttered from beside me.

I quite agreed, but said nothing.

Avriel snatched the cup and sipped. The longest swig anyone had taken yet. Then he lowered it and reaching across the table, passed it to a wiry man who looked older than most of the other contestants, with sharp, bird-like talons in place of his fingers.

The man took the cup eagerly and brought it to his lips.

"Varis," Odessa whispered. "He hates Avriel. He'll be one of the strongest challengers."

Something was happening.

Varis had not passed the cup to the next competitor. Instead, he was staring down at it with a strange expression.

The man across from him, with short fiery orange hair framing his face and red scales covering both his arms like smoldering coals, said something that sounded sharp and impatient.

"That's Brasad," Odessa murmured, sounding almost amused. "Hot head."

In more ways than one, from the look of it.

"What's happening to Varis?" I whispered.

Odessa said nothing, but I had the impression that whatever occurred next wouldn't surprise her.

The chalice fell from Varis's hands to the stone table with a clatter, then rolled off the edge and to the ground.

Varis was next to fall. He toppled like a sapling, first leaning one way, then the other before crumpling to the floor.

There was a murmur of excitement from the crowd.

The Queen Regent stepped forward calmly and stooping low, picked up the chalice.

Then, stepping back to the head of the table, she moved her eyes briefly from Lyrastra to Draven to Rhea and finally to Avriel.

"Some contenders are simply too eager to wait for the games to begin," she said finally, smiling calmly up at the spectators. "Who can blame them?"

There was laughter and a smattering of applause. I heard no protest.

Along the row beside me, Odessa, Crescent, Gawain, and Hawl were silent.

"I don't understand," I hissed to Odessa. "What just happened?"

She spoke without looking at me. "One of the first four must have poisoned Varis."

"Which one?"

"Who do you think did it?"

"Not the prince," I said stubbornly. He might be an infuriating bastard, but Draven would never stoop to a poisoned chalice just to eliminate a single competitor.

He would meet them head on and take pleasure in destroying them brutally but fairly.

"Probably not," Odessa conceded. "But any of the others."

"What if there's still poison in the cup?" I whispered, as the Queen Regent filled the chalice from a tall silver flask and then walked down the row and carefully handed it to the sixth contestant.

Odessa shrugged. "Then I hope they're prepared."

"Prepared? For poison?"

Odessa nodded briefly. "Shhh."

The sixth contestant was a lithe woman draped in midnight blue satin robes. Her skin was a beautiful onyx with an iridescent sheen like the scales of a fish, and her hair swam around her face like the shades of the ocean reflecting the night sky.

"Malkah," Odessa offered.

Malkah drank, paled briefly, but did not fall to the ground as Varis had. Instead, she passed the cup on to the next challenger.

"Selwyn," Odessa murmured, as a towering man gripped the cup. He possessed stormy silver eyes. Majestic antlers sprouted from his temples.

"There are few like Selwyn," Odessa decreed. "He'll be hard to beat."

A woman with chestnut brown hair in a long braid and clever hazel eyes was next. Her hands ended in sharp bird-of-prey talons which she was extending and withdrawing over and over as if anxious.

"Vespera," Odessa whispered reliably.

I nodded, beginning to lose track.

"Zephrae." Another woman, her skin bronzed like burnished copper and her hair a vivid auburn. Delicate prismatic feathers covered her shoulders and stretched down to the tips of her fingers.

"Erion."

Erion's hair was a messy blond nest of waves, while every inch of the rest of his face and body were covered with reptilian scales like the ones Avriel had on his arms. I stared in fascination.

But by the time the cup reached the last contestant, I was leaning forward again, watching as a strikingly lovely young woman with flowing, pale-white hair and sky-blue eyes received the chalice with a graceful nod of her head.

"Celeste," Odessa whispered. "Her sister, Pearl, died in a training accident a few days ago or she would have been a competitor, too."

A training "accident"? Was that what they were calling it? There had been nothing accidental about the way Avriel had crushed the breath from Pearl's body.

Worse, based on what I had overheard, he had been within the rules of this sick game in doing what he did.

Celeste raised the chalice but not to her lips. She held it high over her head.

"What is she doing?" Odessa muttered.

"This court has no true authority." Celeste's voice was shrill and high-pitched, but as she went on her voice grew stronger. "The Court of Umbral Flames is a corruption. A foul perversion. We can never recover from the great sin that was perpetrated against our Valtain brethren. You all know this!" Her arm swept out, encompassing all of the Siabra in her claim of guilt.

"I decree the use of this chalice a sin of the highest order and declare our Queen Regent a pretender. All of you–" She gestured to her fellow challengers. "All of you are pretenders to a throne that should not even exist. The Siabra have no right to exist. Not anymore. Not while the true High King lives!"

There was a commotion by the doors, as if guards were trying to enter but had found the way barred.

I shot Odessa a startled look. Her face was grim.

Celeste's lovely face wore a pious smile. Her arm was still raised high in the air, holding the chalice like a lifeline. "We must rejoin our brethren. We must be made anew. Join me, brothers! Join me, sisters! Here, tonight. Or I swear, you will die for your betrayal."

Her other hand shot up into the air and I heard a crackling spark as if of lightning.

There were gasps from the crowd and not a few people began to stand up.

"Oh, shit," Odessa muttered.

"Stop her!" The Queen Regent's voice called out. "Stop her this instant!"

But it was too late.

"If we die, we die because we had no right to live at all," Celeste screamed direly.

And then a portal opened over her head.

I had never seen such a thing before. The portal shimmered with an eerie, pulsating light, its edges swirling with a dark mist that seemed to defy gravity.

There were sounds coming from the other side. At first, they were faint. Shuffling footsteps. Scratching nails.

But as I realized what they meant, my entire body began to tremble with memory.

The haunting cries of children filled the air. The moans of the undead. The sounds of lifeless yet hungry despair.

Pallid faces contorted in twisted expressions appeared in the portal.

Screams erupted around me.

And then the children fell from the heavens.

They landed upon the stone table, unscathed, and were quickly up on their feet, looking around them with searching starved expressions.

More were coming, more and more falling through Celeste's portal.

"To me!" I heard Draven shout. "Don't let them get into the crowd. If you have weapons, draw them now, challengers! Use everything you have at your disposal."

"The Queen! Protect the Queen Regent!" Avriel roared from beside him. "Into formation. Shield your queen, Siabra!"

My heart was racing. The competitors around Draven and Avriel were doing as they said.

Lyrastra had already engaged a child. Pulling small blades from her gown, she was slashing away mercilessly. Her eyes were wide and disbelieving. Perhaps she had heard the rumors. Today she had learned they were true.

The crowd was panicking. Many were running for the door, only to find it barred. Celeste's doing, I assumed. Or perhaps there were more rebels than just herself.

Other Siabra were pulling out weapons or unsheathing their claws. Some brave ones were leaping over seats to join Draven, Lyrastra, and the other challengers below.

"Odessa," I heard Draven shout. "You know what to do."

His eyes glanced over at me and I saw something unexpected there. Fear. He was afraid. Not of the children. No, he had met them head-on before and prevailed.

Draven was afraid for me.

Odessa was already standing, shouting orders to Crescent and the others down our row.

She was just in time.

As Draven had spoken, Celeste had turned. Her beautiful face was twisted with hate as she looked at me. Our eyes met with a jolt.

"Your prince cares more about his half-blood plaything than his people, Siabra," she screamed over the chaos. "More about power than about redemption. We all know the reason. Is he above you all? Does he think he will be exempt? Kill the girl. She dies here tonight. He will have nothing. For nothing is what we deserve."

"She's mad," Odessa muttered. "How does any of that make sense?"

Celeste sounded as if she were riling the Siabra, expecting rebels to come out of the crowd and join her in assassinating me.

But instead to my shock, she pointed a finger towards me and with a flash of some inexplicable power, some of the horde of children around her turned towards me in unison.

She had control over them. Somehow, they were following her lead. How was such a thing possible? I had no idea.

"Kill Prince Kairos. Kill the Queen Regent. Kill the para–" That was all Celeste had time to say before blood spilled from her lips and I saw Draven's knife protruding from her throat.

Celeste's body fell to the ground as Draven leaped onto the table, charged through the children, and pulled the knife from her body, turning just in time to use it again to slice one of the monstrous children's head's off as it lunged to bite.

A powerful weapon. And to think I had thought it might only be ceremonial or decorative.

I felt naked without my own weapon.

I felt a tap on my shoulder and turned to see Odessa had pulled out her blades. She held one out to me, her scarred face rigid.

"Here. With luck, you won't need to use it."

The sword was forged from black steel and possessed a wickedly serrated edge on one side. The other boasted a series of jagged runes etched in crimson. I took hold of the hilt, wrapped in dark leather, and shot her a look of appreciation.

Odessa nodded. In her own hand she held a slender blade of polished pale steel with a silver crescent moon pommel. Its edge was keenly sharp and it looked perfect for swift strikes and precise maneuvers in closed spaces. Like betrayals in a throne room.

I glanced down the row behind her. Crescent stood by his sister's side. To my surprise, his attention was not on the attacking horde of undead children but rather on the portal still open, hovering in the air despite Celeste's fall. His face was set in concentration as he muttered to himself, his hands twisting in the air in front of him.

With a jolt, I realized what he was doing. He was trying to close the portal. To undo what Celeste had done. I wondered if it would work.

More small monstrosities were emerging from the hole in the sky, falling onto the table below and racing out into the crowd.

I watched as one ran up the aisle towards us, snarling and clawing with outstretched arms and raised my blade.

But to my shock, when it reached the edge of our aisle, it slammed into an invisible force and bounced off hard, landing a few meters away.

I looked back at Odessa and she gestured past Crescent at where Javer and Beks stood, arms out above them.

A shield. They were projecting some sort of an invisible shield over us all.

Beks's small face was solemn and serious as he stood beside his master. Beads of sweat dripped down his face as he concentrated, his dark eyes devoid of playfulness.

Next to him stood Javer, his wings opened wide with a sinister grace, his eyes narrowed, dark pointed brows sharp and calculating as he stared at something over our heads that was too subtle to see. The shield he and Beks were creating together, I assumed.

"Keep steady," he shouted to Beks. "Focus. Concentrate. The barrier must hold."

Beks gave a tight nod, his small hands uplifted.

"Perhaps Javer can fly us all out of here," I muttered. My dislike of the man had not come close to fading, no matter how he might be protecting us at the moment.

Something resembling a smile flickered over Odessa's face. "He can't fly," she said briefly. "They're only for show."

For some reason, that pleased me. I was sure possessing such an extravagant feature that served no utilitarian purpose whatsoever must drive a man like Javer mad.

Javer must have heard us. I caught him glowering at me. Then his gaze went to the sword in my hands and a look of sardonic amusement crossed his face.

I thought I understood why and could even perceive the irony, but still, I gripped Odessa's sword.

Down below, Draven and the other Siabra fought the fae children amidst bone-chilling cries.

Not all of the Siabra in the tiered seats were as protected as us. I watched as some of the children reached a huddled group of seemingly-defenseless nobles in the rows across the room and pounced upon them eagerly, shredding and ripping and screams filled the air.

"Shouldn't we go and help them?" I asked Odessa, gripping my sword more tightly.

"There isn't a chance in hell that they would have helped you," she said darkly. "The prince said stay. We stay put."

"But..." I started to say. Just then Gawain pushed past me, coming to stand on my right. He nodded at me with a small smile. There was a vicious-looking spiked mace in his hands. I stared at it. He had certainly not been wearing it when we'd entered. Perhaps he'd had the foresight to stash it under his seat beforehand. My respect for Crescent's partner rapidly increased.

"The shield should hold," Gawain assured me, speaking to me directly for the first time. "But just in case."

"I can defend myself," I told him, but I understood what he was trying to do. This was more about him and Draven than about me. He was simply doing as his prince had asked.

I glanced down at Draven and saw with shock that he was fighting in a close trio, with Lyrastra and Avriel. The three stood back-to-back, close to the Queen Regent. Crumpled small bodies lay littered around them.

The sight would have been heart wrenching had I not known exactly what those rabid things that had once been fae children were capable of.

They had killed Lancelet. Eaten her alive.

And now they were here. A continent away. I shuddered.

How much power had it taken to open that portal? Part of me couldn't help but be impressed by Celeste's capabilities.

Crescent let out a shout of triumph and we all turned to see him looking gleeful. I glanced up at the space over the stone table.

The portal was gone.

Odessa clapped her brother on the shoulder, with an expression of pride.

"Well done, my love," Gawain shouted to him from beside me.

Crescent gave a modest shrug.

A scream shattered the moment of success and we all looked to where the competitors fought.

One of the women—the one with the bright auburn hair—had fallen to the floor and was desperately trying to ward off a group of children pressing upon her. Her talon-hands were raised and she was slashing with all her might, but it was clear to see it would not be enough. She had no other weapon.

"Zephrae," Odessa murmured. "Shit. She's not going to make it."

My eyes shot to Draven. He was already moving forward but as I watched, his mother the queen gave a shrill commanding cry and he froze, then turned back unwillingly.

He glanced up at where we stood in the seats and beside me, I felt Gawain spring into movement.

There was a spark as he passed through the shield Javer and Beks held suspended around us and then he was jumping down the rows, hoisting his mace and hurrying towards Zephrae.

"Too late," Odessa murmured sorrowfully from beside me.

She was right. I watched as a child gripped Zephrae by her long beautiful feathers, pinned her head back, then lowered their mouth to rip out her throat.

Gawain roared in anger as he reached the woman. Over and over his mace sped through the air, ending the children who had fed upon her.

The chaos was slowly dying down.

Zephrae was the last Siabra to fall to the horde.

With a crunching sound, I watched as Avriel crushed a child's skull in his bare hands just as Draven decapitated another. Both men were covered in dark, thick blood.

The blood of the already dead and damned.

Beside them, Lyrastra, wiped a trickle of fresh blood from a cut on her cheek. She looked fierce and deadly. A true contender for the throne.

The Queen Regent stood behind the three of them looking pale and shaken. She had done nothing to protect herself, I observed.

As the last of the children fell, I watched Azriel—not Draven—rush to her side and take her arm.

"Shield down, Javer," Odessa said briefly, and then she squeezed past me and ran towards the door, Gawain following her and Crescent close behind.

I watched as they spoke, then Crescent raised his hands.

What was the opposite of a portal? Was that what Celeste had done to the doors?

Slowly, the massive double doors opened. A squad of guards stood in the hall, faces frightened as they peered inside, their spears raised.

The Queen Regent glided towards the doors, calling instructions in a regal tone. Evidently, she had already recovered from the attack.

Behind her, the remaining Siabra were rallying impressively. I could already hear titters of laughter and see smiles on some faces. Sure, the smiles were strained and the laughter rather obscene–but evidently the Siabra were preparing to pretend that the invasion and slaughter in their throne room had been simply a dramatic blip in an otherwise pleasant evening.

I stared as nobles and courtiers followed the Queen Regent in an orderly fashion from the room, leaving the bodies pooled in blood behind them, to be cleaned up by guards and servants no doubt.

A hand touched the small of my back very lightly.

"Shall we go?" Draven's breath was warm on my neck. He was standing very close. "Sorry. I'm a mess." He stepped back a little.

I could smell his scent. Musk and blood and sweat. Despite my best efforts, my body was responding to him with an odd hunger. To my horror, I realized I was aroused. Aroused by this man covered in blood, fresh from battle, with his naked blade still gripped in his hand.

"Back to the suite?" I stared stupidly at him. "So, that's it? It's over?"

He nodded. "The ritual was complete. Celeste was the last. What she did won't change anything for the rest of us. But no, not the suite. The ceremony is finished, but we have…" He cleared his throat. "Traditionally, a gala is held in the Queen's Gardens."

I gaped at him. "Your mother is holding a fucking garden party? Even after all of this?"

He grimaced. "I doubt she will change her plans. We're expected there. It will help to cement your place so we'll go."

It wasn't a question.

"Don't you want to… freshen up?" That was an understatement.

Draven's mouth curved up slightly. "I suspect the Siabra will be more titillated than offended if I attend like this–" He gestured to the blood and grime. "But yes, for your sake, I suppose I should change." He ran a hand over his dark hair and touched the gold diadem. Pulling it off, he looked at it with distaste. "My mother's request."

He passed it to me. "Here. Hold it for me. I'll only be a moment. Gawain and Crescent's suite is nearby. I'll go there and clean up, then find you."

Of course. Gawain and Crescent lived here in the palace. Odessa must, too. And Lyrastra. Just how massive was this place?

I had still never even glimpsed the city above. I wondered if I ever would.

CHAPTER II

T he garden was glowing.

Luminescent orbs floated gently through the trees, shining with ethereal light upon walkways lined with delicate blooms.

Unlike the Shadow Gardens, where Crescent and I had left Nightclaw earlier that day, the Queen's Gardens were carefully pruned and cultivated. Artfully trimmed pathways meandered through lush groves of exotic night-blooming flowers, their petals aglow with a soft blue luminescence like the moss I had seen on the stone walls elsewhere. Elaborate topiaries shaped like birds and animals lined the garden, their forms casting eerie shadows.

Seated among the foliage, a group of musicians played melodies on instruments shaped from wood and reeds as nobles and courtiers drifted about, conversing in low tones and sipping from delicate crystal goblets.

Amidst it all, the Queen Regent stood on a small dais adorned with vines and flowers. Holding a goblet in her hand, she scanned the crowd until her eyes fell upon me.

Her lips turned up in amusement as she saw me standing there alone holding Draven's circlet.

"Greetings, Child of the Valtain. Are you enjoying the evening's entertainment? Or is my son's bed the only sport your kind desires?"

She turned away without waiting for me to answer.

I felt hot and cold all over, humiliated with just a few words. This cold, vicious woman was Draven's mother? I wasn't sure what I had expected. A welcome perhaps. Or at least a courteous address.

Queen Sephone had not even shown an inkling of concern for the fallen competitors back in the throne room—nor for those unlucky few who had been ravaged by the undead children.

Was she so jaded to death and blood that they were all but meaningless to her?

Draven's father must have been quite a piece of work, I decided, to have either chosen a queen like Sephone or to have shaped her until she became this... this... monarch of ice.

"We don't require her approval," a deep voice said in my ear. "Ignore her."

I turned to see Draven. He must have just entered.

"Is that an order?"

"I can make it one if you like." He smiled sensuously.

I glanced at the Queen Regent. "We don't require her approval. Are you sure about that?"

"Believe me, I'm sure. I never expected it. That's not... the kind of relationship we have." His deep voice was terse and clipped. "She would never approve of anyone I chose. I have my doubts she even approves of me."

"But..." There were so many problems with this statement. "She's your mother. And also, you haven't *chosen* me. This is all a farce."

There was a moment's pause.

"You're right. She's not my true mother. She's my aunt."

I was stunned. "Your aunt?"

"My father married her when my own mother died," he said casually. "It's common for royal children to be matched with pairs of nobleborn siblings. She was married to my father's brother first."

"Like Lyrastra," I blurted out.

Draven raised a fine dark brow. "Yes."

"And now you and Lyrastra are both free. Why not simply marry Lyrastra?" I asked bluntly. "If it's tradition, wouldn't that be simplest?"

He studied my features. "Who told you that?"

"No one," I said stubbornly. "But it's obvious to anyone that Lyrastra wouldn't mind."

"Wouldn't she?" Draven's voice was quiet. "Believe me, we wouldn't be good for one another. I'm not what she needs. Walk with me."

His hand slid around my waist, solid and warm.

He led us down a darkened path, into a small grove surrounded by softly glowing blue trees.

Glancing behind, he pulled me to him. I let out a little gasp as my breasts hit his chest.

All of this was incredibly strange. We had been sharing a bed for days and yet this felt like the most intimate we had ever been. Something had shifted, changed. Was it because Draven was so fully in control and I was being forced to follow his lead?

A tangled barrier in him seemed to have unraveled and as I looked up into his eyes, I saw a stark longing that shocked me.

None of this was real, I reminded myself sternly.

The problem was that my pounding heart didn't seem fully convinced of that.

I gave a little nervous laugh and Draven smiled slightly, his beautiful lips turning upwards like a radiant arc of light.

My heart gave a pitter-patter that warned me I was treading on dangerous ground.

"What is it?" he said.

I swallowed. "Only that all of this is so incredibly ridiculous, isn't it?"

His eyes were serious and steady. "Which part?"

"Pretending to be lovers. Being here, with you, in this ridiculously perfect garden after your court was just attacked by monsters." Monsters of their own creation. His was a dark court indeed. "It's all... too much. And I thought the Rose Court was a thorny mess."

His smile grew. "Ours is a volcanic mess. On the verge of eruption."

"Very funny. But truly, can't you let me go, take a step backwards, and we'll stop pretending for a few minutes?" I pleaded. "Just go back to being plain old us? You, grumpy Draven and me, angry-at-you-forever Morgan?"

His arms remained around my waist. "What if I don't want to do that?"

My heartbeat thundered in my ears. "Don't make me use an earring," I said, trying to keep my voice light.

I shook my hair a little, showing off the long silver tendrils Breena had placed in each of my ears.

But instead of looking amused or annoyed, Draven's face turned serious.

"You have the most beautiful laugh, you know. You rarely use it, but when you do..." He took a breath and to my shock I felt him tremble. "It shakes the world. My entire world."

I said nothing. Had no idea what to say.

"I didn't get a chance to tell you earlier this evening," he continued, his voice low and husky. "But you look breathtaking tonight in that gown." He raised a hand and gently touched a finger to a strand of my hair. "Your hair is like liquid moonlight, a crown fit for a goddess."

I laughed nervously before I could stop myself, then made a dismissive sound that said I didn't believe him.

"What are you doing?" I whispered. "Stop it."

He shook his head, face set stubbornly. "I can't. Don't ask me to."

He squeezed my waist gently, reminding me of the strength of those large hands and what they were capable of.

"This. The touch of your waist, your hips, your skin beneath my hands? It sets me on fire, Morgan. I'm in awe of you, every part of you. Can't you tell? I'm spellbound. You've awakened something in me I thought was long dead. Something I never thought I'd ever come close to feeling again. And now I live for your presence. For the hope of your laugh, your smile. All of this. The court. The throne. Bringing you here. I know I can never convince you, but it is all for you. What I do is for you, always."

He leaned forward abruptly, breathing in deeply. "Your scent is intoxicating. Do you have any idea what your fragrance does to me? The longing I feel when I'm this close to you?"

An electric shiver danced through my veins, sending sparks through my body.

"Your brother and his court? They had no idea who you really were, what you were capable of. But I see you, Morgan Pendragon. I see you truly for everything you are and everything you will be and I claim you as mine."

I opened my mouth to speak but no sound came out.

He was saying the words that part of me had always wanted to hear. A part of me I had kept locked up and hidden away, too afraid to even admit it was there.

He was Kairos Draven. My enemy. My protector. Sometimes something close to a friend. Sometimes the man I wanted to stab while he slept.

Pretending to be his lover was a terrible joke, yes–but it was also terribly cruel.

Because part of me had always longed to be. From the very beginning. From the moment we had first met.

And now to hear him say these words...

"Stop," I managed to get out. "You don't get to do this. You don't mean any of the things you're saying. It's just courtly bullshit, so stop. Stop it right now."

The heat behind his eyes singed my heart. "How can I convince you I truly do?"

He pulled me more tightly against him and I felt every inch of his body along mine, felt the press of his desire, hard and unmistakable. I gasped. My body reacted by bursting into flame–heat racing over every inch of my skin where our forms merged and touched.

"Perhaps I don't have to say the right words to convince you," he murmured, his emerald eyes burning into mine. "Perhaps all I have to do is this."

His lips crushed mine, like cinnamon and rose petals, like a smoky burst of ash and pine. His taste and scent encompassed me, overwhelmed me.

The world around us faded into dark oblivion as we began to move through the steps of a dance as old as time itself. His touch was a symphony of sensation upon my skin as he gently slid his hands up and down my back, teasing and caressing.

The taste of him sent me lightheaded and spinning, a heady concoction of everything I had always believed forbidden and yet secretly yearned for. With every moment of the kiss, walls between us shattered, leaving only naked vulnerability. Each brush of his fingertips against the thin fabric of my gown sent tremors of desire coursing through my veins.

My hunger for this man left me reeling. His scent enveloped me, musk and leather and beneath it all the lingering hint of blood. He was the most dangerous temptation I couldn't resist. He had killed for me. I knew he would not hesitate to do so again. What was there about that knowledge that filled me with such primal lust and beyond the lust–pure trust?

I trusted him more than I could ever hate him.

I trusted him with my life or I knew I wouldn't have been there with him right now. No, I would have run far away, no matter what it took, if I thought there was even a chance Draven was anything like Vesper.

Draven's lips moved more fiercely against mine, possessing me in a desperate rhythm, beneath it all an unquenchable thirst for more. I let out a moan as his hands slid lower, cupping my bottom more tightly against him and half-lifting me upwards.

"Yes." The word was wrenched from my lips. I could show no restraint. Not now. "Please. Yes."

I arched against him, wrapping my arms around his neck and pulling his lips still tighter against mine.

My breasts flattened against his chest, nipples puckering into hard buds.

His hands cradled my ass, rocking my hips against his. I wanted those hands everywhere. I wanted *him* everywhere.

The world around us was forgotten. The queen and her court, forgotten. There was only us and the night. And the night was ours for the taking.

In that instant, he could have laid me down on the ground and taken me and all I would probably have said was "More, Draven. Harder. Faster."

But I would never know.

For it was not to be.

There was a whisper in the dark behind us. A scuffling of feet.

I broke the kiss, pushing back, and reluctantly felt Draven lower me back down to the earth.

"What was that?" I glanced behind me into the shadows, one hand still touching his neck.

"I didn't hear anything," he replied swiftly.

I froze.

I turned my head back to him.

"You're lying. There was something. You must have heard it. Your hearing is far better than mine." He had bragged of it more than once.

The sound came again. A woman's voice, followed by a man's.

I turned my head back again to see a man and a woman step out of the darkness. They stood in the center of the path for a moment, letting themselves be seen, not even trying to hide the fact they had been spying upon us.

Then they walked back up the garden path towards the queen's party.

"You knew," I said, icy knowledge sending a chill through my veins. "You knew they were watching us the whole time. And you wanted to put on a show. All of that was for them. Everything you said..."

I took a step back, my head spinning. Waves of nausea coursed through me. How quickly infinite pleasure could turn to infinite pain.

"You made me into a spectacle," I said, my voice low. "You used me."

"I'm protecting you, Morgan, like I've always done. I knew they were there, yes, but that doesn't change..."

I held up a hand like a ward against him. "Stop. Enough. No more. No more lies. I can't take another lie from you."

Another step back, then another.

"Are you all right?" It was Crescent. He looked between us, his face conflicted and unhappy. "I saw Avriel and Lyrastra just now. They looked too amused for my liking."

Amused. Of course, they did. I was the prince's toy. This public affection was all a ploy for their sake. But surely, they also knew none of it was real.

Lyrastra probably believed I thought it was though.

She probably thought I'd fallen for Draven, hook, line, and sinker. That every sweet word that fell from his mouth was truth to me. That I was not only his whore but his fool.

I backed up still farther. "I want to go. Now. Away from here."

Draven's face had become sad and weary. Another sham. I didn't care.

"Take her," he said, raising a hand to his brow. "It's all right."

"Of course, it is," I snarled. "You gave them the show you wanted. Unless you planned to lay me down and fuck me in front of them all. Was that what you were hoping for? To finish things off completely?"

I could almost feel Crescent flinch behind me.

Bitter tears were stinging my eyes. I refused to wipe them away, instead praying he wouldn't be able to see them in the dark.

"You must think I'm such a fool," I spat. "To have fallen for all your lies. Protect me? I don't know what any of this is, but I do know there's no way any of it's for *me*. Maybe it amused you to think you could trick me into actually *being* with you, but thank the Three..." My voice trailed off.

In fact, I could think of nothing to thank the Three for at the moment. I was alone, bereft, and broken. Right back at the place I'd been with Vesper. Tricked and betrayed. Broken and wounded. I could think of nothing to be thankful for.

Whereas mere moments ago, I had been filled with such unspeakable light.

"Your court is broken," I whispered. "*You* are broken. I pity you. And I pity myself for being trapped here with a soulless husk of a man like you."

I turned around and fled.

CHAPTER 12

I ran past Crescent, shouldering him aside, crossing down another shadowed path to the edge of the garden and then followed it, searching for a way out.

Tears burned my eyes and now I let myself brush them aside, trying to clear my vision.

But after a few moments of stumbling in the dark, I realized there was only one way out—the way I had come in.

Any moment and Crescent would come around the grove of trees softly calling my name—or worse, Draven.

They would make me go back to the suite, back to that room.

I couldn't. I just couldn't.

"Psst!"

I whipped my head around, searching for the source of the sound.

"Psst, over here," the voice came again, impatiently.

"Beks?" I squinted into the dark. "Is that you? I can't see you.

"Come towards the wall," the voice hissed. "Hurry up."

I did as he instructed even though all I could see was blackness. My hand hit the wall and I felt cold stone.

"Down here. You'll have to crouch. It's a small one."

I looked down and could just barely make out Beks' dark head poking out from an opening.

"Am I going to fit in there?"

"You can stay here if you..."

But I was already on my knees, crawling through the grass as quickly as I could towards the opening. I saw a glimpse of light as Beks backed up hastily to make room for me and then I was pushing myself through a small square sized space in the stone that would have made me feel unpleasantly confined if it hadn't opened right up into the familiar passageway I was growing used to.

I stood up, brushing grass and petals off my gown.

"You have impeccable timing, Beks. Spying on the garden party, were you?"

Beks shook his head and grinned. "No. I'm supposed to be in bed. But I went to see a friend first. And now she wants to see you."

"A friend of yours? She wants to see me?" I hadn't realized Beks had other friends he visited besides me via the passages. I felt oddly offended for a second. "Who is she?"

"You'll see. You'll like her, don't worry. Come on." He turned and started walking at a brisk pace.

"Exciting evening, wasn't it?" I said conversationally, trying to clear my mind of the repugnant scene with Draven.

Maybe I could live in these passageways. I could sleep on that divan I had seen. Beks could bring me food.

I could sneak into other peoples' apartments to bathe.

I could become a ghost, a phantom. No one would ever find me.

It was surprisingly appealing. So what if I never saw the sun again. The way things were going, I doubted I ever would.

"I never thought I'd get to see them." Beks voice was filled with grisly excitement.

"See them? See what? The children, you mean?" I frowned. "I wouldn't have thought anyone would be eager to see those things."

"They're legendary," Beks said, in a voice filled with awe. "When I was younger, I thought Javer had made them up just to scare me."

"Why would he do something like that?" I scowled to myself. "He's supposed to be teaching you, not frightening you to death."

Beks shrugged. "I'm not a very good pupil, I guess. That's what he says. He says I need to learn some healthy fear. I guess he was right."

I rolled my eyes. "I don't know. You don't seem to have been very afraid of anything that happened tonight."

"Oh, that's true." Beks sounded happy again. "I wasn't. It was kind of..."

"Don't say fun," I warned.

"Fun."

I groaned. "People dying gruesome deaths and undead children are 'fun' to you?"

"Well..." Beks sounded considering. "Those children were just like me. So I guess I feel sorry for them. But also, what happened to them happened a hundred and fifty years ago. And they're still standing. So it's also kind of..."

"Don't say 'neat,'" I threatened.

"Kind of amazing, right? Don't you think so?"

I stared at his small back as he continued to march along. "Amazing. Sure. Those amazing creatures..." I swallowed. "Killed my friend."

He stopped. Looked back at me. "Oh. I'm sorry. That must have been horrible."

"It was. More for her than for me."

"I guess so. Well, I guess they're awful, but it sure was incredible raising that shield with Javer."

I swallowed hard. He was right. He had shone tonight and had every right to be proud. I didn't have to take that away from him. "*You* were incredible, Beks. Had you ever done anything like that before?"

"In practice, yeah. But never the real thing like today. We protected people." His little chest puffed out like a rooster's. "We held it as long as we had to."

"You were very impressive," I agreed, hiding a smile. "You protected us extremely well. Just how large a shield can you make, anyhow?"

"Oh, much larger than that. But Javer wanted us to stay small. He said the prince wanted you shielded and there was no point wasting our energy shielding everyone else. But I could have done more," he boasted. "I was holding myself back."

I sighed. "Of course, Javer would say that." But who knew if Beks was right. Doing such a thing must have been draining for them both.

"Besides, it was too late for him to shield the queen. Once those things came through... Well, everyone down below was too close together. We might have wound up trapping her with one of those children instead. Can you imagine?" Beks gave a delicious shudder.

I sort of could. It wasn't an altogether horrid mental image either.

I forced myself to stop fantasizing about the frosty Queen Regent being eaten.

"So, shielding–that's your power?"

"Yep," Beks said importantly. "Someday I'll be a court mage like Javer. The best of the best. We're the rarest power. That's what Javer says."

"I'm sure he does," I murmured. "And you live here in the palace, studying with Javer until then? Do you like it? Are you happy here? Is he... kind to you?"

Beks shrugged casually. "He's not so bad. He was really angry that day when he levitated me. He doesn't do that. The prince talked to him and told him he'd lose me if he ever mistreated me again. I know. I was listening in."

I suppressed a snort. Unsurprising.

"Besides," he continued. "There's nowhere else for me to go. The palace is better than where I was."

"Draven…" Ugh. The name was like poison on my tongue. "The prince mentioned you were an orphan. How old were you when they found you?"

I realized I had no idea who had actually found him. I'd assumed it had been Javer.

"Crescent and Javer found me. Crescent wanted to keep me, but Javer insisted he should have me because my skills matched his." Beks sounded rather wistful. "He went to the queen and she agreed."

I felt stunned. "You could have lived with Crescent and Gawain?"

"Yes. I was seven then. Now I'm almost eleven." He sounded proud.

"You're remarkable for an eleven-year-old, Beks," I said truthfully. "I doubt many eleven-year-olds could do what you did tonight."

"Almost eleven," Beks corrected. "I guess Javer's not so bad. But he's not really like… well, a father. Not like Crescent might have been. Taina might have been my little sister. She's annoying but… I guess she'd have grown on me."

The wistfulness was back.

"I'm sure Crescent still cares for you," I said carefully. "You're a part of the team, right?"

Where had that come from? I didn't want to think of Draven's bloody team.

Because I actually *liked* them. I liked his friends.

Even if I hated that soulless lying bastard.

Beks nodded. "Javer cares for me, too. It's just that he shows it differently. Plus, he's boring sometimes and so I run away. And then he gets mad and yells a lot."

"An endless cycle, I'm sure," I said drily. But still, I was relieved that Draven had warned Javer to take better care of the boy.

"Here we are," Beks announced.

He tapped a spot on the stone wall lightly and a door swung open, much larger than the one back in the garden.

I followed him out the doorway and onto a small landing overlooking a spacious windowless room that must have been farther below ground in the palace. Steps wound down to the main floor.

Polished stone walls were set with brass lamps that burned with the same magic light Beks had conjured in the passages. Around us was an array of impressive, meticulously arranged equipment that reminded me a little of my uncle's apothecary chamber back in Camelot.

Shelves of oak and iron held a vast assortment of crystalline vials and potion-filled flasks, all carefully labeled. Glass beakers and brass contraptions I didn't recognize stood along gleaming white marble countertops, their intricate mechanisms glowing in the lamplight.

Large white polished tables were spread with parchments, notes, and diagrams, intermingled with fine-tipped quills, stirring rods, and precision scales.

A subtle bubbling sound filled the air and I looked to the corner of the room where a glass cauldron filled with a bright yellow liquid boiled and hissed.

In the middle of the work space stood a girl hunched over a parchment spread out on one of the tables.

As we entered, she lifted her head, her gaze unfocused as if she had forgotten we were coming.

I sucked in my breath. The girl had Draven's eyes. Emerald and intelligent, they gazed back at me.

Short cropped black hair framed her heart-shaped face, while a pair of small horns peeked out from beneath her locks. Her light-brown, sun-kissed skin was the same shade as Draven's too. Perched on her nose were a pair of round glass circles, surrounded by metal frames. They made her look like a clever bird, sharp and relentlessly curious.

"Who is this?" I asked Beks, though I thought I already knew.

"I'm Rychel," the girl said, overhearing. Damn, her hearing was as sharp as Draven's, too. "You must be Morgan."

She smiled up as we came down the steps towards her.

"What is this place?" I asked, trying to keep my voice even. "And look, it's been a hell of a night so I won't mince words. Why do you look so much like Draven?"

Rychel's expression became amused. "Beks said you were used to calling the prince that. Kairos is my older brother." She looked around her. "And I believe this was one of my father's torture chambers before I repurposed it for my work."

"Your brother?" I stared at the girl. "Your work? What sort of work do you do?"

I suddenly spotted a table across the room that I hadn't noticed before. It was covered with a white sheet. Dark spots were forming on the fabric from whatever was below. And sticking out from underneath, just the tip of one foot showing was...

"Why the fuck do you have one of those things down here?" I exclaimed, backing up and hitting my hip against a marble table.

"Don't worry, it's very much dead," Rychel said soothingly. "Though I suppose telling you that won't be much comfort. Hmm." She tapped a finger to her lips. "It's really dead this time. It won't be moving again. I swear." Then she shrugged. "Or if it does, not like before."

I stared at her. "What the hell do you mean...not like before?"

"Well, that's part of my work, you see," she said, in a voice far too chipper to possibly be coming from one of Draven's relatives. "I'm trying to undo what our father did."

My eyes widened still more. "You're trying to undo the plague? You must be mad."

"Not mad," she assured me. "Just really stubborn. It's a family trait." She grinned, showing dimples that I wasn't sure Draven possessed.

Damn. I was already starting to like her. Draven's little sister.

"I didn't even know he had a sister. Why wouldn't he tell me?" I could guess. To protect me? To protect her? "More lies and deceptions."

"I know he was going to tell you. He just hadn't gotten around to it yet. I think there's been a lot going on." She tilted her head. "But he's told me all about you and I wanted to meet you. I'm impatient and decided I couldn't wait. I guess I was especially excited after what Beks brought me tonight."

"Wait... Beks brought you that... thing?" I glared at Beks. Then I wondered how he'd carried it. Ugh. Did I even want to know? I imagined him dragging the child's carcass through the tunnels. Even Beks couldn't be that inured to the macabre, could he?

"Crescent helped me," Beks offered. "He opened a portal."

"Of course, he did." I threw up my hands. "And your brother tossed it in, right?"

"No, he thinks I'm mad–just like you said–for even trying to undo the plague," Rychel said cheerfully. "But he can't stop me from trying. He knows me too well for that."

"Those children died one hundred and fifty years ago," I said slowly. "Yet you really think you can somehow reverse this?"

"Well, that's just it, isn't it?" Rychel said perkily. "It's been more than a century and yet these things look surprisingly fresh, don't they?"

"Fresh?"

"Surprisingly undecayed," she clarified. "I mean, they've decayed to a certain extent. But there's still flesh on their bones. Some have eyeballs still in their sockets."

I gave an involuntary shudder.

"Sorry," she said apologetically. "I'm used to all of this so it doesn't bother me anymore. Comes from being down here too much."

"I'm not the easily disgusted type, but I guess I've just had enough of..." I gestured to the corpse on the table. "Blood and death. At least, for one night. It's been a rough night overall," I finished lamely.

She nodded. "I get it. And this probably isn't what you wanted to end your night talking about. But the short answer is—my father didn't just use a plague to do this. He used magic. And anything that uses magic can be changed. Or undone. Even the past. I refuse to believe otherwise." She smiled calmly at me.

"I see," I said. "Well, I suppose it's admirable that you even want to try. Most of your people don't seem to give a shit about those children unless they're being eaten by one."

"Oh, they're not my people," Rychel said. "I don't consider myself Siabra. I'm like you. Except my mother was human. I guess my brother hasn't told you much."

I quirked an eyebrow. "I know the Queen Regent is actually his aunt."

She grimaced. "Right. My father needed another empress. A human woman wouldn't cut it. But a human woman to breed his extra spawn? He had no qualms about that."

"I thought most human women died in childbirth if..."

"They did. Do. He went through a lot. He was nothing if not persistent and prolific, our father. Fidelity might be Draven's hallmark but it certainly wasn't his." Fidelity? Draven's hallmark? No, I definitely wasn't going to ask.

"Brutal. Callous. Perverted. Fiendish. Those words apply, too." She smiled cheerily.

"I'm sorry?" I offered.

Rychel shrugged. "Well, at least he was clever. My mother must have been, too. I credit her with all my best traits. Though my brother has a few acceptable ones. I would have liked to have met his mother. A pity all the good mothers are gone." She stopped and grinned. "I'm babbling aren't I? I have a tendency to do that. I'm not a people person. I like people. I just don't see them very often, but when I do and when I like them... well, I talk. A lot."

She glanced at me. "You're bleeding. Weren't you just at a party?"

I looked at where she was gazing. Sure enough, there was a small cut on my leg. "It must have happened when I was crawling into the passage. A sharp blade of grass or a twig or something."

"Here, I'll take care of that." She came over with a small white cloth in her hand, cleaned the cut, and then pressed a compress over it. "Wouldn't want it to become putrid now, would we? My brother would throw a fit if something happened to you."

"I want to murder your brother," I said conversationally. "So while you seem lovely, Rychel, I'm honestly not sure we can be friends."

"Oh, I want to murder him, too! Please, let me help." Rychel clapped her hands together. "He's infuriating, isn't he?"

I nodded reluctantly, but wasn't sure she was taking me literally enough. "No, I mean, I might go back to our room and if he dares to make an appearance, I plan to stab him in his sleep."

Rychel tilted her head thoughtfully. "Well, just don't stab him in the heart. Anything else, and I can probably fix it. Or he'll heal. He has incredible healing abilities. I'm sure you've noticed. He's pretty hard to kill, but give it a shot if you need to. I'm sure he deserves it if you're this angry."

I stared at her. "I.... thank you."

"Sure, of course. Now, I'm sure you have a lot of questions and I doubt my brother has given you many answers. Probably part of why you're ready to kill him, am I right? So go ahead and ask me. That's part of why I had Beks bring you here."

"You...did?" I thought for a moment. "Why weren't you at the ceremony tonight?"

"Oh, I'm persona non grata. Out of the court's favor." Unsurprisingly, Rychel looked completely unconcerned by this admission. "The Queen Regent hates my guts. So, that means I don't get invited places. It also means I don't have to go to stupid things like her little garden parties."

"It was rather in bad taste," I acknowledged. "Not just failing to invite you, I mean. But having a party after her court was attacked."

"And a rebel exposed in her midst?" Rychel nodded. "But it's all part and parcel with the Court of Umbral Flames. Just keep your chin up, pretend everything is fine, ignore the fact that we decimated the children of an entire people who, by the way, we're still basically related to, forget about how we're now doomed to childlessness ourselves, pretend there's no dissension in our midst until its literally hitting us in the face... or biting us in the face."

I winced at the image. "Speaking of the childlessness, I would have thought that was the problem you would be trying to find a solution for."

Rychel raised her eyebrows. "Why? Because you think I want to help the Siabra?" She tapped the table beside her with a finger. "You don't think they deserve exactly what they got? Or worse?"

For attacking children. Destroying the lineage of a people.

"Well," I said, taking a breath. "Your father was the one primarily responsible for what happened, wasn't he? As the emperor?"

"He had a fleet of advisors to back up the decision, I can assure you. Not that I was alive then."

"Right. Of course, he did. And it was a horrible thing. But the way your brother made it sound... your father didn't know only the children would be affected? Did he? Or what was going to happen?"

Rychel looked at me thoughtfully. "That's what he told you? I suppose he was trying to present the most balanced version. Honestly, I don't think we'll ever know. My father was too much of an asshole to ever admit that he knew exactly what he was doing." I cringed, thinking of how I had been thinking of Draven exactly the same way. Was he more like his father than I'd thought?

"Especially after it came right back to bite him," Rychel went on. "He didn't exactly go down in Siabra history as our most beloved emperor, as I'm sure you can imagine."

"Why does the Queen Regent hate you, anyhow?" I asked, changing the subject.

"Well, I'm not a trueborn child, for one. Not like Draven, who's at least the child of her dead sister." Rychel began ticking off items on her fingers. "I'm half-human. I refuse to marry and try to breed. Sorry, no desire to die in childbirth for this stupid curse, thanks very much. I'm a constant reminder that my dad–Sephone's husband–was a serial cheater who basically fucked half her court. No gender preference either, in case you were wondering about that."

"I wasn't, but that's... interesting," I managed. Definitely not interested in any details of who Draven's despicable dad had or hadn't slept with.

"Oh, and she thinks I'm mad for being down here, conducting my little experiments and trying to undo the mess my father made," Rychel finished.

"I mean, it is a little... bold," I said cautiously. "It's admirable that you want to try though. I still don't see how it would ever be possible."

"Flesh and memory."

"What?"

"Well, if it was simply a matter of restoring the Valtain children's bodies, I could probably do that right now. But it's memory that's the sticky thing, isn't it? Think of a fae child. Say ten years old. They've lived hardly any time at all. Then one day, bam! They're victims of this horrendous plague. And they spend the next one hundred and fifty years..."

"Oh, Zorya..." I was horrified.

Rychel nodded. "Exactly. They wouldn't want to *keep* those memories, would they? No one would. It's a conundrum all right."

I thought of all of the children we'd had to slay just to survive in the ruins of Meridium. "Perhaps it's better if you never succeed," I said softly. "The results could be just as tragic."

For the first time, Rychel looked a little dejected. "Because we've already slaughtered so many, you mean? There is that. Not to mention that I suspect the Valtain themselves must have tried to come up with some way of reversing what happened. And if they failed, then what chance do I have?" She glanced at the body under the tarp. "Still, I'm learning a lot. And faint hope is better than no hope."

She glanced at me. "Draven was the last pure Siabra child born since this happened. Did you know that?"

I shook my head.

"It's a sad story though. His mother was giving birth to him as the curse took effect. She died in childbirth. No one was expecting that. It was very uncommon for fae women to face any kind of childbirth complications before that. They're heartier overall than human women, as you probably know."

"So he never knew his mother, only his aunt." That still didn't mean he had my sympathy. I'd lost my mother young, too. It hadn't turned me into a lying, morally devoid monster.

"He brought back that chalice, you know," Rychel continued.

I lifted my eyebrows in surprise. "The one they used at the ceremony?"

"Right. It binds the contestants to the rules of the Blood Rise."

"What exactly were they drinking from it, anyhow?" I asked

"It doesn't really matter. It might have been water. Or blood." She grinned wickedly. "It wasn't blood. At least, I doubt Sephone would go that far."

"One of the candidates managed to kill another somehow. I still don't get how that was done," I offered.

Rychel rolled her eyes. "Lemme guess. Avriel had already drunk from the cup?"

I nodded. "You guessed it."

"He probably dropped a poison capsule in as he took a sip, then passed it down."

That made a sick kind of sense. "So this sort of thing happens all the time?"

"With Avriel? Hell yes. With the chalice? No, because there hasn't been a Blood Rise competition in... well, a long time. There hasn't had to be one because the succession ran fairly smoothly before..."

"Before Draven killed his own brother to save Lyrastra? Yeah, I've heard the story."

Rychel looked at me strangely. "Have you?"

"Well, yes. Did I leave anything out?"

Rychel scratched her nose in a way I found endearing. "Rather a lot. But I suppose whoever told you that version wanted it that way. Still..."

"What do you mean?" I demanded. "What was left out exactly? Did Draven do something worse?"

Shit. I hadn't thought that was possible, but clearly I'd been wrong.

"Not worse," Rychel said. "They just left out the whole part about how our brother had already murdered Kairos's wife."

CHAPTER 13

S ilence filled Rychel's laboratory.

"You're looking at me as if I just told you I killed your puppy," Rychel said finally.

"No," I said quickly. "I mean, I'm just... shocked. I had no idea Draven was married already. I mean, married before."

Shocked? I was stunned. What was worse than stunned? I was thunderstruck. Why hadn't he ever told me before?

Because he never told me anything. He kept more things from me than he ever shared. He'd rather lie to me and fake-kiss me than tell me the truth or take me into his confidence.

That was the kind of man Kairos Draven was.

At least he had an amazing little sister to make up for part of his awfulness.

"Yep. Married. It was an arranged marriage, of course. Royal ones always are." Rychel's face was still unusually somber. "Tabar took after our father. He was... ruthless."

"Tell me," I said simply. "Tell me the real story." I met Rychel's eyes. "You must know that I'm not really your brother's paramour."

Rychel nodded slowly. "I had an inkling. But I know he still cares for you, very much."

I snorted. "We won't get into that. I don't want us to argue."

I wasn't sure how much longer I was going to be at the Court of Umbral Flames, but for however much longer I was there I had to admit I wanted Rychel and I to be something like friends.

I realized Rychel was grinning at something across the room.

"You're lucky Beks fell asleep a while ago," she said, nodding to where the little boy was curled up under a table. "Or he'd have been devastated. He thinks you and Draven are a true love match."

I felt an odd guilty sensation in the pit of my stomach. "Oh, Beks. I was worried he might be the romantic type."

"You never can tell who is." She sighed as she looked at the boy. "I guess he'd rather sleep here on the floor than back in his rooms with Javer."

"Can you really blame him?"

Rychel gave a quick laugh, then her face became serious. "I suppose not. Well, where were we? The story. This isn't a nice story to tell so I'm just going to make it quick. Like pulling a tooth, you know? Not that the Siabra would have any idea what that was like. Anyhow, Draven's wife. She was Lyrastra's younger sister."

I felt my eyebrows go up but I kept quiet, not wanting to interrupt Rychel's flow.

"Her name was Nodori. From what I've heard, she was really sweet. Very kind. Completely different from Lyrastra."

My heart sank. Sweet. Of course, she was. Probably unspeakably beautiful, too. So that was the kind of woman Draven liked? I had to admit, I was a little surprised.

"Draven and Tabar married on the same day. Our father arranged the marriages. The Siabra like things in pairs. You may have noticed. Sibling marriages are... well, traditional."

"And weird," I couldn't help adding.

"A little weird, but many dynasties throughout history have had similar arrangements. Anyhow, Draven and Nodori..."

"Look," I interrupted, unable to take it. "You can skip over the part where they were so in love and so happy and all of that. I get it. They were so happy that it was a horrible tragedy when his brother murdered her."

Rychel looked surprised. "Well, it was a tragedy. Especially because Tabar killed their baby. But they weren't in love and I'm really not sure they were ever happy. I mean, I don't think Draven was. I've heard Nodori was pretty happy with him. But Draven... Well, he'd known Nodori since they were kids. They grew up together. I think he'd always viewed her as a sister. They were almost the same age. Not a wife."

"Ew," I managed.

"Ew," Rychel agreed. "But he definitely cared for her. That's not in question. He would have done anything to protect her. Well, you know my brother." She shrugged. "Anyhow, Nodori gave birth to their baby—successfully. A Siabra baby."

My ears suddenly seemed to open up. "What? How was that possible?"

"It wasn't supposed to be," Rychel agreed. "And yet no one had stopped trying. Tabar was furious. Eaten up with jealousy."

"And he blamed Lyrastra," I said, understanding.

"Of course. Men always blame women for anything to do with a failed childbirth. It's unfair and irrational, but there you have it. And Tabar was extremely unfair and irrational. It was basically bred into him."

"I can't believe he'd kill a baby. His own nephew. Or niece."

"Niece," Rychel said quietly. "It was a girl. He went into the bedchamber a few hours after the baby had been born and... Well, I don't think you need a description."

"Draven must have been devastated," I said softly.

I thought of how I had accused him back in the forest about murdering infants. He had brushed off the accusation so easily. But then, he'd had years to harden himself to his grief.

"He was. Grief-stricken and furious. He changed that day, Morgan. Everyone agrees. He had always been softer than Tabar. Much more open. Kinder. I suppose that was why he was matched with Nodori. After all, he was never supposed to be in line to the throne. But that day he changed. He found Tabar just as he was about to kill Lyrastra, and he just...struck him down. Tabar tried to fight back, but he was no match for my brother. Not that day."

"Your brother?" I said. "Weren't they both your brothers?"

Rychel's face darkened. "I don't think of Tabar as my brother. Not anymore."

"I can't believe Draven was banished for doing what he did when he was only trying to avenge his family and protect Lyrastra. It seems, well, kind of justified," I admitted.

"I agree. I think most of the court did, too. Killing a Siabra child was the worst crime imaginable. Everyone was horrified. Tabar might have gotten away with killing Nodori. He was the crown prince, so who knows. But killing the child–that was unforgivable. Still, there are rules for this sort of thing and Sephone had to follow them when it came to punishing Kairos."

"So she was glad when Draven... Kairos, I mean... eventually came back?" Even though it was with me.

"Of course. He brought the chalice with him, for one. That thing is legendary. And also, well, he represents hope."

"Hope?" I wasn't sure I understood. "You mean, if he becomes the next emperor?"

"He'd definitely make a better one than Tabar would have. But no, I mean because he's one of two people who showed they were capable of producing a Siabra child. And the other is dead."

Nodori. Draven's wife. What had his daughter's name been? Had she even had a name? I decided I wasn't going to ask Rychel that. Not now.

"My guess is that Sephone is hoping his breeding power won't have been a fluke, that he'll win the Blood Rise, become emperor, get married and hopefully start having babies."

I wrinkled my nose. "Breeding power?"

"I know, right? He's my brother, need I remind you?" Rychel snickered. "But still, it's just a fact. That said..." Rychel tapped her lip considering. "The Queen Regent might have other plans, too."

"What do you mean?"

"I mean, she and Avriel..." Rychel gave me a significant look.

"You mean they...? Oh!" I wasn't that surprised. I had seen the smile on her face when she looked at him. "But he's one of Draven's competitors. Is that allowed?"

"For the Queen Regent overseeing the Blood Rise to be fucking one of the competitors is probably frowned upon. But the court is pretending they don't know. And it's not as if my brother would ever complain about something like that."

It seemed unfair to me. As if it would give Avriel an unfair advantage.

Not to mention...

"If Avriel won, he could make Sephone his empress, couldn't he?"

Rychel shrugged. "He could. I don't know if he actually would. Avriel is a dick. Sephone would have to be pretty stupid if she actually trusted him to do that. He could easily take another bride. One who hadn't already belonged to my father."

"Belonged." Another word I really disliked at the moment. The court thought I belonged to Draven.

"Well, it was nice to meet you, Rychel," I said. "But I don't particularly want to sleep on your floor tonight, so..."

"I suppose this will go down as one of the oddest conversations you've ever had," Rychel observed.

I tried to smile. "Most likely."

I started to move back towards the stairs, debating whether or not I should wake Beks.

"My brother says you got the sword," she said quickly. "Excalibur. How did you open the portal in the lake? What was down there?"

I froze. "Your brother hasn't asked me much about that."

"From what I understand, he thinks doing so might upset you," Rychel said carefully. "Things didn't exactly go as planned, I take it?"

I turned back slowly. "My lover cut me open, dripped my blood into a lake then shoved me into it, stabbed me when I brought back the sword, tried to kill your brother, and then I had to kill him to stop him. My lover. Not your brother. Though I wish I had killed him, too."

"No, you don't." Rychel's voice was gentle. "Though I don't blame you for being angry with him for whatever he's done. But that man who hurt you–my brother's not like that. I promise you."

"We'll have to agree to disagree," I said, not even trying to force a smile. "How did your brother know the sword was down in that lake in the first place?"

"He knew because I told him," Rychel said evenly. "Just because he was banished didn't mean we stopped talking."

I nodded. That made sense. I was sure they had some secret magical way I didn't need to know the details of right now.

I stifled a yawn. I was more tired than I realized. But the night wasn't over.

"Look, I should go," I said quickly, seeing Rychel was staring at me with open fascination and seemed about to ask yet another question. "You've given me a lot of answers tonight though. More than anyone else. I'm truly grateful. Maybe we can talk again another time."

"I'd like that," Rychel said, smiling. "Come back and visit me anytime. Beks knows the way. You'll learn it."

I nodded. A plan had been forming in my head while we talked.

"One last question. How does the average Siabra get to the city above us? They can't exactly just... walk to the surface. Can they?"

Maybe there was some sort of passageway I just had to find out about that would take me there. I could hope.

Rychel gave me a funny look. "They use a stitcher."

"A what?" A passage in one of the books I had read days ago started to come back to me.

"A stitcher. Someone who can pinch the threads of space and time and... well, manipulate them magically. Not everyone has the gift, but enough do that it's easy enough to make sure you always have a few stitcher friends or family to help you get around. Of course, you can always use a gate–" I assumed she meant an arch, like the one Lancelet had traveled through from the temple to get to us. "But the danger with gates is that they can be moved or destroyed, so you never know exactly what's on the other side. And if there's nothing... Well, let's just say some Siabra have had some bad experiences with gates, so stitching is currently back in fashion."

"I don't know any stitchers," I said slowly.

"Of course, you do! Crescent is one. An excellent one."

"Crescent is a stitcher? He can bring me to the surface?"

That seemed like crucial information that he had conveniently left out. But then, I had to admit that before tonight I hadn't been quite as desperate to get the hell out of Draven's court.

But now... I was as desperate as I could get. Wasn't I?

Rychel nodded. "He could..."

"Let me guess... With your brother's permission?" I swore under my breath.

"Why do you want to leave so badly?" Rychel asked softly.

"Oh, you know, just the ordinary reason–my country is at war, my brother is burning down our former allies' villages and slaughtering their people, and I need to get back so I can try to stop him. Nothing really urgent." I felt my jaw clenching hard.

Rychel looked sympathetic. "I see. Well, if you told my brother..."

"I have told your brother," I exclaimed. "He wouldn't believe me. He wouldn't believe what I saw was real. He said..."

"What did he say?"

"He said it was just a dream." I frowned. "But it wasn't just a dream. He doesn't understand. My dreams have changed."

Now Rychel looked intently interested. "How do you mean?"

"They've become more vivid. More real. I still have dreams, but these... I wouldn't even call them dreams. They're more like... visions. Visions that show real things." I looked at Rychel. "I probably sound deranged."

But Rychel was frowning in a way that told me she was thinking hard about what I'd said.

"The gift of true dreaming is rare. I've only known one other person who dreamed in the way you're describing." She turned to the table behind her and started shuffling through some parchment. "In any case, it's been wonderful to meet you, Morgan. I hope we can talk again soon. You've given me a lot to think about. I can see why my brother is so taken with you."

"Taken with me? I think you mean taken me, full stop," I muttered.

It was obvious I'd been dismissed. Rychel must have had more work to do. Maybe she planned to stay up all night dissecting that horrible body.

With a sigh, I went over to where Beks laying snoring and gently gave him a little kick on the ankle. His eyes popped open.

"Oh, hello there," I said. "What exactly will Javer do to you if you're not back in your bed by morning?"

His eyes widened. Then he sat up and started to push himself up off the floor. "Point..." He yawned. "Taken."

"Good. Let's go."

It wasn't that I was afraid to go into the passages alone–not that I knew how to lit those lamps yet–but it would definitely be easier with Beks to lead the way.

But lead the way where? Back to our–no, not *our*, I had to stop thinking that way. Back to *Draven's* suite? I didn't want to go back there. I didn't want to look at that handsome, lying face. I certainly was not about to sleep next to him in that bed.

But I had a feeling if I showed up at Crescent's home and demanded to be stitched to the surface, he would flatly but very, very kindly refuse. And then summon Draven to take me home. I wasn't sure I could handle any more pointless drama tonight.

And besides the suite, I didn't exactly have anywhere else to go.

Did I?

"We're taking a detour," I told Beks as we stepped back into the passageway.

CHAPTER 14

I woke up with my face pressed against the surface of a wooden table, a sticky coating of drool glued to my skin.

So I hadn't fallen asleep under a table like Beks. Just sort of on top of one.

Groaning, I pushed myself up and out of the wooden chair I had been sleeping in, stretching my limbs. As I did so, a blanket fell to the floor behind me.

I picked it up, glancing quickly down at myself. I was still wearing the gown from the night before. Its beautiful shimmering layers were now limp and tired-looking from where they had been squashed beneath me all night.

Looking around, I wondered who had put the blanket over me. When I had entered the library during the night with Beks, no one else had been around.

The palace library was a massive space. Four long arched halls converged in a center square area, where long rows of tables and chairs were set out for librarians and scholars. Not that I had encountered any yet.

Each of the four halls had soaring ceilings and were lined with towering shelves of a fine dark wood. Winding spiral staircases led up to small reading nooks and mezzanines, offering hidden corners for contemplation and study. Impossibly tall ladders on casters glided along the library's polished marble floors, granting access to the highest reaches of the vast collection. My feet itched to climb them.

The air was imbued with the scent of aged parchment, faded vellum, and fresh ink. I had fallen asleep to the familiar lull of those fragrances, almost able to make myself believe I was back in the castle library in Camelot.

But the library in the Rose Court was perhaps a quarter the size of this one and nowhere near as fine.

Heavy footsteps thudded solidly from behind me and I whirled around, afraid for the worst.

"Oh, it's you. Good morning, Hawl."

"It's me." Hawl did not seem particularly thrilled to see me.

"Crescent said you spent a lot of time in the library," I said hurriedly. "Were you the one who put the blanket on me?"

Hawl brought their majestic dark furry head up and down briefly.

"Well, thank you. Does that mean you've been here a while? I didn't see you when I came in."

"I went to prepare food," Hawl said in their low, rumbling voice. "For you and the prince. Then I returned. I often sleep here."

"Oh." I felt a pang of guilt. "I'm sorry. I haven't been back to the prince's suite since before the ceremony. But thank you for the consideration."

"I noticed." Hawl studied me. "Why are you here?"

"I had nowhere else to go," I said, hoping they wouldn't ask more questions. "I had hoped the library would be empty at that time of the night and fortunately it was."

Hawl made a gruff sound. "You were correct in that assumption. It often is. Save for myself and the librarians. They don't like me."

"Why don't they like you?"

"They have their own prejudices, like every race. I have no intention of giving way to them, however. The prince says this facility is open to all and thus, I stay."

From the sound of it, Hawl had rather stubbornly camped out. But who was I to judge?

"Well, that's good to hear," I said. "I don't see any librarians around."

"They keep to their offices and private reading rooms. The sight of a monstrous bear wandering the stacks offends their sensibilities." Hawl didn't bother to keep the sourness from their voice. They motioned to the aisles around us. "What are you looking for?"

"Looking for?"

"What book do you seek? What knowledge do you search for?"

I suspected Hawl would be offended if I said I'd simply needed a place to sleep and hadn't any intention of seeking knowledge specifically. Seeing the puddle of drool on the table, I quickly wiped it with a corner of the blanket, then began to fold the blanket up.

"Well, I suppose a book on training battlecats would be useful... Exmoors, I mean."

"There are five hundred and ninety-one books referencing exmoors, their history, their physiology, their mythology, and their upkeep in this library," Hawl informed me.

I gaped at the Ursidaur. "That's rather a lot. Is there one you would recommend I begin with?"

"Ask the stacks."

"Ask the stacks? I'm not sure what you..."

"The books will tell you, if you let them." Hawl sounded a tinge impatient. "Have you never been in a library before?"

Now it was my turn to try not to feel offended. "Of course, I have!" I frowned. "But not one where the books speak to you."

"They do not speak. Not in words. They simply tell you."

"Without speaking?" I must have looked doubtful for Hawl glowered.

I was beginning to understand why the librarians and scholars had all disappeared.

"They need not speak to choose you."

I gave up. "Very well, if you say so. Why don't you pretend I've never been in a library before and tell me very simply and carefully where to begin?"

Hawl's furred face seemed to be set in a frown, but now it lightened. "An excellent idea. I would begin at the beginning. Row 37, Section E for exmoor. You do know your numbers and the common alphabet?"

I swallowed my pride. "Yes. I do indeed. I believe I can find that."

"Excellent. Enter the row. Open your mind. Listen to the tomes. They will tell you which book contains what you require today."

At the very least, I decided, I should be able to find a book about exmoors in the E section, even if I couldn't hear the books speaking to me in this numinous, nebulous fashion that Hawl was describing so cryptically.

"My quest begins now," I said, bowing low. "I thank you, noble Ursidaur for your assistance. And the blanket."

I laid the blanket on the table and started towards where I hoped I would find Row 37.

"Behind you, to the left," Hawl growled. "They are clearly numbered."

I nodded, moving towards the wing of the library they were indicating, as if I'd had no intention of going anywhere else.

"Pay no attention to the titles," Hawl called. "You won't be able to read them. The book will tell you when it has chosen you."

I had no idea what to say to that so kept walking.

But as I entered an aisle, I rapidly began to understand what Hawl had meant. The books were inscribed with letters I couldn't pick out. In no language I had ever seen before. I might have thought they were glyphs or sigils, but they resembled none I had seen before.

Grumbling with frustration, I paused and tried to think of what to do.

The book would tell me when it had chosen me. How exactly would it do that?

I closed my eyes, took a deep breath, and tried to envision the book I needed.

A book about exmoors. Preferably one that would not only tell me more about how to care for one, but the history of the creature. They had been used in battle, but how? As mounts, I assumed. How did one train an exmoor as a mount? And what advantages would they have compared to horses?

I pictured riding Nightclaw. The prospect was both appealing and a little terrifying. I couldn't imagine anyone putting a saddle on that exmoor.

I opened my eyes. I heard nothing. I sensed nothing. The books were not speaking to me. Perhaps I was doing something wrong.

Or, perhaps it was just plain foolishness to think I might be able to train an exmoor in the first place. After all, from what I'd heard, Draven wasn't having much luck with Sunstrike.

And then I heard a faint whispering, like the pages of many books all turning at the same time, like leaves rustling in the wind.

Opening my eyes, I stretched out my hand, as an impetus propelled me forward.

I walked down the aisle, hand lifted, as a curious sensation beckoned me towards the end of the row.

When I stopped, my finger strayed as if pulled by some outside force, trailing along leather-bound spines until it touched a dark burgundy book embossed with gold lettering.

Lettering which I could suddenly read.

The title, written in faded gold scrolling letters on a worn leather cover, read: "The Legacy of the Fae Royals: Guardians of the Leap of Faith."

I frowned. The book did not seem to be about exmoors. Nevertheless, it was the only one I could read. I pulled it down from the shelf. The volume was heavier than I expected it to be and I nearly dropped it. Glancing around to make sure Hawl hadn't noticed, I carried it over to a table nearby and opened it.

I was pleasantly surprised as I glanced over the chapter headings and realized the book was not merely the annals of ancient fae monarchs but a history of the fae's connection to the exmoor. Gently I touched a black and white engraving depicting one of the majestic cats leaping through the air, its fur battle-scarred and its rider holding a glowing sword stretched high overhead.

The first pages of the book were a basic description of an exmoor's geographical origins and physiology, perhaps written in mind for someone who had never encountered one before.

"The Imperator Felis Bellator Volans, called 'exmoor' by scholars in Eskira, and frequently known by the colloquial title of 'battlecat' is native to the continents of Myntra and Eskira."

Apparently, this volume had been written quite some time ago as the author seemed to be unaware of the exmoor's near total departure from Myntra.

"Standing at an astounding height of at least six feet at the shoulder, the Felis Bellator possesses a regal and commanding presence that demands awe and respect..."

Of this, I was well aware. I skimmed ahead.

"The Felis Bellator boasts a muscular and streamlined build, enabling it to move with unmatched speed and grace. Its fur is a lustrous golden-brown, accentuated by striking black stripes adorning its back and sides. This pattern serves as both camouflage and a symbol of its prowess. One of its most distinguishing features is a tuft of fur at the tip of its tail, which serves as a means of nonverbal communication, conveying its mood and intentions..."

Smiling to myself, I recalled how the exmoor we had found back on Eskira had made good use of her tail. I made a mental note to remember to pay close attention to Nightclaw's tail movements.

"Despite its formidable stature and fearsome reputation, the Felis Bellator is known to exhibit a strong sense of loyalty and protectiveness towards its chosen companion. These majestic creatures form deep bonds with their riders and will fearlessly defend them in times of danger. While they possess a regal demeanor, they are also known for their intelligence and cunning, making them both powerful allies and worthy adversaries..."

Well, now we seemed to be getting somewhere. I leaned forward over the page.

But to my disappointment, the opening section ended rather abruptly.

The next chapter was much less focused on the exmoor and more on the history of the Valtain monarchy. I read carefully, searching for any mention of battlecats. To my surprise, after reading the first few pages, I realized that the book made no distinction between the Siabra and the fae of Valtain. Groaning, I wondered why the stacks had directed me to such an outdated tome, surely at least hundreds of years old.

Still, I kept reading.

"Among the Fae Kings, High King Gorlois Le Fay, revered for his unwavering valor, stands tall in the lineage of the ancients. It is said that his mastery of the battlecat, his trusted

companion and guardian, cemented his reign as a beacon of strength during the age of wars.
The clash of steel and the thundering paws of the exmoors echoed through the realm, carving
tales of heroism into the very earth..."

I was interrupted by the weight of a heavy paw on my shoulder and looked up to see
Hawl standing over me, holding a plate with bread, sliced meat, and cheese.

"Breakfast," the Bearkin grunted and dropped the plate on the table beside me with a
loud clatter as if I were a prisoner in a cell.

But I was too hungry to be anything but grateful. "I'm ravenous, how did you know?"
My stomach making noisy sounds of anticipation, I picked up a hunk of bread and bit into
it, savoring the warm, pillowy interior. Hawl must have made it themselves that morning.
"Mmmm," I mumbled between chewing. "Thank you, Hawl."

The Bearkin nodded towards the volume that lay on the table. "The right book found
you then, I take it?"

I tilted my head doubtfully. "Well... in a sense. There is information about exmoors in
here. Though I'm not entirely sure how much."

Hawl's furry brow seemed to furrow. "The right book always finds the reader."

"Well, in that case," I said carefully. "Your library seems to think I need to know the
history of the fae monarchy of Valtain."

"Such would seem useful for one such as yourself," Hawl remarked, looking me up and
down. "Do your people not value their own history?"

I thought about the question. My people? I was only just beginning to realize my
people were not only the mortal humans of Pendrath but very likely the fae of Valtain,
too.

"I suppose so," I said, still skeptical. "I can't say I learned a great deal about fae history
from the books in Camelot." At least, not entirely reliable information.

"Well, then," Hawl said with satisfaction. "It seems to me the book which chose you
was well aware of your ignorance."

I pursed my lips. "Indeed. Though it would have been more useful if the book contained specific information on how to train an exmoor."

"Perhaps you are not ready for that level of information," Hawl suggested haughtily.
Clearly they would not even consider the idea that the book had made a mistake in
choosing me. I decided not to press the matter.

The Ursidaur turned as if to stalk back down the aisle, then paused. "The books do not
leave the library."

Well, obviously they didn't completely dislike me or they wouldn't have brought me food, I thought to myself, as I nibbled the cheese and bread. The plain fare reminded me of the many meals Draven and I had eaten together on the road while traveling towards Valtain.

Remembering that reminded me of Vesper and Lancelet.

There had been some good times before the bad. Though they had been over too soon. And the time I had spent with Vesper was forever tainted.

I turned back to the pages of my book.

"The Felis Bellator has long been woven into the fabric of fae mythology and folklore. Tales recount epic battles fought atop the Bellators' backs, with warriors harnessing the creatures hidden gifts and fearsome strength to secure striking victories.

Behind the glorious tales of battlecats and Fae Kings, whispers of an ancient prophecy stir. It is said that within the Leap of Faith lies the key to unraveling the veiled truths of the realm. Only those who possess the courage to take the leap, to trust in the unknown, shall unlock the secrets that have long been concealed. The battlecats, guardians of the Leap, hold the secrets of both the past and the future, awaiting those who dare to seek the answers."

This was incredibly cryptic. Perhaps Hawl would enjoy this passage, I thought sardonically. Quickly, I scanned ahead.

"Within the lineage of High King Gorlois, one name shines with a brilliance all its own—Orcades Le Fay..."

My eyebrows shot up as the name seemed to leap off the page towards me.

"... the brilliant tactician, warrior, and daughter of the King. While most famously known for her dominion at sea, Orcades pleased her father by exemplifying the spirit of the exmoor—a tempest of strength and loyalty. Mounted upon her feline companion, she rode fearlessly into the midst of battles..."

"Good book?"

I was prepared. Jumping to my feet, I grabbed an object from the table, holding it out in front of me at an angle.

"I was wondering when you would show up," I hissed. "Don't you know when you're unwanted?"

The Prince of Claws leaned against a dark wood bookshelf, looking none the worse for wear after last night. As he saw what I held, his lips twitched slightly. "Is that... a letter opener?"

"A very sharp letter opener," I clarified. "And I won't hesitate to stab you with it if you come a step closer to me."

"In that case, would you like me to step closer?" His eyes were dark emerald shadows.

I gritted my teeth. "I'd like you to get the hell out of my life forever."

Something flickered in his eyes. "Sadly, that won't be happening. You and I are stuck with one another. At least, for now."

"So you claim," I snapped. "The problem is I just don't believe you anymore."

"No," he said, eyeing the blade in my hand. "I can see that."

"I *will* stab you," I warned, waving the letter opener. It had a mother-of-pearl handle and an edge sharp enough to slice right through skin. When I'd noticed it on the table, I had wondered why the librarians needed such instruments, but now I was armed—and grateful for it. The book I would be returning to its place on the shelf. The letter opener, on the other hand, was coming with me. "I've been fantasizing about it all night."

Draven chuckled. "I'm sure you have."

"You egotistical bastard. You like to think I think of you, don't you?" I challenged. "I'm sure you enjoy believing your entire court is preening for your attention."

Draven looked consideringly at me. "I don't think I'm quite that shallow."

"Only shallow enough to do what you did last night," I retorted.

"We were being watched, so yes, I used that to our advantage. I don't think they even heard a word I said though. The words," he said very softly, holding my gaze. "The words were for you alone."

I tossed my head, absolutely unwilling to believe this, even though it would soothe my pride and my wounded ego to imagine it was true. As I did, I was reminded of how strangely I was dressed for a library. The little crystals Breena had woven into my hair tinkled as the crown moved.

"Considering they were Siabra and have powers just like you do, I highly doubt that's true. I'm sure you said every word for their benefit—and in order to manipulate me exactly the way you wanted. Now why don't you get the fuck out of this library and leave me alone. Unless you're actually here for a book?"

"I do, in fact, read, as you know," Draven said lightly, skimming a finger along a row of books. "And I enjoy being in this library as much as you probably do. But no, that's not why I'm here. I'm here for you."

"Well, I'm not coming," I growled, reminding myself of Hawl.

"I understand that. Let me rephrase. I was wondering if you would consider joining me..."

"No. Stabbing you soon, remember?" I thrust the letter opener out in front of me and Draven jumped back. I grinned. "If you get cut, perhaps you can run and tell Lyrastra."

"I'd rather not. If you'd just let me finish..."

I moved the knife through the air, watching the metal flash. Was I actually going to try to kill him? Probably not. Did I really want him dead? Again, probably not. Did I wish he was *already* dead? It was a tempting fantasy.

"I don't want to let you finish. I already know I don't want to go anywhere with you, Draven. What part of 'I hate you and want to stab you in the face' do you not understand?"

He looked back at me coolly. "I understand you perfectly, Morgan. I understand you don't want to go anywhere with me, not even to the surface." He put up his hands. "Well, I tried."

He turned and started to walk away.

"What the fuck?" I exclaimed. "Stop bluffing. I know you aren't really going to take me to the surface. Besides, wouldn't you need a stitcher for that?"

There, let him see I had managed to learn a thing or two on my own in the few hours we had been apart.

He turned back to face me. "You would. Which is why Crescent is waiting just outside the library for us. He wasn't sure if you would attack us both on sight, so thought it was safer for him there."

"Don't be ridiculous," I snapped. "Why would I attack Crescent? He hasn't done anything to me."

"Well, that's what I said, but you rushed past him in such a fury last night that he seems to believe you find him at the very least repulsive if not blameworthy. He's very torn up."

I sniffed. "I'm sure he is."

"Since you seem so suspicious, let me alleviate your fears," he continued. "You are not being invited to your own execution. Crescent thought you might enjoy a music festival taking place in Noctasia this evening."

I eyed Draven. He was dressed in fresh clothing. A doublet of dark blue brocade, fitted trousers of deep charcoal, and polished black boots with brass buckles.

At least that part of the story seemed true.

"Hmph," I said. "Then why doesn't Crescent take me himself? Alone."

"Because there are matters you and I should speak of. For one thing, I am ready to accommodate one of your most pressing requests."

"Sure, you are," I scoffed. "My most pressing request is that you let me go."

I glared at him. He stared back, without flinching.

"Really?" My voice sounded weak, even to me. "You're going to let me go?" I cleared my throat. "Fine. But I'm bringing the letter opener. If you're bluffing, may the Three have mercy on your soul."

He nodded gravely. "I understand. You shall be armed and I shall be on my best behavior." I snorted. "Shall we?"

I followed him out of the library, our footsteps echoing on the marble floors.

Just outside the main doors, Crescent leaned against the wall. He sprang forward as he caught sight of me, a smile stretching over his face.

"Lady Morgan! You honor us with your presence," he exclaimed.

I tried to smile. "I apologize for not saying good-bye properly last night."

He waved a hand dismissively.

I cleared my throat. "The prince tells me you're taking us up to the city."

Crescent nodded eagerly. "Indeed. I thought it might be just what you needed after a... disappointing evening last night."

"Oh, is that what we're calling it?" I muttered darkly, eyeballing Draven.

Draven poked me in the back. "Play nice."

He was right. This was Crescent. I couldn't bring myself to be mean.

"That sounds lovely," I forced myself to say. "I can't wait to get out of this palace."

There. At least that was closer to the truth. Though far away from Draven would have been even better.

"I can hardly blame you," Crescent said enthusiastically. "I admit, I find it confining today as well. Are we ready?"

"Did you invite... the others? The ones I suggested?" Draven asked.

"What others?" I whispered, suddenly feeling cranky. I was wearing the same dress I had slept in. I did not particularly want to turn this into a large party.

Besides, why did we need company if Draven was taking me up to the city in order to set me free? Only the three of us were required for that.

Unless he had no intention of actually following through on what he'd just alluded to. I wouldn't be surprised. But in that case, a good stick in the ribs with my letter opener would be more than fair.

I'd leave him bleeding in a dirty street while I ran. Far, far away.

I clenched the letter opener in my fist.

"Are you really going to carry that thing with you all night?" Draven murmured.

"It's my favorite accessory," I murmured back sweetly. "Don't you think it compliments my hair?"

He took a step back and looked me up and down, as if seriously considering what I'd said. "You're right. The mother-of-pearl looks lovely with your silver tresses."

"I was joking." I scowled. "Idiot."

I didn't want any more of his fucking fake compliments. My heart couldn't take it.

"I wasn't sure if you were certain about that," Crescent was saying meanwhile. "But if you're sure they won't be in the way?"

"Absolutely not. I want you to have a night off, Crescent. Take us up and then Lady Morgan and I will wander off for a stroll." Apparently, I wasn't going to see much of this concert after all. "You deserve it," Draven declared firmly.

Crescent smiled and looked a little relieved. "Very well. I told them to wait just around the corner in case..." He trailed off, glancing at me.

"In case Lady Morgan was not amenable to my invitation," Draven finished. "Yes, I understand your qualms. I had my own." He gave my letter opener a significant look and smirked. "Well, let's fetch them."

"Fetch who?" I complained. "The rest of your court?" I was put off by his refusal to accept my anger, my hatred, and my intense desire to stab him as anything but serious.

Or perhaps he was so used to having people want to kill him that it no longer impacted him like it would a normal person.

Draven was possibly the least normal person I had ever met. And considering Arthur was my brother, that was saying a great deal.

"Only two members of it." He nodded ahead to where a man and a little girl had stepped out from around the corner.

The little girl looked to be about five or six or so. She was ebony-skinned with dainty features, sweet pudgy cheeks, and tightly curling turquoise hair that was braided into two plaits. She wore a yellow dress embroidered with white flowers and bright blue leggings.

"She's adorable," Draven whispered in my ear. "Isn't she?"

The red-haired man gave a friendly wave and smiled at me. Gawain.

This must then be Taina.

"She's very sweet," I admitted, waving back at Gawain.

"This is my husband, Gawain, and our daughter, Taina," Crescent said proudly, holding the little girl by the hand as she held Gawain's with her other. "I don't think you and Gawain had a chance to formally meet yesterday."

"Pleathed to meet you Lady Morgan," the child lisped. She made an admirable attempt at a curtsy and I stifled a smile.

I crouched down. "Very pleased to meet you as well, Lady Taina," I said solemnly. "Are you excited for the festival this evening?"

The little girl looked up at me, starry eyed and nodded without speaking.

"She loves the drums," Gawain explained with a wide smile. "And the dancing. Crescent is a wonderful dancer. He's been teaching us both."

"I see," I murmured.

Crescent and Gawain were looking at one another with undisguised affection, clearly anticipating a pleasant family evening out.

I glanced at Draven, feeling awkward, not sure of how to proceed. I felt so out of place around their overt happiness. Around a functional healthy family.

Abruptly, I wondered how the stitching process worked. On the face of it, it sounded rather... painful. I hoped the word was more of a symbolic description than a literal one.

"You've never visited Noctasia, have you, Lady Morgan?" Gawain said pleasantly.

"No, I have not yet had the pleasure. I'm so thankful my lord and master... I mean, Prince Kairos... has granted me permission to visit." I shot a sugary smile in Draven's direction and tried to look as humble as possible. Is this what you wanted? I practically screamed with my eyes. The obedient, grateful Paramour?

"Well, you're in for a real treat," Gawain promised.

"If we can all form a circle," Crescent instructed. "We'll be above in a moment."

We had to touch each other? I wasn't sure I was currently capable of touching Draven with anything but the tip of my blade.

I stepped up next to Crescent and he placed a hand on my shoulder. To my relief, Gawain and Taina came to stand beside me. Draven completed the circle, standing between Taina and Crescent.

I watched as he put a hand gently on the little girl's shoulder and smiled down at her.

When he saw Taina did he think of his own daughter who had been so heartlessly stolen away?

They made a pretty picture, standing there. The prince and the little girl.

Like a deadly viper, Draven could be deceptively beautiful when he wanted to be. I forced myself to look away.

"Ready?" Crescent said.

I started to nod. And then, we vanished.

CHAPTER 15

L ike a flash of lightning, one moment we were in the palace corridor and the next, we weren't. I blinked, closing my eyes for a split second, and when I opened them, we were standing in a busy square, surrounded by people amid a roar of sound.

I looked around me, then up, up, up—awestruck and thrilled beyond measure to be under the true sky once more.

Noctasia was a bright jewel of a city. The capital of the Siabra Empire was a blend of architectural marvels and bustling waterways, teeming with energy, excitement, and diversity.

Within moments, I found myself falling in love with it.

Towering structures rose gracefully along the shores of a magnificent blue lake from which tendril-like canals split off into the city. Carved white stone bridges spanned the waterways, connecting the bustling market districts with quieter residential ones. Elaborate buildings with arched windows and carved wooden balconies lined streets full of bright market stalls and brick patios where people sat at small wrought iron tables eating, drinking, and laughing.

There was color everywhere. A kaleidoscope of vibrant hues and eclectic costumes. It was clear that this city was where people from all corners of the empire came together, their cosmopolitan attire reflecting a wide array of cultures and traditions.

At the heart of the city, footsteps from where we stood, lay a wide town square where a musical festival was in full swing. The air was filled with the sound of instruments and the tantalizing aromas of delectable cuisines. A large wooden stage was set up with a band playing lively tunes as a group of dancers in red costumes swirled and twirled at the front of an enthusiastic crowd.

Further along the square, I spotted jugglers and mimes, acrobats and face painters, as well as artisans displaying their wares.

Beautifully-painted gondolas glided across the lake's surface nearby, dropping passengers off at the festival dock or drifting near enough for their occupants to hear the music as it carried out and over the water as the sun set. The soft lapping of the waves against the sides of the boats added a soothing undertone to the atmosphere.

I turned to watch the gondolas on the water, only half paying attention as Draven encouraged Crescent and Gawain to go and enjoy the music. The family was chattering happily as they walked away. Gradually, their footsteps faded.

"Would you like to go for a gondola ride?"

I faced Draven. I wasn't going to admit that for a very brief moment I had been imagining us in a gondola together, him sprawled out with his long legs stretched in front, me leaning back against him as I skimmed a hand over the surface of the cool water.

"No. I want to know why you brought me here. As quickly as possible." I flashed the blade, letting it glint in the dying sunlight.

Draven sighed. "There's really no need for that. Besides, are you really going to murder these peoples' prince in broad daylight?"

"Is that why you chose such a public spot for this meeting? It's almost night. Everyone around us would be too distracted to care. I could slash you open, push you into the water and then–" I mimicked a small splashing sound followed by a gurgling as I clutched my throat.

Draven looked amused. Too amused. I dropped my hand. "Clearly you've really thought this through."

I pursed my lips. Let him laugh. "Look, this was your idea. Just get to the fucking point."

He nodded. "Fine. You're right. Look, walk with me a little way. Just over here." He indicated a stone terrace closer to the water.

Without waiting, he walked over to lean on the low stone rail, gazing out over the lake. Reluctantly, I followed him. The music was not quite as loud over here.

"You've shown me the worst side of myself, Morgan," Draven said, without meeting my eyes. "You seem exceptionally good at that."

"It wasn't hard to do. When there's no good to reflect, it's easy to reveal the worst," I said ruthlessly.

Draven nodded. "I can understand why you'd think that. Bringing you here..." He shook his head as if tired. "I didn't know what else to do. But maybe... Maybe it was the wrong idea."

I raised my eyebrows. "You think?"

"So, go," he said softly, meeting my eyes. "Go and be free. If that's truly what you wish. If you really think I have less than your best interests at heart. If you won't believe anything I have to say in my defense about last night. Then, I surrender, Morgan. I admit defeat."

I was unable to believe my ears.

"If something happens to you after you leave here…" He swallowed. "I'll never forgive myself. But the choice is yours to make."

I clenched my jaw. "I don't believe you."

He nodded, as if he'd expected me to say that. "I'll be clear. Tell me you want to go and tell me where, and I'll arrange your passage. You wish to return to Pendrath? The voyage will be long and arduous. I refuse to trust the arch Lancelet mentioned traveling through–you remember?"

I nodded. "The one in the temple."

"Right. I'm not sending you that way. It would be faster. It might also result in your fast death. We have no idea if the arch still stands or if it's been destroyed or even moved. You might go through and find yourself in the middle of your brother's castle–or the middle of a battle."

"What about Crescent?" I asked quietly, still hardly believing this was real. "Maybe he could help me."

Draven hesitated. "Stitching into Eskira… That's something Siabra do only when they have absolutely no other choice. When we searched for Lancelet, we used an arch. I had a friend familiar with Meridium pull up the plans for the city as we last knew them. It turned out there was an arch I'd never known about. We used that instead of stitching."

I raised one eyebrow. "That sounds as risky as using the one in the temple in Camelot."

"One volunteer went through first," Draven said quietly. "Once we were sure it was safe, the others followed."

My heart quickened. "Who was the volunteer?"

Draven looked at me steadily. "Me."

I glanced away, gazing out over the lake. "Oh."

"Stitching over such a vast distance would also be incredibly draining to Crescent," he said quietly. "I'm sorry, but I don't want to put him through that. And he's the only stitcher I would trust with your life."

"I understand," I said.

But I was still thinking about what he'd just confessed. That he'd risked his life to go back and look for Lancelet. Not only by returning to Meridium, but stepping into an unknown void. He might have gone into that arch and simply disappeared.

What would I have done then? A small voice in my head asked the question before I could stop it.

"There's also the risk of the Valtain fae," Draven said. "We don't know if they're monitoring uses of magic in Eskira. If Crescent tried to send you back using so much power at once..."

"Yes, I understand. I said I understood. I wouldn't want Crescent to put himself at risk for me either. I hope you know that."

He nodded.

"So, I'll go by boat." I tried to control the nervous anticipation in my voice. "How would that work? How long would it take?"

"You'd travel to the coast, then take a boat to Eskira. From there you'd have to cross the mountains. Via Rheged or Cerunnos most likely." He hesitated. "You wouldn't be alone. Odessa has offered to go with you. She'd keep you safe."

"I can keep myself safe," I said automatically. "But... that's incredibly generous of her. She really offered?"

"She did. She understands... She knows what you mean to me."

I refused to take the bait.

"Right. And when would we leave? Tonight?" This was when I'd call his bluff, I decided.

His eyes widened slightly. "Yes. If that is what you wish. I could arrange it."

I rolled my eyes. "Sure. You'd let me pull Odessa, one of your most loyal allies, away from the court, away from the competition, now? Tonight?"

"If that's what you want, yes." He met my gaze levelly. "This isn't a bluff, Morgan."

"Fine," I snapped. "It's not a bluff. Or?"

"Or?"

"There must be an 'or.' Or my other option is to...? What? What's the offer? What's on the table?"

Draven smiled slightly. "There is an 'or.'"

"Of course, there is," I muttered.

"If you stay, I'll see to it that you receive the best training. Training you could never have possibly hoped to receive in Pendrath. There is no one there capable of teaching you what you need to know, Morgan."

"What I need to know?" I repeated. "What are you talking about?"

He gave me a frank look. "You know what I mean. Your magic. You can't just keep pretending it doesn't exist."

I looked away. "Yes, I can. For all you know that's exactly what I have planned."

"Fine. Let me rephrase. You *could* do that. But to do so would be incredibly stupid, selfish, and inefficient."

"Inefficient? You're calling me stupid, selfish, and *inefficient*?"

"I'm not calling you those things. I'm saying that's what that particular choice would be best-described as."

I made a face of annoyance. "Right. Semantics."

"It would be absolutely inefficient, make no mistake, Morgan, for Pendrath's best hope and most powerful royal heir to return without having an inkling of how to properly use or control her own magic. For all you know, it's the very key to undoing this nightmare of a war your brother has entangled your country in."

Fuck.

Damn him, but he had a point. One I hated to admit.

"Most powerful royal *heir*? Really? That's what you're calling me now?"

I felt his hard gaze on me but refused to meet his eyes.

"You want to set a child up on the throne of Pendrath? Be my guest. I'm sure Kaye will have plenty to say about that idea," Draven said. "Make no mistake, you'd be using him. Just like Arthur is doing right now."

I wondered what Merlin would say about the idea of replacing Arthur with Kaye. Or Sir Ector.

"There is no one with a stronger claim to that throne than you, Morgan, and perhaps it's time you stopped avoiding that uncomfortable truth," he continued.

"I'm not usurping Arthur," I said stubbornly.

"No," Draven said softly. "There's no need to. He already did it to you."

There was silence for a moment.

"And if you stay," he continued finally. "You'll go back to Pendrath like I promised you, with a Siabra army behind you. That is not an inconsiderable offer."

I knew it wasn't. A foreign army to back me, to protect me. To even help me get into Camelot in the first place. For all I knew, the city was under siege by Lyonesse or Rheged at this very moment.

But with Draven's help, I could establish diplomatic relations with the other countries' armies. Help them see that all I wanted was a cessation of hostilities and the protection of Pendrath. I could apologize for my brother's terrible mistakes and offer to guarantee some sort of sanctions or reparations for what he had put them through. I could speak for Kaye—at least, temporarily. Perhaps help serve him as some sort of regent. I knew he would understand.

And then there was the part I hated to imagine but knew I had to.

Once I was in Camelot, I'd have to face Arthur.

To do that alone would be suicide, especially if Orcades really had brought him the sword and he knew how to wield it. Based on the legends alone, the sword had inconceivable powers.

But with Draven and his people there... I wouldn't be alone. I wouldn't be the only fae there with powers. Draven would make sure of that.

I knew I was strong, but Draven was right. I couldn't control my power properly yet. I'd only used it twice. And I didn't even want to use it a third time. But I'd have to, in order to face Arthur alone. It was the only way.

And if I didn't want to face Arthur alone, well, that meant bringing Draven and his army to bolster Merlin and her rebels.

One way or the other, I needed to stay put.

"If you stay here, I'll also owe you a great deal," Draven said.

I whipped my head around to look at him. "What are you talking about? You'll owe me? More like you'll make Pendrath pay your court for centuries for the use of an army."

Draven scowled. "That's not even a question. I won't be doing that. And yes, I'd owe you. Because if you leave here now, I'll lose face before my entire court just before the Blood Rise is set to begin. If you leave me, I'll look weak in front of people who would like nothing better than to kill me and defeat me. People who would like nothing better than to maintain the kind of corrupt court my father left behind."

I stared at him, examining his face for any hint he was lying.

Did I know him well enough to be able to tell? That was the question.

Before last night, I had thought I did.

"You really believe that?" I said wonderingly. "But you aren't... afraid?"

He laughed. "I'm not afraid, no. It would be a disadvantage. Not an impossible one to overcome."

"More like an embarrassing liability," I said bluntly.

"Something like that. My court–my friends–they've warned me of this. I'm sure you can imagine who I mean."

"Let's see," I drawled. "Crescent, Gawain, Odessa, Javer, Hawl, Beks, and... Rychel?"

Draven's eyebrows went up and I felt a surge of gratification knowing I'd surprised him.

"You've met my younger sister. What did you think?"

"I liked her. A lot better than you," I said not very nicely.

He grinned. "I'm prettier though, don't you think?"

I ignored the question. "She's brilliant. And attractive enough, if you like women. Lancelet would have been... a better judge."

Draven's face softened. "I'm sure she would have. She was quite charming."

I nodded, clenching my jaw. "Much more than I am. She was always better in taverns. Better at talking to people."

I looked out over the water. The gondolas had lit their lanterns. They made a pretty sight. Like glowing stars in the sky.

A finger touched my chin, turning it slightly. My hand clenched around the letter opener but I kept it by my side.

"Stay," Draven said. "Stay and lead my army to Pendrath. When I become emperor, I will follow your lead."

I scoffed. "The emperor of the Siabra deferring to a half-fae girl with no throne and no title to speak of? I don't think so."

"No one can take away your title, Morgan. Not even your father. I've never believed it was possible."

"Yes, well, you're years too late. That history has already been written."

I stared at him, suddenly not seeing a future emperor, a prince, or even a liar or an enemy.

Instead, I saw a young husband. A father.

I saw a man overcome with grief for his slaughtered family.

I saw a woman lying in a bed with a newborn babe nestled in her arms, cowering from a man who looked like Draven but who had hate-filled eyes and envy in his heart.

"Tell me why you killed your brother."

Draven frowned. "You already know."

"Tell me why you killed your brother," I said simply. "The truth this time. And maybe I'll stay."

He studied my face. "Rychel told you. She told you last night, didn't she?"

I didn't answer.

"Well, then you already know everything." Draven sighed. "But evidently that's not enough. You want me to, what? Say it all again so you can see if I'm lying?"

"You had a wife, Draven." My voice was very soft. "You had a child."

"A daughter. I had a daughter."

"One day old." I shook my head. "I can't even imagine the pain."

"No," he snapped, his green eyes suddenly blazing to life. "You can't."

I swallowed hard. "You could have told me before. If you trusted me with anything at all in your life that was true. But you don't."

His lips thinned. "Oh, I trust you. I just never wanted *that* from you."

"What?"

"Your pity, Morgan. Your sympathy. It was better if you looked at me and saw... nothing."

"A void? A shadow?" I guessed. "That's not trust, Draven. A blank page isn't trust."

"I trust you with my life." He said the words so bluntly that I flinched. "Do you trust me with yours?"

I bit my lip. "I should. You've saved it enough times. You think I don't know that? I'm aware."

"But all this," Draven said bitterly. "Bringing you here. Giving you this stupid title. Forcing you to be false..."

"I'm not good at it," I said simply. "Not like you are."

"I'm not as good at it as you might think," he said shortly, looking out at the lake. "Tell you, you said? Tell you and you'll stay? Fine. Nodori was my closest friend. I grew up thinking of her as a sister. I'd never cared for her in a romantic way–as a wife. But my father didn't care. He saw a matching set of women for his sons. Two girls from a powerful family. Tabar was interested in Lyrastra then, so they fit. Lyrastra... Well, I think she thought she actually loved Tabar back then. I've always pitied her for that."

He clasped his hands, leaning over the railing, as a gondola slowly drifted past.

"Nodori was Lyrastra's opposite. Soft, gentle. Some might say weak. I tried to make her happy, even though I certainly was not. I like to think I fooled her. Some days, I'm not so sure. I hope she died..." He paused and I saw his jaw clench tightly. "I hope she died believing she had made me happy. She had brought our child into the world. She deserved so much more than she got from it."

He looked down at his hands. I looked at them, too. Golden bronze. Strong. Firm. Reliable hands. The hands of a killer. The hands of a husband.

Had he ever even held his living baby? Had he looked into her eyes just once before she died?

I still couldn't get past the fact that Draven was so much more than I had ever expected him to be.

Was he a bad man? I'd be lying to myself if I denied there was some good in him.

"Tabar marched into the birthing room. I had left for a moment and he knew that. He slaughtered them. And he thought he'd get away with it, too. He thought he would take what I had. Kill my wife and my daughter and live to tell about it. He really thought he would still become emperor one day. That somehow, we would get past it. That I'd stay loyal. Fight by his side." Draven laughed mirthlessly. "That should tell you a great deal about how we were raised, right there."

It did. I felt sick.

"Maybe if my mother had lived... Things might have been different. But she had died giving birth to me. My father raised us in his image. Tabar ate up everything he was taught. All of the foulness. All of the cruelty. Me? I played along. Until the day I killed him, I think they'd both always believed me to be rather weak. But that day... That day, for the first time, my father told me he was proud of me."

He lifted his head and looked at me.

I cringed. "No."

"Oh, yes." Draven nodded. "My father—my emperor—said he'd never thought I had anything close to Tabar's strength. But I had proved him wrong. He told me I'd sire more children. Stronger ones. That Nodori and our baby would soon be forgotten."

I shook my head mutely.

"He was a monster," Draven said flatly. "When I told him I refused, that I would never sit on the Umbral Throne and would never sire a child for him, never extend his pitiful lineage, he had a fit of some sort. I watched him die. I did not call for a healer." He breathed deeply. "Not until I knew it was too late."

He looked at me. "Even fae die eventually, Morgan. He was hundreds of years old and yet in the end, what did he have to show for it? You know the rest. Sephone banished me.

In truth, I think she was relieved he was gone, though of course she could never have said so. He had ruled far longer than any man—fae or mortal—should have. Far longer than he deserved to. But as for me? I deserved worse."

"No, you didn't," I said harshly. "You deserved far better than this shitty, toxic court."

He grimaced. "I don't know about that. Maybe I did when I was a boy. But then? Now?"

I shouldn't have asked the question, I realized, my heart beginning to plummet.

I could almost hear Merlin's voice echoing in my head. Don't ask a question until you're sure you want the answer.

Well, I had asked and been answered.

And now?

Now I couldn't leave.

CHAPTER 16

Draven and I wandered about the square, side by side. My letter opener felt hot and cumbersome in my hand, but I had no sheath for it. Part of me was tempted to toss it in the lake, but the other was stubbornly determined to keep it as a symbol of how differently things still might play out.

I think Draven must have known this, for he didn't comment on it once. Not even in jest.

We passed by Crescent and Gawain. The pair were dancing with Taina. The little girl was shrieking happily as they each held her hand and swung her in a circle in time to the fast-paced music. Gawain waved at me, taking his eyes off his handsome partner for a brief moment. I lifted a hand, smiled, and waved back.

There was no denying I envied them. The two men looked at each other with such adoration and trust. What would it be like to be able to be that open with another person? To have the reassurance of their love?

I pushed the thought from my mind, telling myself to appreciate what I had.

It felt good to be above ground. To be in a crowd of people who weren't all bloodthirsty, cutthroat Siabra nobles.

Just ordinary people going about their business and enjoying the pleasant parts of life.

We passed a smaller stage where an older woman with long gray hair was playing a harp and singing.

She had a hauntingly beautiful voice.

As we passed by her, the moon was out, casting an ethereal glow upon the city. The notes of the harp reverberated through the night air, carried on a voice of sorrow and longing.

She sang a song of tragic loss. About a fae king whose favorite daughter was stolen away by her own mother, a queen consumed by darkness.

I watched from the corner of my eye as the harpist plucked the strings, weaving a yearning melody that echoed across the small piazza.

A tale untold, in realms of old,

Where legends dwell and love's farewell,

With sorrow crowned, a grief profound.

A king revered.

A daughter's tears.

A mother feared.

Through veil of night, a stolen bond,

A secret guise in shadows veiled,

As darkened queen took flight with dreams,

And left behind a shattered scene.

The song was too sad for my liking. I'd had enough of sad families and stories of heartbreaking loss for one evening. I shook off the melody, hastening to catch up to Draven who had gotten a few paces ahead.

"Where are we going?" I demanded

"I thought you might like a night spent out of the palace." He continued walking without looking back at me.

"I do," I replied, picking up my pace.

He glanced sideways at me. "Even if it's in another palace?"

"Another palace?" I looked ahead to the building he was leading us towards.

We were back alongside the lake. Ahead of us, a long and narrow, three-story building of pale coral terracotta rose majestically above the lake's serene dark waters. An arched arcade ran along the lower level, supported by tall, slender columns of a soft creamy hue. Pointed windows with delicate tracery and ornate reliefs covered the upper levels. Decorative pinnacles and statues adorned the rooftop.

The building was delicate. Airy and elegant. Completely different from the palace of the Court of Umbral Flames.

"The Summer Palace," Draven said, gesturing ahead. "Sephone rarely uses it, but it's kept ready at all times. I've had suites prepared. I figured, if you decided to stay..."

I understood. It was a small gesture, but one I appreciated.

"What about Crescent and his family?"

"Since we don't require Crescent's services again this evening, I'll have a message sent letting him know. There's a suite prepared for them here as well, if they prefer to stay in the city tonight. But I suspect Taina will sleep better in her own bed."

I followed him into a cool, dark marble hall and up a wide winding staircase to the second floor. Approaching a large set of heavy wooden doors, Draven pushed them open, revealing a large bedchamber where a regal four-poster bed dominated the space.

A balcony beside the bed looked out over the lake. Its wide windows had already been opened to let in a cool night breeze.

I sniffed eagerly, enjoying the fragrance of lake water and wood smoke drifting up from the bonfires that had been lit in the festival square.

"One suite," Draven said quietly, looking at me as if he was waiting for me to lift the letter opener after all. "Two bedchambers."

He led the way through the first bedroom and into a short hallway. Through an open door, I spotted an opulent bath chamber like the one in our suite in the underground palace. Mosaics portraying mermaids and seashells covered the walls, while a sunken tub of silver and white marble took pride of place in the center.

I followed him into the next bedroom. While the first room had been decorated in dark burgundy and gold, the second room was much more to my taste. The furnishings were fresh and bright. A canopy bed was hung with white muslin curtains and covered in a cascade of soft blankets and pillows.

Next to the bed was a small reading nook where pale silver brocade chairs had been posed next to low tables alongside a small library of beautifully bound books.

A huge fresco painted in light pastel shades depicting swimming sea animals covered one entire wall across from the bed.

"If it pleases you, this room will be yours."

I crossed over to one of the low tables and carefully set down my letter opener. "It's beautiful. And when we return to the court?"

"We'll be sharing the same suite," he said flatly.

I nodded. "I figured."

"Perhaps you'd like to make use of the bath chamber? There should be clothes in your size in the wardrobe over there."

I shook my head. "Thought of everything, didn't you? Just in case I stayed?" I looked at him. "Did you ever have any doubt I would?"

He met my eyes and I felt a moment's surprise by what I saw reflected there. "Yes."

He pulled the doors to my room shut, leaving me alone.

I ran a hand lazily along the spines of the books on the shelves, doing little more than glancing at the titles. Then I opened the balcony doors more widely to let in the fresh air, and set off for the bathing room.

It was a relief to finally shuck off the gown I had been wearing for more than twenty-four hours.

A little while later, I returned to my bedroom, opened the wardrobe and pulled out a long robe of satiny blue embroidered with stars. Standing by the mirror, I started combing out my damp hair.

Belatedly, I realized I had left the doors to the bedroom partly opened.

I crossed over to push them closed, just as someone pressed against them from the other direction.

Draven won. The doors opened, nearly smacking me in the face. We collided.

"I'm sorry," Draven said immediately, taking a step back. "The door was open, so I thought... I was just going to ask if you were finished..."

His voice trailed off and I realized he was looking at me. "Fuck."

I looked down at myself, then moved to pull the robe closed, but it was too late.

Believing myself alone, I had left it unfastened.

Now I had given Draven a full spectacle. Me—wet and naked from head to toe, the robe doing little more than showcasing my damp breasts, the planes of my stomach, and the patch of dark silver hair between my thighs.

Even now the thin satin clung to my damp breasts, my nipples pressing against the fabric in the cool night air.

Belatedly, I realized Draven was breathing hard. I looked at him. He was stripped to the waist. His skin was perfectly smooth, a shade of dark honey. A thick lock of black hair tumbled carelessly over his forehead. He always wore it longer than most men. My fingers clenched. I realized I was resisting lifting them to push it gently off his face.

His disarmingly green eyes were set in a face of such ideal male beauty that he looked like one of the sculptures carved into the facade of the Summer Palace itself. Some warrior from ancient days, preparing to don his armor.

But clearly Draven had been taking his clothes off, not putting them on.

With that thought a rush of heat went through me. I stared at his tautly muscled chest and the swirling black hairs.

We were alone.

But more alone than we were normally in our suite. Somehow here, in this place, away from the court, I felt very differently tonight. I wondered if he did, too.

No one was watching. It was only the two of us.

I felt paralyzed with indecision and heady with the knowledge that anything might happen.

Even the wrong thing.

"Fuck, Morgan," Draven said again, his voice hoarse. "I can't unsee that."

"Why should you?" I said flippantly.

I flicked my damp hair over my shoulders, even though I knew doing so meant raising my arms, letting my breasts lift higher against the satin and giving him a better view. "I'm through with the bathing room. Was that what you came to ask? You can go ahead."

I started to turn away, but a hand shot out and grasped my arm, pulling me back again.

"Fuck," Draven said for a third time. The crude word was like poetry coming from his lips. "This is a very bad idea."

"What is..." I started to say.

And then his lips descended on mine, crushing them mercilessly.

This was happening. Draven's arms closed around me, one hand gripping the back of my neck.

I felt myself going limp as I molded against him, letting the heat and scent and power of him engulf me. He pulled me closer. I could hardly breathe. I didn't really care about breathing anymore. The kiss was everything.

I drank deeply, taking in more. Distantly, I felt his hands fumbling with the belt of my robe.

I let him.

He pushed the satin fabric from my shoulders and I felt my breasts hit his chest, bare skin against skin. I moaned.

Then the robe was being pushed onto the floor and Draven was lifting me up and carrying me to the bed.

My legs wrapped around his waist, and I writhed against him shamelessly, arching myself back, desperate for every bit of contact.

When we reached the bed, I cringed, not wanting him to put me down.

He lay me on it with absolute gentleness, then stood above me for a moment, looking down with those fathomless green eyes.

He looked godlike and beautiful. The air around him practically thrummed with sexual tension. He was hard and flinty, rough and powerful, beautiful and full of grace.

He made my heart ache in every sense. Being near him was an exquisite torture and always had been.

He was every contradiction, soft and hard at the same time, brutal and yet gentle.

How gentle he could be with me. How gently deceptive, too.

From the corner of my eye, I caught sight of the letter opener.

I could reach for it. Stab him now, unsuspectingly. Watch the blood run from his body. I could end all of this. The conflict. The torment. The pain in my heart.

But suddenly, fighting Draven was the last thing I wanted to do.

I was fighting myself instead... and it was a fast-losing battle. I knew I wasn't being rational. Wasn't being intellectual. Wasn't being at all wise.

Nothing good could come of this.

But he was stepping closer, gazing down at my naked body as if it was the most jaw-droppingly gorgeous thing he'd ever seen. He was so near now I could see the black stubble on his jaw. I was light-headed, giddy, drunk with my proximity to him, and oh, fuck, I wanted this so badly. Too badly to try very hard to resist.

He leaned over me, and I tried not to flinch. Then he opened his mouth and flicked his tongue slowly over one of my breasts, trailing it over my nipple, down over the soft swelling curve, to my ribs, then down my belly all the way to my navel.

I let out a shaky gasp.

"This is a very bad idea," he said again, almost conversationally, barely lifting his lips from my stomach. I watched his eyes roam up the hills and valleys of my body. "But hell if I'm going to stop now."

"We definitely should stop," I breathed. The words were teasingly torturous as they rolled off my tongue.

"We should. We absolutely should. Tell me to stop." He licked lower down, past my navel and over the curve of one hip.

I knew what he'd find if he descended any lower with that hot, wicked mouth of his. Part of me was nervous at the very idea of his mouth there. And part of me was aching for him to find out just how wet I already was for him.

"I... can't," I gasped, as his mouth trailed still lower, while one of his hands began playing with my breasts. "I can't do that."

Somehow my hands had become tangled in his hair. It was so thick and so soft. Softer than someone as tough as Draven had any right to be.

"What are you d-doing?" I managed to get out.

His head was hovering over my hips now, his breath hot between my thighs.

"Wouldn't you like to find out?" His voice was deep and gravelly. My nipples puckered into even tighter buds just hearing it.

"Now be a good girl," he murmured, as his hands came down to caress my thighs.

I glanced one last time at the letter opener, almost longingly. We were both being driven by sheer lust, pushed to the brink by all that we'd been through.

We were poised on the edge. I knew soon there'd be no going back.

In some ways, stabbing him would have been easier.

"Get your eyes off that letter opener, Morgan. We both know you're not going to use it," he murmured. "Especially now."

"Now?"

He slid his hand between my legs and I let out a gasp, my hips arching up against him.

"Do you taste as good as you feel? You're beautiful, Morgan. Just fucking look at you, lying there naked and bare. You're spectacular. I bet you taste as good as you look." He stroked his thumb slowly against my clit and I groaned, grasping the bedcovers with my hands. "And I bet you taste as good as you feel, so soft and wet."

He stroked my clit again with those hard, strong fingers and I let out another cry, feeling myself running up against a wall of pure bliss.

"Not yet," Draven murmured, the words gentle and lazy. "Not yet. Be a good girl and wait."

And then he smirked up at me, raised a hand to his lips and licked it.

I wanted to say something smartass and sarcastic. But all I could do was stare at him as his tongue moved over his finger, tasting me, breathing my scent in.

He looked glorious. Half-naked and sprawled there beside my naked body.

I could almost have come just from that.

And then his wicked beautiful mouth lowered, moving between my legs. His tongue stroked me, running up and down the full length of me as I arched my hips and cried out.

I could almost taste my climax. It was so fucking close.

"That's it," Draven growled approvingly. His voice was like thunder, rumbling between my legs, and sending electric shivers over my skin like a crackling surge of lightning.

He lifted my legs, hooking them over his shoulders, pulling my body flush against his mouth as his tongue dove inside me.

I screamed, my hips rocking against him, as I came near to shattering.

"There's a good girl. Fuck me back like you mean it."

I did as he told me because I could do nothing else. My body had taken on a will of its own. My hips arched against him again and again. I was trembling, melting. His mouth worked over me, tongue licking, teeth just barely scraping, driving me mad with a pleasure close to pain.

"Please," I cried into the void, hearing the helplessness in my voice but unable to do anything about it. I was lost. I had fallen. Fallen so hard under this man's fucking spell. I could never let him know how much. "Draven. Enough. Please."

"Enough? It's never going to be fucking enough." There was an edge to his voice that I had never heard before. Almost like desperation.

He cupped my ass in his hands, cradling me against his mouth. I writhed beneath him as his tongue circled my clit, then dipped inside me.

He savored me. Feasted on me.

Holding me beneath him, keeping me on the edge, saving me from falling when I most wanted to fall... and then... finally, when I was almost crying from pleasure, sobbing from desperation, he slid his fingers inside me as his tongue circled my clit and thrust. A brutal, rhythmic thrusting that sent me bursting, screaming, climaxing under him, clawing at his hair, at his back.

And then he was doing the same. His hands covered my breasts, the same but different. Claws had shot out from his fingertips, caressing my breasts, moving over the soft mounds, scratching lightly. A claw slipped over a sensitive nipple and I let out a moan that turned into a long, ragged gasp as my orgasm ripped through me, pulsing through my veins, making my bones rattle and my knees shake.

When it was over, Draven was beside me.

His fucking trousers were still on.

His claws moved leisurely over my stomach. He was very gentle.

I rolled onto my side, and thrust my hips against his. He made a grunting sound low and deep in his throat.

"Just as I thought," I said, with satisfaction. His desire was more than manifest. "Take them off."

"Take them off?"

"Take your fucking pants off, Prince of Claws. Fair is fair."

He grinned and my heart beat faster. "I don't think that's a very good idea, do you?"

"I don't think I care what you think," I said flippantly. "Do it."

I thought I knew what he was worried about. But I also knew I'd manage to find just enough restraint not to mount him once he removed them. Just barely enough.

I only wanted to see him. Well, maybe more.

I moved my hand to the front of his trousers and ran my fingers over his length. His not inconsiderable length. He was long...and hard. Despite my best efforts, I was impressed.

"Take them off," I demanded again. "Don't make me reach for the letter opener."

He didn't even smirk this time, just moved his hand to his pants and undid the fastening, then slipped them down his hips.

Was this real? I wondered. My heart was pounding.

Kairos Draven was suddenly lying beside me naked and there was no doubt in my mind that he was the most gorgeous thing I'd ever seen in my life.

His cock was rigid, springing free from his trousers with a mind of its own.

I looked at it. I swallowed hard.

There was a musky scent in the air between us. The scent of our bodies. Not unpleasant. Like sea salt and spices. I credited Draven for the spices. I wasn't sure I'd ever smell as good as he did, with such apparent effortlessness.

I leaned forward and licked Draven's chest, as slowly and lazily as he had done mine. I made sure to bring my tongue directly over one of his nipples, feeling the curling wiry hairs beneath my mouth. He grunted as I took his nipple between my teeth, moving my tongue over it in a slow rhythm as my hand slipped between his legs, grasping his cock carefully in my hand.

He didn't ask what I was doing or even if I knew what I was doing.

Which was good, because I had absolutely no idea.

Vesper and I had never gotten quite this far. Now I realized that was a good thing.

Better that I'd saved myself for the dark, deceptive assassin prince instead who had lied and told everyone I was his mistress. Much better.

All of my knowledge of male bodies and what to do to them came from dirty tavern talk... and listening to Lancelet when she joined in, which was quite frequently. Since Lancelet had preferred women, her contributions weren't a lot of help now. Still, I believed I had grasped the basic concept. Thank the Three for naughty tavern maids who had chimed in with their own tidbits as they passed the ale between tables of rowdy men and women.

I lifted my mouth to Draven's and his lips fell upon mine hungrily. Now came the question I had been dreading.

"What are you doing, Morgan?" he murmured against my mouth. "Do you even know?"

"Be a good fucking boy and maybe you'll find out," I drawled, pulling my lips from his and giving him what I hoped was a smile at least partly as wicked as some of the ones he'd given me.

I pushed him onto his back, then sat up.

He gazed at me with stark desire, his eyes roaming my body from head to toe. The knowledge of how much he wanted me was gratifying. It gave me the extra confidence I needed.

I ran a hand down his chest, feeling him tremble under my fingertips. He was waiting, trying to anticipate what I'd do next.

I didn't give him a chance to ask again.

I moved down his body to straddle his legs with my hips, then lowered my mouth to his cock. I wrapped my hand around it, running my fingertips up its length, feeling the silky smoothness. It was shockingly soft. So incredibly soft and hard at the same time. I wondered how it was even possible. I ran my tongue tentatively around the shaft, and Draven let out a groan.

"You don't have to do this, Morgan." His voice was raspy. That was how I could tell just how much he wanted what I was going to give him.

I licked the tip of his cock, tasting brine and he groaned more deeply. "I know. Now shut the fuck up and let me."

Without looking, I ran a hand down one of his thighs, my nails out like his claws had been. I wasn't as gentle. I was purposely rough and as I scraped against him, I heard him let out a groan that I wasn't entirely sure was all pleasure.

Then I filled my mouth with him. Taking in the swollen head of his cock and sucking him hard. He was big. Which I supposed might be a good thing under other circumstances. I knew women placed undue value on size. Draven would certainly have lived up to any of the highest expectations.

But in this case, I was worried size was a detriment and I wouldn't be able to do this. That I'd choke. That I wouldn't be able to give him anything close to the pleasure he gave me.

I didn't have to worry. Swallowing my fear, I took him in, my body quickly finding a rhythm. Soon he was thrusting into my mouth, his hips in tandem with my lips, unable to help himself–as out of control as I had been just moments before. I stroked him with my tongue, swirling it around the head of his cock, then moving my mouth down as far as I could, up and down, again and again.

The repetitive movement was driving him to the brink.

Draven's entire body was clenched, tense and taut. I watched the muscles in his stomach rippling as they clenched and unclenched. His hands worked against the sheet, gripping it in his fists.

This huge, indomitable man was sprawled beneath me, desperate for what I was giving him and the power I felt was utterly intoxicating.

I wanted to bring him pleasure. I wanted to make it as good for him as he had for me.

And deep down and maybe most importantly, I wanted to do it because I knew he would never, ever have fucking asked or expected me to.

He would have walked out of the room and kept going before he asked me to put my mouth on his beautiful cock.

So it made me want to do it even more.

He was close now. Something had changed. I could feel it.

I stroked more firmly, speeding up just a little, and that was it. With fascination, I watched as Draven utterly lost control.

His hands reached for my head, fingers running through my hair, as he rocked against my mouth. His fingers slid down the back of my neck, every place they touched setting me ablaze in the best way.

And then he moved back, surprising me, pulling his cock out of my mouth and spilling his release on his stomach with a sound of such primal satisfaction that even though I felt partly cheated–I hadn't gotten to taste him–I couldn't help but ultimately feel pleased.

I had done this to him. Pleased him. Brought him some release.

I gazed down at him. His eyes had briefly closed. One of his hands was still in my hair, gently caressing, while the other sprawled over his chest.

He looked so innocent. So vulnerable.

Was this how Nodori had seen him?

Something tugged painfully at my heart at the thought of his first wife.

She had not been loved. Not in the way most women would want a man to love them. Was he even capable of loving a woman in that way?

I felt a stab of strange sorrow for the woman who had been his childhood friend and then been forced to become his bride. Had she gone into the marriage willingly or simply out of duty as he had?

And yet I knew somehow beyond a doubt that she had loved him deeply. And to love Kairos Draven and not be loved in the same way in return... Well, I couldn't imagine a worse fate.

I wasn't jealous of Nodori. No, I pitied her. Because she had died in the most tragic way possible. Though she must have known he would avenge her, it would have been small comfort at the time.

Draven's eyes opened. "What are you thinking?"

I struggled to clear the truth from my face.

"Just what a terrible mistake this all was and how I'm already regretting it."

The words were cruelly flippant, but for a split-second I registered shock in his eyes.

"I was joking," I said quickly. I rolled off him, lying on my back. "I mean, it was a terrible mistake, of course."

"Of course," he murmured.

"But if you're going to make a fucking mistake, may as well make it a good one."

He grabbed a tissue off the nightstand beside us and applied it to his stomach, then turned on his side to look at me. "That doesn't sound like the Morgan I know. Did Lancelet's spirit enter your body when she died?"

There was silence, then, "I'm sorry, I don't know why I said that."

I could hear the genuine regret in his voice. He thought he'd gone too far. But in a way it had been a relief to hear him say her name. I wanted to speak of Lancelet sometimes.

And he was the only person here who had even met her.

"No, it's all right. I know what you mean." I was quiet for a moment. "Maybe. Or maybe I've just changed."

"Oh, you most definitely have."

"In a good way?"

Now it was his turn to be silent. "I think so. But you're the one who has to live with yourself. What do you think?"

"I'm not as... well, innocent as I was when we left Camelot." I thought of the heads in the box that Arthur had shown me that night. The hunters. "Not that I ever was," I amended.

"You were more innocent then though. It's true. You've seen more horror," Draven said softly. "I wish that hadn't been the case." I felt his eyes on my face. "What are we doing here exactly?"

I gave what I hoped was a nonchalant shrug. "We've just made the Prince's Paramour thing real. We played it out. Now we know. Now we're going to sleep. You in your room, me in mine."

"That's how it is?"

I sat up and looked around for the robe that had started this all. It was halfway across the room, in a puddle on the floor. I made myself rise, cross over, pick it up and pull it on, without thinking of how his eyes were on me all the while. "That's how it is."

"Right." Draven swung his legs off the bed and stood up. He grabbed his trousers off the floor and slung them over one shoulder, completely at ease with his own breathtaking nudity. "Goodnight then."

"Goodnight," I said, trying to keep my voice easy as he walked out the door.

I stole a glance as he crossed through the doorway. His back was straight. No hint that anything I'd said had hurt or surprised him.

Nothing hurt the Prince of Claws.

He was impervious. And soon, I would be, too.

I lay on the bed for a long time after that, wrapped in the satin robe.

When hours passed, I began to resign myself to the idea I might not fall asleep that night at all. So much for having a better rest in the Summer Palace.

But finally, a comfortable dozy state came over me and I crawled under the covers, pulling them up around my chin as I had done when I was a child.

It was strange to be sleeping alone. That was all that was wrong, I told myself. I simply wasn't used to it anymore.

I hadn't truly slept without Draven nearby in a very long time. Months in fact.

Eventually my eyes closed.

I dreamed.

I dreamed of my mother.

She was running through the city of Numenos with me in her arms.

BOOK 2

PROLOGUE

The City of Numenos

The warm sun bathed the streets in light as I walked along. Morgan's laughter echoed through the air as she ran ahead.

Around us, most of the city's inhabitants were carrying on with their lives, unaware of the impending doom that threatened on the horizon.

There was no panic yet. But soon there would be. The truth song rang in my heart.

Whispers had already begun to circulate in the marketplaces. And marketplace whispers moved fast as wildfire.

We had days. Perhaps only hours.

A plague had emerged in the neighboring city of Meridium in the midst of a festival.

Its merciless grip had fallen upon Meridium's children.

The rumors were too horrific to be believed. Some said the children died painlessly. Others spoke of wild, nightmarish things worse than death. A gruesome tapestry of pain and torment.

My heart was full of fear, heavy as a storm cloud, for I knew today would be my undoing.

My husband Gorlois ruled Valtain with an iron fist.

Within me, hatred and fear for him intertwined like ivy strangling a once-proud oak.

My hate and fear ran as deep and as true as the love he bore our daughter. An affection he concealed, even from me, for he could not afford to be seen as weak.

His other children were fully grown and had come into their power.

Lorion, indulgent and arrogant, served his father's whims with blind loyalty as the most brutal general of his armies.

Sarrasine, with her haunting melodies and captivating voice, was traveling through Aercanum, no one knew quite where. She cared nothing for the ongoing war, oblivious to everything but the sound of her own ballads.

Orcades oversaw a fleet of ships. Her heart was fierce. She was the boldest and most clever of her father's generals, his right hand in the battle we waged with Myntra. Orcades could be reasoned with. But she was not here now. If she were... Well, perhaps she might help me. Or perhaps she would see me bound and chained.

But the others, the progeny of a High King who had defied death for millennia, were little more than idle symbols of power. Spoiled and consumed by their own desires. Children of a sovereign who had lived for thousands of years, choosing wives who would sate his lust and caring nothing for their own needs or desires.

My own union to Valtain's High King had been arranged in my childhood. Gorlois's keen gaze had selected me from a crowd, seeing within me a fragment of the daughter he had lost long ago.

In me, he said, he would plant the seed of that child again and see it come to fruition.

In Morgan, our precious daughter, his dreams had materialized, breathing life into the legacy he thought he had lost forever.

She was his dream come to life.

The daughter he had lost.

The dream I was now contemplating taking away.

Because for all the love he bore our daughter, more than any of his other children, I knew Gorlois would never protect her.

The fear of appearing weak and vulnerable consumed him, clouding his judgment. My desperate pleas to close the city gates had fallen upon deaf ears, met with nothing more than laughter. He silenced the truth song that resided in my heart, dismissing it as a mere distraction.

All the people of Valtain were his people and Numenos must shelter them, he said. No matter what the cost.

With a chill in my heart, I had forced myself to a calmness I did not feel. When I had said I was taking Morgan for a walk, he had not even tried to stop us. Even knowing what I had told him, he saw no need to shelter this girl so young and precious to his heart.

Stupid, stupid man. Cruel father to fail to guard something so infinitely precious.

To him, Morgan was his legacy. To me, she was my whole world.

And so I walked with my daughter, my small one, my sweet, straight through the city, straight through the very market where I had first heard the whispers.

We marched through as the foresight grew deep in my heart where the seed of knowledge had fallen, its roots immediately taking hold.

The truth of it grew, unchecked, as I walked through my beloved Numenos.

This plague would kill our children.

This plague would kill my daughter.

Gorlois was making a terrible mistake.

I would not let Morgan pay the price.

The weight of my power, concealed from Gorlois all these years, pulsated within my clenched fists. It coursed through me, ready to shield, protect, and keep my child safe.

Gorlois had never known the extent of it, how deep it ran. He had never questioned how I had borne him a daughter so reminiscent of the child he had lost ages before. Like a man, he had accepted it as his due. To him, it was merely the outcome of his own might.

Today, that power would flow through me, into my child.

Today, I would defy Gorlois's terrible mistake, for the life of my daughter outweighed the destruction of my own legacy as a queen of Valtain.

We would enter a place the plague could not touch us, hidden between worlds, concealed in the fabric of time itself.

And we would not emerge until the world was safe for us once again.

With each determined step, the anticipation of a better future coursed through my veins, an unyielding flame that burned brighter than all of Gorlois's wrath, brighter the sunlit streets of Numenos itself.

CHAPTER 17

I prowled beside Nightclaw, my body as tense and on edge as his own seemed to be.

My heart had not stopped pounding since I had woken that morning.

The journey from Noctasia back to the Umbral Court had been swift–and for my part, silent. Draven had given me one strange look, then accepted my reticence.

Now Nightclaw and I walked through the Shadow Gardens, tolerating one another's presence, each wrapped up in our own separate misery.

I was shaken by my dream.

The woman had looked like my mother Ygraine.

For the span of the dream, I had been *her*. I had seen all that she had seen.

All of it had been so very real.

Everything about her had been familiar and true.

My mother's shimmering waves of hair, like spun gold. Her eyes, wise beyond her years, brimming with secrets. *My* eyes.

Secrets I was beginning to realize she had kept from me my entire life.

For if my dream was to be believed, I was not who I thought I was.

I was not even from *when* I thought I was.

But who would be so great a fool as to believe a single fleeting dream? Especially one as far-fetched as the one I'd had last night.

My mother had not lived one hundred and fifty years ago. *I* had not lived one hundred and fifty years ago.

I was not the daughter of the High King of Valtain.

Such a thing was completely impossible.

I thought of what Rychel had said. How she had known only one other true dreamer. And how she had swiftly changed the subject.

Perhaps because that dreamer was now dead and she did not want to frighten me by telling me of their fate?

Regardless, she was the only person I could think of to ask about any of this.

"Are you training the cat or simply exercising him? He doesn't require your presence to pace about." Hawl's wry voice broke through my reverie.

I spun around, scowling. "Don't sneak up on us."

"I only snuck up on *you*. The exmoor has been aware of my presence since I entered his domain." Hawl nodded respectfully at Nightclaw. "Well met, Bellator."

The exmoor had stopped when I paused. Now he sat down on his hind legs and seemed to incline his head towards the Ursidaur.

I sucked in a breath. "He understood you."

"Of course, he did." Hawl shot me a look of unmistakable disdain. "Not a word is said in this creature's presence without his perfect comprehension. Never fail to remember that."

It wasn't that I had taken Nightclaw's intelligence for granted. I had simply not spent enough time with him. That had to change. He could not simply live alone and neglected in the Shadow Gardens, exchanging one prison for another.

I realized Hawl was holding something. "What is that?"

My eyes widened. "Is that... a saddle?" I glanced at Nightclaw, not bothering to hide my skepticism. "You really think he'll let you put that thing on him?"

"As I'm not Master Rodrick, I think there are a great many things Nightclaw will permit us to do," Hawl said mildly. "Besides, I have an inkling about you, Bellator." He spoke directly to the battlecat. "You cunning cat. You rapacious warrior. You fooled the old fool, didn't you? And perhaps Prince Tabar, too."

"Tabar?" I said sharply.

Hawl nodded. "Tabar is the one who brought the exmoor back. Ropes tied to every limb, holding him down as they paraded him through the streets of Noctasia on the bed of a wagon."

The vision sickened me. "Nightclaw had not wished to come?"

Hawl shook their head. "Fought tooth and nail to remain free. Tabar tried to break his spirits, thinking that was the way to make a proper mount of him. When he failed, Rodrick took over."

I looked at Nightclaw, sick at heart. "To think I had the audacity to think I might be able to train him. He should be left alone. Or better yet, set free."

Hawl surprised me by shaking their head. "There was a reason the cat would never have accepted Tabar. I think you know it, too. Besides, I have a hunch about Nightclaw. If my hunch is right, he won't need much training."

My heartbeat quickened. "What do you mean?"

Hawl lifted the saddle. Nightclaw's eyes followed it carefully. "Nightclaw's already been trained. Haven't you, Bellator?"

"By whom? How?" My voice was sharp. "How is that possible?"

"As I said," Hawl said easily. "Just a hunch. But with your permission..." He took a step towards the exmoor.

I knew he wasn't talking to me. I stepped aside, watching in fascination.

The Bearkin was massive, easily capable of saddling the exmoor alone. I watched how it was done, making careful mental notes in the unlikely chance I would one day have to do it by myself.

"You're going to ride him? Here? Now?"

Hawl gave a laugh that sounded like the grating of tree bark. "No." The Bearkin tightened the last buckle and stepped back. "You are."

"Me?" My voice came out as a mouselike squeak. "Now?"

"Unless you think you need some training of your own first? You *do* know how to ride a horse, don't you?"

"I probably need more training than Nightclaw, if what you say is true," I admitted. "I can ride, yes. But I'm not an expert rider."

I thought of Draven's skill in the saddle and wondered how he was getting on with Sunstrike. But I shouldn't have thought of him at all, because suddenly the memory of his handsome face dipping between my legs swam in my vision and was all I could think of.

"Well, he hasn't had a rider in a very long time, if I'm right about this. He'll go easy on you. Won't you, Bellator?"

Nightclaw made a sound halfway between a growl and a meow. I wasn't sure if this was supposed to be reassuring or not.

"It's all about earning his trust," Hawl promised. "He may not accept a new rider. But then, you probably went a long way towards proving yourself just by getting him away from Bastard Rodrick."

I giggled at the play on words. "You mean, Master?"

"I said what I said," Hawl huffed. "That man has no true mastery over any beast. He's as competent as a shepherd with a blindfold on."

"You should take over." As soon as the words were out, I knew I meant it. "I could ask the prince..."

Hawl scoffed dismissively. "I cook for you, I help you find books, I bring you a saddle. Now you want me to run a menagerie. I have enough to occupy my time, thank you, Lady."

"I'm sorry," I said, feeling like an idiot. "You're right, I didn't mean..."

Hawl made a rasping sound that might have been a chortle. "Enough, girl child. Now are you going to mount your steed or not?"

I looked up at Nightclaw. He would be the tallest "steed" I had ever ridden. He was higher than Hala by at least a head.

I looked at the saddle. There were stirrups and a pommel to grip, but they were currently out of my reach.

I gulped.

Nightclaw was observing me. As I swallowed nervously, he let out a sound that made me think of a patient mother's sigh and stretched out his body along the ground.

"Thank you," I whispered gratefully. I reached for the pommel, just barely getting my foot into the closest stirrup. Part way up, I slipped, my other foot kicking into the exmoor's ribs. "I'm so sorry. I'll get better at it, I promise."

Nightclaw said nothing. I assumed he was being stoic. He'd certainly had a lot of practice.

"Well, you're up," Hawl said, not sounding particularly impressed. The Bearkin crossed their arms over their dark furry chest. "How does it feel?"

"Good," I said, to my own surprise. "Right. Secure."

"Excellent. Now where will you ride him?"

"Uh..." I thought for a moment. "Where does the prince ride the female?"

"Now that's the right question," Hawl said approvingly. "There are areas, outside of the palace, within the shield. Open plains where an exmoor might run about. Or if you happen to know a stitcher, you might request that they bring you both to the surface. There are royal hunting grounds just outside of the city."

"That sounds preferable," I said immediately. Nightclaw's ears twitched. "I think Nightclaw would prefer that, too."

"Good. Then you'll speak with Crescent about it later. For now, these gardens are room enough for you to at least practice riding at a trot." Hawl began to walk away.

"Where are you going?" I asked nervously.

"You don't need me for this part. Make sure you take care of that saddle. There's not another one like it." Hawl paused and looked back at me. "Tabar would never have been able to ride this creature. Bonding an exmoor takes trust and respect. If I'm right, Nightclaw's already had one rider. It's up to him to decide if he wants another. If he finds you worthy, you'll know. If he doesn't..."

"Thanks for the vote of confidence," I called sardonically as Hawl strode out of the gardens. The Bearkin waved a paw without turning around.

I gripped the reins, feeling all too aware of my precarious place perched atop such a large creature. It was like riding a house.

Nightclaw stepped forward, taking cautious steps as if as worried he would displace me as I was of being displaced. Yet with each paw forward, his movements became more fluid.

As we slowly trod along one of the wild garden paths, I could feel the subtle vibrations of the exmoor's purrs resonating through his body.

A purr had to be a good sign, I thought. Cats purred when they were happy, didn't they?

We hadn't had many cats in the Rose Court. Arthur wasn't fond of them. But Kaye was. And I remembered him sneaking a kitten into his room once when he was younger. He had managed to keep it there for months until it finally got out when a servant left the door open. We hadn't found it again. Kaye had been devastated. We had searched everywhere. Eventually I had promised my younger brother that the kitten must have snuck out into the woods and found a new family.

But the truth was, I hadn't put it past Arthur or Florian to have done something far nastier to Kaye's pet.

I recalled lying on Kaye's bed, stroking his kitten's sleek little stomach one day. She had been purring up a storm. Suddenly she had leaped to her feet, tail up, hissing at the door. She was still purring. If anything, her purr had become louder.

When Kaye peeked out into the hall, he had seen Florian striding past.

Cats could purr for all sorts of reasons. When they were happy, yes, but also when they were anxious or afraid.

I wondered which it was with Nightclaw. I certainly hoped he knew he had nothing to fear from me.

Taking a deep breath, I reached a hand out tentatively and lay it along the exmoor's shoulder, feeling the rumbling vibrations pass through me.

Our connection felt even more real like this, skin to fur. A lump formed in my throat.

"I will never let anyone hurt you again," I promised. "And if you would rather be free, I swear I will have you released."

The problem was, I had no idea if that *was* what Nightclaw would prefer. It wasn't as if I could read the cat's mind.

But as if in response, Nightclaw suddenly leaped forward. I let out a shriek holding onto the pommel, as the exmoor burst into an loping trot, taking us through a shadowy path full of vibrant foliage where the scent of blossoming greenery filled the air, intermingling with the earthy aroma of the garden.

As we trotted along the rough winding path, Nightclaw's eyes seemed to gleam with a vitality that had not been there that day in the menagerie. His tufted tail swayed gently behind me.

"Eager for a run, are you?" I murmured. "Shall we go a little faster? Or will we risk running into a tree?" Gently, I nudged my legs and gave the lightest of touches to the reins.

Nightclaw responded instantly, shifting into a rhythmic canter. His sleek golden-brown fur shimmered in the dappled light that filtered down through the canopy of vines and trees above us. He sped down a path, entering a grove, never breaking into anything as fast as a gallop but still going fast enough to send my pulse racing.

I had no need to worry about my riding skills, I realized tardily. Nightclaw was skilled enough for us both. He easily darted between tree trunks and hanging vines, avoiding tall bushes and never losing his footing even when the path was a mess of brush and loose pebbles.

Vulnerable as I felt in the saddle as we sped through the garden, I suddenly realized the ride was a dance of trust and understanding.

Nightclaw *wanted* to be ridden. Perhaps had even yearned for it.

It was a strange honor, coming from this creature who seemed to embody the very essence of the wild in his majestic being, to know that I was wanted as I perched so small and frail in the saddle above.

When I left the Shadow Gardens, I was tired, dirty, and sweaty but also vastly satisfied.

There was something incredible about seeing how much happier Nightclaw was out of the menagerie and knowing I had done that for him—gotten him away from his cruel prison, away from Master Rodrick.

I still couldn't believe how long he had been confined. If Tabar had captured Nightclaw then that meant the exmoor had been in the underground palace more than twenty years.

Twenty years of agony and hopelessness.

I had left Hawl's saddle in the gardens, hanging from a tree in an area full of soft grass that Nightclaw seemed to use as his bed.

I hadn't wanted to walk with it through the palace corridors, and as I turned a corner and saw two figures coming towards me with an entourage of guards and courtiers behind them, I was glad of my decision.

"Well, look who it is," Avriel drawled. "The Valtain..." He paused to look at his companion. "I'm surprised she's allowed to wander unaccompanied. Wasn't she supposed to have guards? What exactly are we calling my cousin's prize again?"

He made a striking figure. Dusky bronzed hair and amber skin that hinted at the power that simmered just below the surface. My eyes went to the glimmering gold scales adorning his forearms. A porcelain hand lay resting lightly along one arm.

Beside Avriel, the Queen Regent's velvety crimson lips curved upwards slightly. Waves of cherry hair cascaded down her back, interwoven with delicate strands of gold. Draperies of silk billowed around her. A regal cape of sapphire blue was fastened around her shoulders. Her ivory complexion, flawlessly fair, seemed to glow in the dimly lit hallway.

"Why, our royal guest, of course," Sephone replied. She looked at me as if she were already bored, then tapped Avriel's arm playfully. "The Prince's Prize. I mean, Paramour." She tilted her head. "I wonder how long she will be with us?"

There was something ominous to this statement.

"I have a name," I said tightly. "You may address me as Morgan."

Avriel laughed. "The Prince of Claws's prize may have claws of her own."

"Tiny ones," Sephone allowed. "Like a sweet kitten." Her smile widened, beautiful and cruel.

"Nowhere near as sweet as a kitten, I'm afraid," I replied. "And where are you two off to? Just out for a pleasant family stroll? Do you always hold hands? Now that's rather adorable."

Sephone's eyes narrowed to slits.

"The Queen Regent does not answer to you, captive whore," Avriel snapped, showing his true colors in a heartbeat. "It is none of your business where she deigns to go or not go."

I smiled slowly. "No, but you answer to your cousin, don't you, Avriel?" I stared at him, holding him fixed with my eyes, reminding him of the moment of utter weakness he had shown on the mat that day when Draven had dominated him in a matter of seconds. "I suppose some men only get off on bullying those weaker than them. Like Pearl."

"What the fuck do you know about Pearl?" Avriel's eyes narrowed.

Sephone's hand pressed down slightly on Avriel's arm. "Sister to the rebel traitor. She would have died in the Blood Rise if Avriel had not put her down. From what I understand, it was a mercy killing."

"That's funny," I bluffed. "Because I've heard it called a coward's way of cheating before the competition has even begun. But then, I suppose it's all right if some of the challengers have it easier than others. As long as they're favorites of their queen."

I held Sephone's gaze intently for as long as I dared.

She returned it with a cool, detached stare. "You bore me, my dear. I honestly don't know what my son sees in you."

"She must be a good fuck at least," Avriel said snidely. "There must be something special about her—or at least between her legs—or he wouldn't have brought her back. He gets off on it, I suppose. Bedding the enemy. We all know how frigid Kairos used to be. Perhaps that's what he needed to get him going. Why, I'm surprised he could bed his own wife..."

"That's enough," Sephone said sharply. "You'll speak more respectfully of your prince." But I suspected she had only berated Avriel because of the fleet of onlookers behind her.

I noticed Ulpheas in the crowd of courtiers. He was watching me with a puzzled expression.

"Bedding the enemy?" I gave Sephone a significant look, refusing to meet Avriel's eyes. "Is that what it's called? Regardless, Kairos will win the Blood Rise. You'll see."

"Your faith is admirable, little Valtain," Sephone replied. "Though I fear it may be misplaced."

"If only you shared it," I said bluntly. "Especially as you claim Kairos as your son. But it's clear where you're laying your bets." I nodded towards Avriel, then stepped aside to let them pass.

Avriel bared his teeth and hissed as he stepped past, then whispered something in the queen's ear that sent her into a peal of laughter.

I let out a breath I hadn't known I'd been holding.

Then I realized I wasn't alone.

Lyrastra was standing before me with a curious expression. She must have been trailing behind at the back of the group.

"I hadn't realized you were part of the procession. Hoping for another chance to freeze me to the wall? I warn you, you'll meet with resistance if you try. I won't hold back."

Now I was really bluffing. I had absolutely no desire to let my powers loose, even on Lyrastra. Not after what I had dreamed last night.

The snake-eyed woman shook her head slowly. "It wasn't cheating, you know. What he did to Pearl. Just poor form."

"So I'm told," I said bitterly. "What merciless rules you all play by."

She looked at me strangely. "Do you really care?"

"Why wouldn't I?" I snapped. "Perhaps more of you should."

She glanced up the hall in the direction the queen's procession had taken. "Pearl was Ulpheas's cousin, you know. The queen doesn't believe he didn't know Celeste was a traitor in advance. But he's too stupid for Celeste to have taken into her confidence."

"Aren't you all cousins?" I said tiredly. "Besides, I thought you were friends with Ulpheas."

"We are." Lyrastra looked surprised. "It's still the truth. As for Avriel." She shrugged wearily. "It's how it's always been done. His cheating will be more blatant, just wait and see, once the real thing begins. And why shouldn't it be? *She* certainly won't care."

I knew she meant the Queen Regent.

"They're sleeping together, aren't they?" I said bluntly. "The queen and Draven's cousin?"

Lyrastra gave me a small smile. "She's his aunt, too, you know. His father was Sephone's brother."

She was obviously trying to shock me so I tried not to let my revulsion show too plainly. "Well, you Siabra really are something, aren't you?" I said as blithely as I could manage. "Keeping the royal bloodlines nice and tight, I suppose."

"Something like that." Lyrastra looked down the hallway where the royal procession had disappeared. "Still, he's the top contender. He and Kairos."

"What about you?" I said, surprising myself. "You seem fairly... competent."

"I am. But I'm no match for Avriel. I won't cheat, you see."

I snorted. "You did the other day."

She looked at me. "That was different. We were playing."

"And you're not going to play when it comes to the Blood Rise, when your very life is on the line?" I shook my head. "Forgive me if I don't see you as particularly honorable. Why are you even telling me this?"

"Kairos already knows his cousin. What Avriel is capable of. And he knows me, too." She lifted her chin. "Tell him I don't need his protection when it all begins. I can hold my own. Tell him not to get himself killed trying to save me. I'm not Pearl. He can't save us all."

I stared. "That's what this is about? Weren't you supposed to be trying to kill me the next time we were alone? Aren't you wasting your chance?"

"Just fucking tell him. If you even talk." She gave me a look of derision that reminded me it was the same old Lyrastra. "And there's plenty of time."

She turned and marched away.

CHAPTER 18

When I got to Rychel's workshop, it was evening. I had gone back to the suite I shared with Draven and opened the passage in the sitting room, thanks to Beks' instructions. I hadn't wanted to always have to rely on him to get around but I also didn't want to use the main corridors and risk running into Avriel or Sephone again. Once had been enough.

Beks had been reluctant at first. I think he liked sharing his secrets with someone. But he liked sneaking away from Javer even more. Still, I didn't want the boy getting into trouble constantly for my sake.

I also didn't need him there, listening to every question I asked Rychel. Not that I didn't trust him, but he was just a child and he was already too worldly wise for a boy so young.

Rychel was wearing a set of bulging eye pieces rimmed in black and peering at something on the table in front of her as I entered.

As she stepped back, I saw what it was. The goblet from the opening ceremony the other night.

"Why do you have that?" I asked, as I descended the flight of stone stairs to the workshop floor.

Rychel turned. She didn't look surprised to see me. "I stole it. From the treasury. Sephone had it locked up as soon as Draven brought it back. She only took it out for the ceremony then it was back in its place and waiting for me to rescue it."

"I still don't understand the fascination with that thing." I stared at the chalice. It was a simple wooden cup.

As I stepped closer and peered over Rychel's shoulder, I saw that the cup had an interior of polished gold. Still, it was hardly the most lavish goblet I had ever seen.

"It bound the competitors to the terms of the challenge. How exactly?" I asked

"It did that, yes. But its capable of much more." She spoke of the chalice almost as if it were a living thing, I noticed. "Before the opening ceremony, each competitor provided a drop of their blood. The blood went into the cup. The cup remembered. When Sephone said the words, the rite was enforced and the participants bound."

"So if someone decides they suddenly don't want to compete in the Blood Rise...?"

"They'll die. It's simple really," Rychel said, still studying the cup. "They have to show up for each challenge and they can't exit a challenge part-way, no matter how much they might want to. They have to see it through now that it's begun."

"All of them except for Celeste," I reminded her.

"Right. Celeste." Rychel grimaced. "Brave but stupid."

"Brave? How so?"

"I can understand the desire to rebel. The desire to denounce this court for its crimes," Rychel said mildly. "But obviously from the moment she opened her mouth, she was doomed to die." She looked thoughtful. "She probably knew that. It was a gesture, nothing more. I'm sure she hoped the children would take out Sephone. It was a nice idea."

"And you got your body to experiment on, after all," I said coolly.

"I did. Not that much has come of it," Rychel said, her face falling. She perked up. "I have more hope from this."

"So, Draven brought the chalice back?"

"We had it. He took it. He brought it back again."

"Wait, wait, wait..." I said, suddenly grasping something. "This cup..."

"This cup is the grail," Rychel clarified. "You might have heard of it."

"*The sword, the spear, the grail's mystery*," I said, repeating the lines I had seen etched into the stone in Orcades' underwater prison.

Rychel wrinkled her nose. "Right. The grail is mysterious all right."

"Why did your brother take it?" I demanded. "What did he want with it?"

"He's not exactly forthcoming, but if I had to guess, he wanted to destroy it. After all, my father used it to craft the plague."

Fuck. I hadn't realized that. "Why didn't he? Destroy it, I mean."

Rychel shrugged. "Probably because he couldn't. Do you have any idea how much magic went into creating this thing? You do know it's said to have been created by the goddess Marzanna herself?"

"But that's just a legend," I said slowly.

Rychel rolled her eyes. "Everything is just a legend. But legends hold truths. Sometimes frightening ones. Which is why the Siabra have a temple to the gods that they now treat as nothing more than a museum. Because they're too afraid of what the gods will do to them if they ever return one day, they've turned their backs on the gods first instead."

"What do you mean?"

"The gods were probably just powerful fae who lived long ago, Morgan. But the legends say they're immortal–really immortal. So, if you're a true believer, then they could still be around. Floating up in the sky somewhere. Or maybe on another plane. Who knows." Rychel shrugged.

Or hiding inside the fabric of time itself?

I swallowed. "Who knows." I looked at the grail. So plain and unassuming. "He could have tossed it into the ocean. Buried it deep underground. Why bring it back?"

"Maybe he didn't want to risk someone innocent finding it and setting off the next cataclysm. Imagine this thing washing up on the shore one day and being picked up by a poor fisherman."

"So it's back where it started. The Siabra had the grail. They used it to do something horrible. The Valtain had the sword. They buried it with Orcades. And the spear?"

"Oh, the Valtain probably have that, too. Supposedly it's their High King's favorite weapon. It sounds like it gets the most use out of all these three things. Excalibur can't be used by just anyone, you know. It has to like you."

"Excuse me?"

"It has to like your blood," Rychel clarified. "All of these things are bound by blood. The grail is the greediest. It will do a lot for blood. New blood, old blood. That's why it cooperates with the Blood Rise. It gets to taste each competitor. Sephone takes a sampling of each challenger's blood and mixes it in. You didn't see that part of things at the ceremony, did you?"

I shuddered. "You make it sound as if it's... alive."

"They all are. Each of the objects the gods created. That's what makes them special. They have... well, minds of their own. At least, that's my theory."

"How is that possible?"

"How is magic possible at all? We use it and we still have no idea. There are powers in Aercanum that the fae can harness but mortals can't. How is that fair? How does it all work? Maybe someday we'll know. I hope I live that long."

"What are you going to do with it... with that... thing?" I said, staring at the grail with dislike.

"Well, if our father could use it to turn a plague into something so powerful and terrible that even he didn't understand it, then..."

"Then you think you can use it to undo the same plague?" My eyes flashed. "Now that's stupid."

"Is it?" Rychel mused. "Probably. But I'll study it nonetheless. See if I can learn more about what makes it tick."

"Get killed in the process," I muttered.

"You don't like it." Rychel stared at me. "That's smart. It's not a good idea to become enamored with magical objects that hold untold power."

I looked at her meaningfully.

"Oh, I'm not enamored," she assured me. "Just curious."

"Small difference," I snapped.

She laughed. "I'll be careful. I promise." She eyed me curiously. "Why are you here, by the way? I assume it's not because of the grail. You're not going to tell Sephone I stole it from the treasury, are you?"

"Certainly not. Sephone can go fuck herself for all I care." I crossed my arms over my chest.

"Not enamored with our fair queen either, huh?" Rychel snickered. "She's not particularly warm and cozy. So what then? Not that I'm complaining. I've lost track of how many days I've been down here alone..."

"I had a few questions," I admitted. "I wasn't sure who else to ask..."

"I am a wealth of knowledge," Rychel said cheerfully. "Ask away."

I tapped my foot nervously. "Well, first, I had another dream. It was... very vivid. I think it was a memory."

"We talked about this before. True dreaming is very rare." Rychel studied me. "But... it's possible. You seem very certain."

"I wish I could be." I took a deep breath. "When I met Orcades, she looked at me. She looked into my head somehow, Rychel. And then she touched me and said the word 'Remember.'"

"And? Did you?"

"Not right away," I admitted. "But now... I think I'm starting to. I think this dream was part of what she did to me. She made me start to remember things. Is that even possible?"

Rychel tapped a finger to her lips. "I don't see why not. If you had repressed memories..."

"Repressed?" I said sharply. "I didn't repress anything. At least, not voluntarily." I wracked my mind, trying to remember exactly what Orcades had said. "She took Excalibur. She called it something else though."

"Iron of the Goddess?" Rychel suggested. "*Ferrum deae* perhaps?"

My eyes lit up. "That's it! That's what it means?"

"That's what the Valtain prefer to call it."

"Perun's Blade. Vela's Blade. Excalibur. Iron of the Goddess. Too many names for a single sword," I complained. My face hardened. "Whatever it's called, Orcades wanted to kill the Siabra with it. I think she thought I was planning on taking it back to you. But I had no idea who the Siabra even were then."

"Her mistake," Rychel quipped. "But that doesn't surprise me. She led Valtain's armies, you know. I suppose when she failed, she was punished with imprisonment. At least, that would be my guess."

"Why are my memories only starting to come back now when Orcades touched me weeks ago?" I demanded, knowing it was unfair to expect Rychel to have any real answers. I thought of something else. "She said someone had made a mess of me. Of my memories. My head. What could she have meant?"

"Maybe you haven't been repressing anything. Maybe there are things in there someone didn't want you to remember," Rychel said thoughtfully. "But who would have done that?"

My own mother. But I couldn't say that out loud.

"The dream I had last night... The answer may have been in there. But I don't know if I can trust the dream." It was all so frustrating.

Rychel looked sympathetic. "Ultimately, until you dream something that's verifiable, only you can decide whether these are true dreamings or not."

"You said there was one other person you knew who had the gift of true dreaming. Who was it? What did they do with it?"

"Did I call it a gift? Some might call it a curse." Rychel sighed. "They were like you. Unsure if what they dreamed was true."

"And then they realized it was?"

Rychel nodded slowly. "But only when it was too late to change what occurred. After that, they learned to block them out. I haven't talked to them about this in a very long time, you understand."

I understood. I also understood she wasn't going to tell me who this person was.

"So they saw something in a dream but they didn't trust it to be real? Until it was too late," I said slowly.

She nodded. "If it's a gift, then it's a treacherous one, Morgan. A gift that could drive you mad. Never knowing if what you see is real. Be careful. Don't let the dreams sweep you away."

This wasn't helping. I was almost certain what I saw in my dreams was real. But I had no way to verify what was truly going on along the border of Pendrath and Tintagel any more than I could verify my dream of something that may have taken place more than a century ago.

"Right," I said hollowly. "I'll be careful."

"What was the other question?"

"The other?"

"You said there were two."

"Oh. Right." I blushed slightly.

"*That* kind of question is it?" Rychel crowed. "If it's about my brother, this might get awkward."

"I'll keep it as un-awkward as I can, but I really do have to ask this. I'm sorry," I said quickly. "I know the Siabra can't have children. But I'm afraid I can. And I don't want to. Is there anything you know of..."

"I can give you something," Rychel cut me off. "There's a spell and there's a herb. Or you can be on the extra safe side and do both. But if it's my brother you're worried about, don't be. He's already dealt with his side of things."

"I-it's not..." I stuttered, feeling my cheeks suffuse with heat. "I mean, I honestly don't know. I just want to be... safe. I don't want to bring a child into this world. You can see the state of things just like I can."

My brother was busy trying to take over a continent. Undead children ran rampant in an abandoned fae city. I had accidentally unleashed a powerful Valtain general from prison and now she thought we were enemies. Oh, and I was trapped in a court filled with people who thought I was scum to be stepped on and wouldn't care if I was knifed in my sleep.

Those all seemed like pretty good reasons to avoid ever bringing a child into the mix.

Rychel nodded. "Oh, I'm with you. This is why I plan to never mate. I'm happy like this. Alone."

I raised my eyebrows. "Really? Never? That's an awfully long time."

"That's the plan," she chirped. "Anyhow, after what happened with Nodori, my brother felt pretty much the same as you do. I made the mistake of bringing up the subject when he got back to court with you."

"And?" I was very interested now.

"And he basically said to mind my own business but that the Siabra wouldn't be getting any more babies out of him." Rychel smirked in a way that reminded me of Draven. "Sephone won't be pleased, if she ever finds out. I'm sure she still has hopes for Lyrastra."

I thought of what Lyrastra had said and the way the queen had touched Avriel so brazenly. "I'm not so sure about that. But maybe."

Rychel cocked an eyebrow. "Oh? Well, you can tell me another time."

I nodded. Suddenly I was very tired. And yet, if I went back to the suite and fell asleep... What if I had another dream?

The very idea made me even more weary.

It was one thing to run from danger but when the danger was *me*... there weren't many places to turn.

CHAPTER 19

T he Blood Rise began just a few days later.

Draven had been avoiding me since we got back from Noctasia. Part of me thought I'd offended him by ignoring him the day we returned. Even though my silence had had nothing to do with him, I knew he didn't know that. I'd been meaning to say something, but suddenly I was out of time.

I woke up to find Draven gone and Breena knocking furiously at the bedroom door.

"Let me guess," I said blearily, rubbing sleep from my eyes. "Another garden party? I'll pass."

"Not a garden party," Breena said, looking offended by the very suggestion. "Can you really not know?"

"Know what?" I wasn't going to come out and say that the prince didn't exactly keep me well-informed. Besides, it was probably pretty obvious.

Breena hemmed and hawed a moment. "Prince Kairos didn't explicitly say so, but I know he will want you there."

"Want me where?" I demanded.

"The Blood Rise," she hissed. "It begins in an hour. Surely you wish to watch the first challenge..."

"I do," I cut in sharply. "Of course, I do! What do I need? Where do I go?"

"Let me dress you and then I've asked for an escort to meet you at your suite," Breena said.

"Perfect. Let's hurry. I want to leave as soon as possible."

The thought suddenly struck me that Draven could die today. Then I shoved it away. That was an impossibility if there ever was one. He was as hard as nails, as strong as steel, and as infuriatingly stubborn as a brick wall. He'd be fine.

But regardless of how fine he'd be, I wanted to watch whatever was taking place. I didn't trust Sephone as far as I could throw her and Avriel even less.

There had to be someone there for Draven. Someone watching who was on his side, no matter what.

With not a little irritation, I realized that person had somehow become me.

Maybe I'd tuck the letter opener in my boot, just in case. I'd brought it back from Noctasia. A memento, if you will.

"You need to look your best," Breena was muttering, half to herself, half to me, as she swept through the pile of clothing she'd carried in, then flung open the doors of my wardrobe. "Something striking. Something fearless."

She had the right idea, I had to admit. I wondered what she'd put me in.

She lifted a long gown from the pile she had carried in. It was a dove white, as pure as freshly fallen snow.

"White?" I said dubiously. "Are you sure this will strike fear into the hearts of our enemies?"

Breena shook her head stubbornly. "It's not about striking fear. It's about showing how different you are from them."

I stared at the dress. "It's rather... elaborate."

"You don't have to blend in. Stand out so he can see you," Breena insisted.

"He'll certainly be able to spot me in this." I sighed. "Very well."

I let her pull the gown over my head. The fabric was as delicate as a moth's wings. There were designs cut all over, and with every movement I made, ripples went through the fabric, revealing glimpses of my gold-tinged skin beneath.

I glanced in the mirror. The gown enhanced my curves, draping over my bodice and hips alluringly, hugging my figure like a second skin.

As I walked, the material billowed and danced, reminding me of the cloak Sephone had been wearing the day before.

The neckline of the dress was modest, only hinting at the soft expanse of my collarbone, while delicate straps graced my shoulders, attaching along the sides of the dress and leaving the expanse of my back bare.

The fabric felt weightless, as light as feathers. The skirt fell like a waterfall around my feet.

Breena slid pearlescent slippers onto my feet before I could protest, then fastened a gold choker around my neck.

She left my hair down in a simple braid, sweet and maidenly, then stood back clasping her hands.

"There," she said with satisfaction. "Very different from anything the court will be wearing."

I nodded, suddenly nervous. "What should I expect?"

The little maid frowned. "Someone always dies on the first day. Sometimes more than one."

"And the court?"

"Oh, they stand around gossiping, enjoying refreshments and pretending not to watch."

Unsurprising. "They don't want to watch even though the outcome determines their future emperor or empress?"

She chuckled. "They know there's quite a way to go."

"How many challenges are there in total?" I had never asked Draven.

"Three in all. By the last one... Well, there won't be much competition. They get worse as they go on."

I wasn't sure if she meant the competitors or the challenges themselves.

"The prince will make it through them all. I know he will," I said stoutly.

Breena shot me an odd look that made me think she was surprised by my show of faith. Perhaps she had found the letter opener in my drawer.

There was a tapping at the door.

"Come," Breena called.

I wasn't surprised when Odessa's form filled the frame.

"Ready?" Her tone was even terser than usual, as if she was worried about something. About Draven?

I nodded and followed her out into the hall, then turned back to Breena. "Will you be there?"

She shook her head. "The viewing area is for nobles and courtiers. We hear the results second-hand. Usually quite quickly." She smiled slightly. "Thanks to that scallywag Beks."

"He's quite a little rogue, isn't he?" I tried to smile. "Well, then... Thank you for everything, as always, Breena."

Odessa led the way through the palace to a new wing I had never been in before.

Pushing open large glass doors, I followed her into a spacious gallery filled with crystalline light. Luminous stalactites hung over us, hanging down from a cavernous stone ceiling.

The space was already full of Siabra, milling about holding beverages and sampling from trays carried by passing servants, just as Breena had predicted. They looked cool and bored and completely unphased by the prospect of whatever bloody spectacle we were about to witness.

On the far side of the gallery was a long low rail. I walked over to it.

Below us was a series of caves. I leaned forward to get a better look and my forehead connected with cool glass. A translucent shield had been erected around the edge of the gallery, keeping the spectators firmly separated from the contenders below.

Odessa stepped up beside me. "They enter the caves. If they make it out, they live. If they don't, they die." Her voice was flat.

"What's in the caves?"

"No one but the Queen Regent knows in advance," she replied. "Illusions. Tricks. Death traps. That sort of thing most likely."

"Easy peasy," I muttered.

Odessa nodded tightly. "He'll be fine. It's an elimination round."

I wondered who Avriel would eliminate this time.

"There you are." It was Crescent, looking calm and cheerful. Javer and Beks were beside him. "Ready for the bloodbath?"

"Don't even say that," Odessa said sharply.

For a warrior, she didn't seem keen on the brutal sport we were about to observe. Not that I blamed her.

"It's an absurd legacy from millennia ago," Javer drawled, looking already bored.

"It certainly doesn't seem like the most efficient or intelligent way to select a monarch," I admitted.

Javer raised a dark brow. "You think we pick them for their wisdom? Or perhaps their benevolence?"

"I think I know the Siabra well enough by now to know that would be a naive hope," I replied dryly.

Javer smiled slightly. "She learns. Excellent."

"She's a fast learner," Odessa said, surprising me. "She's doing well in Steelhaven. Not bad at teaching the younger girls a few tricks either."

I flushed with pride, knowing how rare Odessa's compliments were. "I'm behind myself, that's all." I'd lost some of the skills I'd been working on while on the road with Draven–though I'd gained others. "The younger girls are the easiest to spar with. I don't have to ask them to go easy on me."

"I've watched you. You're doing fine. Making noticeable progress. You must have had good teachers back in..."

"Pendrath," I supplied. "Camelot. The best. Sir Ector and Dame Halyna." I smiled slightly. "You'd like them."

"Thrilled to hear my new pupil is capable of learning," Javer cut in, with droll wit.

"New pupil?" I didn't like the sound of that. "What are you talking about?"

"I'm talking about your first lesson in magic. Which begins tomorrow."

"I don't think so..." I started to say, just as Crescent hissed, "Shhh. It's beginning. Here they come."

The lights in the gallery suddenly dimmed as the ones in the cave system below us flared to life.

I spotted Sephone stepping up to the rail. She looked as if she were trying to perfect an expression of perfect ennui, but she didn't fool me. I noticed she had not made any introductory speeches or given a welcome address to the courtly crowd. Perhaps she was as eager to see this over with as I was–and to see Avriel and Draven come through it safely.

There was a hum of excitement from the Siabra nobles around us as the eleven remaining challengers stepped out.

Some of them glanced up at us. Rhea, the smallest of the group, even smiled and waved. Her long curly blonde hair had been pinned and fastened in a practical braid. She seemed eager to begin, even cocky.

Avriel glanced up at the gallery, his eyes going right to the queen. He did not wave.

Draven didn't look up at all. His eyes were focused on whatever lay ahead.

Or perhaps he was angry with me for ignoring him since we'd returned, I thought with a stab of guilt.

"They have weapons," I murmured to Odessa. There was a bow strapped to Rhea's back, while I saw other contestants carrying blades, bows, and swords.

Selwyn, the large man with the stormy silver eyes and majestic antlers, hoisted an ax over one shoulder, while Erion, the fair-haired reptilian Siabra who was covered in scales, carried a long spear.

Avriel had two wicked-looking sabers criss-crossed on his back. I had no doubt he had others, hidden in his armor.

"In this challenge, they are permitted to bring whatever they wish to carry. In future challenges, it may be different," she whispered.

Draven had a sword strapped to his back. I knew just how effective he was with it. Like the other challengers, he wore leather armor–light and easy to move in. Part of me wished he were wearing steel, but I supposed that wouldn't have been a wise choice, not without knowing what he was going up against.

"What will they face?" I murmured impatiently.

"I have an inkling," Odessa said, but her face was unreadable. "There." She pointed.

The cave system below was filling up with mist.

Shouts rang up from the challengers below as the mist reached them. I heard Draven yell out, calling his fellow competitors to form a ring, back-to-back.

Soon we could no longer see them at all.

There were murmurs of complaint from the nobles around me. Their show was being spoiled.

I glanced down the balcony at the queen. She looked unperturbed.

The sounds of fighting rang out. Whatever was down there, the contestants were facing it blind.

There was a scream. The sound of blades running through flesh. The grunt of warriors fighting hand to hand.

I clutched the railing. Was this how the entire challenge would go? Us looking down into the mist with no idea what was unfolding?

Then the mist cleared. We could see the challengers again.

Most of them had done what Draven said. They had formed a group with him, defending themselves and each other. I saw Lyrastra to his right. She seemed unhurt.

Others were not so lucky. Brasad, the small man with short fiery hair and red scales, was favoring one arm while his other dripped blood. I watched while he laughed and shrugged, evidently not put off by the injury.

Nearby, Selwyn put a hand on Malkah's shoulder–the woman with the onyx fish-like scales whose hair was all the colors of the ocean. She clutched at her stomach, then she straightened and tried to clear a look of pain from her face.

"She's hurt already. Shit. She would have been a good one," Odessa muttered.

"A good one?" I was confused. Didn't we all want Draven to win?

"More than one challenger can make it through, though only one will become ruler," Crescent said quietly. "If someone comes in second or third place, they'll often be appointed to the emperor or empress's council–a prestigious position. Malkah is fair-minded, balanced, wise. She would be a good person to have."

I nodded my understanding.

Avriel, I noticed, had not joined Draven's group. He stood a ways off, licking a drop of blood from his lips, grinning as he stood in a fighting stance.

At his feet lay one of the creatures that had attacked in the mist.

"Fucking goblins," Odessa muttered. "Nasty brutes."

I looked at the bodies littered around the challengers in fascination. They were humanoid but larger even than the average fae, roughly six to seven feet tall. Their bodies were a greenish tinge, hunched and emaciated, with sinewy limbs and twisted postures. Their skin was rough and covered in scars and blemishes, giving them an eerie appearance.

The goblins heads were elongated, with sharp, jagged teeth jutting out of their mouths. Their ears were pointed, like a fae's, but twisted and deformed, with ragged edges.

"They hunt in packs," Odessa informed me. "Their bite is venomous."

I glanced at Malkah. The wound on her stomach hadn't seemed so bad, but if it was infested with poison...

"She'll need to clear the caves quickly and get to a healer," Odessa said grimly.

I looked along the cave system. When the mist had sprung up, the goblins had entered. But the ground had also changed. Pools of dark water now covered large patches of the cave floor.

"That's where they need to go," Crescent said in a low voice, pointing to the opposite side of the cave where a perilous-looking stone cliff loomed. "They make it to the far side. Climb up."

"And the pools?" I thought I already knew.

"Goblins love caves and dark places, including water. They'll be infested with them."

I looked at the path the challengers would have to take. It would be impossible to avoid all of the water. At some point, they'd have to step into a pool–or even swim across, depending on how deep the water was.

Draven was already moving forward. So were most of the others.

Only Malkah hung back, with Erion and Selwyn beside her.

I watched as Draven called something to them, then approached the first pool.

Avriel, I noticed, was skirting around the edge of the caves, not coming close to anyone else. I supposed I should be grateful for that at least.

A head popped out of the water, then another. And another.

Draven swung his sword almost lazily, lopping off heads as fast as they poked up.

Beside him, Lyrastra took up a position at his back, her eyes scanning around them.

Despite what she had said, she seemed intent on guarding him. Or perhaps she simply knew Draven's back was the safest place for her to be.

Sure enough, a group of goblins emerged from around a pile of stones. They moved towards Lyrastra with surprising quickness.

I watched as she moved into a low stance, then slashed out with a pair of daggers, cutting them down as quickly as they came towards her.

There was a shrieking sound and one of the challengers swooped towards her. The woman called Vespera, whose hands ended in sharp bird-like talons.

As Lyrastra used her daggers, Vespera attacked the goblin pack from the rear, slicing them to pieces with her talons.

"She doesn't even need weapons," I observed quietly.

Crescent nodded from beside me. "Though she might wish she'd brought one eventually. The prince could use his claws as well, but a sword is easier and faster when fighting a larger group."

I clapped my hands. "He's across."

Draven had cleared the pool. I watched as he waded out of waist-high water and clambered up over some boulders, then gestured to Selwyn and Malkah to move ahead.

"He can't shield them all the way across," Odessa murmured. "But it's an honorable attempt."

I glanced at Javer and he met my eyes, his lips thinning into a cold smile. "There are no bonus points for chivalry, Lady Morgan. The survivor takes all." He inclined his chin and I saw that Avriel was at the front of the group, the furthest ahead, still edging along the border of the caves.

Rhea was close behind him. She had left the main group and was following Avriel. A small smile played on her lips as she leaped and bounded like a graceful gazelle over rocks.

"She's following him. Avriel won't like that," Odessa noted.

I watched as Avriel and Rhea neared a pool of black water that came right up to the border of the caves. There was no way to skirt this one. But there were large rocks spaced out across the pool, wide enough to stand on.

In a flash, Avriel leaped to the first one. Then the second.

The water around him remained still. If there were monsters in it, Avriel had yet to awaken them.

Behind him, Rhea followed. I watched as he turned back to look at her, a scowl marring his handsome face.

"She's bold," I observed.

"She's smug and she's cocky and she's getting too close to something far more dangerous than goblins," Crescent murmured.

Sure enough, as Rhea reached the middle of the pool, her arms out as she balanced on a rock, Avriel stepped onto solid ground. He turned, grabbed a small rock from the ground beside him and threw it back into the pool where it landed with a splash near Rhea.

Instantly the waters around the blonde girl erupted.

Goblins surged up from the depths, churning the water with their frenzied movements.

I watched in horror as clawed hands reached out, grabbing at Rhea's feet. She hopped, moved back, but there was nowhere to go. The rock was small. And the goblins had her completely surrounded.

"Her bow is useless," Odessa muttered angrily from beside me.

"Not useless," Crescent corrected. "But she's forgotten she has it."

She certainly seemed to have.

A shout rang out over the caves. Draven's voice.

Rhea's head shot up, looking across the water at the other challengers who seemed to be shouting suggestions and encouragement.

On the opposite bank, Avriel stood, his arms folded over his chest, grinning and watching.

He was fucking enjoying this. Of course, he was. What did he care that there could be more than one winner? That these Siabra could be his advisors and helpers if he ever managed to win.

He wanted to be the sole survivor. The one and only.

His ego demanded it. His vicious nature called for it.

And that was why he could never be emperor of these people. A man like Avriel would spell their certain doom and ensure another tragic mistake like the one Draven's father had made would soon be repeated, tenfold.

Rhea had pulled out her bow. She was notching an arrow with shaking hands.

A goblin had her by one ankle. She kicked it off. My heart beat faster. Maybe she could do this.

She took a shot. An arrow pierced through the face of the goblin nearest her. She started to notch another.

A goblin's hand shot out, wrapping around one of Rhea's ankles, then around her other. She tried to kick out but it was no use. Her footing faltered. As she stumbled forward, her feet literally pulled out from beneath her, she let out a piercing scream that echoed through the caves.

Her body slipped down the rock. She dropped her bow, hands clawing out, clutching at the wet rock behind her. But a hand hold was impossible.

Her body was half in the water now. The goblin's collective strength was too much. One greedy creature lunged forward, mouth opening hungrily to reveal jagged teeth as he tore a hunk of flesh from Rhea's midriff.

Her scream echoed through the caverns.

And then she was gone. Her body disappearing beneath the surface, disappearing amidst the swarm.

Only ripples remained, spreading outwards before finally dissolving into stillness.

A residue of red appeared on the surface of the water.

I looked away, my stomach churning.

"A little too close to the undead children, don't you think?" Crescent muttered.

"Are you saying our fair queen has shown poor taste?" Javer inquired, looking utterly unphased by Rhea's demise. "I'm shocked."

Odessa shrugged. "Chances are high that anything she threw at them would try to eat them."

She was right. Harpies. Fenrirs. Goblins. They were ravenous for blood and flesh. Just like the undead fae children. It wasn't like it got any better–or worse–than this.

I hoped Rhea had drowned quickly and not had to experience the torment of being devoured alive–like Lancelet had.

Avriel was already moving on.

"Does it matter who gets to the top of the cliff first?" I asked.

Odessa shook her head. "Not this time. But that could be a factor in the next challenge. In the past, some of the trials have been timed."

"And if you don't complete the trial in time?"

She glanced at me briefly. "Then you don't come out. The spectators leave though. Eventually."

I swallowed. "Lovely."

Avriel was in the lead.

I watched with interest as Brasad followed Rhea's path, copying the route she and Avriel had taken, right down to the very rock she had fallen from. But as Avriel had already gone ahead, Brasad was in no danger this time as he crossed the pool. He reached the other side, breaking into an eager run. If his arm still bothered him, he wasn't showing it.

Behind him came the others. Draven and Lyrastra, with Vespera close behind. Erion and Selwyn had stuck with Malkah in a way I thought was admirable. Draven seemed to have committed to clearing a path ahead.

Together he and Lyrastra and Vespera cleared the next pool, throwing rocks in to bring out the goblins, then slaughtering them as they emerged.

Draven entered the pool first. It was deeper than the last one he had waded through. My heart sped up as I saw he would have to swim.

But he reached the other side untouched, with Lyrastra and Vespera closely following.

Together, they urged Selwyn, Malkah, and Erion on. I watched as Malkah stepped into the pool first. She swam across it effortlessly, even under the pain of her injury, skimming over the water like a fish.

Behind her Erion and Selwyn followed, her loyal guardians.

Draven, Lyrastra, and Vespera had already gone on ahead.

Which was how Malkah came to be alone when she reached the far side of the pool and emerged only to be ambushed by a pack of goblins who raced out from the shadows of one of the caves, slathering and snarling.

Malkah did not shriek or scream like Rhea had. She simply stood up slowly, wearing a look of grim resolve on her face.

"Where are her weapons?" I asked, leaning forward. Selwyn and Erion were swimming as fast as they could towards where Malkah stood but I feared they would not reach her soon enough.

"Just watch," was all Odessa said shortly.

The goblins pounced. Malkah raised her arms. Blades shot out—directly from along her wrists. They were thin and pointed and white like bone. Sharp, fish-bones.

She pierced through the chest of one goblin, then whirled to slide a bone-blade through the eye of another.

Selwyn and Erion were climbing out of the water. Raising his dripping ax, Selwyn decapitated the closest goblin to Malkah while Erion threw his spear into another.

Then Malkah shouted a warning. More goblins were appearing from the pool they had just swam out of.

"How is that possible?" I muttered.

Odessa tapped her fingers on the rail. "They're endless. The pools are connected, down below. You can never truly clear them. I'm sure Draven figured that out already, don't worry."

The trio was quickly becoming surrounded. I watched as a look of panic came over Erion's face.

Malkah was faltering. The pain from her wound seemed to be finally overwhelming her. She continued to fight but her movements were slower. I watched as she stabbed a bone blade out towards a goblin too slowly and it jumped away, teeth bared in a hungry grin.

Selwyn was fighting fiercely. He shouted something to Erion.

But Erion was backing away, clearing his own path with determination.

"He's leaving them," I said with shock. "He's abandoning her."

Javer gave a mocking laugh from where he stood next to Crescent. "Smart man."

I glowered at him.

Crescent nudged me. "Look to the prince."

I did. Draven was coming back. Lyrastra and Vespera were going on ahead, but Draven was doubling back, following the same path he had just taken. He passed Erion without a word.

"It's pointless. She'll never make it up the cliff, even if she gets there," Odessa said softly, almost sadly as we watched Malkah and Selwyn continue their fight.

I couldn't help but think she was right. Malkah had sunk down to her knees. Her bone blades were still up, but it was clear she was failing fast.

Selwyn prowled around her, his ax picking off the goblin horde one by one.

Then Draven reached them. Together, he and Selwyn cleared the remaining few.

When it was over, he and Selwyn crouched down by Malkah, conferring.

Draven's face was hard and angry. I didn't understand why. Then he rose, tried to pick up Malkah by the waist. She resisted, pushing him away.

Selwyn stood by, his expression grim.

"She won't let them be slowed down by her," Odessa said quietly.

"Good. She should never have entered the challenge in the first place," Javer said calmly. "She nearly got them all killed."

"It was bad luck. She's a good fighter. I've seen her," Odessa countered.

Javer shrugged, but said no more.

I wanted to slap the smug expression off his arrogant face. This man thought he was going to teach me magic? He had another thing fucking coming if he thought I would ever become his pupil.

My eyes widened. "What's Malkah doing?"

The beautiful onyx-skinned woman was pushing herself along the stone on her hands, back towards the water.

Selwyn shouted something and leaped towards her, but it was too late.

With a small splash, Malkah slipped into the water.

For a moment, she floated there, her scales shimmering.

Then gnarled hands reached out, pulling her down into the depths.

Draven and Selwyn turned away, moving slowly back the way Draven had come from.

Draven was too far away for me to make out his expression. What had he thought as Malkah had slid into the water? Had he believed her foolish or brave?

She had died with dignity, sacrificing herself lest she risk the two men. Had Selwyn meant something more to her? Was that why he had stood by her so faithfully until the very end?

Watching the challenge play out, I realized I had never once truly considered that Draven could actually die. But now, watching him take risk after risk for other peoples' lives, I was becoming frightened.

Maybe it wasn't Avriel I had to worry about. Maybe it was Draven himself and his stubborn determination to try to help everyone else.

I looked at the people closest to me–Odessa, Crescent, Javer. They were here because of Draven. Because he had made a deep impression on them–even on fucking Javer.

And because they thought he was fit to lead an empire. More than fit, uniquely qualified.

He could be a ruthless bastard. He was capable of lying, manipulation, and murder.

But he also inspired loyalty. He believed in protecting the weak. He could be generous and kind.

And he slept in my bed.

An idea began to tumble through my mind as I forced my eyes back on the scene below.

To my surprise, Lyrastra had reached the cliff first. She was nearing the top with Vespera close behind her.

Erion was just below them both. He had made it past the pools alone and was starting his ascent up the cliff face.

Avriel had been cornered by a pack of goblins on the opposite side of the cavern near the cliff base. He had both of his sabers out and was fighting with impressive skill, holding off creatures on each side.

Brasad had caught up to him. Now he called something harsh and mocking to Avriel, then skirted around the pack of goblins and began climbing the cliff.

Avriel's face darkened in fury as he watched Brasad pass him by and begin his ascent.

Meanwhile Draven and Selwyn were passing through the last pool. The water in this one seemed shallow–deceptively so.

Draven had nearly crossed it when Selwyn let out a cry and sank forward suddenly. Ominous bubbles began to erupt from around him. Goblins rising to the surface.

Draven swerved back, reaching out a strong arm and grasping Selwyn by the hand, pulling him up and towards the edge of the pool just as goblins emerged from the waters around them.

The two men pushed themselves up and out, then stood back-to-back, dealing death blows to the monstrous creatures as they lurched and snarled around them.

Within a few moments, it was over. I took in Draven's appearance. His leather armor was slashed to pieces along one arm. There were scratches and cuts on his face. But he was whole. Alive. Nowhere near as injured as Malkah had been.

Selwyn was limping. His fall in the pool must have twisted his leg. But he followed behind Draven closely as they approached the cliff and began to climb.

Avriel had freed himself from the pack. Now he ran towards the cliff and began to climb, quickly gaining on Brasad who was just above.

"Lyrastra's up," Crescent murmured from beside me.

The dark-haired woman stood at the top of the cliff, looking down at Vespera who was just below her. Vespera had withdrawn her talons and was climbing with her hands. Her long brown braid hung over her back.

My heart hammered. Would Lyrastra help her? Watch her reach the top? Or take the opportunity to eliminate another contestant?

To my relief, Lyrastra reached down and grabbed Vespera by the hand, helping her up the rest of the way. The two women stood looking down at the four men below. They had made it. Through one challenge at least.

"Good for her," Crescent said, his tone somewhat admiring.

I couldn't find it in myself to say anything so outrightly positive about Lyrastra. Not yet. But her behavior in this trial had certainly altered my impression of her a little.

"She'd be better than Avriel, that's for sure," Odessa said quietly. She met my gaze, looking awkward. "We all know the prince will prevail. But Lyrastra would be an...interesting...addition to his council. Should she survive."

I nodded. "Interesting is a good word choice."

The woman who claimed she wanted to kill me, on Draven's council?

"Now what?" I stared at the two women at the top of the cliff. "They just... wait?"

Odessa shook her head. "They'll be pulled out. Watch."

A door was opening at the top of the cliff where there had been only plain stone a moment ago. Lyrastra and Vespera turned and went through, then it closed again.

There was a tittering sound from the crowd behind us and I turned to see the two women enter the gallery.

Lyrastra's head was held high, but I caught a glint of unmistakable pride in her serpentine eyes.

She had come out in first place. And what was more, she had earned it. She hadn't shoved anyone to the goblins to get there. She had even helped her fellow contenders—more than I'd ever expected her to.

Behind her Vespera was nodding to nobles she knew, her face set in a tight-lipped smile. Perhaps the challenge had been more brutal than she'd expected it to be. Still, she had made it through.

I turned back quickly to see how the others were doing. Draven and Selwyn were on the opposite side of the cliffside from Brasad and Avriel. If all went well, they should reach the top soon—and be able to keep far away from Avriel while doing it.

Brasad was not so lucky.

Avriel was climbing with preternatural speed. His gold-scaled forearms shooting out over and over to grab subtle hand holds, his strong legs moving up and up.

Soon he was parallel with Brasad.

Another moment, and he was above him.

And then, the crowd around us gasped as Avriel ascended the clifftop, pulling himself up and over the edge.

He stood there for a moment, breathing hard, his hands on his hips.

Then he grinned, leaned down to say something to Brasad, and held out his hand–just like Lyrastra had done.

I held my breath. Was Avriel actually going to show some fucking sportsmanship?

The murmurs around me said the crowd of Siabra were as surprised as I.

Brasad was grinning back. He reached a hand out to take Avriel's extended one.

Avriel gave a sharp yank and suddenly Brasad was hanging in the air, suspended by Avriel's arm.

His face seemed frozen in terror.

Then Avriel leaned forward, his teeth bared like the goblins. With a quick movement, he slashed at Brasad's wrist with his teeth, drawing blood.

Brasad let out a sharp yelp, but didn't fall. He hung suspended as Avriel placed his mouth over the bloody wrist and, to my horror, seemed to begin to suck.

When he lifted his head, Avriel's mouth was rimmed red. He grinned up at the crowd.

Then he let go of Brasad.

Shouts of shock erupted around me. I heard murmurs of anger, too.

"What the fuck was that?" I hissed, turning my head back and forth between Odessa and Crescent.

They were looking at one another, too, I realized. The brother and sister held each other's gaze. Finally, "It's symbolic," Odessa said slowly.

I stared at her. "Symbolic? What the hell does that mean?" Abruptly, I recalled one of my worst fears about my fae heritage. "I thought fae bloodlust was a myth."

"It is," Crescent said quickly. "At least, fae don't require blood in any sense. Especially the blood of other fae."

"Which isn't to say that some don't want it." Odessa's voice was biting.

"Your prince approaches," Javer cut in. "Perhaps you wish to watch this bit?"

My heart hammered as I watched Draven put his hand over the top of the cliff, mere feet away from where Avriel stood, his mouth still painted with blood.

I knew there wasn't a chance in hell Draven would take a hand Avriel proffered, but still, that didn't mean Avriel couldn't make things very difficult.

Draven's face was stony as he reached his other hand up, his eyes fixed on Avriel.

But Avriel just laughed, said something none of us could hear, then tapped on the wall behind him.

The door appeared again. He turned and passed through.

I breathed a sigh of relief.

Draven pulled himself the rest of the way up, then stood back and waited while Selwyn reached the top. He didn't offer Selwyn a hand. I supposed Avriel had rather ruined that gesture.

There was a crowing sound and I turned to see Avriel strutting through the crowd behind me.

People stood back, giving him a wide berth as he passed. The gallery had become unnaturally quiet.

I heard no congratulations.

The Queen Regent stepped forward.

Avriel sank to his knees. "I hope our performance has pleased you, my queen. May the blood of all who fell here today bring honor to the Siabra Empire."

The Queen looked at him in silence for a moment, then extended a hand serenely. Avriel took it and rose to his feet with a smile.

"You fought very well," I heard Sephone say as they turned away.

I spotted Lyrastra on the edge of the crowd, her lips pursed tightly. The Queen Regent had not commended her or offered her a hand. Or Vespera, for that matter. Did Lyrastra care?

Our eyes met. I watched as her serpentine gaze flickered over me.

"Well done," I mouthed across the crowd, knowing she would be able to read my lips.

Lyrastra's eyes widened briefly. Then she opened her mouth and hissed, her tongue briefly snaking out.

I rolled my eyes and turned away, just as Draven and Selwyn entered the gallery.

CHAPTER 20

I n a split second, my heart was in my throat and the world around us had melted away.

Draven's eyes met mine, cool, green, and familiar, and I felt my face splitting into a smile wider than any I could remember as tears pricked the corners of my eyes.

He was whole. He was alive. He had made it.

What folly was this?

At times, I had wanted to kill this man.

And yet I couldn't seem to live without him.

He walked towards me and my body screamed out warnings. But looking at him was like returning home.

I was trapped in this palace, but worse, Draven was trapped inside of *me*.

He was in my heart. In my very soul. Cracking me into pieces. Shattering the girl I once used to be. Creating me anew.

Had I had even a fraction of the same impact on him? Did it matter?

His face was grave as he walked towards me, his gaze intense and unswerving. I shivered a little, under that hard stare. But it was no wonder he wasn't smiling. He'd fought a battle while we'd all stood on the sidelines and watched, as if the lives and deaths of those below were merely for our entertainment.

And unlike Avriel, I had no doubt Draven would mourn the ones who had fallen. Rhea. Malkah. Brasad.

He would see their deaths not as Avriel's doing or the goblin's doing but as his own failure.

Because that was the sort of man he was. A man who was made to lead empires.

And as for me? Who was I in all of this?

A bystander. An outsider. A woman trying to get back home.

But for now? At this moment? I had a role to play.

And fuck it, I decided. I was going to start playing it well.

I moved towards him, feeling the gossamer fabric of the snow-white gown swaying around me like the wings of a butterfly.

I knew with every movement I made the cuts in the gown gave teasing glimpses of bare midriff and curving thighs.

Like the Lyonessian woman I had watched with not a little envy at the Rose Court ball that night so long ago, I felt filled with the knowledge of my own power and allure.

There was silence around us as I reached Draven, my slipper-clad feet light on the marbled floor.

He looked down at me, a line of dried blood along one side of his jaw, and I lifted a hand up and did what I had wanted to do so many times before.

I pushed away a falling lock of dark hair from his brow, then lifted my chin and kissed him full on the mouth.

I kissed him as if no one was watching us, as if we were the only two people left in all of Aercanum.

I kissed him as goosebumps sprang up all over my skin and until I could barely breathe.

I kissed him as I remembered the touch of his lips hot on my skin as I climaxed under his mouth.

For a moment, Draven seemed frozen and I doubted the wisdom of what I had done.

Then he kissed me back.

Reaching out his arms, he pulled me towards the sanctuary of his chest. Strong hands delicately cradled my jaw. His thumb slid along the nape of my neck, sending tremors of bliss along my skin.

Boundaries blurred and worlds collided as I relaxed against his touch, leaning into him in a daze of pleasure.

When we finally pulled apart, I made sure to steel my face into an expression of careful serenity as I glanced around the gallery.

The crowd around us had exploded into a cacophony of conversation. I assumed most of it was about us. We had stolen the show from Avriel and Sephone. From the corner of my eye, I caught Avriel watching us closely from where he stood near the queen's left shoulder.

I looked away and was just in time to catch Lyrastra as she swept out through the double glass doors and into the hall beyond.

And then everyone was crowding around us.

Beks had appeared from somewhere. He was grinning and congratulating Draven and winking at me at the same time, as Crescent chattered cheerfully to Javer while Odessa stood nearby, a faint smile on her normally stoic face.

I felt giddy and lightheaded, filled with relief. I could only imagine how Draven felt. To come from a pit of death to this gala-like setting, surrounded by people and praise.

Selwyn stood stoically behind him, his arms crossed over his huge chest, his face flinty. I wondered if he was thinking about Malkah. How close had they been? Friends or more?

Across the room, Erion was speaking to Vespera. I watched as he glanced at Selwyn, then away again.

Erion wasn't responsible for Malkah's death. No one was. But I couldn't help but feel impressed by Selwyn for refusing to leave his friend behind—and put off by Erion's desperate decision to save his own skin. Though the truth was, I couldn't imagine what I would have done in the same position. Hadn't I already come precariously close to being just like Erion once?

A buzz of anticipation was going up in the gallery around me and I realized the glass doors had swung open yet again, but this time to allow new guests entrance.

Hawl stood there with Rychel beside them.

Rychel raised a hand in greeting, then marched towards us. She was dressed in a long flowing coat of a deep shade of violet, embroidered with botanical patterns, and a pair of tailored black trousers. Shoving her hands into her pockets as she walked, the belt around her waist jingled, drawing attention to an assortment of pouches and vials. Hopefully none filled with dangerous or noxious substances. The round glass circles she favored were still perched on her nose. As she came towards us, she freed one hand from her pocket and pushed them up higher.

Behind her, Hawl followed. The proud Bearkin did not spare a single look for the Siabra who were openly gaping and tittering around them. Their broad snout and black nose were held high, quietly confident, while clever dark eyes peered out from under their shaggy brow.

"What the hell are you wearing on your face?" Draven demanded as his sister came up to us.

I grinned, realizing this was the first time I was seeing them together. Side by side, they looked even more alike. Dark hair and green eyes mirroring each other.

"Oh, these?" Rychel touched a hand to the frame on her face. "I call them glimmer-glasses."

Draven sputtered. "You call them what?" His eyes narrowed. "I've seen humans wearing something similar. They improve their vision. I know for a fact, however, that you have perfect sight."

"I do, it's true. But these give added... clarity." Rychel grinned. "Besides, what do you care what I have on my face? You're not embarrassed by me, are you?" She nudged him playfully, but I noticed her stealing a glance in Sephone's direction.

The Queen Regent seemed to be studiously ignoring Rychel and Hawl.

"Of course not," Draven said gruffly. "You can wear whatever you please..."

"Thank you," Rychel said smoothly.

"No matter how foolish you look."

"Ouch. I've missed you, too, brother." She looked at me and winked. "Lovely to see you, Morgan." Then she clapped her hands together. "Now are you all ready? Hawl has prepared refreshments. I think it's time we left this hellhole, don't you?"

"More than ready," Hawl's voice boomed out. "Already overstayed our welcome, I believe."

"If we were ever welcome in the first place, which I highly doubt," Rychel muttered. "Well, move along then, follow me."

Abruptly, she beamed at me, then pointed downwards.

I looked down and realized that somehow in the last few minutes, Draven's hand had become intertwined with mine.

"Don't forget what I told you," Rychel muttered, leaning towards my ear. "He's absolutely safe. Nothing to be concerned about."

"Oh, Zorya," I groaned with embarrassment, feeling my cheeks flushing pink. "Hush, Rychel."

Fortunately, Draven seemed not to have heard. Or if he had, he was pretending to not have. What she had said had been cryptic enough that I hoped he would have no idea what we were even talking about.

Our party followed Rychel and Hawl out of the gallery where she paused and looked at Crescent. "It would be so much faster..."

"Really, Rychel?" Crescent rolled his eyes. "I still have to fetch Gawain and Taina."

"Yes, and won't this save you time? Just stitch us over to my suite and then go back and fetch them, too," Rychel said sweetly.

"Oh, very well. It won't take much, I suppose."

We formed a circle. My hand was still in Draven's. Warm and solid. I squeezed slightly and felt the reassuring press of him squeezing back.

It was all part of the facade, I reminded myself, trying to suppress the butterflies swooping around my stomach. If it felt natural then so much the better. My part would be easier to play.

I blinked. I hadn't learned my lesson. Not that I supposed there was much to see when one stitched.

We were in a different hall, standing outside a doorway covered with very bright, very messy paintings of birds reading books.

"This is my place," Rychel said cheerfully. "Well, everyone come in." She pushed the door open and stepped back to let us pass as Crescent vanished again, presumably to collect the rest of his family.

I wandered in, peering around curiously. Rychel's living area was as much of a refreshing change from the rest of the Siabra court as she was. The suite was entirely different from her white and stark workshop.

The foyer of the suite was a domed courtyard where delicate vines cascaded from trellises hung with flowers blooming in hues I had never seen in the natural world. The uneven stones beneath our feet were covered with colorful splashes of paint, as if someone had simply tossed pots of the stuff around, determined to produce a chaotic mess of rainbows. Around us, three balconies jutted out from various levels, leading back into other rooms of the suite.

Walking across the courtyard we entered a disorderly but cozy sitting room full of overstuffed chaises and stained velvet chairs, where towering stacks of books teetered precariously alongside tall wooden shelves overflowing with thick tomes. Piles of parchment littered the floor in places, covered with hastily scrawled notes and sketches.

A spiral staircase led up to another level where I saw a large, unmade bed strewn with patterned silk pillows.

"Don't mind the mess," Rychel encouraged. "Step into my chaos. All are welcome here. Well, all of *you*, at least."

She gestured towards a wall of glass doors leading out onto a terrace on the other side of the living space. Outside was a long wooden table, set with a charmingly mismatched assortment of plates and goblets.

"Help yourselves," she said, gesturing to the piles of food and steaming dishes. "I'm sure Crescent will be here in no..."

"Time at all," Crescent finished from behind her.

Gawain stood at his shoulder, grinning. He had probably become used to all of Crescent's stitching jokes, I thought, smiling at them. In front of them, little Taina hopped back and forth from foot to foot as she stared at the mounds of goodies on the table.

"I'm starving," Beks announced loudly.

Everyone laughed and suddenly that was all it took. We pulled up seats around the table and dove in.

Hawl had outdone themselves with the feast. There were skewers of shrimp coated in dragonfire, a fiery blend of spices that Hawl claimed were a secret recipe. The shrimp had been delivered with Crescent's help from the coast that morning.

It turned out Draven was a seafood lover. As I watched as he devoured skewer after skewer, his eyes closing in bliss, a bolt of affection passed through me like lightning.

I glanced away, just in time to be offered a plate of tartlets Gawain was holding out. Taking one, I sank my teeth into a sweet velvety creamy concoction infused with crushed berries.

Across from us, I watched Javer pop a stuffed quail into his mouth, then slap Beks' hand in the next instant, just as the boy was about to pour himself a goblet of nectarine wine.

Beks's face took on a sulky expression.

I choked on my tartlet, trying to suppress my laughter. It wouldn't do to have my personal guide think I was laughing at him. Not when he had been so generous about sharing secrets with me.

"Mermaid's Song, Morgan?" Rychel asked. She was standing beside me, holding a silver pitcher. Before I could answer, she filled my goblet to the brim with something blue-green and cold. She leaned down to whisper in my ear, "This should make your night more memorable."

"What exactly is this stuff, Rychel?" Draven demanded, eyeing my goblet suspiciously as his sister filled his own.

"My own special brew," Rychel said, her eyes sparkling with mischief. "Crafted from the melodies of mermaids caught in seashells and the tears of phoenixes who lost their way home."

Draven snorted. "Stuff and nonsense."

"But there is no such thing as mermaids, is there, Rychel?" Taina asked innocently from across the table with wide eyes.

"Well, who can ever say for certain?" Rychel responded diplomatically. "I prefer to believe they may exist."

"And phoenixes?" Draven asked drily.

Rychel shrugged. "Perhaps I caught one. Why don't you visit my workshop sometime and maybe I'll show you?"

Draven rolled his eyes.

Laughing, I took a small sip from my goblet. It may not have been made of mermaid songs, but whatever it was, it tasted delicious.

A warm sensation flowed through me. I looked around the table, feeling lighter and more at ease.

Beside me, Draven was talking quietly to Odessa. They seemed to be discussing the next round of the competition.

I leaned back in my chair, trailing a hand lightly over Draven's arm. He caught it and squeezed my fingers gently.

I was playing my part perfectly and would continue to do so. It was surprising just how easy it had been so far.

Across the table, Beks was entertaining Taina with a lurid tale of a monster he had supposedly seen in the bowels of the palace–a wizened old man with holes where eyes should have been. I doubted there was any truth to the story but Taina let out a petrified squeal that drew Gawain's attention. He leaned over and tapped Javer who quickly scolded Beks with a few choice words.

Beks sat back in his chair, arms crossed, looking sulky once more.

I caught his eyes and gave him a playful wink. His expression cleared and he winked back. Then he gestured to the terrace wall behind him, where loose stones were exposed behind a shield of vines. "Want to get out of here?" he mouthed.

I grinned and shook my head. "Not now," I mouthed back. "But good to know."

There was a commotion by the terrace doors.

Beside me, Draven and Odessa leaped to their feet.

Startled, I rose with them.

Lyrastra stepped onto the terrace. She had changed out of her fighting leathers and wore a silky black tunic over silvery leggings. Her jet-black hair fell in waves behind her back. Grudgingly, I had to acknowledge once more how lovely she was. Her uncanny eyes moved around the table, a mesmerizing kaleidoscope of golden, yellow, and purple hues.

When she caught sight of Draven and me, they paused.

"Well met, Lyrastra," Draven said quietly from beside me. "You did well today."

Lyrastra nodded. "As did you." She bit her lip. "I am sorry... about Malkah. I should have turned back."

"You did a great deal more than most," Draven replied.

"Malkah had already been poisoned," Javer added. "She would never have made it up the cliff. When she went under the water, she did the right thing."

Maybe he was right, but it angered me to hear him say it so bluntly. The man seemed as unfeeling as a rock.

Lyrastra slid into a seat beside Rychel who welcomed her warmly.

"Are you all right?" Draven murmured beside me.

"What do you mean?"

"I mean Odessa told me about Steelhaven."

I looked at him. "You mean how Lyrastra wrapped a snake around my legs and then threatened to kill me?"

Draven raised one brow. "Odessa didn't mention that last part."

"That's because I didn't tell her," I admitted. I stole a glance at Lyrastra. She was smiling at something Rychel had said. She looked almost... happy. "I suppose she was very brave today."

"She was. She has a bold spirit." I felt his hand touch my face, pushing a strand of my hair back behind my ear, and I shivered. "Almost as bold as yours. Perhaps that's why she dislikes you so much. You're more alike than either of you want to admit."

"Oh, I think we both know there's another reason. One that's tall with black hair and green eyes."

"Rychel?" Draven said innocently. "I think Lyrastra prefers men."

"Very funny. I'm well-aware of her preferences."

"She doesn't hate you, you know," Draven said softly. "Rychel wouldn't have invited her here if she believed that. My little sister is a surprisingly good judge of character for someone who spends so much time in a basement."

"I heard that," Rychel called out from down the table. "It's a workshop."

Draven grimaced at her, then lowered his voice. "So, we're back at playing the game again?"

"The game?"

"This." He leaned over and brushed my lips with his. "The game. You're playing your part very well tonight."

"Am I?" I said lightly. "Should I say thanks?"

"After Noctasia, I had thought... Well, I suppose it doesn't matter." He frowned, his expression briefly turning brooding.

"Look, I wasn't ignoring you. I had a lot on my mind the next morning." I hesitated. "I had another dream that night. It was very vivid."

Draven's brow furrowed. "Another dream about the war in Pendrath?"

"No, I mean..." I paused. How could I possibly tell him what I had seen? He hadn't believed me about the other dreams. Why would he believe me about this? It was so far-fetched. "I mean yes, another dream about the war. I think... I think it's getting worse. I'm worried about Kaye."

None of that was a lie.

He nodded as if he understood. "With luck, this will all soon be over. We'll soon set things right in Camelot. Together."

"Do you really think so? There are two more challenges..."

But something was happening. Crescent and Javer were pushing back their chairs and rising to their feet, their faces grim and clouded.

Avriel strode onto the terrace.

He had changed his clothing, too. He wore a crimson cloak around his shoulders, lined with black leather. The gold scales on his forearms glistened in the light, reminding me of gleaming armor. He moved towards the table, sculpted muscles rippling under the fabric of a bronze-colored tunic. He looked stomach-churningly regal and arrogant.

Rychel rose to her feet. "Get the fuck out of my house."

"My, my, look at all of the pretty little misfits, you've assembled," Avriel crooned, ignoring Rychel and looking straight at Draven. "It's almost endearing how you cling to one another for support. The weak seek out the weak, I suppose. And that's why you, my cousin, will never make an emperor."

"Is that what it was today, Avriel?" Draven's tone was deceptively mild. "When you benefited from Lyrastra and Vespera's generous decision not to throw you off the cliff like you did to Brasad?"

I hadn't even thought of how the women might have turned on Avriel together, but Draven had a point. Lyrastra had proven herself capable, and with a companion's help she might have managed it.

They would all have been safer if she had, a voice in my head said. So why hadn't she?

Avriel glanced at where the black-haired woman sat near Rychel listening quietly. "Forgive me, Lyrastra, my dear, but it's laughable to think two women like you and Vespera could have taken me on. So, yes, it was a weakness," he said, looking back at Draven. "They did nothing because they had no other choice. It would have been sheer idiocy to have tried to thwart me."

Lyrastra said nothing. Her face was as still as ice as she watched the two men.

"Now as for you, my dear cousin, the presence of that Valtain woman beside you tells me everything I need to know about your utter lack of real ambition." He sneered at me. "I suppose it's fitting for a prince who knows nothing of true power to show such blind and pathetic devotion to someone so insignificant. What does it feel like to hang on the prince's arm, Lady Morgan? Is it like clinging to a big strong rock?"

Draven slammed his hands down on the table. The sound echoed through the room. "You like to laugh, don't you, Avriel? There's something about a smile that can goad most of your opponents, isn't there? It makes your job easier as you pick off those you perceive as weak. But while you're laughing all alone, I'll be here thanking the gods I have a woman beside me who leaves me with no doubt that she is my equal in every way. Morgan Pendragon is far from insignificant. She's a force of destiny and you would do well not to trifle with her or ever let her name cross your lips again."

"Insults only hurt when they come from people I actually respect, Avriel," I added quickly, trying not to think of how Draven had just described me as his equal in every way... and a force of destiny. "You're certainly not one of them."

"Shall I find him a short route back to whatever hell he came from?" Crescent asked, stepping forward.

"This is a fun game," Rychel chirped. "Can I play? You're an insufferable egotist, Avriel. You're one to talk about being a hanger-on when you toady up to our stepmother as if you would suck on her teat like an infant if she let you. I'd punch you in the face with the greatest of pleasure if I wasn't already so confident my brother would be doing it on behalf of us all soon. Lyrastra took pity on you today but I pray she doesn't the next time. She's worth a dozen of you put together."

Rychel leaned forward, her palms flat upon the table, her normally calm face a mask of rage. "Now get the hell out of my home before I show you just how badly this little group of misfits can fuck you up."

Hawl let out a deep, ominous growl, as Rychel glanced down the table at where the children sat. "My apologies, Taina, Beks."

Gawain already had his hands over the little girl's ears. She looked scared and nervous.

Beks' face was solemn. He was far too astute a child not to grasp everything that was happening around him.

I glared at Avriel, fury running through me—for Beks and Taina's sake but also for Rychel and Draven's. He had ruined something lovely here tonight. He had tried to make everyone present feel less-than, beneath him.

Why?

"You mistake arrogance for strength and true companionship for weakness, Avriel." My voice carried across the terrace. "You look down upon us? Despise us? But unlike you, we stand together. Look at you—alone and exposed in your twisted ambition and cruelty." I gestured to the table of people around me. "You show up here only because you're desperate, envious, and bitter. And worse, you have nowhere else to go. You can't fathom the power of friendship because you've never come close to experiencing it. And in the end, that's why they'll beat you. Because you lack qualities you can't even comprehend."

Lyrastra's eyes flickered to mine as she took in the fact I had said "they" and not simply "he."

But Avriel's sneer only deepened. "I pray you aren't about to say 'love.' I may have to vomit all over this floor if that trite word passes your lips."

"Why would I say something so pointless?" I said calmly. "When your mind is too small to grasp the concept." Beside me I felt Draven make a slight movement. "You're a bully and a coward who picks on the weakest link to make himself feel strong. The prince doesn't need to do that. He knows his own strength and he knows protecting the weak only makes him stronger." I leaned forward and spoke the last words very clearly and slowly. "That's why his legacy will live on long after you're dead."

Avriel's smile fell away. His eyes narrowed.

"Don't," Crescent said from behind him. "Say another word except 'good-bye.'"

"Good-bye?" Taina piped up.

But Avriel and Crescent were both gone.

Crescent reappeared a moment later, his usually cheerful face besmirched by a frown.

"Where did you leave him?" Gawain inquired, as Crescent sat back down beside his family with a sigh.

"An empty stall in the menagerie," Crescent replied, perking up a little and giving me a meaningful look. "It was locked so it may take him a while to get out. I don't think Master Rodrick was around."

Hawl burst into a gruff growling laugh, slapping their leg with one paw. "Fitting."

I raised my glass in a faux-toast. "Well done."

Draven's hand touched mine. "I think it's time to go."

I nodded, my heart speeding up a little. "I'm ready if you are."

"Wait." Rychel's voice carried down the table. "First, a toast if you will." She quirked her lips. "I find the Mermaid's Song inspires me."

We all rose, holding our glasses, even Beks and little Taina.

Rychel held her goblet aloft. "Here's to the fae and mortals alike, united by starlit dreams that span the skies. Gazes ablaze with stardust, their dreams become tapestries of hope as they envision guardians of realms and leaders of empires who are truly worthy. May their dreams find refuge."

Rychel paused, looking at Lyrastra beside her, then down the table at her brother. "May we all dream of a future sovereign whose noble heart heeds the aspirations of the oppressed and who safeguards the dreams of the vulnerable, igniting Aercanum in infinite possibilities."

It was evident who she had in mind. My hand slipped into Draven's again and squeezed gently.

"May their dreams find refuge," Draven echoed from beside me, nodding at his sister a little awkwardly. He raised his glass and drank.

"Hear, hear," Gawain chimed in. "To the Siabra Empire and to Aercanum. May we find true and worthy champions for our people."

"To the fae and mortal dreamers," Lyrastra said, looking down into her goblet. "To the hope that lies in dreams."

"To those who possess the heart of a dreamer," I murmured so quietly I felt certain no one else could hear.

I feared I did, whether I wished to or not.

CHAPTER 21

J aver was waiting in the courtyard as Draven and I came out.

"If I might? A moment of your time, Lady Morgan." Javer exchanged a glance with Draven and I realized he'd been expecting this.

I watched Draven walk away, already beginning to seethe.

"The prince has requested that you train with me, Lady Morgan," Javer said smoothly.

Not requested that *he* train me. That *I* train with him. As if I should be honored by the great opportunity.

"No," I said bluntly.

Normally I'd have said something like, "No, thank you." But there was something about this man I couldn't stand. So why be bothered with the niceties?

Javer lifted his hand to his pointed beard and stroked it as he studied me. "From what the prince has told me, you possess considerable power. How many times have you managed to wield it?"

"He had no business telling you that," I said furiously.

And the answer was twice. Once in Nethervale when Draven had been essentially passed out on the floor from his poisoned wound. The second in Meridium. When I'd turned Vesper to ash.

"The prince postulates that your magic is elemental. Can you confirm this?"

"He postulates?" I crossed my arms over my chest and glared at the closed door where Draven presumably stood waiting in the hallway.

"Apparently he was present the first time you used your powers, but was in no state to accurately describe them."

"That's right," I snapped. "Have I mentioned my powers are none of his business? Or yours?"

Javer's eyes narrowed. "He is our prince. If all goes well, soon to be our emperor. If he chooses to use us as tools of the Siabra Empire, who are we to decline?"

"I thought you served the Queen Regent," I said.

"I serve the Empire. And whoever rules the empire. The queen's regency is merely a stop gap. A temporary measure while we await the beginning of the next imperial age."

"I'm surprised you don't serve Avriel, to be honest," I said bluntly. "Isn't he more your type?"

A look of distaste came over Javer's face. "He's a brutal, clumsy instrument of violence and nothing more."

"And you prefer Prince Kairos because he's what... subtler?"

"I follow the prince for a great many reasons, not least of which is the fact that he is the true and rightful heir. Furthermore, subtlety is an undervalued quality in a monarch and the prince does in fact possess it in abundance, yes."

I thought of Arthur. Definitely lacking in subtlety. Perhaps Javer had a small point.

"Fine. I believe you're loyal. And you're doing what he told you, which I can somewhat respect. But I'm declining the opportunity. I have no wish to be your pupil. No offense."

I started to turn away.

"Perhaps you'd like to wait until your powers can no longer be suppressed and you burn yourself and whoever happens to be nearby to death in your sleep one night," Javer said smoothly.

I turned around. "Is that really... That's never actually happened. Has it?"

Guilt flooded through me as I remembered a promise I had made months ago.

A promise to myself. A promise to the power that lay within me. I had sworn I would never deny it again. Would never hide it away for another person's comfort or convenience ever again.

But back then, I had been thinking of Arthur and my uncle. Of those who had forced me to hide my mother's fae heritage.

This was different. Now I was suppressing my magic for a different reason.

Which was?

Being too afraid to use it?

No! It wasn't that.

Yes, it was that and more. I had no wish to wield it. I had no wish to kill with it.

Javer ignored my question. "Or perhaps," he continued. "You would rather find your-self in a situation where your life is at risk and the prince is nowhere around to save you. There you will be, waiting to see if your power will choose to manifest when you desperately need it. How many times can you deny a gift before the gift no longer comes when you call it?"

The words hit too close to home. "I..."

"Or perhaps," he went on ruthlessly. "Your power *will* come when you finally summon it. But it will come as a tidal wave does–sweeping away everything in its path, leaving nothing behind but destruction. And you'll be left as nothing but a burned-out husk once the magic has been stripped away."

I stared at him. "You're not a very pleasant person. Has anyone ever told you that?"

Javer smiled coldly. "I don't need to be pleasant. I am very good at what I do and I find that is enough. For most."

"But not for me. Because I'm not letting you near my magic. I'm certainly not going to trust you to instruct me in how to use it. And I'm certainly not going to believe any of your bullshit fearmongering words."

"Nevertheless, I will expect you in the Invocation Chamber tomorrow morning. I'm looking forward to it."

"In that case, you'll be waiting a very long time, won't you?" I whirled away, pushing the door open then slamming it hard behind me.

Draven was leaning against the wall outside, his arms folded over his chest. "So, how did that go?"

"You asked him to teach me? He's a fucking monster. You saw how he treats Beks."

Draven grimaced. "That one day... He was very annoyed with the boy. I agree, he went overboard. We've talked about it." He ran a hand over his chin. "I have to say, I'm not sure what your tutors were like in Camelot, but mine were often a lot harsher than Javer."

"Harsher than Javer? They pulled you out from under a bench and made you hover in the air frequently, did they?" I demanded.

"No, but they didn't hesitate to use canes or whips. And their words could be even crueler than their weapons."

I thought of Draven as a child, being whipped and scolded by a harsh tutor. I shook my head. "It doesn't excuse Javer's behavior. That's no way to teach a child."

"You might be surprised to find that Javer agrees. His own childhood was by no means a happy one. Have you noticed how an unhappy childhood can often lead to an unhappy person? He struggles."

I snorted. "Sure. Forgive me if my sympathy lies more with Beks, who is a child, than his master, who is a grown man."

"Javer isn't used to children, Morgan, but he's trying. I can see it. And Beks needs something of a firm hand. He's a wily little fellow. It's one thing to play and sneak off sometimes, but Beks's possesses a considerable amount of power and he needs to learn how to use it. I've weighed the options and, look, it would be much more dangerous for everyone if Beks was simply left to his own devices and grew up without Javer for a mentor. The very future of this empire may depend on people like Beks some day."

"What do you mean?"

"Well, he and Javer have a rare ability. They can shield. It's considered a very valuable skill here because so few Siabra were born with it. And to find it in a human child..." Draven shook his head. "He may be even more powerful than Javer one day."

"Well, I can't shield. So I don't see how Javer is the right person to teach me," I said stubbornly. I thought of something. "Maybe we could ask Crescent."

"Javer isn't only a shielder. He's something of a savant. He can access a range of powers, which is why he's so unique. Not to mention such a valuable ally. It's also why I specifically asked him to try to teach you. Crescent can stitch, but that's the limit of his skills. I know you like him and he likes you, but he's not what you need right now."

"Perhaps you should have asked me what I needed before you asked Javer," I said, starting to lose my temper again. "Did you ever think of that?"

"Maybe I should have. You're right. But to be honest, I'd hoped Javer would be more... persuasive."

"He basically said I was going to send us up in flames," I muttered.

Draven's lips twitched. "Well, you haven't so far."

"Count your lucky stars."

"You do have considerable power though, Morgan. Why deny it? I'm just curious." Draven's voice was calm and quiet. "Don't you want to learn about it? Learn how to use it more effectively?"

"More effectively than burning my former lover up? I'd say I was pretty effective," I snapped.

"Did you feel like you were in control at that moment? As if you could decide when the power began and when it would stop? Or did it simply... overwhelm you?"

I looked away.

A finger touched my chin. "You don't want to talk about this. I get it. Why do you think I've tried to keep my nose out of it? But Morgan, your powers are your best defense weapon against anyone who tries to hurt you or the ones you love. And right now, you don't even know how to wield them. That..." He paused. "That *kills* me."

I looked at him in surprise. The look in his eyes shocked me. He was telling the truth. I saw fear there.

"I won't always be there to protect you, as much as I want to be. But knowing you were more than able to protect yourself..."

"I'll think about it," I interrupted.

He nodded quickly. "Good. That's all I ask."

We walked back to our suite, side by side, hands brushing against one another.

Draven might have won this round, but he had no idea I was determined to win the next one that very night.

Draven had kept his armor on all through Rychel's dinner. Now he began to remove it in the sanctum of our suite. With each buckle and strap he unfastened, his powerful frame was unveiled.

I watched him out of the corner of my eyes as I sat on the edge of the bed, brushing out my hair.

He was a masterpiece sculpted from strength and grace.

Black hair hung around his face, tousled and sweat-stained, framing his chiseled features. His bronze-kissed skin shone with the day's exertion. With practiced ease, he let the pauldron slip from his shoulders. Next came the cuirass, then the close-fitting doublet, worn underneath.

I held my breath as I glimpsed his chest. It was covered with dried blood and bruises.

"You were injured today," I said sharply, taking in the wounds.

He shrugged, as if too tired to care. "A little. Most of these–" He gestured to his torso. "Have closed up already. I heal fast. You know this."

"A Siabra power?"

He nodded.

I knew. I also knew his rapid healing abilities weren't always enough. Back in Eskira, when Arthur's man had poisoned him with bloodwraith, Draven had become very ill indeed. Even now, he had no idea I was to thank for his rapid recovery.

"Very convenient," I mused as I watched him. "Claws, horns, cat-like reflexes, rapid healing. What else do you have that I don't know about?"

He grinned wickedly and I blushed.

"That's *not* what I meant."

He shrugged. "I suppose it depends on who you ask. If you spoke to a cleric–there are a few left, though the Siabra seem to have lost their devotion for the most part–and you might be told we have the gods to thank for these traits."

"And if I asked someone who wasn't a cleric?"

"They might say one of my ancestors had fucked a cat."

"Very funny." I threw my hairbrush. It landed at his feet with a thunk. I hadn't really been trying to hit him.

"No, but really, I have no idea."

"Cats don't have horns," I said primly.

"Excellent observation, milady." He smirked. "Perhaps more than one animal was involved in the... um, process."

I wrinkled my nose in disgust. "Oh, for fuck's sake, you've evidently given this a great deal of thought. What a dirty mind you have, my prince."

He laughed, then lifted the discarded armor up and hung it on a wooden stand near the wardrobe that held his everyday clothes.

I watched him run a hand over his face as he turned back to me, his handsome face in profile as he brushed his fingers over the shadow of dark stubble that clung to his rugged jaw. He shrugged his shoulders, loosening the muscles in his back, and I could see the weariness there. Every line and every sinew spoke to his commitment to defending his people with an unwavering resolve.

And his commitment to defending me.

No wonder the Siabra held an entire continent within their grasp. This man could conquer worlds if he had to.

But every battle he fought was a sacrifice, too. He fought with unyielding strength because he believed he had no other choice. Not because he wanted to. Beneath it all, I saw his weariness, his vulnerability.

He had called me a force of destiny. Which was funny, because these days I frequently felt as if I were simply being relentlessly swept along in Draven's destiny.

I wondered if he longed for solace and respite as much as I did.

He turned to face me, his bare chest rising and falling with each breath. I swallowed hard as our eyes locked.

"I'm going for a bath," I said hurriedly.

He nodded. "I think I'll turn in. Long day training tomorrow."

My jaw hung open for a split second before I managed to close it.

Kairos Draven had just told me his plans for the next day.

"Right."

I left the room and drew a hot, steamy bath, taking my time as I lathered away the metaphorical grime that had come from being in the presence of people like Avriel and Sephone.

Draven could have died today.

Others had died.

Then there was me. The supposed Prince's Paramour. The one he had delegated to stand by his side—and to sleep in his bed.

Until recently, I had resisted the label with every fiber of my being.

But that night in Noctasia... It had opened my eyes to a world of new possibilities.

If we were going to perpetuate this relationship fraud, why not go all the way?

Especially when every day with Kairos Draven felt like a matter of life or death.

Was I really going to let him go into the next challenge without another taste of the potential between us?

And if I could bring him some small measure of comfort from the burdens he bore, so be it.

I fucking wanted to.

I wanted him.

I was done dancing around.

I finished my bath and patted myself dry, then slipped back into the bedroom.

Draven had dimmed the lights. His back was to me and it looked as though he was already asleep.

Exactly how I wanted it.

I lifted the covers on my side, and slid underneath, completely naked.

Tonight, I wasn't staying on my side of the bed.

I moved over to the center of the mattress. I had never gone past this point before. It felt as if I were crossing an invisible line in the sand.

Taking a deep breath, I moved closer towards Draven's back. From past experience, I knew he'd be wearing something underneath. But he was bare from the waist up.

I pressed up against him, my breasts flush against his skin.

He wasn't even awake yet but I was already feeling flames shooting through me merely from this much contact.

I reached out one arm and curled it around his chest, brushing my hand over his nipples lightly.

I felt his body go perfectly still. He was awake.

"Morgan?" His voice sounded funny. Hoarse and constricted. "What are you doing?"

"Oh, you know," I said conversationally. "Sharing your bed."

"This... isn't how we usually share it."

"I thought I'd change things up."

I squirmed a little closer against him, pressing my hips against his firm buttocks. He groaned.

"Morgan..."

"What?"

"If I turn over, you'd better not scream," he warned. "I'm turning over now."

I didn't think he'd realized yet just what he'd be turning over *to*.

"All right," I said innocently. "You do what you need to do."

He moved onto his back, then flipped onto his other side to face me.

I didn't move away.

I heard his quick indrawn gasp of breath.

"Fuck me."

"I'm trying to."

"You're fucking... Morgan, where the hell are your clothes?"

"I seem to have misplaced them."

"You misplaced them?" He swore. "I'll kill Breena."

"That's not very nice. I'm sure there are clothes somewhere. Just not here. On me."

I wiggled my body against him, pressing my breasts flat against his hard chest. I couldn't help it. I let out a little moan. He felt so good.

And down below? Fuck, he was so hard already. I could feel him, bulging against me. I arched my hips a little, trying to increase the contact.

His hand shot out, grasping the swell of my waist.

"Yes, please," I gasped.

"What is this?" His voice was rough and demanding. Perfect. That was exactly how I wanted him tonight.

"This is what I want. If you want it, too, then I don't see a problem. Isn't this what we're supposed to be doing after all?"

"Stop playing around," he snarled. I could hear the tension in his voice. "This isn't part of the game."

"Isn't it?" My tone became more serious. "I think it is, Draven. You're the one who put us in this position after all... I mean, not this position precisely, but the one where we have to pretend we're fucking."

He groaned.

"What?"

"Don't say that word in that way."

"What?" I said innocently. "Fucking?"

"That's the one." His breathing was ragged. "Fuck."

"So you can say it but I can't?"

"Does it make you want to fuck me when I say it?"

"A little," I admitted. "Yes."

"Oh. Well..."

"So we're agreed then? We both want this? You want to fuck me?"

There was exactly one split second of silence and then I found myself flat on my back.

Draven straddled me. His hips ground against mine. It was my turn to let out a raspy little gasp.

"Yes," he growled. "Yes, I want to fuck you, Morgan."

"Good," I gasped. "Maybe we could move things along."

I thrust my hips upwards a little, hoping he'd get the idea and take off his pants.

"Since when did you get so eager?" His teeth nipped at the sensitive flesh of my earlobe, then moved downwards, brushing over my neck.

"Oh, you know," I stalled.

Draven's face hovered over mine. "Did you and Vesper ever...?"

I frowned. "Is this really the time for such personal questions? Look, I don't want to talk about Vesper. Just promise you won't try to kill me like he did and we'll be fine."

"I think I can promise that," Draven said levelly, his emerald eyes locked with mine.

He slid off the bed abruptly then, shucked off the thin black pants he'd been wearing.

"Yes, that's better," I said, my voice strained as I took in the sight of him, long hard length showing his readiness for exactly what I had in mind. "Who knows, maybe you can teach me a few things."

Where was this coming from? This was not in the script, Morgan. I wasn't brash and cocky. Yet now, I suddenly was. I could tell how much it was driving Draven crazy, too.

Gradually, I realized he was still standing beside the bed.

"We can't do this."

"What are you talking about? I think we've just established that we absolutely can."

"You don't understand. We can't do this. Once we start, I won't be able to stop."

"I think that's the point, if I understand things correctly," I said slowly.

Draven leaped onto the bed, straddling me again. His hands were on my breasts, covering them, playing with my nipples as I tried to focus on what he was saying.

"You don't understand, Morgan. I want to teach you everything," he said, his voice thick with need. "And once we start, I might not be able to stop. I don't know if I can just do this the one time... Not with you."

"I'm sure we can negotiate seconds and thirds." I gasped as his fingers tweaked one puckered nipple. "Maybe fourths." I paused. "Did you mean all in one night?"

"One night. Two nights. We could make this a nightly thing. I wouldn't complain." He ducked his head to my neck, biting slowly and I moaned.

"Fuck, that feels good. Draven, please..."

He reached a hand down and I felt what I'd been looking for. The touch of his cock at my slick entrance.

He looked down at me. "Are you sure you're ready? You don't want..."

"I don't need anything but you, this, right now," I said, my voice a little higher and more desperate-sounding than I would have liked. "I'm ready. Very ready."

I moved against him, but he moved away.

His lips found mine. His kiss was surprisingly soft and gentle. "I just want this to be good for you. I don't know who you've been with before, what you've done. I don't need to know any of that. I'm just saying, I want this to be good. Between us. Tonight."

"I do, too," I said, suddenly shy.

He was being sweet. I didn't want sweet. I hadn't planned for sweet. I had planned for fast and rough, surprising and quick. That was all I had been able to imagine ahead of time.

"I want this, I do. Please, believe me. And it will be good. Because... it's us," I said softly. And I knew it was true. Irrefutably true.

He nodded.

Then he slid into me as his lips touched mine again.

My thighs wrapped around his waist instinctively as he pushed inside, stretching me to my limits, taking me and making me completely his with one long stroke.

I lifted my hips, meeting him as he thrust, fucking him back, and forcing him deeper.

He lowered his mouth to mine, hungrily, desperately, kissing me with a fierceness that left me shaken and panting.

It wasn't the fucking I should have been worried about, I realized with a jolt.

It was his kiss.

He kissed me as if he couldn't get enough of me. As if he couldn't fuck me without kissing me. As if he needed me, every inch of me, as if my body were a part of his own and we were becoming one.

His hands slid along my body as he stroked his cock in and out. My skin was on fire, pleasure sending me spinning and soaring. The bliss was so sublime it was rapidly becoming unbearable.

I could feel the heat simmering over my skin, sizzling and steaming.

This had never happened with Vesper, I thought hazily. Not like this.

Draven took me again and again, his cock hard and relentless as he held my hips with a surety and possessiveness I secretly adored.

I wanted him deeper still. More and more and still more. Never ending. Never stopping.

The simmer became a boil. The pleasure grew inside me, building to a powerful point as our bodies collided over and over.

I touched my hands to his chest and then gasped. My golden-hued skin was glowing. More than it usually did. The silver markings were moving over my skin, rolling and swirling like liquid fire in a cauldron.

I removed my hands quickly, grasping the bed sheets instead.

"Draven," I said, my voice a little frantic.

He gave a long, slow, beautiful thrust and I gasped, arching my back.

"You're mine," he growled. "All mine."

"Don't stop," I gasped, forgetting about the sheets. "Don't ever stop."

And then he was thrusting deeper, pushing me over the edge, and I was begging, groaning, cursing, sobbing, crying his name and the flames were shooting out of me as my body clenched around him and a climax tore through me so deep that I was lost.

I heard Draven let out his own sound of rapture as pleasure crested through him. His forehead came down to rest against mine, his breath hot on my face as I felt him spill into me with a groan.

There was silence for a moment.

I was afraid to move my hands.

Finally, I lifted them.

"Draven," I said, my voice small. "I think I've scorched the sheets."

He sat up, looking down at the bed where my hands had just been clasping the fabric. Black marks were seared into the silk on each side of us.

"Well, that answers that question."

"What question?"

"You've been suppressing your power and it needed to come out. Somehow." He met my eyes and grinned. "You didn't set us on fire, don't worry."

"Yes, but..." I began.

"No buts," he growled playfully, nipping at my breasts. "You needed this. In more ways than one."

"True," I agreed. "But..."

But Draven was already flipping me onto my stomach. One hand reached between my legs, then slid up to make a slow teasing circle around my clit. I gasped.

"How many scorch marks do you want to leave Breena?" he asked in a lazy voice.

"How many do you think is the right amount?" I gasped again as his other hand cupped my breast, rubbing a thumb over a puckered nipple.

"I'd say at least five sets to make it even," he whispered, his breath hot against my ear. "We'd better get started."

CHAPTER 22

I woke up the next morning alone. My hair was in knots and I smelled of sex. A great deal of it.

Padding to the bathing room, I reluctantly washed Draven's scent from my body, then pulled on a sleeveless white tunic and loose-fitting black pants with a silver belt.

I was just fastening the belt around my waist and contemplating breakfast when there was a knock at the door.

"Good morning." It was Crescent. Behind him stood Odessa, looking faintly bored.

"Did we have plans today?"

Crescent's eyebrows lifted. "Yes, I thought you already knew."

"Knew what?"

"Apparently the prince has something he'd like to show you in Noctasia. I'm to take you." He nodded at Odessa. "She's along for the ride."

Behind him Odessa waggled a hand.

"Oh." The surprise on my face must have been manifest for Crescent cocked an eyebrow. "This is news to me," I explained. "The prince didn't mention it. Do you know where exactly we're going?"

Crescent shrugged. "Some obscure shop in the market district. I was given the message this morning." He snapped his fingers. "Perhaps one of the servants was supposed to deliver a similar one to you this morning but forgot?"

"Perhaps," I agreed. "Well, I'm dressed so let's go."

We stitched into the city, appearing on a bridge overlooking the lake. Crossing over it, Odessa and I followed Crescent as he began to walk in the direction of a crowded part of the city where narrow alleys led into shadowy streets.

"Not the best neighborhood," Crescent observed. "But the prince probably has some trick up his sleeve. A present for you, no doubt." He grinned at me playfully and I tried to grin back.

"No doubt," I echoed.

The night's activities were fresh in my mind. Draven's touch still resonated through my body. I could feel him inside me even now if I tried.

I shook my head and attempted to focus.

"The prince said he had training today," I remarked.

"He must have decided to take part of the day off," Crescent suggested. "No doubt he feels well-prepared by now."

He walked a few feet ahead as Odessa trailed behind me. As we entered a shaded alley full of shops, our footsteps were silent as we padded over the cobblestones.

Crescent took a sharp turn, then another. Nothing around me looked familiar. We had come quite a distance from the lake.

"We're close to the shop," he assured me, looking over his shoulder.

I nodded and glanced back at Odessa. She was frowning and looking around, perhaps wondering as I was why exactly the prince was sending us to this shadowy corner of the city. It seemed an odd place to deliver a gift–or a surprise.

I turned back to Crescent to ask him what kind of shop we were searching for exactly just as an object whizzed past my head buzzing like an angry bee.

Behind me, Odessa let out a sharp yell.

"Odessa!" Crescent whirled around with an alarmed expression.

I turned to see Odessa standing with her arms outstretched, a thin dagger caught between two of her fingers. Her face was flinty. "We're under attack. Crescent, get her to cover."

But it was too late for that.

They encircled us. A ring of assailants from either side of the alley, their faces hidden beneath black masks that exposed only their eyes. They were dressed from head to toe in the same color. Most wore gloves as well.

There were weapons in their hands. Gleaming daggers. Curving swords. A sharp-edged mace.

"She comes with us," one attacker said menacingly, stepping forward. Their voice was too distorted for me to make out anything else about them.

From behind me, I heard the sound of two blades being drawn swiftly.

"No," Odessa said, her voice low.

Immediately a skirmish began as Odessa's lithe figure spun into action, engaging the three attackers at my back.

Just in front of me, Crescent was frozen as he looked at the assailants blocking our way out the other side of the alley.

"I could stitch us out," he whispered indecisively, taking a step backwards.

He reached for my wrist.

"No!" I hissed. "We can't leave Odessa."

Yet I was all but weaponless. There was a blade tucked into my boot. A small dagger I had recently pilfered from Steelhaven in case I ever needed it. Now I cursed myself for depending on others for my protection. If I had been carrying a sword, I would have been engaging our assailants already.

I reached down slowly to pull the dagger out, just as a masked attacker lunged towards Crescent.

In an instant Crescent was thrown to his feet, tossed down like a feather as his attacker stood over him, a booted foot planted on his chest.

"Let him go!" I shouted. My dagger was in my hand. I swallowed as the two assailants behind the one holding Crescent down moved forward. Could I do this without Crescent being hurt?

The masked assailant leaning on Crescent's chest turned slowly as if daring me to stop them.

From beneath their concealing mask, only dark eyes showed. I let out a string of curses under my breath.

"Let him go," I demanded, making my voice as imperious as I could. But I knew it would be no use.

I wasn't even sure they wanted me. Perhaps this was simply some game. Murdering courtiers from the palace for sport—and robbing them of their goods. In any case, Crescent was a far more valuable hostage than I was considering his unique talent.

I was considering mentioning that, just as Crescent's attacker moved their foot to his neck and began pressing down slowly.

In an instant, my stomach was in my throat.

My heart drummed in my ears.

I saw Pearl, her neck compressed by Avriel in the training ring as the life was squeezed out of her.

Crescent's eyes were desperate. His mouth opened soundlessly in a wordless plea. He wasn't getting enough air to be able to speak. I watched his eyes darken and then begin to close.

"No!" I screamed. "You can't do this. No!"

Around me, the ground began to shake.

The assailant glanced around nervously but did not remove their foot.

Rage was building in me like a torrent of water beating against the walls of a cracking dam.

"No!" I shouted again.

The attacker's head turned towards me. But their foot remained on Crescent's throat, heavy and oppressive.

It didn't matter. It was already too late.

Tendrils of power were flowing through me, lapping at my ankles, whirling around my waist.

The ground beneath us was trembling, cobblestones shaking and splitting apart.

I reached out my arms, closed my eyes, and screamed as I erupted in a torrent of flames.

Around me energy crackled and hissed. The air was suddenly filled with the sound of splitting wood and falling rock and above it all the high-pitched screams of terrified people being scorched alive.

I couldn't control it. This was beyond anything I had felt before. The power was shooting out of my hands, my feet. Was it screams coming from my mouth or was it flames?

I was the inferno. I was the scorching wave, consuming everything in my path.

Cries echoed through the alley and then died away.

I felt as if I were floating, levitating in the air. The heat rushing from me wasn't painful. It was a sweet relief, like the refreshing coolness of a storm after a hot day.

And then it was over. As suddenly as it had begun. I was empty, falling to my knees.

The air crackled once with a final malefic swell of energy and then there was silence.

I opened my eyes to a scene of death and destruction.

The outer walls of the buildings around us were crumbling.

In front of me, Crescent was slowly sitting up, coughing hoarsely as the smoke cleared around us. His clothes were singed and a layer of ash covered him, but he was alive.

I looked at the ash, my stomach churning with comprehension.

A hand touched my shoulder.

Odessa's eyes were wide. Her face was painted with soot.

Behind her lay the burned corpses of the assailants she had been fighting.

I turned, seeing the bodies of our other attackers lying prone and blackened up ahead.

They had been running to flee the alley in the other direction. But they hadn't been fast enough.

My powers had erupted and swept them into the firestorm.

Odessa moved to pull down the sleeve of her tunic but it was too late.

"What is that?"

Slowly, she pulled the sleeve back up.

Burn marks. Raw exposed skin ran from her wrist to the top of her shoulder, angry and red. The leather of her armor had been melted to her shoulder on one side. It looked incredibly painful.

"I did that?" I felt the bile rising in my throat. "I did that to you?"

Odessa cleared her throat. "It's all right. It's nothing. I'll see a healer. It will be fine."

I shook my head, bitter tears stinging my throat. "It's not nothing. It's not fine. Your armor is fucking melted to your skin. Are they gone? Is Crescent all right?" I turned to him. He was pushing himself to his feet. "I'll fucking slaughter them if they touch you again."

Odessa's hand touched my shoulder again gently. "They're gone, Morgan. You... took care of them all."

"I'm so sorry," I said, looking between brother and sister. Their eyes were wide. Were they scared of me? "I'm so sorry I did this to you."

The sound of someone clapping slowly came from behind us.

I whipped my head around.

"You!"

Javer walked towards me, a small smile on his bearded face.

Behind him, Beks followed slowly, his head hung low.

In a flash, I understood. "You did this. You set this up."

"Why would I do such a thing?" Javer asked, his piercing eyes holding my own. It was not, I understood, a denial.

"It was a fucking test," I said, gritting my teeth. "People died."

"*Mercenaries* died," Javer corrected me. "Not people. Blades for hire. They knew what they were getting into. They shouldn't have been in this line of work if they didn't."

"Did they?" I demanded. "Did they really understand? You told them they'd be facing someone with uncontrollable magic who might mercilessly burn them all to death?"

"From what I saw, you controlled yourself quite well," Javer replied. "After all, Odessa and Crescent are still standing. In fact, I'd say you held back too long. I would recommend acting more swiftly the next time. Not waiting until your friend almost dies with a boot to his throat."

I looked past Javer at Beks. "You. You told him what we saw."

Beks looked as if he were about to cry.

"It's all right, Beks," I said wearily. "It's not your fault."

Instead of looking relieved, Beks burst into tears, then whirled away and ran back down the alley.

"The boy is fond of you," Javer observed. "We could work together, the three of us. I could train you both."

I clenched my jaw. I took a menacing step forward and Javer backed up one. "Never. I will never work with you. You almost got Odessa and Crescent killed today. And for what? Do you even care?"

"It's their job to protect you. I'm sure the prince would be eager to know how quickly they failed. And we've learned a great deal from this, you and I," Javer said, not even glancing after Beks. "As I suspected, you have a notable flaw."

If I roasted Javer where he stood, would anyone care? Would Draven chastise me? I knew the empire needed shielders, but just how much trouble would I be in?

I curled my hands into fists then slowly uncurled them, feeling Javer's eyes on me. "Oh? And what's that? Caring for other people?"

Javer tilted his head then lifted his huge, eagle-like wings behind him. The feathers fluttered impressively, then folded back again. I recalled what Odessa had told me. He had wings but could not fly.

He also had a heart he wasn't using.

"You care, yes, but not about yourself. Your sense of self-preservation is dangerously lacking." Javer's black eyes were shrewd as he looked at me calculatingly. "Tell me something. On the two occasions prior to this when you used your powers, was it in your own defense or in defense of someone you cared about?"

My mind raced. The first time was in Nethervale. I had been protecting myself and Draven. Would I have been able to access my powers so swiftly if I hadn't known that Draven was lying there behind me, utterly defenseless?

The second time... I was in Meridium. Vesper had already stabbed me once. And Draven... Draven was coming. Vesper was going to ambush him. Strangle him with a wire. A coward's attack.

I'd stopped him. But I hadn't saved myself.

No, Draven had saved me. Somehow, he had gotten me back to the palace in time to reach a healer.

Javer was watching me steadily. "As I thought. You used your powers to save the prince both times."

"I didn't fucking say that," I snarled.

Nearby, I saw Odessa nervously step back. I didn't blame her.

"You didn't have to. It's written all over your face." Javer's face twisted into a smile. "The word you refused to say to Avriel. It's what drives you to use your powers. You won't use them otherwise, not even for your own good. How absolutely charming. How incredibly fascinating. But of course, that has to change."

He nodded past me to where Crescent was slowly rising, his sister's arm wrapped around his waist. "I wouldn't have let anything actually happen to him, you know. Beks and I were close by. We would have shielded you all before it came to that."

My face contorted with fury. "I don't believe you. Look at Odessa. Just look at her!" I took a step towards Javer, backing him up against a wall. "You egotistical, abusive, maniacal bastard. You might have killed us all and for what? To prove a fucking point?"

"What the hell is going on here?"

I whirled around.

Draven had entered the alleyway. Behind him Ulpheas followed at a slower pace.

I watched Ulpheas's baby-blue eyes expand as he looked around him, taking in the crumbling buildings and charred bodies.

"Morgan." Draven reached me and gripped my shoulders. "Are you all right?" His face hardened as he looked past me to Javer. "What the hell happened here?"

I could feel myself shaking under his hands. I took a deep breath, trying to steady myself. "What happened is your court mage thought it would be a good idea to give me an unplanned test." I looked past him to Ulpheas. "He's a stitcher, isn't he?"

"Yes," Draven said distractedly. "Lyrastra sent him to me. She suggested I find out where you were."

"Lyrastra? I suppose that makes sense. She wouldn't want anyone to steal the pleasure of killing me before she had a chance to do it," I said bitterly.

Draven let go of my shoulders abruptly. His green eyes darted around the alley, taking in Odessa's shoulder, the bodies, the crumbling walls, Crescent's stunned expression.

"My lord prince," Javer said hastily as Draven's eyes fell upon him. "I can explain. If this was a test, she passed with flying colors. Why, look at these two. Hardly injured at all. Somehow, she managed to kill all of the others while your friends remain unscathed."

"Yes," Draven said slowly. "My friends. Your friends, too. Not merely Morgan's guards. Friends. And as for Morgan herself? My paramour? You set armed men upon her? You had her ambushed on the chance she would be able to defend herself? What if she had failed?"

"I knew that would never happen," Javer said swiftly. "She's incredible. You were absolutely right to demand she receive training."

"No," Draven said. "I was wrong. And so were you."

Javer paled.

Draven lifted his arms as if about to deliver a blow. I saw his hands were trembling. Slowly, he lowered them again. "You know what I would do to most men in your stead, Javer. I have given you more chances than most ever would."

Javer straightened his back and lifted his chin. "I live to serve. I die to serve. I accept the error of my ways, though it was not my intent to cause harm or offense, my prince. Do what you will. I accept your judgment. You have my loyalty, always, even to the death."

Fuck.

Javer was managing to impress me, even after all he had done.

I still wanted to kill him slowly. But he had fucked up and admitted it. Just as Draven had done. That took guts.

Or he simply knew the right words to say to get himself one last chance.

"Go back to the palace," Draven said, his voice low and menacing. "Morgan will not be receiving training from you. If you come near her like this again, I will not hesitate to kill you."

"I understand." Javer bowed his head.

He scurried out of the alley like a rat from a sinking ship, his large wings fluttering behind him.

Draven turned back to where Odessa, Crescent, and I stood silently waiting.

I watched as he took a deep breath. "Odessa, Crescent. I pray you will not blame Morgan for your injuries. Javer erred greatly. But my error was still greater. I should never have asked him to become involved in Morgan's training." He met my gaze. "Can you forgive me? I should never have gone to him. It was my fault this happened."

"It was Javer's fault." I shook my head stubbornly. "Not yours. And no one is to blame for Odessa's injury but me, the one who gave it to her. Whether I meant to or not, I did that."

"Does this mean there's no gift?" Crescent piped up. I was shocked to see a smile already playing at the corners of his mouth. "I was told there would be a gift."

"You're rallying quickly, aren't you?" I grumbled. "There's obviously no gift."

Draven raised one dark brow. "Gift?"

"Crescent was given a message saying to bring me to a shop nearby where you'd be waiting with a gift," I explained. "All part of Javer's neat little ambush."

"Ah, I see." Draven glanced down the alley. "As it happens, there is a gift. But I wasn't planning on giving it to you until after the next challenge." His lips twitched. "If I survived."

I punched him on the arm. "Don't you dare fucking say that."

"Of course, you'll come through the next round admirably," Odessa agreed stoutly.

Draven's eyes narrowed in on her burns. "Odessa, what are you even still doing standing here?" He snapped his fingers and Ulpheas came running. "Get Odessa to a healer back in the palace."

Ulpheas bowed his head. "At once."

Before they vanished, the blonde man looked at me. I thought I caught a glint of something resembling respect in those blue eyes. But then, I told myself, it was probably just dust.

"Crescent, my apologies. I should have asked if you wished to go with your sister," Draven said, clapping a hand to his forehead.

Crescent shook his head. "I can remain above. I assume you'll need me to get home."

"Find us here in an hour then," Draven instructed, listing an address I didn't recognize.

Crescent turned to go, then hesitated. "I'd rather follow you both, if you don't mind. I failed Morgan once today already. Let me stay where I can be of some use. Just in case?"

Draven's face turned sympathetic. "Of course. If that's what you want."

"I'll stay a good distance behind," Crescent promised. "Give you your privacy."

Draven smiled. "That sounds good." He looked at me and held out his hand. "If you're ready?"

We walked out of the alley. I flinched as we passed the two burned bodies of the assailants who had been trying to run.

"Ulpheas will send someone to take care of... all of this," Draven said, his voice low. "The city will be notified that you were attacked and defended yourself with the help of your guards. That's all they need to know."

I nodded tightly.

His hand squeezed mine. "I truly am sorry. I fucked up. Hugely. I know that."

"You did," I agreed. "Hugely." I glanced at him. His face was wry. "But at least you admitted it. And you did say Javer was the best."

"He is the best," Draven agreed. "But there's someone else who's also uniquely qualified. I thought it would be arrogance to suggest they could train you at first. But now I think it was a different kind of arrogance not to."

"What do you mean?"

"I mean if you'll let me, I'll take Javer's place. Let me be the one to help you, Morgan. I won't even say 'train.' Just... let me help you find your way. You have power. But it clearly frightens you..." He paused, his expression questioning.

"It does," I admitted. "Now more than ever. You saw what I did back there."

He nodded. "Your powers are... intimidating. I won't deny it. And you're right–you might have killed Odessa. Or both of them."

"Thanks," I said drily.

But in my heart, I knew we were both right. I truly might have. Or worse. What if I had gone beyond the walls of the alley? What if I had managed to take out entire buildings of people? What if I had harmed children?

"If you ever hurt anyone you cared about or an innocent, you would never forgive yourself, Morgan," Draven said softly. Clearly my face was too easy to read. "So, let's make sure that doesn't happen. Let's get you to the point where you feel in control. I imagine it doesn't feel very good not to feel in control of your own body."

"It doesn't. It's awful. And... last night..." I glanced behind me. Crescent had stayed true to his word and was two blocks behind us. "I stupidly thought that might be enough. That I had purged some of this."

"So you fucked me to get your powers out?" Draven joked. "I'm sorry it didn't work."

"Well," I teased. "There were scorch marks. But I guess it wasn't enough." I sighed. "I don't mean that in a naughty way either."

"I know," he said quietly, squeezing my hand again. "Not that I'm not willing to do my part to help. In any way you need." He winked. "But I think what you really require right now is guidance. You have to learn to direct your powers, to shield yourself and others from its effects. When you use them, what happens?"

"I erupt. I lose control. I'm barely aware of what's happening. If I hit a bad guy, it's luck and instinct, not a matter of having good aim. And I have been lucky so far," I acknowledged. "With Vesper... I just... burst. Like a dam. All I knew was I had to stop him."

"But you couldn't." Draven's voice was very gentle. "You didn't stop him, Morgan."

"But I did."

I watched his eyes widen in surprise.

I scowled. "That was what Javer was so cleverly pointing out."

"What do you mean?"

"I mean..." I licked my lips. Had I really never told him? "I wasn't trying to save myself from Vesper. I was trying to save you. And I did."

"Tell me everything," Draven said, his eyes intense as he looked at me.

I sighed. "We heard you coming. Vesper was going to ambush you. He had a length of wire. It wasn't going to be a fair fight." My eyes locked with his. "I couldn't let him do that."

"So you killed him. To protect me."

I nodded. "I didn't know who else was with you. I had hoped... maybe Lancelet..."

He looked away. "No such luck."

"That wasn't your fault. I know you tried." There was a lump in my throat.

"I thought you killed him to protect yourself." Draven shook his head. "You did it for me."

I snorted disdainfully, thinking of how easily Vesper's blade had sliced through me. "I did a poor job if it was to protect myself. I don't know if shielding is supposed to be part of this, but I have no idea how to do it if so."

"Elemental wielders often can shield, but not all," Draven mused. "We'll have to give it a try and find out."

He stopped. "Here we are."

I looked up to see a quaint, half-timber shop. Curving bow windows framed in delicate ironwork protruded out into the street, laden with an assortment of trinkets and pretty curiosities. Weathered stone steps led up to a heavy oak door where curling gold letters displayed the shop's name.

"Arcane Masterpieces of Myntra," I read out loud. "Really? How arcane can they be if they're being sold in a shop in a major city?"

Draven swatted my arm playfully. "Please keep your skepticism in check. The owner of the shop does not take kindly to critics."

He pushed open the door and stepped inside as the bell over the doorframe rang out with a soft tinkling sound.

A woman stood with her back to us, bent over a stack of books she was sorting. Her dark red hair fell loosely over a tight-fitting black silk dress that accentuated her curving figure. Polished black leather boots and lace stockings peeked artfully out from under the knee-high silk skirt.

As she heard us enter, she began to turn, catching sight of Draven first. "Oh, it's you. I thought you weren't coming until later in the week."

"Plans changed," Draven replied, just as I exclaimed, "Laverna?"

My hands were fishing for the knife in my boot before I could say another word.

Draven's hand shot out and grabbed my wrist. "Stop, Morgan. It's not what you think."

"No?" I said furiously. "Are you sure? Because I *think*—no, I'm pretty fucking sure—that she was working with Vesper all along."

"I know. But she wasn't. I checked."

"What do you mean 'you checked'?" I demanded. "You've met with her before this?"

"Of course, he has. He had to. In order to prepare your little surprise." Laverna came towards me, a beguiling little smile on her lips.

"If it's a gift from her, I don't want it," I spat, turning back towards the door.

"Morgan, wait. You burned her inn down. Don't you think you at least owe her a moment to hear her out?"

I turned back slowly. "Oh, that's low. *I* burned her inn down, did I? As I recall, she and Vesper arranged that ambush. An ambush where you almost died, might I add."

"Vesper arranged it," Laverna said smoothly. "I would never have risked my inn. I knew he thought you might be attacked that night and that he planned to follow you, nothing more. That man always had more tricks up his pretty sleeves than I could ever keep track of."

"Right," I said sarcastically. "You knew nothing about his plan to use my blood to open a magic portal in a lake to get a priceless enchanted sword and then murder me."

"No," Laverna said simply. "I didn't. Meridium... Vesper and I went there once, looking for treasure. He probably told you. Once was enough." She shuddered.

"Fine, you don't like Meridium or undead children. That doesn't mean you weren't in on his plan," I snapped.

"Morgan, look at me." It was Draven. His green eyes were reassuring. "I knew as soon as Laverna arrived in Noctasia. I make it my business to know these things. But also, she wasn't bothering to hide. Her story checks out. I've known Laverna for a long time." He glanced at her. "She's a lot of things, but not a murderer. I mean, not like..."

"Not like Vesper," I finished. "She'll kill for money though, like he did. Wasn't that the entire point of her inn for assassins?"

"*Rogues* and assassins. Personally, I prefer theft," Laverna said, studying her nails. They were lacquered in a bright bold red. "But I'm an honest woman now. I'm starting anew. This is my latest project."

I looked around the shop, still disbelieving. "Is this all of your stolen merchandise? Arcane objects you and Vesper collected?"

For a moment, Laverna looked sheepish. "Some of them. I also make my own." She crossed her arms over the black silk bodice of her gown and leaned back against the polished wood shop counter.

"That's what I commissioned her for," Draven explained. "To make something for you that no one else could." He glanced at Laverna. "Look, can I just take Morgan to the back?"

She nodded. "If the interrogation is through..."

Laverna smiled sweetly at me as I passed.

"Strange place to purchase a gift, Draven," I hissed as I followed him through a doorway hung with ribbons and beads that clattered as we passed through.

I stopped talking abruptly as Draven led the way into a marvelous little room that resembled an armorer's workshop.

The air was filled with the scent of cured leather. Sunlight filtered through small, dusty windows high up on one wall, casting beams that danced over the worn stone floor. Shelves lined the walls, displaying an array of tools, dyes, and rolls of supple leather in various textures and shades. Patterns and sketches covered one entire wall. Detailed designs for armor and various accessories. Pauldrons, helmets, cuirasses. Racks and hooks hung from the ceiling on one side of the room, displaying beautifully crafted leather pieces glistening in a multitude of dark colors and intricately engraved with cryptic sigils and runes.

In the center of the room lay a large workbench, where a pair of gauntlets sat.

They were molded from gleaming black leather. On the back of each hand was an embossed motif of dyed-red roses, each petal meticulously etched with lifelike precision. A pattern of gold and silver flames wound up the sleeves.

I froze. "Are those... for me?"

Draven was already picking them up and holding them out. "Yes. I had Laverna make them. She's an excellent leather-worker, but she also has another rare gift. She's a true arcanist, able to work sigils and spells into the armor she crafts."

"So these have... special powers?" I said slowly, reaching out my hand and taking the beautiful objects. They were incredibly lovely gauntlets. My hands itched to put them on.

Draven nodded. "In a sense. I had her imbue these with aiming sigils."

I smirked at him. "Smart."

He grinned. "No offense. But maybe they'll help a bit."

"So we're going to start practicing? Together? You and I? You aren't afraid of being scorched?" I asked dubiously.

He tilted his head. "I think I already am."

My heart skipped a beat.

I forced myself to look down at the gauntlets. "They're lovely, Draven. Really. Thank you."

Not as lovely as you, I wanted to say. But he beat me to the punch.

"They're not nearly as beautiful as you are, Morgan Pendragon," he said quietly.

His eyes roamed my face then passed onto my body, finding my curves and lingering on each one with a raw, possessive hunger.

A simmering heat sparked deep inside me. Answering the desire in his eyes like a fire fed flaming coals.

"Do you know how hard I've tried to stay away from you?" he whispered. "Do you know how long I've waited? And in the span of a few nights, all of it has been undone. I can't keep away. I know I don't deserve you. You've forgiven too much already. But I'm not strong enough to resist. You're my every weakness, my every temptation. And I..."

"Shut up," I whispered. "Just shut up." And then my mouth was on his.

I didn't want to hear it. I didn't want to risk it. He was saying too much. And in the end, when this all fell apart, like we both knew it would, it would be so much harder.

Better to keep pretending. Playing the game.

None of this was real.

It worked because of who we were, yes.

But it also worked because I knew it was just a lie.

I moved my lips from his, licking my way along his jaw, kissing a path to the cleft in the center of his chin. I rubbed my cheek against the roughness of his stubble. Enjoying the slightly painful burn of it against my soft skin. He was all hard edges and flat planes. Strong and savage, the toughness I needed.

His lips found mine again, kissing me greedily as his hands cupped my breasts in a gesture of total possession. I gasped as he lifted my arms over his shoulders, then grabbed my hips and lifted me up onto the workshop table, pushing all the small tools Laverna had there to the floor in one sweep of his hand.

"What are you doing?" I asked weakly. "We shouldn't. Laverna..."

The door bell tinkled as if in response and then I heard the heavy oak shop door slam shut.

"I think Laverna's gone out," Draven muttered between kissing his way down my neck to the opening of my tunic. "Very wise of her." His hands were already fumbling with the fastenings of my trousers.

I moaned as his hand slipped inside, fingers dipping into my wetness with an expert touch. Draven growled low in the back of his throat as he kissed my breasts through the thin fabric of my shirt then bit down gently on one nipple, moistening the material with his lips and sucking hard.

His fingers played along my cleft, rubbing small circles along my clit with his thumb that made me mad with desire as heat began to spread over every inch of my skin.

One finger slid inside me, thrusting very slowly. I spread my thighs apart a little more, reckless and wanton and no longer caring about being seen or heard.

"More. Please," I managed, as his thumb slipped over my clit and circled it gently.

A second finger slid inside me and I ground against him, letting out a moan so loud I wondered if the people in the neighboring shops would hear.

"That's it," Draven said, his lips brushing against my cheek. "Let it go. Let yourself go."

He plunged his fingers inside me and I cried out, opening to him, desperate for more.

"That's it," he murmured. "Come for me, Morgan. There's a good girl."

And as his thumb circled my clit again and his fingers thrust into me hard, harder, deeper, more deeply, I did. I came. I came for him. I came *hard*, shattering against his hand, my fingers gripping his shoulder so tightly I thought I would leave bruises.

"Lift," Draven commanded as his eyes blazed down on me. I scooted upwards without a second thought, letting him shimmy my pants down my hips and over my thighs, then onto the floor.

He pulled my tunic over my head, and suddenly I was naked before him, my ass cold on Laverna's workshop table, my thighs spread wide, dripping and wet.

But Draven's eyes were higher up. He gazed at my chest, just above my breasts.

Self-consciously, I put a hand to my chest, to the scars, to the place where the name "Florian" could still be faintly seen. The marks had faded, but I wasn't sure they would ever disappear entirely.

"That fucking bastard." Draven stared at where my hand rested. He lifted his eyes to mine. "If you hadn't killed him, I would have. You did the right thing, you know. Killing the motherfucker."

I nodded. But satisfying as they were, those weren't the words I wanted him to say right now. The ones I needed to hear.

He looked me up and down slowly and I saw the anger leave his eyes. He shook his head. "You're beautiful, Morgan. Nothing that bastard did could ever change that. You're exquisite. Do you have any idea what you fucking do to me? I want you. Very fucking badly."

"I want you, too," I whispered. "You're beautiful." I reached out a hand and stroked his cheek. "I've never wanted anyone this much. So badly."

That was the closest to the truth I was going to give him. I bit my lip, forcing the flow of words to a halt.

Within seconds, he had freed himself from his own trousers. His cock was long and hard, the head bulging red.

I licked my lips, aware that my breathing had turned ragged from lust.

Then I gasped as he pressed himself slowly against my opening, while his lips plundered my mouth with another slow, heavy kiss.

He pushed himself inside me in one thrust and I arched backwards on the table, already lifting my hips in eager response.

"Yes," I cried. "Draven, please. Yes."

He cupped me from below, lifting me more tightly against him then kissed me in a way both savage and tender, and thrust more deeply inside.

His hands were stroking my body, moving across my breasts, as his cock slid in and out of me, thrusting in a perfect rhythm.

I was aroused and soothed all at once, closing my eyes as he moved over me. His mouth found my breast, tugging my nipple into a turgid bud then flicking, and I let out a sharp gasp.

His hands held my wrists, pushing them behind my back, forcing my breasts more fully against his chest as he took me again and again.

"Look at you. Lips parted. Gasping for more." His tone was utterly admiring and I gave a shiver of shame mingled with delight. But there was nothing demeaning about the words when he said them. "You want this, don't you, Morgan? You want more and more, don't you?"

"Yes," I whimpered, feeding into the fantasy completely. "Fuck me on this table. I don't care if anyone hears us."

He gave a sharp thrust and I moaned loudly. It was true. I was too lost to be embarrassed. Laverna might have come and leaned on the counter and watched for all I fucking cared at this point.

"You're fucking exquisite. You're gorgeous, Morgan. Do you hear me? You're a fucking beauty. And any man who ever tells you otherwise, will die a painful death should I ever hear them." He bit my neck and I hissed with pleasure.

"You certainly love to kill, don't you?" I writhed a little under him, enjoying the look in his eyes as he watched my breasts thrust upwards.

"I love to kill for *you*," he said, emphasizing the word before setting his mouth to one of my nipples and sucking hard.

He pushed into me again, then moved his mouth to mine, kissing me more fiercely than ever. He was close now, I could tell. I wrapped my legs around him, drawing him against me more tightly.

"Fuck," he said hoarsely. His gorgeous emerald eyes glazed as he looked down at me, his beautiful lips parted slightly with pleasure and longing.

I raised my hands and grasped his horns, wrapping my hands around them, then pulling his head down towards mine and biting his lower lip so hard I could taste the blood.

He gave a guttural groan and then he was coming and I was coming with him. His mouth covered mine with a brutal desperation, teeth clashing, tongues twining. I arched hard, crying out as the climax tore through me. I felt him shudder over me, his broad chest rubbing against my breasts.

"You're mine," he growled, as he set his mouth to my neck. "You're mine, Morgan. Here, now, always." He bit down. "You were fucking made for me. Do you understand?"

I shifted against him, suddenly not able to look him in the eyes. The words set a new feeling shuddering through me. One I could not describe. There was a rightness to the words.

But more than that, a finality to them that I couldn't help but rebel against.

If I was his, then was he mine? Did I dare lay claim to this warrior prince, this dark fae brute of a man with honor in his heart and fire in his veins?

And so I said nothing.

We dressed swiftly, pulling on our clothes.

I tried to change the subject. "Are you nervous for the next trial? What if it's fenrirs? Or harpies? Do they have monsters like that here in Myntra?" I could hear myself babbling.

Draven shrugged as he tugged his trousers over his lean muscled thighs.

"Not really nervous, no. The most terrifying thing in the world isn't monsters, Morgan. It's other people."

"You mean Avriel," I shot back.

He grimaced. "Do you think I'm afraid of Avriel?"

"I don't know. Are you? Maybe you should be. A little?"

"And why is that?"

"Because cowards are more dangerous than honorable men," I said. "Because Avriel won't hesitate to lie or cheat or do just about anything to beat you."

"You're right about that," Draven agreed.

"You should have killed him when you had the chance," I muttered.

"And when was that?"

"Back in the training room, before this ever started. Before he even had a chance to compete," I said before I could stop and think.

Draven stared at me. "You were there that day? Watching us?" A look of understanding crossed his face. "Of course, you were. Beks and his little excursions." He chuckled.

"It's not fucking funny," I snapped. "He killed Pearl."

Draven's face turned somber. "You're right. I didn't think he'd really do it. It's been a long time since I've been around Avriel, you know. I'd forgotten just how merciless he could be."

"I doubt he changed for the better in your absence," I said bitterly.

"Not at all. He's cruel. More vicious. More ready to show it, too. He's had a taste of power, thanks to my stepmother. Now he's more desperate than ever to keep it."

I thought of Sephone, cool and composed but not above playing favorites. "Is that what she wants, I wonder?"

"I honestly have no idea," Draven admitted. "But if I'd saved Pearl that day, do you really think it would have helped? She wasn't going to back out. Avriel would have gotten to her eventually." He ran his hands through his dark hair and scowled. "I wanted to keep them all safe, Morgan. But I couldn't. This fucking game wasn't designed for that. It's brutal and cruel."

It was brutal and cruel that a man with a heart could do nothing to save his people from being slaughtered. It was brutal and cruel that he had grown up in a court led by the greatest villain in Aercanum. It was brutal and cruel that his brother had followed in his father's footsteps and murdered Draven's wife and child.

"I know that," I said, my face softening. "I do. You can't... You can't save everyone. What matters is that you care. That you try." I put my hand on his chest. "There's a beating heart in your chest. Not all the Siabra are so lucky."

"Maybe they're luckier," he said sourly.

I shook my head. "Don't ever think that. This." I pushed against the heartbeat under my palm. "This is what sets you apart. It's why you deserve to win. It's why you'll..." I hesitated. "It's why you'll be a better ruler than my brother or your father or Sephone. You could really fix things, Draven."

He was quiet as he looked down at me. Then his hand covered mine. "Thank you."

I nodded, then pulled away. "We should go."

My body burned for this man. I couldn't have my heart burning, too.

I walked out of the workshop without a backwards glance, the gauntlets hanging by my side.

Ironic that he had chosen gauntlets when my heart was in his hands.

CHAPTER 23

P erhaps it shouldn't have surprised me so much that Draven was a very good teacher.

In a way, he reminded me of Sir Ector. He could be equally as patient.

He was a lot better looking though, which was distracting at times.

I stood in a secluded training room of the palace, clad in my newly crafted rose and flame gauntlets. Unlike some styles, these were fingerless. Thick leather covered the back of my hands and wrists but left my sensitive fingers exposed, presumably to allow for better aim and control.

With a mix of determination and apprehension, I extended my palms and conjured a flickering flame that danced at my fingertips.

Targets were set up across the room. Most of them bore scorch marks from where I had managed, over the last few days, to hit them at least once.

Most of them.

I extended my hands, willing the flames to shoot forth, focusing and guiding them.

Frustration etched upon my features as flames shot out a few feet in front of me, then veered off course, missing the mark and hitting the stone wall.

Which was also covered with scorch marks.

I clenched my fists in frustration, feeling the thick leather fill my palm.

Draven watched from the sidelines, leaning against the wall near the doorway with one foot up, his arms crossed over his chest. I had made him wear armor. I had wanted him to wear a helmet, too, but he had laughed and refused. Instead, he held a small round shield in one hand, tossing it up and down in the air like a ball.

He thought it was a joke. But if I burned his pretty face off, it would be his fault not mine.

So far, I'd managed not to.

Again and again, I tried, my concentration waning with each failed attempt.

My control was improving. Yesterday the flames had responded to my will, arcing towards the targets with shocking accuracy. I had hit them one after another, feeling myself surge with mastery.

My confidence had bloomed. I had fallen asleep thinking this was it. I had done it. The next day would be even better.

But today it felt as if I had taken a large step back rather than leaping forward.

I sighed deeply and tried again, lifting my hands, willing the flames to come, watching them dance first on my fingertips, then shooting them forward.

There was a loud clash at the door and I turned in confusion.

Startled, I felt the flames flare up uncontrollably and shouted out as a searing blast launched across the room.

Someone in the doorframe ducked and rolled out of the way, letting the door close again with a crash.

Draven raised the shield he had been playing with, just as the flames engulfed his body.

I was already running towards him, heart pounding in panic.

"No, no, no."

His armor was blackened. I could see where part of the cuirass had melted away, exposing flesh beneath.

"Fuck, no, no," I cursed.

He hadn't fallen. He was still leaning up against the wall.

Could a corpse still lean? Maybe his body had been so desiccated by the fire that he was no more than a hollow log.

A log could lean.

The shield lowered. For a second, I thought I saw pain stamped across Draven's handsome face. Then it was gone and I watched as he laughed loudly.

"Why the fuck are you laughing?" I demanded furiously. "You're bleeding!"

He shrugged. "I've bled before. It's nothing new."

"That looks painful. Very painful," I insisted, staring at the raw, red burn and the melted armor.

"A little. You might remember I've had worse."

"You need to go and see a healer," I said stubbornly.

"I doubt they can do anything for me I can't do for myself, but if you insist. Just as soon as we see who that was at the door." He turned as the heavy wooden door was pushed tentatively open a second time.

Vespera stepped through. Her face was stricken.

Her eyes widened as she saw Draven's chest. "I'm so sorry! I had no idea... I was just bringing a message." She glanced at me. "Did you do that?"

"I'm partly responsible, yes," I said through clenched teeth, glaring at her.

"I'm so sorry, Prince Kairos," she said. "I thought you were practicing but I had no idea what sort of practice you were engaged in..."

"Yes, Morgan here is a flame wielder. Rather unusual in the Court of Umbral Flames, which is funny, isn't it?" Draven sounded vastly amused and none the worse for wear.

Vespera nodded nervously. "I was just carrying a message for your mother. The Queen Regent, I mean."

"Pity she didn't come herself," I muttered. "Pity I didn't hit her instead."

Draven's lips quirked but he ignored me. "Yes?"

"The next round of the competition is tomorrow," Vespera explained. "She's moved it up a day."

"Are you serious?" I exploded. "No. He can't compete like this. Go and tell the queen what just happened..."

"I'll be fine," Draven cut in. The tone of his voice said there was no room for argument. "Tell Sephone I'll be ready."

Vespera nodded and scuttled out the door again.

I turned to Draven. "You can't compete like this."

"I heal fast. I'll be fine."

"Odessa will take weeks to heal," I said, my nostrils flaring. "She's still healing. But you expect to be fine by tomorrow morning?"

"More or less," Draven replied. "It's fine. Have I already said that? Don't worry, Morgan. Training accidents happen. I've been expecting this."

My eyebrows shot up. "You've been expecting this? Yet you wouldn't wear a helmet?"

"You didn't hit my head. Thank you for that, by the way. And I had this." He waved the blackened shield which looked as if it was about to disintegrate at any moment.

"Wonderful. Now I've put you at a disadvantage. Avriel will love this."

"She seemed so sincere, didn't she?" Draven said, glancing at the door.

"Who? Vespera?" I stared at him. "You don't think..."

He made a face. "Who knows."

"I thought you trusted Vespera. Lyrastra helped her..."

"Oh, so you trust her because of Lyrastra? Fascinating." Draven smirked.

"That wasn't what I meant," I said hotly. "But I thought you trusted her, yes."

"The only ones I trust are Selwyn and Lyrastra," Draven said thoughtfully. "Vespera is a wild card."

"You don't think she'll attack Lyrastra, too?"

"Do you think Lyrastra deserves her loyalty?" Draven asked. "Interesting."

I lifted my chin. "I'm sure Lyrastra can take care of herself."

"I'm sure you're right. As can I." He leaned forward and surprised me by kissing the center of my forehead gently. "Don't worry, Morgan."

"Right. I'll magically stop worrying that you might die tomorrow now that I've gravely wounded you," I muttered, trying not to think about how wonderful his lips had felt pressed to my skin, tender and soft.

Each night we fell into bed together, tired and excited. Each night was better than the one before.

I had never been so happy.

I had never been so afraid.

Tomorrow it might all end.

"Gravely wounded?" Draven snorted. "Don't give yourself so much credit. It's a scratch."

"Don't make me stab you in your sleep tonight."

"We both know you're going to be far too tired for that after I'm through with you," Draven said wickedly, waggling his dark brows in a way that made me want to kiss him on the lips and giggle at the same time.

I chose neither, striding towards the door and pushing it open instead. "Practice is over. You need a healer."

"I need you in my bed," Draven muttered from behind me. "Preferably naked and on top of me."

I pretended I hadn't heard him.

CHAPTER 24

A creature of nightmares stood before Draven.

Clad in tattered, threadbare garments that draped from bony shoulders, elongated hands tipped with razor-sharp claws twitched in eager anticipation as the creature held them clasped in front of themselves, as if in a silent prayer.

A thin veil of pallid white skin covered a hairless, eyeless skull.

Thin lips stretched into a sinister grin, exposing four rows of serrated, needle-like teeth.

Wisps of black smoke curled from its nostrils, carrying the scent of unnatural decay.

I leaned forward where I stood at the railing. My forehead once again collided sharply with the invisible barrier making a loud smacking noise.

Some of the Siabra further down covered their mouths to hide laughter.

I glared at them, rubbing my head.

"You'll never learn, will you?" Odessa looked almost amused.

"Hush," I said crossly. "I do it because I care."

"You care too much. Spare your forehead. He's not going to die at the very first trial."

"It's not the first trial. It's the second and it's not fair that there are three trials in a single trial in the first place," I snapped loudly, not caring who heard me.

"It's the first trial of the second challenge, and you know, I don't believe anyone has ever described Sephone as 'fair' before," Odessa mused.

"Your wound has made you even more cantankerous than before," I complained.

"Has it? I'm fairly sure it's just you who is peevish today. I've always been like this."

"Very funny. Ha ha. Hush. Something is happening."

Sure enough, the creature was opening its cavernous jaw very slowly, as if about to speak.

"In shadows deep, my secrets lie. Unveil them now, or surely die."

The creature paused ominously.

"Oh, just fucking get it over with," I spat, feeling murderous.

"It's a good thing it can't hear you. Would you like to go down there and do it yourself?" Odessa asked with a surprisingly saucy grin.

I bared my teeth and snapped at her. She laughed.

The caves that the gallery had overlooked at the first Blood Rise challenge had vanished. Today we stood in the same gallery but above a shadowy network of narrow tunnels leading to larger rooms. Only one room was illuminated for our view at a time.

At the moment, the competitors were convened in an entrance-like chamber, waiting their turn to approach the creature one by one and be granted passage into the tapered opening that lay behind it, blocked by the monster's body.

Lyrastra, Avriel, Erion, and Selwyn had already passed the riddle-giver. Now it was Draven's turn.

Vespera waited behind him.

The creature's voice rang out again, clear enough for all watching above to hear.

"In the night's embrace, I come to play..."

"I don't like how it's starting," Odessa whispered.

I tried not to snicker. "Stop. You're being highly inappropriate."

"A phantom figure that won't betray," the creature's voice boomed out. "What am I, hidden in the gloom, a presence that dances in twilight's room?"

"What the fuck is the answer?" I hissed at Odessa.

She shrugged. "Fuck if I know."

"Oh gods. Oh, Zorya." My stomach was queasy. "I would be terrible at this."

"Good thing we're not down there. He is. Just watch."

"What if he gets it wrong?"

"Then he lops the thing's head off and makes it easier for the next contestants."

I nodded, pretending a confidence I didn't feel. "Right. Easy."

"A moonbeam," Draven's voice rang out clear as a bell.

There was silence.

I held my breath.

"That is correct." The creature slowly moved aside.

I watched Draven move through a cramped tunnel and then into another large stone chamber where the other contestants waited. Some sort of staging area perhaps?

"When the last contestant is through, the next challenge will begin," Odessa murmured. "I've heard of it being done that way with some of the trials."

Vespera was next. We watched as she almost danced up to the riddle-giver, rubbing her taloned hands together eagerly.

"She's nervous. Her palms are sweating," Odessa observed. "She needs to be careful, not too hurried or she'll make a mistake."

The eyeless horror faced Vespera unmoving.

Gradually, Vespera's hands stopped twitching and she relaxed into stillness. But from a distance, we could all see she was trembling.

I pitied her. I was terrible at riddles. How could she have known she would face this sort of a challenge? It wasn't exactly the kind of thing any of the contestants had been training for.

Unless they'd been secretly spending time in the library.

Then I remembered how Vespera had burst into my own training the day before, resulting in the injury to Draven's chest which he had downplayed and tried to hide. Admittedly, I couldn't see it impacting him so far. But then, he hadn't faced a physical challenge yet today.

Had she been sent in to distract me, as Draven had suggested?

Even so, facing the monstrous riddle-giver was something I didn't think I'd wish on my worst enemy.

"Step forward, child," the riddle-giver said with a hissing voice.

Vespera took a small step towards the creature.

The riddle-giver's mouth curved up slightly into a cruel, jagged smile, then opened again.

"With midnight wings, I take flight,

'Cross a canvas of ebony night.

Silent as whispers, I soar unseen,

A creature born of night serene.

A specter in the dark,

Essence of shadows, an ember's spark?

What am I?"

Vespera licked her lips nervously.

"Think," Odessa whispered. "Take your time."

I said nothing.

Below, Vespera was tugging anxiously on her long brown braid, and clearing her throat.
"You... You are..."

"Yes?" The creature's hands jerked and shuddered, as if impatient for the answer.

"You're... a raven," Vespera said, her voice growing louder.

She glanced up at the crowd watching and I saw her smile.

She looked confident. She believed she had the correct answer. Good, I decided. I had no wish to see her fall to this miserable creature of shadowy horror.

There was a pause. It stretched, becoming longer than the one which had followed Draven's answer.

I glanced at Odessa.

"False," the creature's voice hissed. "Owl is the answer."

There was a swift motion, then a piercing scream.

The scream went on and on. It seemed as if it would never end.

The crowd was murmuring around me. Had the creature even moved?

I blinked.

Vespera stood below, clutching her hands to her face. Blood streamed down her cheeks. Her mouth was still open, screaming in wordless horror.

Across from her, the creature chewed.

"It took her eyes," I gasped.

The riddle-giver's fingers were dripping with blood. A wide, cracked rimmed smile with bloody jagged edges covered its face as it chewed and chewed on its prize.

"What can she do now?" I asked Odessa wildly. "Can she try again?"

Odessa's face was impassive as she shook her head slowly.

The crowd around us was relaxing into silence once more. They had accepted what was about to happen. Even if I hadn't.

The creature's claw-like hands shot out again. This time slow enough that we could all see as the riddle-giver grabbed Vespera's right hand and forced her talons to extend.

Swift and ruthless, the riddle-giver slashed Vespera's own talons across her throat.

The cut went deep.

For a moment her head wobbled on her neck.

Then it fell.

The creature caught it up greedily in its own hands, lifting Vespera's head to its mouth like one might do with a juicy ripe fruit.

I looked away, gagging.

Behind me, I glimpsed a few of the Siabra turning aside in horror and disgust.

Fury and revulsion churned within me in equal measure. This was part of this people's culture? I couldn't have dreamed such nightmares up. And yet they watched as if for sport.

I was a spectator, too. But I was forced to be. I had to bear witness. How could I look away when Draven was down there, risking everything for a chance to rule these spoiled, craven people that he believed he could somehow redeem?

Something was happening in the next chamber. The cavern with the riddle-maker grew dark. It's part of the story was over now.

The stony room where Draven was became brighter.

Around him stood Avriel, Lyrastra, Erion, and Magus. The final five.

I could now pick out an object on the opposite side of the room.

Shadows fell away as a tall oblong frame was revealed.

The second trial. A mirror.

The mirror was rimmed in pristine silver so pale it was nearly white. Its polished glass surface gleamed with a radiant clarity.

As we watched, the looking glass slowly filled the small stone chamber with a beautiful light.

The mirror seemed innocent and inviting. Nothing like the riddle-giver in the room before.

But I knew better than to expect anything sweet or innocent from the Blood Rise by now. My heart sped up as I looked at the mirror.

Who would be the first to find out what this challenge involved?

Lyrastra and Avriel both moved at the same time.

But Lyrastra was quicker.

She reached the mirror and stood before it, silent and waiting.

Were there words she was meant to say, I wondered? How would she know what to do next?

But something was already starting to happen. A mist was moving across the surface of the mirror.

A voice emerged from the mirror. Whispering a single word I wasn't confident I had heard correctly.

Lyrastra didn't waste time. We saw her nod. Then she pulled a blade from one of the belts strapped to her thighs and slashed it quickly across one of her palms.

Squeezing her bleeding hand into a tight fist, she raised it so that the drops fell against the glass of the mirror.

Instantly the surface began to change. Red clouds spread faintly across the surface.

Lyrastra stepped through, as if the mirror were a doorway and as if she knew exactly what lay on the other side. She vanished.

There was an appreciative titter from the crowd. They liked Lyrastra, I realized. They might have liked her even more than they liked Draven or Avriel. She was something of a court favorite–bold and decisive. She wasn't as brave or as strong as Draven. She wasn't as cunning or cutthroat as Avriel.

But she did what needed to be done.

I found myself hoping Lyrastra survived. Draven would need people like her around him.

Had I really just thought that?

I shook my head and looked back at the room below.

Selwyn had beaten Avriel to the punch and was approaching the mirror. Or had Avriel purposely decided to linger? He stood nearby, watching closely, his scaled arms folded over his muscular chest.

"That seemed very easy," I whispered to Odessa, feeling relieved. "Blood to pass through."

To my surprise, she grimaced and shook her head.

"What?"

"Wait," was all she said. "I pray I'm wrong."

Selwyn glanced back at Draven who nodded as if in encouragement. The antlered man nodded back, then faced the mirror.

"He let him go first," Odessa muttered.

"Why not?" If all that was required was a handful of blood… A feeling in the pit of my stomach said that it could not be that easy.

"The prince is too generous for his own good," was all she said, her face grim.

The mirror swirled. A voice emerged. We could not hear what it said.

Selwyn's large hands curled into fists by his side.

Whatever he was being asked for, it wasn't simply blood this time. And he wasn't happy about it.

Turning, he shouted something up to the gallery. To my surprise, the queen turned sharply to a group of courtiers standing behind her. Two of them broke away from the group, nearly running in their haste to reach the gallery doors.

"Where are they going?" I asked, bewildered.

"Wait. We should know in a minute."

I sighed. Odessa was being annoyingly obtuse. Evidently, she had hunches of her own but didn't wish to share. Was she afraid of being wrong? Or afraid of frightening me if she was right?

There was a lull, like the calm before the storm. Around us, Siabra were chattering and laughing. Vespera's death had swiftly been forgotten.

A table with lavish refreshments had been set up in one corner of the room, replete with crystal tableware and a tinkling fountain flowing with a pink-tinged wine. I recognized a face as a man crossed a room and filled a glass with the pink stuff.

"Javer is here," I told Odessa.

She nodded as if not surprised. "He'll keep his distance." She met my gaze. "But he wouldn't stay away. He's loyal to the prince, regardless of how furious the prince may be with him."

"I understand." And I did. I even grudgingly respected it. In that same vein, I was about to ask where Crescent and Gawain were when there was a commotion from near the entrance.

The doors had opened again. Four people stepped into the gallery.

"Fashionably late," Odessa said, rolling her eyes as Rychel, Hawl, Gawain, and Crescent walked towards us.

"What did we miss?" Rychel asked, her keen eyes darting down to the room before.

"Vespera..." Odessa began.

"We heard," Crescent interrupted, a look of distress crossing his face. "That much we've heard."

"Selwyn has sent to the menagerie," Hawl's deep voice boomed out. "Why?"

"We'll know in a moment," Odessa replied. "Here they come."

The Queen Regent's two courtiers pushed through the doors, carrying something between them.

My eyes widened. "A verdantail."

The pretty deerlike creature was wriggling against its captors, shaking its antlered head back and forth frantically. I watched as it raised its emerald-green furred head and made a plaintive flute-like sound.

The hairs on the back of my neck stood up.

The creature and courtiers disappeared through a hidden door near the queen's corner.

A few moments later a panel opened in the stone door of the room where the competitors waited down below and the little green verdantail tottered in.

Selwyn stared at it for a moment, then crossed over and picked it up.

He stroked the small deer's fur gently for a moment. Then reached for something strapped to his back.

My breath caught in my throat. It was a sharp hunting knife—like the one Draven usually carried at his hip.

With a swift stroke, the knife swept below the little deer's dainty chin.

Selwyn stepped closer to the mirror, holding the deer aloft as its heart's blood trickled down onto the glass surface.

The blood cleared. The mirror clouded once more, darker red clouds swirling along its surface.

Selwyn cradled the verdantail's dead body to his chest and stepped through, following Lyrastra's path.

It was just a deer, I reminded myself, my heart hammering. We ate deer. Crescent had said verdantail were a delicacy here. It was just a deer. We ate animals all the time.

But the mirror hadn't eaten the deer for nourishment—or demanded that Selwyn do so. It had wanted Lyrastra's blood. And then it had demanded...

"Did the mirror ask for the verdantail specifically?" I demanded, elbowing Odessa.

She looked at me. "I don't know. Probably not. It probably wanted some sort of beast, without specifying the kind. But killing any innocent living creature went against everything Selwyn stands for."

I thought of the large man's own antlers. Had he chosen the verdantail for its symbolism? Because the deer mirrored himself? "But he did it. He's killed before. He killed the goblins."

She nodded. "Yes, but they weren't innocent. Selwyn is part of a rare group of Siabra who refuse to consume the blood or flesh of any innocent creature. They eat only the fruits of the earth."

Plants and vegetables, she meant.

"The opposite of Avriel, you mean?" I said hollowly, thinking of Avriel's brutal gesture of bloodlust as he'd held Brasad aloft then fed from him.

"Pretty much," she agreed. "Malkah was the same."

Two gentle souls in a brutal game. "Draven let him go first. Because he knew the mirror would want more."

"The mirror is a living being. A cursed spirit," Hawl spoke up. "Once fed, it grows greedy for more."

"Quiet," Rychel murmured as she stepped up beside me. "Look. It's my brother's turn."

Draven approached the mirror. From nearby, Avriel waited and watched. I was surprised he hadn't shoved his way past Draven and Selwyn to go immediately after Lyrastra. Instead, he seemed to be biding his time. His very presence so close to Draven made me nervous.

But Draven ignored him.

The mirror was speaking again. Words only the competitors were close enough to hear. I clenched my hands into fists, heart pounding impatiently. What would it ask of him?

Slowly, Draven turned and lifted his head, his eyes going up to where we stood in the gallery.

Our eyes met. Time stood still for a moment as I drank in the sight of the man who had become my entire world. Obsidian hair cascaded around his face, enticingly disheveled. When was the last time he had bothered to cut it? I was sure Breena would have loved to get her hands on those overly-long locks.

His sun-kissed skin seemed so out of place in the damp stony cavern.

While the mirror gave off a bright radiant light, it was no longer beautiful. I now saw it for what it was—a false, cold promise of light.

Whereas Draven's skin held a captivating warmth that I had felt, touched, kissed, licked. The secrets of a thousand brilliant sunsets lay in that bronze-tinged skin, a thousand hours sprawled in our bed, a thousand kisses placed all over my body.

He wore a supple leather jerkin over his chest, hiding the burn-marks I had given him the day before. The dark brown material hugged his face, accentuating his broad shoulders and sculpted waist.

A lump grew in my throat. Every contour and sinew of his body spoke of raw power and primal strength. He was a warrior. A killer. A brute of a man.

So then why was he looking at me in that way? As though he were peering into my soul with unsettling ease.

As if in answer to an unspoken question, I felt my mouth beginning to open, my lips forming a silent "yes."

But Draven was already turning away.

He spoke something to the mirror. Then he pulled out the blade from his belt.

"What's he doing?" I demanded of Rychel and Odessa sharply. "Why did he look at us?"

Rychel shrugged helplessly from beside me.

Odessa was quiet. "Not at us," she said finally. "At you. What were you about to say?"

"I was about to say 'yes.'"

"Why? To what? What question did he ask you?" she demanded.

I opened my mouth, closed it, then opened it again. "He... didn't. And yet."

"It was the mirror," Hawl said decisively. "You said 'yes.' But that's not enough. It's what *he* says that matters. I'm surprised you were asked at all."

"But...what did I say 'yes' to?" I asked, in confusion.

"A question you should never have had to answer." Odessa's face was furious as she glared at the mirror. "And your answer was worthless, without even understanding the question."

"But he understood. Look." Rychel pointed.

Down below Draven was shaking his head and looking at the mirror with a mutinous expression.

He spoke again, then seemed to be waiting.

Finally, the voice from the mirror answered, as clouded as its surface.

Draven nodded decisively. He raised the blade.

"What is he doing?" I demanded of the others.

One of Rychel's hands slipped into mine.

The blade was lifted higher.

"What is he doing?" My voice was filled with panic.

I held my breath as Draven began to saw at something on his forehead.

Crimson drops fell to the ground around him. Red liquid trickled down his face.

"No," I breathed.

With a massive amount of force, Draven's blade was slicing through the strong, dense material of his own horns.

The sound of cracking and splintering filled the air as the blade cut its way through the tough shards of horn. Blood ran down Draven's cheeks to his jaw as the horn came away in his hand.

Wordlessly, he held it out to the mirror, letting the blood from the jagged horn dribble across the greedy glass.

Then he dropped the horn to the ground and lifted his blade to the other.

"No," I whimpered. Tears were running soundlessly down my cheeks.

"It's all right," Odessa said quietly.

She was trying to be comforting. I understood. But this *wasn't* all right. This would never be all right.

Draven continued the grueling process, cutting through his other horn with brutal determination. Each incision was a visceral reminder of his commitment to this sick game.

And of his refusal to offer the mirror its first choice.

Me. It had wanted *me*.

I watched him hold his second horn up to the mirror. The blood fell onto the pane again.

Still, he did not step through.

"What?" I clenched my jaw until it hurt. "What now? Why isn't he moving?"

The second horn fell to the ground at Draven's feet. He crouched down, placing his knife beside the two bloody, severed horns, then stood back up and began unbuckling his jerkin.

My heart thudded against the walls of my chest. "What the fuck is he doing? Odessa?"

No one else spoke. Odessa seemed to be holding her breath.

Slowly, Draven undid the fastenings of the leather armor and pulled it off, then stripped off the protective linen tunic he wore beneath.

When he was bare to the waist, he stooped and picked up his knife again.

Holding it aloft, he said something to the mirror, then he looked back up at the gallery. Our eyes locked.

"What are you doing, Draven?" I whispered. "Please, just stop."

I could feel the eyes of Sephone's court on me, knew they were watching hungrily, hoping to pick out the words I was saying. I didn't care.

"Please. Stop," I mouthed against the glass, leaning my head against it hard.

Draven's lips turned upwards slightly. His eyes were saying not to worry. While his blade... His blade was curving down towards the bronze-skin of his chest.

I didn't scream. I didn't blink. My gaze was as firm and unwavering as Draven's hand as he impaled the knife through his own flesh directly over the center of his heart.

"He'll kill himself." Rychel sounded dazed.

"No," Odessa's tone was clipped. Short and to the point, just like the warrior herself. It was simple. No, he would not.

But he might come fucking close, I thought silently. That was undeniable.

Around me an eruption was occurring. Apparently even for the Siabra, this was an extreme act.

Draven shifted, turning his back slightly and obscuring our view.

I was humiliated to know I was relieved. Relieved I could not see whatever he was doing.

When he turned back towards us, I could see the sheen of sweat on his brow.

The blade was still gripped in one hand. In his other, he held a severed fragment of pulsating heart. The pale flesh was a mixture of delicate colors, pale pinks, fragile blues, and beneath it all the dark tinge of heart's blood beating through where Draven had severed this piece from the rest of the precious organ.

Flinching in pain, he stooped low one last time, sweeping up his leather jerkin in the hand that gripped the knife, and then stepped forward towards the mirror.

In a flash, Avriel was at his back, gripping his shoulder with one hand, just as Draven stepped into the mirror.

They both vanished.

"Fuck," Odessa said, very carefully and precisely.

"He cheated." I couldn't believe it. "He fucking cheated. How? How could he do that? How is he allowed to do that?"

"He piggy-backed," Rychel mused. "Very daring." I glared at her. "Very dangerous, too," she added hastily. "He may not have made it. It was a calculated risk."

Around us the crowd had burst into raucous noise. Were they praising Draven's mind-blowing resolve? Or lauding Avriel's audacity?

I couldn't tell and what was more I didn't care. I hated them all. None of them had a stake in this game. Not really. Not like we had.

In that instant, I pitied Lyrastra. Where were her people? Who stood waiting for her? Who would weep if she did not emerge?

We couldn't see where Lyrastra, Selwyn, and Draven had ended up. Or if Avriel's sleazy maneuver had succeeded. He might have been swallowed up by the mirror for all we knew.

Not that anyone would care. Save Sephone, at least.

Erion was all alone now.

He walked up to the mirror. The pristine shimmer of the frame was gone, clouded with a rust-like hue that reminded me of dried blood. The reflective surface was swirling with tendrils of black and red.

The mirror was greedy and whatever it ate was clearly not good for it.

I wondered what would happen if it ate too much. Would it cloud up forever? Or burst and shatter, spilling blood and bones like a grotesque breaking dam?

"What will happen to Draven?" I demanded. "How can he live like that? With a literal hole in his fucking heart?"

There was silence around me.

"He's stronger than we could possibly know," a voice said from behind. "I don't believe in false hope. You know me well enough to know that by now, I think?"

I turned around to face Javer. "Yes."

Something like relief darted through his eyes. "Well, then. Please believe me, Lady Morgan, when I say he could live. Even like that."

"But if the next challenge is physically demanding..." I let my voice trail off.

This was ridiculous. Was I really pleading with Javer of all people for comfort and reassurance?

There was an awkward silence.

"Well," the court mage said at last, raising a hand to touch the tip of his pointed beard. "Yes."

My heart sank. I turned back.

Draven had stabbed himself in the heart. He had carved off his own horns. He had mutilated himself, nearly destroyed himself. Why?

The alternative had been clear.

The mirror had wanted me.

What would it want from Erion and what would the reptilian man be willing to give? A lung? An arm?

We watched, we waited.

The mirror spoke to Erion.

Even through his dark scales, I could see Erion's face shifting into an expression of dismay as whatever the mirror had requested–demanded–sank in.

Then he turned to the gallery, looked up in the direction of the Queen Regent, and like Selwyn before him, he shouted up a request.

The silence that fell across the gallery was worse than the noise.

You could have heard a pin drop. A horn fall. A blade clatter.

Then a courtier went running to the gallery door. I saw them call to the guards stationed outside in the hall.

If guards would be required, this must be serious. I glanced at Odessa and Rychel. They were quiet. Rychel's bronze face was paler than normal.

Within minutes, a wailing filled the air from the corridor outside.

I felt a chill run down my spine as the doors to the gallery opened and two of the Queen Regent's guards entered, dragging a young girl between them.

She must have been no more than thirteen or fourteen. Her hands had been bound behind her back.

Like Erion, the girl's hair was blonde and wavy while her body was covered with gleaming reptilian scales.

Behind her came a man and a woman. The woman was wailing as if her heart was breaking. Which it probably was.

Erion's sister. And his parents. Unless I was mistaken.

"How can this be allowed?" I demanded harshly, grabbing Odessa's elbow. "How can we allow it?"

I watched her swallow hard. "It's part of the rules of the game," she said, licking her lips. "When a contestant enters, their family is bound by the same rules they must follow."

"Fucking Siabra," Rychel spat from beside me.

And then she really did spit. Her saliva sprayed the guard nearest to us. He paused to wipe his face, glaring at her with a look of intense dislike.

Rychel didn't even notice. She darted forward, her long black hair whipping behind her, as she stood in front of the girl.

"All of you are fucking monsters," she cried, the fury in her voice palpable.

I longed to join her. Longed to scream my protests in the Queen Regent's face. But I couldn't risk being removed from the gallery. Not when Draven's fate still hung in the balance.

"You really haven't had enough child sacrifice yet?" Rychel shouted, her voice carrying across the gallery. "You haven't learned your lesson? Who agreed to the Blood Rise? Who sets the terms? Who do you think?"

"Silence." The Queen Regent stepped forward. Cold and imperious. Her face was anything but, however. Rage creased her beautiful features.

"When is this going to end?" Rychel demanded, her voice low and intense.

"I suppose that depends on who wins," Sephone answered smoothly.

"Spiteful bitch. Cruel queen. You might have ended all of this. There were other ways."

A look of disdain crossed Sephone's face. "Not Siabra ways."

"Fucking Siabra," Rychel cursed again. A glob of spit landed on the shoulder of Sephone's glistening silk gown.

Rychel whirled around and slammed through the doors of the gallery, shoving them open so hard one cracked.

Beside me, Odessa, Hawl, Crescent, and Javer stood very still, watching the queen.

They would not leave. Though they likely longed to turn away from this horror as much as I did, they would not leave Draven.

And neither would I.

I watched as Erion's little sister was dragged across the gallery.

More guards had entered. They held back her struggling parents.

The girl's mother finally escaped the guards' cruel grasp as she sank to the floor, sobbing in unspeakable pain.

In the cavern below, Erion stood waiting, his face blank as his sacrifice was delivered as easily as Selwyn's verdantail had been.

Except this was a girl. A Siabra girl.

I wondered if Draven could see what was happening here in the room behind him. Was he beating his fists against the stone wall even now as he realized Erion was going to comply with the mirror's horrific demand?

Or was he lying prone on the ground, his blood flowing out of him as he took his last breaths?

"He could have said 'no,'" I said to no one in particular. "Why didn't he say 'no'?"

Javer stepped up beside me, squeezing his slender frame in between myself and Odessa.

I knew I could have turned him away, demanded he be ostracized from our group. But the funny thing was? I didn't have the heart for anymore unnecessary cruelty.

"Most men are cowards beneath it all," Javer said simply. "Erion accepted his cowardice quite early on, I believe."

"When he left Malkah, you mean?"

Javer nodded. "Under tests such as this, friendship either frays or fortifies."

My heart leaped. Where would that leave Draven? He had helped so many others. But most were dead now. Except for Lyrastra and Selwyn.

On the other side of the mirror would loyalties remain or would they dissolve as easily as Erion's ties to his family had? Given up for a ruthless shot at personal survival?

I cheated.

As the guards shoved Erion's sobbing sister across the room and he caught her up against his chest with the desperate eagerness of a rabid, starving animal and then stepped into the mirror, I closed my eyes for a brief moment.

CHAPTER 25

When I opened them, the scene below had changed once more. Like the rise and fall of a curtain over the stage during a play, the room with the mirror was gone. A new space was illuminated.

Gone were the stony caves.

We looked down onto another world.

A grove of trees stood on the edge of a cliff. A frayed and weathered wooden bridge hung over the side of the cliff, spanning a deep rocky chasm. Below the bridge, a torrent of rushing water roared, threatening to swallow anything that fell into its depths.

At the foot of the bridge, at the border of the grove, Draven sat crouched on the ground.

His skin was a sickly shade of gray. A sheen of sweat covered his body. The leather jerkin he had been wearing lay abandoned on the ground nearby. Dried blood coated his face in a death mask.

The stumps of his once-beautiful horns were jagged and rough. Blood still trickled down his forehead. I could hardly look at them.

And his chest... A mortal would have fallen long ago. I had no idea how he was still breathing. What sort of a creature, mortal or fae, could rip out part of their heart as he had done and still be alive?

I knew he had healing powers. But I also knew they had not been sufficient in the past when it came to the bloodwraith.

Selwyn was kneeling beside him, trying to staunch the gaping hole in Draven's chest with what looked like a mixture of mud and moss. I had heard of hunters using such makeshift poultices in times of extremity before. I wondered if there was a chance in hell it could work.

Beside me, Odessa drew in a sharp hissing breath.

"What?" I demanded.

"Something's wrong." Javer's voice was surprisingly gentle.

"Besides the hole in his heart, you mean?"

The mage nodded. "Something else."

"Poison," Odessa said briefly.

"Avriel touched him on the shoulder. He touched Draven's bare skin." I looked at her in horror. "You think..."

"I think he's a conniving bastard and that was the way he got past the mirror." Javer sounded almost admiring.

My hand flew to my mouth in shock. "He offered it to Draven."

I looked down at where Draven sat. The man who had offered the mirror a piece of his own heart rather than do what despicable Erion had done and offer it me instead.

It had been within his rights. I hadn't signed up for the fucking Blood Rise.

But clearly, I was somehow still bound by its rules.

Draven might have sacrificed me, used me, to get ahead. And it would have been permitted.

My eyes shot to just beyond the treeline. Erion stood there. He was alone.

There was no trace of the dead verdantail either.

"What did the mirror do with Erion's sister and Selwyn's verdantail? Where are they?"

"I don't think you really want to know the answer to that question, Lady Morgan," Javer replied, his voice surprisingly gentle. "Selwyn... Well, at least he was merciful to his offering."

The clear implication was that Erion had not been.

He had gone through the mirror with his living sacrifice in his arms. His own sister.

He had not had the guts to do what Selwyn had done and ensure his sister experienced no pain. No greater pain, I reminded myself, than what she already had experienced by being betrayed by her own brother.

I said nothing. Javer was right.

"Focus on the prince," Javer suggested. "He's all that matters."

"It's incredible that Selwyn is helping him. You said friendships fray."

I thought I caught the hint of a smile behind the dark beard. "The prince forges powerful loyalties. It's one of his greatest aptitudes. Where others break and destroy, Prince Kairos creates."

I drew a quavering breath. Fuck if it didn't kill me to admit it, but Javer was right.

I only had to look around me, at the people by my side, to know he was right. Amidst a cold court, Draven had created his own. He had forged a community.

"If Draven doesn't die, the mirror won't have gotten anything from Avriel," I said hopefully. "Maybe it'll kill him."

"We can hope," Javer agreed. "But I doubt it. Its range is unlikely to extend into the third arena. And you forget, Avriel did give it one thing, though I'm sure it wasn't what the spirit truly desired. The prince's pain."

My eyes went to Draven's face. Was he in pain? His jaw was clenched tightly, his eyes narrowed. He hid his pain well. He always had.

"Back in Eskira, he was poisoned with bloodwraith," I told Javer, my voice tight. "Could that have been what Avriel used?"

Javer's expression turned thoughtful. "Avriel would have had to have known he was susceptible to that. Not all Siabra are. Fascinating. I wonder if…"

He broke off as we both looked down to see Lyrastra shouting at Avriel. He had tried to approach the trio.

But Lyrastra was standing guard. Her blades were out, one in each hand.

As we watched, Avriel tipped his head back and laughed, then gestured to Draven.

"Probably saying something pragmatic about how they should put the prince out of his misery," Javer suggested. "Oh, she'll kill him first if he tries to even come close, don't worry."

I nodded, nervously. Would she?

Avriel took another step.

To my horror, Lyrastra lowered her blades to her side, then sheathed them in a swift movement.

She backed up, closer to where Selwyn was still working on Draven, forcing the leather jerkin over Draven's injured chest and buckling it tightly.

Avriel took one step closer. Lyrastra smiled at him.

My heart thumped. Was she changing sides? Had she ever had a side, really?

Her hands shot out. A familiar sight appeared. A shadowy serpent slithered from the palms of her hands, shooting towards Avriel with incredible speed.

Before he could move, his legs were out from under him, just as mine had been.

Lyrastra moved her hands in a swirling pattern and the wraithlike serpent's body constricted, squeezing Avriel's legs painfully.

He shouted angrily at her, but she kept smiling and tugging with her hands, the serpent's bonds growing tighter and tighter.

There was a flash of green. Erion was moving from the edge of the forest.

Selwyn shouted something to Lyrastra. She nodded, glancing briefly at Erion with an expression of bored annoyance.

There was a cracking sound as Lyrastra swiftly pulled her hands apart, then shoved them hard together. Avriel yelped in pain.

"She broke one of his fucking legs," I said with delight. Then I frowned. "Why didn't she break his neck?"

I thought it was a fair point. Avriel seemed ready to kill her if it came down to it. Why hadn't she taken him out when she had been given yet another chance?

"I have a theory about that," Javer murmured from where he had maintained his position in between Odessa and I. "Why don't I tell you once it's fleshed out."

I glanced past him at Odessa. She met my eyes but simply shrugged.

Down below, Lyrastra was finally showing the full range of her serpentine powers and demonstrating without a doubt that she might have done far worse to Avriel than simply leaving him with a broken leg.

Her shadow serpent furled forward, wrapping itself around Erion's neck just as he leaped past Selwyn and Draven and placed his foot onto the wooden bridge.

In an instant, he was yanked back, his body falling to the ground. His hands clawed uselessly at his throat, falling through mist and shadow as the wraith snake curled around and around his neck, squeezing the breath out of him mercilessly and swiftly.

There was a crack. It wasn't a leg this time.

Erion's body collapsed limp on the ground. He was dead.

Lyrastra strode up to the body, looked down at it with distaste, then kicked it off the edge of the cliff into the churning waters below.

She didn't even glance up at the onlookers in the gallery.

I wondered how Erion's parents felt about Lyrastra's particular brand of justice.

Draven was rising to his feet. There was a scowl on his face that seemed to be more to do with some disagreement he was having with Selwyn than the pain he was in.

Selwyn was gesturing to the bridge. Draven pointed at Lyrastra, then called to her.

Clearly, he wanted her to go first.

She shrugged and started over the first wooden slat, then turned and waited for the two men to follow.

Avriel was slowly pushing himself up from the ground, his useless leg twisted at an unnatural angle, a look of anguish on his handsome face.

Good. Let him suffer. He deserved it. There was no doubt in my mind when it came to Avriel that the world would be better off without him.

Draven staggered to the bridge. For a moment, I thought he was going to fall over the side. I gripped the rail so hard my hands hurt. I reveled in the discomfort. A miniscule version of the pain Draven must have been in.

Selwyn was guarding Draven's back, blocking the bridge, as he watched Avriel struggle to gain his footing. I watched as Selwyn drew the heavy ax from his back and held it at the ready.

Meanwhile, Draven was following Lyrastra slowly across the bridge.

They had nearly reached the midway point.

I glanced at the opposite cliff–their destination. There was nothing special there that told me anything about what might await them. Simply rocks and grass and low shrubs. If there was a way out over there, like the door that had opened in the first trial as each contestant reached the top, I couldn't see it.

Avriel had managed to stand up. He was moving slowly towards Selwyn, dragging his broken leg behind him.

Selwyn watched with a faint smile on his lips. He was plainly unconcerned.

A shout rang out from Lyrastra. She had paused on the rickety wooden rungs and was pointing upwards.

A shrill, avian cry pierced the air.

Harpies!

Monstrous birds twisted through the air with deadly grace, converging onto the spot where Draven and Lyrastra stood.

There was a sharp shout of pain. For a moment, I stared at Lyrastra and Draven in confusion.

But the cry had not come from them.

Selwyn!

I watched in horror as the large man dropped his ax and sank to his knees, clawing frantically at his face.

Avriel stood a few feet away, grinning with malice. Then he licked his lips, opened his mouth wide and a green liquid sprayed out, coating Selwyn's hands and every part of his face still left uncovered.

Selwyn let out a piercing scream of pain and his hands dropped away.

I gasped and around me heard many Siabra doing the same.

Selwyn's face had been destroyed. His flesh dripped from his bones.

Avriel had shot some sort of acid from his mouth, dissolving Selwyn's skin.

I looked wildly at Javer, waiting for some sort of explanation.

"Fascinating," the mage murmured, his eyes wide with horror. "The torment must be exquisite."

I gritted my teeth. "How is he fucking doing it?"

"Some sort of reptilian reserve from a pocket in his throat. It must be a very limited amount or he would have used it against his other opponents before now. Evidently, he's been saving it for a moment of desperation like this..." Javer gestured to Avriel's leg. "When he knew he would need the upper hand."

"The upper hand?" A bitter laugh broke from my lips. "Selwyn's face is *gone*. I suppose you could call that gaining the upper hand."

Selwyn was a pitiful sight. A terrible keening sound was coming from the antlered man's throat as he clutched it with his acid-burned hands. The acid was still doing its evil work. The flesh on his face and hands continued to bubble and melt away, pieces of skin falling like leaves to the ground around him.

On the bridge, Draven and Lyrastra watched horror-struck. But they had problems of their own. The harpies were nearly upon them. And besides, it was far too late for them to help Selwyn now.

The large man fell onto his side, his body spasming and twitching.

Avriel watched and waited. When Selwyn seemed to be dead, he stepped forward, straightening his body. He was not as badly hurt as he had pretended to be, I realized with shock. As he began to step forward, Avriel was still able to put some weight on his broken leg.

He stepped over Selwyn's prone form, and touched a foot to the first rung of the wooden bridge, then paused, watching in what seemed like amusement as the harpy flock descended on Draven and Lyrastra.

I knew better than to think he would engage in the fight. He would hang back, waiting for the other two challengers to clear the bridge. Only then would he dare approach.

Was there more acid in his throat? Was he saving it for Lyrastra and Draven? Or was Javer right and that had been his only reserve? I imagined Draven's face melting away as acid burned through flesh and bone and shuddered, wrapping my arms around myself.

The harpies had reached Draven and Lyrastra.

The monstrous birds looked exactly as I remembered from when they had attacked us at Meridium. A grotesque fusion of woman and bird, a macabre and deformed caricature of two originally beautiful creatures.

We had fought them off at Meridium, but had been forced to seek shelter inside the ruins. How would Draven fare against them now, poisoned and wounded as he was?

The harpies' bodies were sinewy and gaunt, covered in mottled feathers of red, gray, and brown. Their razor-sharp talons were out as they flew towards the pair on the bridge, their wings beating with a relentless fury.

Lyrastra stood ready, her knives in hand. As the first harpy flew over, she leaped into the air, slicing through its wings with swift and precise movements like the ones I had seen her practicing in the training arena what felt like ages ago. The harpy plummeted past her into the chasm below with a furious scream and was swallowed up by the rushing waters.

She leaped again, a jump that left me holding my breath as the bridge shook underneath her and she poised midair. Then bloodied feathers floated past as two more harpies fell, screeching, their wings hanging at their sides.

Draven seemed frozen. He was slumped against the ropes of the bridge, barely standing. He had made no move to unsheathe a weapon.

Lyrastra glanced at him nervously as she took down another harpy.

My heart was in my throat. Would she abandon him there?

The largest harpy I had ever seen flew through the air, cawing loudly. Her face bore the remnants of feminine features, high cheekbones and a pair of lovely eyes. But a sharp, jagged beak protruded from where a woman's mouth should have been, curving downwards menacingly.

I watched as the harpy spread her wings wider then circled high above Lyrastra, avoiding her high leaps and sharp knives.

The harpy's eyes gleamed with a yellow eagle-like hue as she stared down at Draven with malice.

I understood what she saw. Draven seemed like the weakest link. The easiest prey to pick off.

The harpy dove.

Lyrastra moved forward, her knives already extending.

In a flash, Draven was upright.

He let go of the ropes, placing his body between Lyrastra and the enormous harpy.

As the harpy screeched and lunged, her wings beating and flapping, Draven slowly raised his hands.

He lifted his arms towards the sky.

My heart was beating wildly. What was this? Some sort of plea to the gods? Draven had never seemed devout before. What was he doing? Why wasn't he pulling his blade?

His own claws had extended.

But compared to the harpy's talons, Draven's claws seemed decorative. Not deadly. His horns were gone, too. He couldn't slash with those.

What was his plan?

His palms stayed up.

The harpy swooped towards him.

A burst of fire crackled around the winged monster, engulfing her in a blaze of heat.

She spiraled past Draven, her fearsome form swiftly becoming a charred remnant as she hit the water with a splash and went under the swirling blackness.

"What the fuck?" Odessa demanded. She turned to me, her dark eyes huge. "What the fuck was that? How did he do that? Did you know he could do that?"

Mutely, I shook my head.

More harpies were diving towards Draven and Lyrastra. The dark-haired woman was staring at Draven, her mouth agape. She seemed as shocked as we were.

Draven, on the other hand, was radiating perfect calm.

With a twist of his body, he extended his hands again, shooting flames at the two harpies closest to him. They screeched and sizzled, their feathers bursting into flames.

Three harpies flew in on his left. He turned with a deliberate slowness I found almost infuriating. Flames flew from his palms. The burning harpies spun downwards and sank into the rapids at the bottom of the chasm.

The flock had been decimated. Two last harpies swooped overhead, then turned and beat their wings frantically, speeding away in surrender.

On the bridge, Draven watched them go. Then he sank to his knees. His dark head fell to his breast.

The air began to resonate with the rhythmic pulse of wings in motion. Another flock of harpies was incoming from the opposite direction.

It would never end, I thought hollowly. Draven had pushed himself too far.

Perhaps Sephone had decided to simply kill them all. Or was she paving the way for Avriel? Just how much was she controlling all of this?

"He over spent himself. He did too much. Fuck, fuck, fuck," Odessa chanted beside me, her voice filled with a panic I had never expected to hear. "Lyrastra... Please, if you ever cared for him at all. If you ever cared for this empire, for our people, please..."

I froze. Was this what it came down to?

Was I really going to pray to whatever gods I believed in and beg them to soften Lyrastra's heart? Beg her to give her own life saving Draven?

It should have been me, not her down below with him. I finally let myself say it inside my own head.

I should have been beside Draven. Not her. Protecting him. Shielding him. Not Lyrastra, me.

The irrational fear and jealousy filled my body like poison. I could hardly breathe.

He was mine. I was his. We belonged to one another. It couldn't end like this. Not with us separated. Not like this. We had so much more to say. There was so much I still had to tell him. The words I had been hiding...

Lyrastra slowly lifted her head. She looked up at the onlookers in the gallery.

Her eyes searched across the crowd, then found mine.

We stared at one another as the sound of beating wings filled the air.

I could have mouthed the words. Begged her to save him.

But the moment was over as soon as it had begun.

She broke her gaze from mine and with a movement quick as lightning, pushed Draven off the bridge and into the chasm below.

CHAPTER 26

I watched Draven's body plummet downwards, my lips sealed together.

He hit the water with a splash and disappeared beneath the swirling dark waves.

On the bridge, Lyrastra was moving back and forth, her blades speeding to and fro.

I saw her glance across the wooden slats in the direction of the grove and then I understood.

Avriel had advanced.

He was halfway between the midpoint and the cliff. Now he stood, frozen in indecision, his eyes moving between the flock of harpies rushing towards the bridge and Lyrastra's knives.

She was swifter than the harpy's beating wings.

Ruthlessly, she sliced through the ropes that held the bridge together.

The ropes frayed and split apart, first on one side then the other.

For a moment, Lyrastra hung on, gripping a wooden board. Then she raised her arm and cut through the last rope holding her.

The bridge split.

Lyrastra fell.

And so did Avriel.

He caught at a wooden slat as his half of the bridge swung dizzyingly downwards, then slammed into the side of the cliff.

For a moment, I held my breath, hoping the force of the impact would take care of him once and for all.

Then I looked away. He was still alive, hanging there.

Lyrastra had fallen down into the waters below. Her head broke the surface. She gasped, then dove down.

Seconds passed.

Minutes.

Around me, the crowd began to murmur.

I imagined what they were saying. Had the Blood Rise just become much simpler? Would Avriel win by default?

On either side of me, Draven's friends stood silent and still. Rychel's elbow touched mine. A jolt of connection. I unfurled my fists and forced myself to take her hand in mind.

I had no words of comfort to offer. I had no words of resignation either. I refused to accept it.

Draven *couldn't* be gone. It was an impossibility.

So we said nothing. Simply watched and waited and if some of us prayed, who could ever say who had done so?

Time stretched. The air was heavy with uncertainty.

The murmurs around us slowly became a roar.

Below, the chasm held its secrets.

With every second, I chanted a silent plea. Not to Zorya. Not to the Three. Not to any god or goddess I knew, but to all of them together. To everything. To Aercanum itself. To the blood in my veins. To the chance of goodness, if it had ever existed. To hope, that fleeting spark that had preserved me thus far.

To something more tremulous and fragile.

To a word I had never brought myself to say even when I knew I had felt it.

For down below, my heart was lost in the waters.

If Draven never surfaced, would I?

Then, as if the world had held its breath with me, a wave crashed onto the beach below, sweeping two figures onto the sand.

Gasps and shouts filled the gallery around me. The spectacle had just soared to new heights.

Lyrastra stirred first, pushing herself up onto her knees, and coughing.

Slowly, she crawled across the sand to where Draven lay on his stomach.

Unceremoniously shoving him onto his back, she began to pound on his chest.

I didn't dare to breathe.

Not until the moment he coughed and sputtered, water trickling from his mouth out onto the sand.

Rychel's hand clenched mine tightly as her brother's chest began to rise and fall.

Somehow, Lyrastra got him to his feet.

Staggering over the sand, she half-dragged, half-carried him to the door that had suddenly opened behind them and then they were gone.

On the other side of the chasm, Avriel dropped into the water from where he had climbed down the cliff face and began to swim towards the beach.

I had no doubt he would reach it. Fate had evidently decided that this was not his day to die.

The second trial was over.

CHAPTER 27

I raced through the field on Nightclaw's back, trying to clear my head.

It had been three days since the trial had ended. Three days since Lyrastra had brought Draven back to me, still breathing but not much else.

Dripping wet, the pair had sunk to the floor of the gallery–Draven's weight pulling the serpentine woman down. Rychel and I had been there in a heartbeat, with the rest of our small group close behind.

Gawain and Hawl had carried Draven out of that hellish gallery and back to our suite where the best healers in the court had been summoned to attend to him. Rychel and Javer looked on all the while, their gazes hawkish for any signs of treachery or foul play.

When the healers had failed to ascertain just what was wrong. When none could come up with a reason for why Draven was breathing but hadn't opened his eyes, my hope had flickered like a candle. Gradually, everyone departed one by one.

When the suite was finally empty, I had crouched by Draven's bedside and touched him, calling my powers forth as best I could.

I had healed him once before when I hadn't even been trying to do it.

Surely, I could do it again.

A piece of his heart was missing. His fucking *heart*. Selwyn had used clods of earth and moss to close the breach. The healers had peeled the mess out again, cleaning and stitching the wound.

Now jagged stitches traced a path across Draven's chest, holding his damaged flesh together. A puckered scar was forming around the wound.

His features held a weary pallor, the vibrancy of life drained from his normally sun-bronzed skin. Shadows danced beneath his eyes. Beads of sweat clung to his forehead, glistening in the light.

His breathing was shallow and labored, yet steady. His heartbeat was shockingly regular.

One of the healers claimed he had entered a kind of stasis and simply required time to heal.

The rest said he shouldn't have been alive at all. Not with the injury to his heart. Not with the concoction of bloodwraith they had found traces of on his skin. Even a Siabra, apparently, could only endure so much.

As for how he had managed to get onto the bridge still standing, fight the harpies, summon flame from his hands?

They had no answers. None that made any sense at least. One had used the word "miracle." Another had muttered that he would have made a fine emperor.

Would have.

So, they had left. And I had stayed.

I had touched his skin, tracing the stitches gently with my fingers. Then, putting my palms against his chest, I had summoned whatever part of my powers had healed him once before.

I had felt something come.

Tendrils of power flickered forth from me and into him.

For a moment, I had been hopeful.

Then the tendrils had curled up like wisps of smoke from a dying candle and vanished.

I tried again. And again. And again. Until I was drenched with sweat and exhausted.

Each time dealt the same result. It was as if my magic had hit a solid wall of stone and been repelled.

I threw myself against the wall, over and over, not caring when my body was bruised and battered.

Until Breena and Hawl had finally found me panting and crying on the floor of the bedroom in the dark like a child and forced me out of the room. Made me eat some of the food Hawl had somehow managed to find the will to cook. Made me bathe and dress. And then, Hawl had shoved me none-too-gently out into the hall where Crescent had stood waiting.

I had followed the stitcher in silence as he took us above to the city on the surface and led me towards the only creature who could possibly need me as much as Draven did.

In a field just outside of Noctasia, Nightclaw stood waiting for me.

With Hawl's help, I had arranged for him to be rehomed. An old hunting lodge as well as the grounds around it had been set up for his use.

The former gamekeeper, a benevolent woman named Tiana who was the opposite of Master Rodrick in every possible way, had been charged with his care and had embraced her new role. She had woven a bed of soft grasses for Nightclaw to sleep in and had arranged the delivery of fresh meats and tender greens from city markets every day to supplement Nightclaw's newly rekindled hunting skills.

The exmoor had taken to Tiana, leaving her presents outside of the lodge. Dead rabbits and partially-skinned deer. Tiana was delighted and ate everything he brought. After cooking it, of course.

Now, under the cover of the moonlit night, I wove my fingers gently through Nightclaw's golden fur as we galloped through an endless field of wheat and barley. The saddle had become a part of me. My legs wrapped securely around the exmoor's muscular form, feeling his latent strength pulsating beneath me.

With each stride Nightclaw took, the ground quivered beneath us. His large, padded paws propelled us forward, leaving deep imprints in the earth as we streaked through the open field.

The wind rushed past, tangling my hair and rustling Nightclaw's fur as his swift movements sliced through the cool night air.

I leaned forward, running my hands over the battlecat's coat. He was so vital. So alive. I thought of Draven, lying prone in the bed. It was unnatural to see him like that. Every fiber of my being screamed out the wrongness of it.

But here, above ground, running over the surface of Aercanum on Nightclaw's back, I could forget for a few moments. Or, if not forget, try to remind myself of the most precious parts of the life I wanted Draven to return to so badly.

On Nightclaw's back, my heart was more at ease than it had been in days. Filled with the exmoor's own excitement and exhilaration... and beneath it all a quiet satisfaction. Nightclaw had yearned for this freedom, I suddenly understood. He had chafed at the confines of his cage, yes, but more than that he had hated being below ground. To an exmoor, it was as unnatural as being fed one's food rather than hunting for it.

Now Nightclaw's true instincts were being honed once more. He was learning how to hunt for himself again. Remembering how to be free again.

I felt this on some visceral level, as I touched my hand to his body. Together we were becoming a single force, melded into one.

A sense of peaceful understanding was passing between us. As if Nightclaw's emotions, untethered by words, were finding a conduit in my very soul.

I could sense his unwavering loyalty to me, his fierce protectiveness. His *love*. The feelings were deep and intense and they moved me. I felt undeserving of such devotion and allegiance. But as quickly as the thought passed through me, it was followed by Nightclaw's swift rebuttal.

I was more than worthy, the exmoor said. I was his warrior. His rider.

I kept my emotions in check, my heart pounding. How was this possible? Was my imagination running wild or was I truly sensing the battlecat's feelings?

Perhaps it was wishful thinking, I told myself, only to receive a quick tap on the back of my shoulder from Nightclaw's tufted tail as a rebuke.

I laughed aloud as a sense of awe washed over me. There was a hidden reservoir of potential here, waiting to be unleashed.

And yet I couldn't focus on it fully. My mind was consumed with thoughts of Draven. Nightclaw's happiness warmed my heart and yet also only smoothed the surface of my grief for a little while.

It was all right, Nightclaw said through our bond.

A companion shares the path, no matter where it leads and no matter how painful.

I gasped aloud with shock. The words had rung so clearly in my ears, as if they had been spoken by someone beside me.

A moment later, Nightclaw turned back to the hunting lodge. Someone was there, I understood. Waiting to speak with me.

I saw Rychel huddled in the dark on a bench outside the lodge as we approached.

She raised her head as Nightclaw came to a skidding halt and smiled slightly. "Playful beast."

"He does love to show off," I admitted, sliding off and giving Nightclaw one last pat along his sleek side.

"I hear he's making good use of my father's hunting grounds," Rychel remarked, standing up. "All of those poor rabbits."

Nightclaw let out a little snarling growl as if to say, "I was hungry. What would you have had me do?"

"Tiana says the rabbits were out of control. Basically a pest," I said primly. "Nightclaw did her a favor. Besides, he says he was hungry."

"Ha," Rychel said. "He said that, did he? I'm sure he did."

I colored. "You're far from home."

Rychel stared up at the moon. "I found out how Avriel knew to use bloodwraith."

I raised my eyebrows. "That's what you've been doing? Tracking down leads?"

"Among other things." She shrugged. "Why? What would you have suggested I do? I can't help my brother in any other way and I can't sit still."

It was probably more useful than what I'd been doing. "What did you find out?"

"Ulpheas told him." She scowled. "The snitch."

"But how would Ulpheas even have known that?" I said slowly. I couldn't imagine Draven telling him. Nor telling anyone else who might tell Ulpheas—no, not even Lyrastra.

"That's what I can't make heads or tails of. Nor why he would tell Avriel either. He's something of a neutral, Ulpheas. That's what happens when you're too cowardly to pick a side, I suppose."

"He's a stitcher. Your brother used him to find me in Noctasia the other day."

Rychel grimaced. "He sure is. And that's how he got away from me."

"Away from you?"

"You know, before I could get my hot pokers out and really give him a piece of my mind," she clarified. "He stitched away. Little fink."

"You have hot pokers?"

"It's a euphemism."

I didn't ask what for. She looked too grim and angry for me to believe she was entirely joking.

If Ulpheas had told Avriel something so critical, then Ulpheas had harmed Draven by proxy. I couldn't see Rychel forgiving something like that easily.

"I suppose it's good to know who we can't trust, but it doesn't help us help Draven," I said quietly.

Rychel nodded. "I've been experimenting in my workshop."

My eyebrows went up. "With?"

"The grail." She met my gaze then looked away. "It's not necessarily evil, Morgan."

"It corrupted the fae children. You use it for the Blood Rise. I'm sorry, I must have missed the part where it had healing properties."

"But it does. It can do anything. In the right hands. It has limitless potential. I just..." She shook her head, frustrated. "I'm not the right hands. It won't respond to me. No matter what I try."

My expression softened as I looked at her. "At least you're trying, Rychel. Unlike most of the Siabra. At least you still care." The idea that she could undo what her father had done to the fae children was, well, lunacy in my humble opinion. But it was also admirable.

Rychel was looking past me, at the moonlit field. "I thought it would work. But his body wouldn't even let me bring it near him."

"You brought the grail to Draven?" I asked sharply.

She nodded. "It was like a shield was up. Which is impossible. He can't shield. And yet I couldn't even bring the cup to his lips." She looked at me. "Perhaps we should ask Javer..."

"Keep Javer away from Draven and no, even better yet, keep Javer away from the grail. Do you really think that man mixes well with limitless power?"

Rychel nodded. "You probably have a point. But if shielding is involved..."

"It's not. That's impossible. Besides, Javer has seen Draven. I'm sure he would have said something if that were the case. He was there when the court healers examined him."

I didn't tell Rychel I had come up against the same thing. The invisible wall I had felt when I had tried to use my magic. The tendrils bouncing off something hard and unyielding.

Crescent arrived and soon we were back in the palace.

I stiffened as we approached the door to the suite. Someone was waiting outside.

Avriel peeled himself away from the wall, a grin on his face. The leg he had injured in the last trial looked fine. How disappointing.

I stared at him coldly. I could kill him, here, now. Fry him to the floor like an egg in a pan. It was tempting. Disgusting to clean up, but tempting.

But the Blood Rise wasn't over yet. Was it? Draven was still alive. Even if there was no way he could compete.

"What the fuck are you doing here?" I demanded. Behind me I could feel Crescent tense and waiting.

"Just came to see the look on your face," Avriel drawled, folding his muscular scaled golden arms across a white linen tunic.

"You saw it." I turned to the door of the suite.

"When I told you the next trial is tomorrow," Avriel finished.

I paused. "You're a man of lies, Avriel. Why would I believe such a stupid one?"

"Because it's not a lie. The Queen Regent grows tired of waiting for her...son... to awaken." Avriel didn't bother to hide his smirk.

Sephone had never behaved as if Draven meant anything like true family to her, though from all I had seen he treated her with courtesy and respect. Overall, I knew people who had closer bonds with their baker. Or their dogs.

So, I wouldn't have put it past her. Still, it was clearly a blatant lie.

"Well, you've told me," I said blithely. "Now go. Before your toxic aroma stains the hall."

"You don't believe me," Avriel crowed. "But it's true."

I lost my patience.

Whirling around, my hands shot out.

A ring of fire sprang up around Avriel. I watched him hop and dance, his back to the wall as the flames flickered.

"Here's what I know," I said, holding the flames steadily in place. "You should be dead already. Lyrastra should have killed you. Draven should have killed you. Selwyn should certainly have killed you. You're weak and craven and haven't the heart or the stomach to lead an empire. You're thirsty for power but like an infant, you'd drink it up only to spew it out again. You're weak, Avriel. So weak it makes me sick. And if I had the chance..."

"What?" Avriel challenged, his scales flashing as he leaned forward, taunting the flames. "You'd what?"

"I'd kill you myself," I said truthfully. "If the prince dies, you won't live to see the next dawn." Suddenly, I saw the truth behind his brazenness. "You think you're invincible because you have the favor of the queen. That's why Lyrastra held back. That's why they all did. What did Sephone do? Threaten them? Threaten the contestants' families?" I waggled my finger and the flames climbed a little higher. I could feel their heat from where I stood. "That's not very nice, Avriel. Tampering with the Blood Rise. Hiding behind the queen's silk skirts."

I enjoyed the look on his face. Unbridled fury that he could do nothing with.

"Get me out of here."

"You'll find your own way out. You're good at that, aren't you?"

I pushed open the door to the suite, leaving him in the ring of fire.

Lyrastra was sitting in a chair by the bed, with her head leaning on one hand. She seemed tired as she stared at Draven's prone form.

As I entered, she looked up.

"Good. You're back. We need to talk."

CHAPTER 28

L yrastra rose from the chair and strode past me, her hands extended and fingers splayed. Energy danced as an intricate pattern formed in the air, criss-crossing over the door I had just come through, pulsing with a faint glow.

"There. I've set a ward," she said, turning to face me. "Against prying ears."

"Considering Avriel is lurking outside, that seems wise."

"Lurking? He's lurking now?"

"He may be on fire right now. Or more likely he got the flames out and has scampered away. Back to Sephone's side no doubt." I cast a hard look at Lyrastra. "What does the queen have on you? Why didn't you finish Avriel off when you had the chance?"

She tilted her head. "That's what you're going to ask me? Not what I'm doing here?"

"I can ask you both, can't I?"

"You could ask him the same question," she said, pointing to where Draven lay immobile in the bed. "He could have finished Avriel."

"He would have," I said quietly.

"Why didn't he do it before?" she challenged. "Aren't you curious?"

"I have a feeling the answer is simple. It's Sephone's game. And you're all pieces on her board. Draven would have scattered the pieces. But you're right, he waited. Too long." I glanced at the bed. "But it's not too late."

"Actually, it is. The third trial is tomorrow."

My eyes flew to her face. "Avriel claimed the same thing. I thought he was lying."

"For once in his life, he wasn't. Sephone announced she's bored. It would seem that three days is long enough for even her own son to recover from losing a piece of his heart and being poisoned."

"She knows he's nowhere near recovered. She must know."

"She doesn't give a fuck, Morgan. Do you really think they're anything like a family? Maybe there are families back where you're from who genuinely care for one another, but do you think that's common here? In this court?"

"It seems common enough above you," I said, thinking of the city of Noctasia and then of Gawain and Crescent. There were exceptions to every rule.

"Sure. Among mortals. Not among the Siabra. Not among the nobles. Not among those of us who grew up below ground thinking any of this was... normal." She threw up her hands, then placed them on her waist and began to walk back and forth. "If Kairos hadn't come back, what do you think would have happened?"

"Avriel would have ascended," I said slowly.

"Right. With Sephone by his side. But Kairos returned. And so Sephone had to institute the Blood Rise. Make no mistake, she's had fun doing it. She loves this sort of spectacle. So does most of the court. But Avriel was supposed to win all along. And now he's so close, they can both taste it."

"What's the fun of a rigged game?" I demanded. "The court wouldn't stand for it. Surely they'd find it boring. Wouldn't they?"

"Some are ready for a change. They don't want Avriel as emperor. He's a return to the ways of Draven's father. They see it as a regression. But most Siabra? The status quo is fine with them."

"Even when it's meant their slow decline? The loss of their bloodlines? I mean, you're all going to die eventually, aren't you? And what will be left?"

"That's hundreds of years away. Do you really think many of these people care about babies? Besides, they'll keep doing what they've been doing. Believing a cure is out there. Believing they can sow fae seed in some mortal woman and that eventually it'll stick."

I blanched in disgust. "That's madness."

"There's no other word for doing the same thing over and over again and expecting a different result," Lyrastra agreed. "But that's what they'll do. You're right. The court is dying. It's withering like an infected vine. And Kairos? He'd have cut it off, right at the root."

"You wanted him to win." I stared at her. "You really did."

Her lips twisted. "I would make a good empress."

"You probably would," I agreed, enjoying the look of shock that came over her face. "I wouldn't have said that when I first met you, but now? You're daring. Brave. You're *very* fucking brave, Lyrastra. And you're loyal. You saved him. Don't think I'll ever forget that."

"Don't think I care what you think of me," she snapped, reminding me of the first day we'd met.

Me lying frozen in the bed. Her standing over me with hate in her eyes.

I smiled. "Just like old times, isn't it?"

She looked away. "He's not as ruthless as he likes to think he is."

"No," I agreed. "He isn't. That's why he's there." I felt disloyal for even saying it but I still couldn't get over that. Some truth I had taken for granted about Draven that I was now forced to question. I remembered when I had believed he really was simply a ruthless, mindless killing machine. It had been easier then, in a way, to finding out he had a soul. A heart.

"There's a way around it." Lyrastra interrupted my train of thought. "A way he can still win."

"He can't even talk or walk and you think he can still win tomorrow?" I shook my head. "No. We'll go to Sephone. You and I, together. We'll demand she summon the court. The entire court. Surely in Siabra law there's something that says the rest of the court gets some kind of a say in all of this. We'll beseech them to reconsider, to move the trial date."

"No," Lyrastra cut in. "We won't. There's no such law. There's only one gambit here to play. There's only one way to save Kairos. There's only one way he can still win. And it doesn't involve beseeching the court." She shook her head at me as if I were a naive idiot.

I raised my hands. "Fine. Let's hear it."

"There's a stipulation in the rules. It only applies to those of the royal house."

"What is it?"

"A Royal Paramour or Consort may stand in for the original challenger."

I stared at her. "You're joking. You want me to take Draven's place?"

But the words were sinking in fast. Wasn't this exactly what I had wanted as I watched Lyrastra at Draven's side?

Except now I would be at Lyrastra's side, not Draven's.

"You want me there? You trust me there?"

She tossed her glossy black hair. "Do you trust me?"

"I honestly have no idea," I said frankly. "You're something of an enigma."

She looked pleased at that.

"What happens if I don't do this?" I demanded. "What then?"

"Then the prince dies. Either by forfeit or from his injuries."

"Forfeit? I'd hardly call it forfeit. He hasn't given up," I protested.

"Can he compete tomorrow? No. Then he forfeits. He'll be executed. Maybe Sephone will be merciful and wait until he finally wakes up to do it. Or maybe she'll have her personal healer ensure he never wakens at all. Do you want to wait around and find out? Either way, he'll be dead and Avriel will be the next emperor."

I swore softly. "Fuck." Then I looked at her. "I don't just have to compete. I have to win."

"Unless you'd prefer to let me win," she said sweetly. "You know there's a high probability I will."

I nodded. It seemed pointless to deny it. "You're right."

She looked taken aback. "Either way, I want a seat at the table."

"Draven said it was traditional for the follow-up winners to become advisors. I don't think he'd deny you the position. He respects you a great deal." I studied her. "But why are you really doing all of this? For the good of the empire? Or is there a particular rule you're keen on changing?"

I saw my arrow hit home. Lyrastra's face flushed.

"I'm tired of being viewed as nothing more than a discarded vessel for a dead prince's spawn."

"You want to be free," I guessed. "Free to wed."

"Free to choose." Her lovely serpentine eyes fixed upon me as her face softened. "There's someone above. In Noctasia. They're not Siabra."

"Someone you care about."

She nodded reluctantly.

"What happened to wanting Kairos? To wanting me dead?"

She looked away. "It would have been simpler. It was what Sephone claimed I deserved. In keeping with tradition. But..." She looked back at me. "Things change."

"In other words, you met this someone fairly recently," I guessed, a grin forming on my lips. "Well, good for you."

The blush crept across her cheeks again. She tossed her hair.

"So how do we do this?" I asked. "Do I go to Sephone now...?"

"No," she said swiftly. "Don't do that. Don't leave this room until we send for you tomorrow. I'll summon Javer when I leave. He'll keep the wards up."

My heart sank. "Because if we told Sephone now..."

"I doubt she'd let you live until morning," Lyrastra said bluntly. "But if you show up at the challenge, there'll be nothing she can do. Everyone knows the rules. They're brutal but simple. In the meantime, I'll start the rumors. Crescent will help me. We'll whisper in the right ears. Remind the court that a chance for Prince Kairos still remains if the woman he loves chooses to take it."

I tried not to let the sound of the word shake me too much. It was Lyrastra's word, not mine. Not his.

"The court is merciless," she continued. "They won't care about love, but they'll understand the motivation and they'll be eager for a chance to see you bleed. Others will wonder why Sephone didn't approach you herself. It'll get back to her. When she sees you there tomorrow, she'll be resigned. She'll know there's nothing she can do."

"This is really within the rules? Has it ever happened before? Is there a precedent?"

Lyrastra looked at me consideringly. "I had Hawl look up the history of this particular stipulation. It's always been on the books. But it seems it's only been used once before. By a Prince's Paramour."

My heart sped up. "What happened to her? Did she win?"

Lyrastra's lips twisted into a familiar cruel smirk. "It was a man. And of course not. He died. Quite spectacularly, too. I believe he tried to catapult from..."

I held up a hand. "Never mind. Don't tell me."

When the door closed behind her, I went back to the bed, sitting on the edge as I watched Draven's chest rise and fall.

Somehow his vulnerability had revealed a deeper truth. We were linked, he and I, bound by something that went deeper than I could have ever have imagined.

He had stood beside me, guarded me, protected me, shielded me in every way he could. Now it was my turn to do the same for him.

I wasn't worried that Draven wouldn't wake up again.

Somehow, I knew he would.

What worried me was what he would wake up to. A death sentence or an empire waiting to be ruled?

His black wavy locks cascaded over the pillow, framing his face. The silver ring nestled in his left ear glimmered faintly, his only adornment. It was strange not to see his eyes open, to feel those intense emerald orbs graze my face. I swallowed hard as my eyes fell upon the broken stumps of horns that protruded from his forehead.

His heart and his horns. He had given both freely. Even though doing so had left him in agony and susceptible to Avriel's ploy.

He had never been one to take the easy way out.

Even in his stillness, there was a serene strength emanating from him.

Unable to resist the pull of my emotions, I lay down on the bed beside him. Reaching out trembling fingers, I lightly traced the outline of his features, gently caressing his skin.

This bond between us defied logic and reason. It had led me from wanting to stab him to wanting to do far different things.

Now the urge to protect him from harm rose above all else.

An image came unbidden. Draven wielding flames as he brought down harpy after harpy on the bridge.

My skin prickled. How had he done such a thing? Had he known he was capable of it until that moment? If so, why had he never told me?

How could he have offered to train me without confessing we shared such similar powers?

He had to wake and soon. For this infuriating man had secrets upon secrets and one by one I was determined to uncover them all, no matter how hard he resisted.

When an hour had passed and there had been no alteration, not that I had expected any, I rose and I changed out of my clothes, bathed, and put on my nightclothes.

Lying down on the bed beside him again, I closed my eyes and tried to sleep.

But all I could think of were the horrific deaths that I had witnessed in the Blood Rise. Tomorrow, I would enter the final trial alongside Avriel and Lyrastra. They were more prepared, probably better trained, had a multitude of finely honed magical abilities, and one of them would stop at nothing to kill me at every opportunity.

I flipped onto my back, folding my hands over my chest.

I was decent with a sword. More than capable with a bow. I could throw a blade. I was fairly quick. I was smart.

I could wield flames, if I was permitted to use magic. Though who knew how well.

Then I thought of the ring of fire I had left dancing around Avriel and smiled to myself.

Whatever happened tomorrow, I knew one thing for certain. I would not be Avriel's easy prey. I was no Rhea or Brasad.

He would find me much harder to kill... for I would be trying my best to kill him right back.

I closed my eyes and willed sleep to come for me.

CHAPTER 29

I followed my mother as she raced up the stairs of the Temple of Vela, my small hand caught in hers.

We burst through the temple's ancient wooden doors, our footsteps echoing through the hallowed halls. Inside, the air was thick with sweet-smelling incense, swirling wisps of fragrant smoke curling around the towered pillars that lined the vast rotunda.

My heart pounded as my mother hurried us towards the heart of the temple.

There, a massive stone arch stood behind a pristine white marble altar.

My mother let go of my hand. Drawing a silver dagger from inside her cloak, she pressed the edge to her own palm.

A drop of crimson welled forth.

Holding her hand high, she let the blood fall onto the altar.

The hair along my arms prickled as a rush of wind blew through the rotunda.

I stepped forward, already knowing what would be required of me. Holding my small palm outstretched, I tried not to flinch as the dagger cut into my flesh.

My mother squeezed a drop of my blood upon the altar, then caught me up in her arms and squeezed me tightly. I could feel her shaking as she held me.

Her fear was infectious.

But we were together.

Holding me on her hip, she went around the altar and to the stone arch behind it.

For a moment, we stood upon the threshold.

My mother stepped forward into the arch.

For a moment, the space inside was dark and terrifyingly empty.

Then thousands upon thousands of stars sparkled to life around us. I reached out a hand, trying to grasp one, laughing out loud as pinpricks of light surrounded us.

My mother's arms were still around me, enfolding me in her timeless embrace. I felt her boundless love, her unwavering protection.

Overcome by weariness, my eyelids flickered as my head drooped against her chest.

The starlight faded.

My eyes closed.

Someone was calling to me.

"Morgan!"

I knew the voice. Boyish and high-pitched. Heart-tuggingly familiar.

"Morgan, I see you. Can you see me? What is this place?"

Kaye. It was Kaye's voice.

I struggled to open my eyes. A trickle of light filtered in, blinding me.

"You have to stop him. Morgan, he's going to kill us all..."

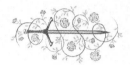

I woke in a cold sweat with the certainty that every one of my vivid dreams had been real.

The village I had seen burning in Tintagel.

My mother running through the streets of Valtain. My mother, the High King's wife.

I woke with the knowledge that I was improbably, impossibly, but truly somehow 150 years old, that Uther Pendragon had never been my real father at all, that Kaye was not my true brother but that he was calling for me, his sister, beyond time and beyond dreams and with the wild hope that I would hear him, that I was still alive, and that I would get to him.

I woke with the knowledge that I would probably die today in the Blood Rise but if by some precious gift of the Three I managed not to then I would leave the dark Siabra court and seek Kaye that very night.

I woke with the realization that someone was knocking at the door.

No, not the door. The wall in the sitting room.

I sat up.

Beside me, Draven slumbered like a prince in a fairytale.

Nothing had changed. He could not help me now.

I crossed the bedroom into the sitting room.

The panel by the bookcases had opened. A small face peeked out.

"Beks?"

His shiny hair fell across his face, almost obscuring his eyes.

Slowly he clambered out and stood before me.

"Not going to invite me in?" I asked, a little amused.

"You're taking Prince Kairos's place in the Blood Rise."

Was it any real surprise he had already found out?

"That's right. The Queen Regent has set the next trial to begin today. Lyrastra tells me I can take the prince's place. There's no other option if we want to save him, Beks."

The boy's lower lip quivered slightly. "It will be... very dangerous."

"Yes, I know." My voice was quiet.

"I had to make sure you weren't still angry with me," he burst out. "I didn't want to tell him anything."

"Angry with you?" I stared at him. "Oh, Beks. I'm not angry with you. I never was."

"But I told him," he said, miserably. "About what we saw. About Avriel killing Pearl and how he did it."

"Did he force you to tell him?" I demanded.

But Beks shook his head. "He heard me, crying out in my sleep. I had a nightmare. He was trying to comfort me."

I was pleasantly shocked to hear Javer would be so tender.

"No wonder you had a nightmare." I touched the boy's cheek, feeling its soft childish smoothness. "You should never have seen such a terrible thing, Beks." I thought of the opening ceremony and the way he had shielded us alongside Javer. "You've seen far too many awful things for a child. Javer should protect you better."

"Javer says there's no point in shielding a shielder. It's my job to protect others, not to be coddled," Beks declared, standing up a little straighter and puffing out his chest. "Besides, he says it's pointless to try to contain me because I'm as slippery as an eel."

That last part was certainly true. Perhaps Javer was coming to terms with the boy's impetuous nature and learning to accept it. I hoped so.

"You have a very important role to play here, that is true. But you're still just a child, Beks. Every child deserves a little coddling. And more than a little protection."

"Javer protects me," Beks said stubbornly.

I smiled slightly, amused by this abrupt show of loyalty. "I'm glad to hear that. He should. He's been entrusted with something incredibly precious."

"What?"

"You, of course." I pulled Beks towards me, embracing him before he could protest. He stayed stiff for a moment, then I felt his body relax against me. Small arms reached around my waist.

"I don't think you should do it, Morgan." The little boy's voice was muffled against my shoulder. "It's too dangerous. I really don't want you to."

"The trial?" I asked gently. "Oh, Beks. I have to. It's the only way to protect the prince."

He nodded wretchedly. "I don't think the queen is a very good mother."

"I don't think so either," I agreed. I held him by the shoulders. "I think that if you ever become a parent, you are certain to do a much better job of it."

He perked up. "Maybe you and the prince could hide somewhere. Like in the tunnels. I could bring you food. It wouldn't be so bad."

I tried not to smile. There was a time not so long ago when I would have considered it. "That's a very kind offer. And I'm sure you would take excellent care of us. But I also don't think Prince Kairos would want to hide. Do you?"

Beks shook his head reluctantly. "Will he ever wake up?"

"I know he will." The resounding certainty in my voice surprised even me. "I just don't know when. But I think it will happen soon. His body must be healing itself. He just needs... more time."

Time that I could buy for him. No matter what it took.

I looked around us, wondering if it was anywhere near morning. I sniffed. I could smell food cooking.

The familiar smell of bacon.

"I think Hawl is here. Are you hungry?"

Beks took a tentative sniff of his own. His eyes widened. "For bacon? Always."

I led him into the dining room, then stopped.

Odessa was already in the room. She was laying out objects on the large table, inspecting each one carefully as she put it out.

As we entered, she looked up. "There you are. I was just about to wake you. The trial begins in an hour."

Suddenly the desire for bacon dissipated. I couldn't imagine eating anything at all.

Beks was not so affected. He ran past me to the kitchen, obviously intent on snatching some of Hawl's cooking.

I looked at the objects Odessa was arranging.

"Armor. For you." She ran a hand over her long braids. The dark strands hung around her shoulders loosely today. "The best we could come up with on such short notice."

The armor on the table was the most beautiful set I had ever seen. Made from supple, ebony leather, it consisted of a cuirass, greaves, boots, and thigh-guards. Leggings and an under-tunic in a brilliant ruby shade were set out alongside them.

All of the leather pieces had been crafted to match my gauntlets, which were there as well. Dyed-red roses were intricately etched onto the surface of the cuirass. Gold and silver flames danced along the edges of the greaves and thigh-guards. Rose-shaped cutouts had been carved into the greaves, allowing glimpses of the fiery red fabric underneath.

"It's beautiful. How could this all have been made so quickly?"

Odessa looked uncomfortable. "I believe the prince had already commissioned the set for."

I stared at her. "Laverna made all of this, you mean?"

She nodded. "Some of the pieces were ready. The rest... Well, she worked all night to finish it. She told me to tell you it's called the Flamebloom Armor."

The name was as lovely as the pieces themselves.

"Why don't I help you put it on now?" Odessa suggested. "If you're like me, you probably don't feel much like eating before a battle."

That's what this was. A battle.

I had never been in battle.

Then abruptly, I thought of the fenrirs, the ambush in Nethervale, the undead children of Meridium.

But those I had fought unknowingly. Not like this. Not with foreknowledge of precisely what I was going up against. *Whom.*

Avriel.

I slipped on the tunic and leggings, then stood still as Odessa approached holding the cuirass.

"We know a little about the trial today," she said, as she began to buckle me into it. "No weapons are allowed. Any other ability is permitted. Physical or magical. No limits."

I nodded.

"Avriel will have plenty at his disposal. We already know his penchant for poison. There's a chance he'll try to sneak it in again. I doubt the queen will penalize him if he does. She seems to be taking a hands-off approach."

"Right."

"As for Lyrastra... Well, you've already seen her skills."

"I have. Now to discover if she plans on using them against me." I met Odessa's eyes. "Her turnaround from enemy to ally has been startling to say the least."

Odessa cleared her throat. "She fetched this armor for you, you know."

I raised one brow. "Should I be checking it for poison? Is that what you're saying?"

Odessa smiled slightly. "No. I think she wished to visit someone on the surface. It was an opportunity to do both, help you and..." She shot me a significant look.

"You mean Laverna? Lyrastra wanted to see Laverna?" My jaw dropped. "*That's* who she's interested in?"

Zorya, what a pair those two women would make.

"Stranger things have happened." Odessa finished buckling my greaves. "Lyrastra wants to live. She wants things to change. I don't know how much she cares about winning outright anymore at this point."

"She claims not a lot. But still..." Still, Lyrastra could easily betray me today. For all I knew, this was all a ploy just to eliminate me entirely, once and for all.

"We'll all be there," Odessa said softly. "Watching you."

She didn't say anything trite like "We know you can do this." Or "Make us proud."

Just letting me know they'd be there was enough. Just like they had been for Draven.

"Thank you." I pushed past the lump in my throat. "That's good to know."

The hour was nearly gone.

I followed Odessa out into the hallway where Crescent, Gawain, and Javer were waiting, solemn and silent.

The path to the gallery was already familiar.

As we entered, a hush fell over the Siabra inside.

The crowd parted as I stepped forward. Avriel and Lyrastra were already standing near the Queen Regent.

Sephone's face was glacial as I approached.

"Your Majesty," I said carefully, bowing as low as I could manage.

What was I supposed to say, I wondered? Thank you for giving me this opportunity to try to save your stepson and nephew's life? Thank you for ruthlessly moving up the last trial in an obvious attempt to show just how little you care and how desperately you want him dead?

I closed my mouth and waited.

For a moment, Sephone seemed expectant. Perhaps she really did expect my thanks.

"Our third contestant," she said finally, in minimal acknowledgement, her lovely lips thinning.

Then she turned away. The time for speeches had passed.

I started towards the other two contestants, then was shocked as Avriel reached an arm out and cinched the queen by the waist, pulling her towards him for a long open-mouthed kiss.

I was sure the Siabra were drinking it in. Their Queen Regent and her lover, not bothering to hide their lust–for each other or for the throne.

The rules were skewed and Draven must have known it all along. What was the point of even playing along with the game if everyone was going to cheat?

But I was trapped now. I was bound through Draven as much as if I had participated in the Blood Rise opening ceremony myself.

Because I was the Prince's Paramour.

Nearly the closest fucking thing to family he had.

As I thought this, my eyes met Rychel's. She had been standing near the edge of the room near Lyrastra. As her eyes found mine, I thought I saw her flinch. Then she stepped towards me.

"I couldn't. I'm sorry, Morgan."

For a moment, I didn't understand what she meant. Then I suddenly I did.

"You could have taken his place. It didn't have to be me."

She nodded, her expression miserable. "I wasn't cut out for it. I'm not saying you were. But..."

"It's all right." I forced a smile. "What's done is done. I'll do my best. Everything... Everything is going to be fine." I touched her arm, then stepped past her, oddly shaken.

Rychel was probably right. She wasn't cut out for this. Had she ever even been in a fight? Or had most of her young lifetime been spent in her workshop, looking for answers to problems created by a father she would never know and never love? Looking for answers that didn't exist, no matter how hard she might wish they did.

A passage in the wall was opening up. It led into a long shadowy hall.

I followed Avriel and Lyrastra as they stepped in first.

The entrance sealed behind me.

I took one step, then another. In front of me, Avriel and Lyrastra were collapsing to their knees.

I opened my mouth to cry out but a mist swam before my eyes.

CHAPTER 30

My eyelids fluttered open, revealing a scene of entwined torment.

My body was ensnared. A cage surrounded me.

Wicked brambles and sinuous vines embraced my body.

I twisted and turned and they grew tighter. Sharp thorns poked into every exposed bit of my flesh, scratching my face and tearing at my hair.

Through the web of vines, I could see movement. Were my competitors facing the same thing I was? Or had they already freed themselves?

My gaze fell upon my hands, pressed tightly to my chest. The gauntlets were etched with sigils that Draven had promised would give me better control.

Would I be able to control my flames in such a confined space? Or would I burn myself to death?

As I possessed no other weapons and couldn't have moved far enough to grab them even if I did, it didn't seem as if I had much choice but to find out.

Summoning my will, I extended my arms as far out as I could towards the constricting mesh of entangling foliage.

A tempest of fire lashed out with wild abandon, igniting the brambles.

I turned my head away from the heat, gritting my teeth as the flames seared the exposed skin of my hands.

Agony seared through me as the fire that was burning through the vines dipped back against my fingertips. The cage was too constraining. I had nowhere to go. I had never had to wield in such close quarters.

I closed my eyes tightly, my breath coming in short panting gasps, unable to do anything but endure the pain as the fire burned through the thick fortress of vegetation.

A few more moments and a space opened up. I lowered my hands and shoved my shoulder through, then twisted my body, and ducking my head, squeezed out of the opening.

Relief coursed through me, intermingled with searing pain. I held out my hands. My fingers were scorched raw.

What were the chances I wouldn't have to use my hands for the rest of the trial?

Slim to none, I thought, shoving down a wave of nausea as another wave of pain swept over me.

I looked around.

To my left, two similar cages to mine lay empty and open. One had been literally split in two. The other was covered in traces of familiar green acid.

Avriel and Lyrastra had beaten me out.

Now where were they?

There was no sign of the gallery of spectators as there had been in the previous two challenges. I could not simply look up and see my friends like Draven had. I had no doubt we were being observed, but in this final round apparently the view went only one way.

I turned to my right. A wall stood before me, tall and imposing. Its surface was unlike anything I had encountered before. Smooth and unyielding, it looked almost transparent, shining with a lustrous quality like grains of sand on a beach.

Stepping forward, I touched the surface gingerly with my least injured fingertip. The wall was as smooth and glossy to the touch as it looked.

Lifting my head, I scanned upwards. It was high. At least seventy feet by my measure.

And there, above me, more than half-way up already, were Lyrastra and Avriel. They climbed on opposite sides of the wall, as far from one another as they could get.

Avriel seemed to be using some sort of substance on the bare palms of his hands and feet to adhere to the wall. He moved slowly, lifting first one hand and smacking it down again before cautiously lifting the next. I wondered if his hands and feet were adapted to climbing, perhaps bearing specialized pads that I had seen on small reptiles that allowed for powerful adhesion as they clung to surfaces.

His progress appeared slow but he seemed in no danger of falling.

Lyrastra's movements were slightly faster and even more impressive. Using serpentine agility, she slithered and coiled against the wall, her body impressively flexible. Undulating and maneuvering her muscles she slowly slid up the wall's burnished surface.

My heart sank like a stone as I watched them.

Frustration mingled with curiosity as I traced my fingers along the seamless facade, searching for any hidden recesses or grooves that could aid my ascent. But the wall remained unyielding, revealing no secrets or footholds to exploit.

Clearly some sort of natural abilities must be required.

I had none that were relevant. I couldn't exactly burn my way up the wall.

But with that thought I decided there was no harm in trying.

Stepping back, I lifted my hands, cringing as the reddened skin on my scorched fingers shifted with the movement. Bubbling blisters were already forming, their delicate surfaces pulsating with the trapped heat.

I clenched my jaw and ignoring the pain, forced flames forth.

The wall in front of me erupted with fire.

I saw Avriel shoot a brief curious glance downwards, then continue his climb. Evidently, I was too far behind to be of much concern.

The flames cleared. I inspected the wall. It was unscathed. My flames had absolutely no effect. Any hopes of burning grooves or hand-holds into its surface vanished. The wall was essentially fireproof. There were no hand-holds or any way to grip the wall's surface that I could see.

A throbbing sensation from my fingertips drew my attention. I looked down, flexing my hands gingerly.

They already hurt less, if that were possible.

Instead of seeing more blisters forming, the ones that had emerged seemed to already be shrinking.

I turned my hands over.

The ugly, painful rawness was dissipating. A healthy color was returning to my skin, as if the flesh were regrowing as quickly as it had been burned away.

As the pain slowly subsided, I felt a peculiar sensation in my fingertips. As if something were awakening inside the very bones.

Instinctively, I stepped up to the wall and placed both my hands along it with my fingertips extended.

And gasped in disbelief as claws snapped out.

The claws flashed with a natural sheen, formidable and thick. Their curved tips glinted with a razor-sharp edge.

I positioned my fingertips carefully against the smooth wall, then tried to dig in.

The claws found purchase, sinking into the material with remarkable ease.

I lifted one hand then another, pulling my body upwards, then kicking the grips on the toes of my boots against the wall to leverage my lower body as I ascended.

My progress was slow but steady. With each extension of my claws and each well-placed kick and grip of my boots, I advanced.

Above me, Lyrastra and Avriel had disappeared from view.

I distributed my weight as strategically as I could, balancing my body as I ascended. Still, every inch gained was slow and painstaking. My muscles screamed as I edged my way higher, readjusting my weight and repositioning my limbs.

My claws were like anchors, puncturing the wall and holding me in place. But the strain on my muscles grew more intense with each moment. The exertion required to maintain my grip, solely relying on the claws and grips on my boots, sent waves of burning sensation coursing through my arms, shoulders and back. Every sinew and fiber strained under the weight of holding up my body, urging me to give in to the discomfort.

But step by step, clawhold by clawhold, I fought back the pain and fatigue.

Sweat trickled down my face, stinging my eyes. I drew on my reserves, gritting my teeth and pushing past the throbbing ache and burning strain.

The pain became a constant but familiar companion. I stole brief glances at my hands, seeing the delicate skin healing over, the blisters drying up, as over and over my claws extended and dug in, extended and dug in.

Finally, I reached the ledge at the top.

With trembling limbs, I hauled myself up and over, the strain in my muscles forgotten as exhilaration washed over me.

My chest rose and fell in labored breaths.

Gradually, I took in what was before me.

A makeshift stable with three stalls stood in front of me. The first two spots stood empty.

Unbelievably, in the third stall stood Nightclaw, his yellow eyes gleaming as he watched me clamber awkwardly to my feet.

Just outside the stall lay his saddle.

And beyond the makeshift stable... A distant island in the center of a vast field. A pillar rose out of the island, tall and narrow. There was something resting atop the pillar that I couldn't pick out.

The field around the island gleamed like a mosaic of glimmering glass cobblestones.

Across this strange terrain, Lyrastra galloped on a nimble black mount covered with snake-like scales. I had never seen any creature move so fast.

Behind her, Avriel seemed to have just entered the field. He rode a massive wolf-like beast covered in thick white fur that shimmered as if it had been touched by the breath of winter itself. As the creature sped over the gleaming cobblestones, I caught a glimpse of ice-like claws and frosty footprints left on the ground beneath.

I raced towards the saddle and yanked open Nightclaw's stall. With trembling hands, I strapped the saddle onto his back, ducking beneath his massive chest to fasten the buckles, then mounted quickly and fumbled for the reins.

We set off swiftly across the peculiar field. My eyes were fixed on the figures in front of us.

Lyrastra was gradually losing her lead. Avriel and his white wolf were closing in on her.

At this rate, she would still make it to the center of the field before them.

I looked beyond to what awaited us. A network of rope bridges extended towards a small central island where a solitary pillar rose upwards. Atop the pillar, a golden object gleamed.

It didn't take much to imagine what it could be.

A crown. The crown of the Siabra empire.

Only one of us could claim the object. What would happen to the other two if they survived but failed to grasp the crown?

But then, I didn't have to worry about that because I was already dead last.

It didn't matter that I had managed to fight my way out of a cage of brambles or claw my way up a perilous wall.

I had already lost. All I could do now was watch and try to guard Lyrastra's back.

Which was growing more and more impossible to do the further away from me she galloped.

I urged Nightclaw forward and he responded eagerly, his soft padded paws flying over the ground.

Ahead of us, Avriel was urging his own mount to increase its speed, lashing at it with his hands and kicking it with his feet in a reckless display of fury and desperation that made me pity the animal.

That is, I nearly pitied it... until with a shout of command from Avriel, the frosty beast opened its maw wide and leaped ahead towards Lyrastra.

In an instant, a blast of icy breath shot forth from the wolf's mouth, engulfing Lyrastra and her black serpentine steed.

For a moment, they were enveloped in frost, frozen in time, suspended in an icy tableau.

Then I watched in horror as Lyrastra tumbled from her mount, falling to the ground in a hard landing.

Avriel looked back at the dark-haired woman's prone body, his face split in a laugh. Then he urged the wolf forward, racing up alongside the frozen black steed and tapping it briefly with his hand.

In response to that touch, the mount shattered. Breaking into countless icy splinters and falling to the ground in a cascade of frozen fragments.

I stared ahead, stunned, then glanced at where Lyrastra lay, her body encased in frost.

Was that her fate? Was she already dead? Would she crumble into pieces if I tried to touch her?

But it didn't matter. Because there was no time to stop and check. If I did, we would both die for certain.

I would go back for her. I wouldn't leave her here. Somehow, I would get her out, I swore to myself.

Nightclaw raced on. I caught only a glimmer of icy blue cheeks and frost-covered lashes before we had raced past.

Ahead of us, Avriel and his frost wolf raced swiftly on. The path to the island lay open before him now. He could easily beat me and seize the crown.

But as he neared the end of the field, I watched him turn and catch sight of me.

A glimmer of sly cunning crossed his face. With a commanding gesture he tightened his grip on the frost wolf's reins, pulling the mount to a halt.

He was stopping. Why?

Nightclaw and I raced forward, even as foreboding filled my heart.

He couldn't just win. Not while a single other contestant was left standing.

The wolf was unleashing its freezing breath once more. With a swift gesture, Avriel raced the wolf around the perimeter of the island. The creature's breath became a swirling gust, forming a wide ring that enveloped the glassy cobblestone field.

As the wolf's frost-laden breath settled over the glistening stones, it coated them in a glacial sheen.

What was he up to, I wondered?

Avriel's gaze locked on mine, a devious smile playing on his lips. With a sharp gesture, he urged the wolf to rear onto its hind legs.

Briefly, the beast towered over the frozen cobblestones.

Then with a crash it lowered its powerful front legs back to the ground with bone-shaking force.

A resounding crack echoed through the air.

The ground all around the island was shattering like fragile glass.

Piece by piece, the ground was falling into a dark chasm that yawned wide beneath.

A treacherous abyss had lain under us all this time, I realized, my heart speeding up as Nightclaw continued to fly forward.

Beneath the glass surface was *nothing*. Absolutely nothing.

A void stretched out before us. A void Nightclaw was still running straight towards.

CHAPTER 31

I tugged desperately at the reins, panic coursing through my veins.

"Stop! Nightclaw, stop!" Raw fear laced through my voice.

The cat moved forward resolutely, his feral power overwhelming my pleas.

We hurtled on.

The chasm's gaping mouth loomed ever closer.

Through the bond I had briefly sensed the other night, a flicker of reassurance passed. The barest whisper of emotion carried on a current. A wisp of calm. A wordless message claiming all would be well. An attempt to assuage my mounting dread.

But my mind echoed with terror, already vividly imagining our impending fall into the abyss below.

I screamed again, pleading for Nightclaw to halt, already knowing it was too late.

The cat pressed ahead, driven by an unyielding determination that surpassed my comprehension.

My eyes widened, pupils dilating with fear as the edge drew near, the dark depths threatening to engulf us whole.

The battlecat's muscles tensed beneath me.

I squeezed my eyes shut as my stomach plummeted.

We fell into oblivion.

And then we began to soar.

My eyes popped open.

The impossible was unfolding before my very eyes.

It was a day for impossibilities. A day for leaps of faith.

From beneath Nightclaw's muscular frame, concealed beneath his thick fur coat, a hidden secret had been unveiled.

Wings unfurled from his sides, stretching outwards like a revelation. Bones elongated and sinew stretched as with a surge of energy, hidden mechanisms within Nightclaw's powerful frame extended. The wings had a membranous structure, nearly translucent. They were veined with threads of gold and covered with soft, short golden fur.

The wings expanded, catching the currents of air and casting a long shadow beneath us where Avriel stood gaping.

I couldn't help it. I grinned and waved.

Beneath me Nightclaw was emitting a low, rumbling, his body vibrating beneath me. To my delight, I realized he was purring.

We circled the island, each wing beat a symphony of strength, as the powerful muscles beneath me propelled us upwards. Nightclaw's wings cleaved through the air with a soft whooshing sound as we soared above the chasm.

From the corner of my eye, I glimpsed Avriel darting about below. He ran to the web of rope bridges encircling the island. I assumed he was frantic to cross to the pillar before we could reach it.

He fumbled about with something under the thick ropes.

When he stood upright again, there was something in his hands. I caught sight of smooth wood and a glint of black metal.

A crossbow.

I cried out as the bolt was released, urging Nightclaw upwards.

The bolt sliced through the air with deadly intent, just as Nightclaw shifted upwards, beating his wings with a vengeance.

The projectile clipped one outstretched wing. I felt it as if it had pierced through my very own skin.

Nightclaw let out a guttural growl, carrying with it the essence of both fury and suffering.

My heart clenched, a gush of fury filling me with determination.

I could feel Nightclaw's rage and anguish echoing in my own soul.

I urged him downwards, sensing his grim determination as he complied.

Avriel was looking up at us in alarm, frantically loading a second bolt.

I held out my hands, gripping the battlecat's body tightly with my thighs.

With all my focus, I channeled my inner fire, willing the gauntlets I wore to help me aim. A crackle of sparks danced along my fingertips.

A concentrated torrent of searing fire erupted from my hands, narrowing into a stream resembling the lash of a whip.

The fiery torrent cascaded downwards leaving behind a trail of shimmering embers that painted the air.

Within seconds, Avriel was encompassed. Flames licked at his body, ensnaring him in an inescapable inferno.

I had only a moment to take in his screams of agony before he stumbled backwards, his arms flailing as he pitched into the gaping chasm and was claimed by its depths.

Did he turn to ashes as he fell as Vesper had done?

He was my enemy, but as he fell into the abyss surrounded by a maelstrom of heat, I felt nothing. No satisfaction. No newfound sense of safety.

I simply wanted this to be over. I wanted to be done.

Somewhere, Kaye waited for me, alone and afraid.

Would Draven understand what I had to do? Would I ever be able to tell him?

Nightclaw swooped downwards, gliding effortlessly towards the pillar where the golden crown rested. I leaned forward in the saddle and plucked it up as we passed by, holding it warily in one hand as if it were poison.

There was no way I was putting the thing on my head. I longed to drop it into the chasm with Avriel but settled for hooking it over the pommel of the saddle.

Nightclaw was already flying back in the direction we'd come from. Towards the frozen figure of Lyrastra lying helplessly on the far side of the glassy field that had not been shattered.

The battlecat landed soundlessly and I slid down from his back, running towards the woman.

Crouching beside her frost-covered figure, I reached out a tenuous hand, then withdrew it.

Would I shatter her with my touch as Avriel had done the steed?

I had to do something. I couldn't just leave her there, to be battlefield carrion.

The gauntlets had worked once before. I stared down at them, urging them to help me, praying the sigils Laverna had embedded in her handiwork would enable the delicate work I needed from them now.

Then, ever so gently, I touched Lyrastra's hand with mine, letting the smallest bit of warmth extend from me.

I watched in excitement as subtle coils of heat fed through me and into the ice encasement.

Slowly, the frozen shell began to melt, revealing Lyrastra's features underneath.

Lyrastra coughed, her eyes fluttering open.

All over her body, the ice was melting. I watched as she groaned, then moved her legs. It was all right. She was going to be all right. Relief flooded through me.

Lyrastra's gaze shifted down to her right arm. Confusion mingled with hope in her eyes.

Steadily, I continued streaming heat into her body, holding my hands steady. But a glimmer of fear filled me as I saw what she was looking at.

A spiderweb of fractures was forming over her right arm, tracing patterns over the frozen limb like cracks across a frozen pond.

Wretchedly, I watched the fissures spread. I dared not feed more heat into Lyrastra's form for fear she would ignite.

A gasp escaped Lyrastra's lips as the fractures multiplied.

I reached out one of my hands, about to touch the arm, but it was too late. Lyrastra lifted her head in a wordless scream as the sound of splitting ice reverberated through the air.

Brittle shards cascaded downwards, glistening in the light.

Lyrastra's expression had morphed to one of horror. Her eyes widened as she beheld the shattered remains of her arm.

I watched as pain, raw and unrelenting, surged through her body, radiating from the mangled stump. She began to writhe, in the grip of unforgiving shock, her groans of anguish terrible to hear.

Around us, something was happening. The very fabric of our surroundings was crumbling.

The glass cobblestones beneath us began to shake.

I leaped to my feet, my heart pounding with urgency. Ignoring my own weariness, I mustered every ounce of strength and caught Lyrastra up by the waist, ignoring her sobs of pain as I brushed against her fragmented shoulder.

Dragging her over to Nightclaw, I hoisted her up and into the saddle then climbed up behind her, grabbing the reins.

Nightclaw was already beginning to run. A great, leaping gallop that nearly sent me sliding off his back. I gripped the cat more tightly, clutching the reins and wrapping my arms around Lyrastra who had hunched forward pitifully like a broken doll.

As ominous rumblings filled the arena, Nightclaw's wings unfurled, lifting us into the air as the floor below us disintegrated, crumbling into a void of chaos.

We soared above the destruction.

With every motion Nightclaw made, I could see Lyrastra's agony intensifying but there was nothing I could do. We had to get out. Get her to a healer.

My gaze darted across the crumbling expanse, searching for an escape route.

Had Sephone planned this? Had the event been timed?

Or was it simply that once Avriel was gone, Sephone was content to let the rest of us die? Was the Siabra court watching even now from some hidden recess camouflaged from view?

Unlike Draven, I could not simply glance up and make eye contact with my friends. The gallery window was nowhere to be seen. I was utterly alone.

We flew through the air. Time seemed to warp and distort.

"There," I shouted, pointing ahead as if Nightclaw could see me.

High on the opposite side of the arena, an opening had suddenly appeared, shimmering in the air.

A glimpse of freedom.

Nightclaw veered towards the beckoning passage, wings beating against the roaring winds surging from below that threatened to engulf us.

I clung to Lyrastra, shielding her as best I could from the onslaught of debris whipping through the arena.

As we neared the exit, the sound of collapse faded into the background.

Nightclaw soared through the corridor into the dark and we were out.

CHAPTER 32

We flew out a towering doorway.

As Nightclaw landed, his paws softly thudding on the floor, my gaze was seized by the sight that unfolded before me.

This was not the gallery.

Instead, a new, resplendent room stretched out before us.

The room resembled the throne room where the opening ceremony had been held but was even more striking and grandiose.

Stone rows of seats flanked the hall like in an ancient amphitheater, rising up towards a vaulted ceiling, every one occupied by Siabra. There were literally thousands of them, their eyes all fixed on me.

Across the room in front of me, the Queen Regent stood on a dais. Her dark beauty was shrouded in an aura of cold fury as her eyes met mine.

Behind her lay the Umbral Throne, transported to this new location. Hewn from the depths of dark volcanic rock, its imposing form radiated foreboding power. Jagged contours like the serrated teeth of a predator bordered its edges where glittering crimson rubies pulsated with unsettling energy.

The throne's dark and lethal beauty chilled me as I imagined Draven seated there as emperor.

Below Sephone's feet, lava coursed under an enchanted glass floor, casting an eerie red glow over the chamber. Pillars carved from black marble veined with gold lined the hall. Above us, towering stalagmites hung from the ceiling, jagged and daunting. Red crystals embedded in the rocky spires pulsed with light, shadowing the crowd in dark hues.

The juxtaposition of grandeur and darkness did not escape me as I half-slid, half-fell from Nightclaw's back, then turned around to help Lyrastra down.

The semi-silence morphed into a sudden burst of sound as the crowd watched one of their own helped down from the battlecat, Lyrastra's missing limb evident to all.

She let out a moan of pain and fell into my arms.

Instantly, Crescent and Gawain were there beside me, emerging out of the crowd. Gawain scooped up Lyrastra, hoisting her effortlessly into his strong arms. I had only time to glimpse the look of questioning horror on Crescent's face before the red-haired man swept her away.

Across the room, something was happening. Tall doors at the opposite side of the chamber behind the dais had opened.

My attention was captivated by the figure materializing before my eyes.

Time seemed to slow as Kairos Draven Venator, the Prince of Claws, strode into the throne room.

He was clad in a uniform of lustrous black linen. The fabric clung to his muscular form, emphasizing the breadth of his shoulders and the power coiled within. His black hair had been slicked back with precision, highlighting the hard angular planes of his face. The familiar silver ring glinted against its bronze-hued setting in his pointed left ear.

There was something embroidered along the collar of his jacket. Symbols of some sort. As he came closer, I caught sight of a red rose on a backdrop of dancing flames and caught my breath.

The emerald shards of his eyes pierced mine, then swept through the crowd, penetrating and intense.

A shiver ran down my spine. Gone was the warmth I was used to seeing in Draven's face as he looked at me. It had been replaced by an enigmatic coldness that nearly matched Sephone's.

A stranger stood before me wearing the visage of a man I thought I knew.

The flickering flames and roses embroidered on Draven's jacket seemed to echo the riddle he had suddenly become. Why had he chosen such a crest for his reign?

With every calculated step he took across the room, he exuded a palpable sense of power and mastery.

Trepidation stirred within me.

How was any of this possible? He had been practically comatose when I had left that morning.

Now he was the picture of health and strength, his presence more formidable than ever been before.

My heart nearly stopped as I realized this was truer than I had thought.

The small horns on his head had grown back.

In the span of hours, they were fully formed and whole. There was no trace of the bloody stumps they had replaced.

A sickening rage filled my throat. How had he done this? Why?

I turned away, reaching up to grasp the golden crown that hung from Nightclaw's pommel. Clutching it in my hand, I faced the room again and tossed it onto the floor.

The Siabra crown fell with a loud clatter, then tumbled across the lava-illuminated glass and came to a halt at the base of the dais.

"I believe this is yours, Prince Kairos," I said loudly, striving to be heard over the murmuring of the crowd.

"No," Draven replied. His voice carried easily. "It's yours."

All hell broke loose.

"Silence." Sephone's crystalline tone cut through the noise. "What is the meaning of this?"

Draven walked forward, passing the dais then pausing in the center of the room between Sephone and myself.

"Morgan Pendragon is not merely my paramour as I have led you all to believe." His eyes rested on me. "She is also my wife."

The words hit me like a shockwave, shattering my understanding.

My breath caught in my throat.

I touched a hand to Nightclaw's warm side, feeling as if the ground beneath my feet had disappeared.

My eyes searched Draven's face, scanning for any signs of jest or deception. But all I found was the cold, impassive expression of a stranger.

He believed what he had just said.

The realization crashed over me, leaving me gasping for air. My mind raced, trying to understand how the world could have turned so abruptly upside down.

"That's impossible." I held up my hand to try to silence the crowd and raised my voice. "We are not married."

Sephone's eyes met mine with something like relief. "I was about to say the same thing. Prince Kairos, your recent illness has clearly addled your mind. If you are not fit to be crowned today, you should return to your rooms and rest. I'll see that a healer is sent to you. We can continue this ceremony at another time."

Draven smiled slightly. "I thank you for the consideration, but that won't be necessary." He turned to face the crowd. "My marriage to this woman did occur and it was indeed valid."

"That's impossible," I hissed.

He ignored me. "Morgan Pendragon was gravely wounded in the Valtain ruins of Meridium. I reached her as she lay dying."

All this was true. So far.

"All of the Siabra here know of the blood bond that once joined mated pairs," he continued.

My heart hammered.

"The bond is everything. The blood is everything."

"The blood bond has not been carried out in centuries," Sephone interrupted. "It requires the grail to complete. We all know this." Abruptly her eyes widened, as if she had remembered.

"Conveniently, Queen Regent, I possessed that, too. As you'll recall, I brought the chalice back to you when I returned. It was used to conduct the opening ceremonies weeks ago. We all witnessed its presence that night."

Draven's words hung in the air, resonating with truth.

"A marriage cannot be conducted without the consent of both individuals," I declared, casting my voice loudly to be heard. "What you're describing is not a marriage."

"Perhaps not a mortal marriage. Or even a Valtain marriage," Draven agreed, his voice deceptively calm. "But as you know, Morgan, we Siabra have our own savage ways."

The fucking bastard. I gripped Nightclaw's fur, trying not to teeter where I stood.

"I did not," I said through clenched teeth. "Consent to be married."

"You did consent. With your blood. With your life–which I saved and restored to you. And furthermore, in the presence of an honorable and unimpeachable witness."

"What witness?" I spat. "Where is this witness?"

"You'll recall the presence of Odelna."

My eyes widened in disbelief. "A child? That is your witness? She was no more than ten years old."

"As it turns out, she was... not. Nor was she a child at all."

There was silence for a moment as I tried to process this. Finally, I shook my head. "What the hell are you talking about?"

Raising his voice, Draven seemed to ignore the question. "Any mage or magic user present here today may test the bond between us to verify its validity. They will see that it was created in the presence of a sacred witness whose authority is by any imagination virtually boundless. Blood was exchanged and the grail vessel consecrated it, binding Morgan and me together irrevocably." He gazed at me, his face dispassionate. "Surely you have felt the bond before this, Morgan. A hint of it. They say the connection grows stronger with time."

I thought of the flames Draven had used against the harpies.

The claws that had extended from my hands.

And the weight of the truth settled on me like a heavy cloak, threatening to suffocate me.

"What did you do to me?" I whispered.

Some semblance of emotion briefly flickered over his face. "I saved your life by giving you part of my own. And now that you've survived the Blood Rise, the crown of the Siabra Empire is yours." Draven raised his voice. "Behold your new empress, Siabra. May her rule be long and prosperous."

A roar burst from the crowd as it erupted once more.

I opened my mouth to tell them all not to worry. That I didn't want their fucking throne. That I would never accept it.

But Sephone beat me to the punch.

"No," the Queen Regent screeched. She stepped off the dais, her face white with rage. Striding forward, she practically ran towards me, her fingers outstretched.

I could hear Draven shouting but my eyes were fixed on Sephone's fingers, so long and white. They came towards me, gripped me by the shoulder.

The room around us disappeared as she seized me.

CHAPTER 33

S ephone was a fucking stitcher.

I fell at her feet, hard stone beneath my hands.

The wind whipped through my hair as I struggled to get my bearings.

The ramparts. We stood at the top of an open fortified stone tower overlooking the palace. Down stone steps to each side, the wide ramparts continued, lining a vast fortified wall.

Why a palace like this one, underground and concealed, would ever even *need* ramparts was beyond me, but there we were.

Around us stood a group of astonished royal guards, their mouths agape as they glanced nervously between me and the queen.

"Queen Regent," said one bold soul stepping forward, a tentative smile on her face. "If we may assist you both, merely say the word. News has spread quickly of the new empress..."

The word was a death sentence.

Sephone parted her lovely lips and roared.

But instead of sound, a silent mist emerged from her mouth, swirling and billowing towards the group of guards.

I pushed myself to my feet, backing quickly away until I felt the edge of the cold stone parapet. Shaking I gripped the top of the low wall, watching as a deadly fog engulfed the guards.

As the mist seeped into their lungs, agonized cries filled the air. They fell, clutching at their throats and convulsing, faces contorted in anguish.

The Queen Regent turned to me as the last of the guards twitched behind her, eyes rolled back in his head.

"Nicely done," I commented, hiding my shaking hands behind my back. "Avriel only had green spit. I prefer the mist. Much more subtle."

A chill smile curled upon Sephone's lips.

"So, Draven wasn't the only one to get married, was he?" I said, stalling for time. "You and Avriel decided to use the grail, too. How incredibly romantic. Except, you know, he's dead, so... What now?"

Sephone snarled.

"This wasn't how it was supposed to play out for you, was it?" I said, with false sympathy. "You told Avriel you'd share power in every way, I suppose. And then down the line? When he conveniently died a few years after becoming emperor? Let me guess, there's another caveat for that?"

Sephone glared and took one step forward. On second thought, I didn't really want her to open her mouth again. Not after what I'd just seen.

"I have powers of my own you know," I said hastily.

"Elemental magic," she said disdainfully. "But can you fly, I wonder?"

She lifted her hands and behind me the stones began to drip with acid and crumble into dust.

I suddenly felt much less secure.

"Get the fuck away from my wife, Sephone."

I looked up to see Crescent and Draven had appeared across the battlement. They were not alone. Nightclaw stood just behind Crescent. The exmoor's teeth were bared, sharp feline fangs protruding as he stared at Sephone with the eyes of a predator.

"I'm not your fucking wife, Draven," I shouted.

This was ridiculous. Was I really going to fight with this man before falling to my death?

"I hate you." The words shot out before I could stop them. "I trusted you. I could have died. Do you even fucking care?"

Draven stopped in his tracks, his eyes darting between me and Sephone.

"I stood in for you so that you could rule," I went on. "And for what? So you could hide in the background and avoid the danger?"

His face hardened. "In all the time that you've known me, have I ever tried to avoid danger, Morgan?"

"I don't know. I don't really know you at all. That's what I've realized." I laughed. "Husband? It's a joke, right? This is all lunacy. We can't possibly be married." I shook my head. "I was right about you all along. From the very start, I was right."

BRIAR BOLEYN

"I assure you, it's no joke," he said, taking another step forward. "And you were only right about some parts. You know this already."

In front of him, Sephone gave a reptilian hiss of impatience.

Draven's face flickered with annoyance. "Stand down, Sephone. We both know you're not going to kill her. To do so would be suicide."

"I don't know," I remarked. "She had no problem murdering her own guards just now."

"A temper tantrum," Draven snapped. "Believe me, she's done worse. But she knows if she dares to lay a hand on my wife, it will spell her immediate end."

"I'd be more worried about the mist from her mouth than her hands," I said. "And stop fucking calling me that."

"What?"

"Your wife!"

Behind Draven, there was a movement. Not from Crescent or Nightclaw.

One of the guards was stirring. The female guard who had smiled at Sephone. The one who had called me "empress."

I watched as the guard began to push herself slowly to her feet, unable to believe my eyes.

"You are my wife, like it or not. I did what I did to save your life," Draven was saying. "Besides, it might have been worse. Who would your brother have married you off to, I wonder? Some ancient nobleman? Or was he planning to give you to that bastard Florian?"

"There's only one bastard standing here that I can see," I snapped. "And he claims we're already married." My eyes widened. "Draven, behind you!"

The words rushed out. Not necessarily because I wanted to protect him but because I needed someone else's confirmation that I was truly seeing this.

"Are we back at Meridium?"

The guard who had been dead mere moments before was now standing up and opening her eyes.

Draven shook his head. "I don't think so."

"Something else? Something *worse*? Fuck."

"Calm yourself, child," the guard said, slowly blinking her eyes.

"It can talk, Draven," I observed. "This isn't good. Talking undead guards are not a good thing."

Sephone's face was transfixed as she watched the guard walk towards her. Then it became ashen. "Wise One," she whispered. "Is it truly you?"

The guard seemed amused. "I'm surprised you recognize me, child. The Siabra are not exactly known for their devotion."

Sephone's beautiful eyes widened. If I hadn't known any better, I'd have thought she was about to fall to her knees. "I recall the stories, Wise One. I grew up hearing them."

Then she shocked me by doing just that. Sinking to her knees, she lowered her head as if in reverence. "Mother of Fate, you honor me."

"Don't get too excited," the undead guard chided. "You won't like what I have to say. I'm not here to see you crown yourself." The guard glanced over at me, then snickered slightly. "Besides, if I'm the Mother of Fate as you say, then *she* is a daughter of destiny."

"Daughter of destiny?" Sephone followed the guard's gaze until her eyes rested on me. "I don't understand. This one? She cannot possibly rule us."

"For once, I agree with Sephone," I remarked. "Not interested in ruling. Not interested at all."

The guard sighed, as if exasperated. "Little one, it matters not what you want or do not want. Your blood was bound with his. I witnessed it myself. I strengthened it with my own hands." She glanced down at herself and cackled macabrely. "Not these ones."

My eyes widened. "You? But..."

"Enough," she snapped. "When one such as I tells you a thing, the thing is true. There is no questioning. There is no denying. There is certainly no undoing the bond. Your husband is your destiny and you are his. I have said this. Thus, it is so."

Sephone moved, her mouth parting ever so slightly and I flinched.

The guard rolled her eyes. She raised one hand and Sephone froze, quite literally, her mouth stuck open, her eyes panicked and wide. "You both have larger problems on your hands than destroying one whose hands hold so many threads, Queen Regent. Look to the horizon. They are coming."

The words had barely time to penetrate when the guard fell to her knees, toppling over beside Sephone, lifeless once more.

"Well, that was..." I began.

Thunder boomed out.

Thunder? Here, beneath the earth? I looked across the red-hued vista at the volcanic mountain beside the palace, but the structure was unchanged. The sound had not emanated from there.

The thunderous sound rang out once more, assaulting my senses and sending the rampart walls trembling with powerful vibrations.

Draven was staring into the distance with a grim expression.

My gaze followed his, sweeping across the palace walls, over the rocky landscape and upwards.

Emerging one by one with each thunderous boom were a flock of riders on flying beasts. With sinewy frames covered in leathery skin, the creatures flew through the makeshift sky towards the palace, their wings undulating with a hypnotic rhythm. Long, slender talons extended from their wingtips, honed to lethal points. Their limbs, long and muscular, reflected a raw power that spoke of formidable strength and speed.

Mounted upon them were riders clad in armor as black as night. Spiked pauldrons rose like jagged peaks from their shoulders. Ghostly mists swirled around them, trailing behind like remnants of forgotten sorcery. The riders' helmets were crafted in the image of death itself. The metal formed skeletal features, where hollow eye sockets housed dark orbs that burned with an unholy glow.

A movement from further down the ramparts caught my eye.

The figure of a girl running along the fortifications.

The dark metal rimming her eyes gleamed in the light.

"Rychel," I shouted.

The figure paused, then turned. I watched as Rychel's eyes widened as she took us in—Draven and Sephone and myself, with Crescent and Nightclaw behind us.

"What are you doing?" Draven was already moving towards the steps. "Get back here, Rychel. It's not safe."

But Rychel darted backwards quickly. "You don't understand," she called, over the thunderous boom. "They're here for me." Resignation filled her face.

I watched as Draven's expression turned to horror.

"What is she talking about?" I stepped up beside him, my fury temporarily paused. Behind me, Sephone was still frozen from the effects of whatever the strange visitor had done to her.

"She's let the wards down. The palace is unprotected. Noctasia, too."

"Why?" I demanded. "Why would she do that?"

"She summoned them here. She believes they won't harm us." Draven's face said he didn't share the same belief. "She thinks they can help the children."

The children? I didn't understand.

He moved then, racing forward like an arrow shot from a bow, propelled with desperate urgency.

"No," Rychel screamed as he ran towards her. "Stay back! You don't understand, Kairos."

"I do," I heard him shout. "Believe me, I want the same thing you do. But not like this. Don't do this, Rychel. Don't give it to them. We'll find another way."

"There is no other way! You know I've tried. I've tried so hard. But I'm not enough. I don't know enough."

Only then did I belatedly see what she held in one hand.

The grail.

She raised it high over her head as her brother sped down the battlement, then stepped towards the edge of the wall.

"They won't use it for what you want, Rychel. Nothing can undo what our father did. Don't throw your life away. Stay with us. Don't do this."

"I have to know. I can't live like this anymore," Rychel said, her voice pleading. "We're the monsters, Kairos. Don't you see? He made us this way. We're all his creations. My mother died bearing me. His tainted fruit."

"You're not tainted, Rychel. And no matter what you might believe, they're worse." Draven's voice echoed over the stone, sending chills through my veins as I heard the fear there. "You don't know what you're doing, Sister. I beg you, please stop."

"Let me give them the grail." Rychel took another step backwards. "That's all I'll do."

"No, it's too late. You've let the wards down, Rychel. We have to get back inside."

My breath hitched as one of the riders reached the outskirts of the palace walls.

Swooping low, they dove towards Rychel.

Draven raced forward, his hand outstretched, reaching frantically for her.

But it was too late. The dark rider extended a gloved hand, fingers curling like talons as they grasped Rychel, lifting her slender form off the rampart walls and holding her suspended in its clutches. I gasped as the rider ascended, speeding back into the incoming flock and disappearing in its midst.

Draven whirled to face me, fists clenched, knuckles turning white.

"Crescent," he bellowed, looking past me. "You know what to do."

Behind me, Crescent vanished, then reappeared in the blink of an eye with Javer and Beks.

"Gawain's staying with Taina," he called to Draven who was speeding back up the steps. I watched Draven nod.

Javer looked around appraisingly, taking in the dark riders flying towards the palace, then beginning to bark orders to his small ward.

Together they raced to the edge of the wall with their hands up.

"We can't recover the wards," Javer bellowed to Draven. "There's no time to mend them. All we can do is try to shield the palace if they…"

A malevolent energy crackled through the air.

The dark riders were nearing. Arcs of black lightning shot from their fingertips, striking the palace walls nearby with explosive force.

Stone shattered and splintered under the onslaught, sending debris cascading down around us in a rain of destruction.

"No, forget the palace. Get up top. Go to the city. Shield Noctasia," Draven instructed. "Take them up now, Crescent." He met my eyes. "We'll look after the palace then join you."

With shock, I realized he was including me in that statement.

Crescent touched Javer and Beks on the shoulders and the trio vanished.

"You expect me to fight by your side?" I snarled. "After everything you've done?"

"Your exmoor can fly?" Draven was looking past me at Nightclaw.

"He flies for me. You're not touching him."

Belatedly I remembered he had been training Sunstrike.

"My prince." It was Odessa. We turned to see her beside Ulpheas, a group of soldiers alongside them. "What is this?" She stared up at the riders.

"Valtain," Draven said briefly. "The High King's Hunters. Rychel… She's gone with them. She's given them the grail."

Odessa's eyes widened with shock, then she nodded swiftly. Turning to the soldiers around her, she began shouting orders.

"Ulpheas, keep doing what you're doing," Draven commanded, clapping the fair-haired man on the shoulder. "We need archers all along these walls. Bring up every soldier you can find. Tell those inside to go deeper underground or better yet, have them stitched to Noctasia. If it hasn't been attacked yet, I fear it will be. We need people above, aiding the city."

Ulpheas nodded shakily, then glanced past us at the Queen Regent who still sat frozen, her lips parted. "What about her?"

"Oh, for fuck's sake," Draven swore, looking at Sephone with distaste. Evidently, he had forgotten about her. "Take her, too. Put her somewhere safe. I have no idea when whatever spell was put on her will wear off. Sephone, try not to kill anyone else on our side today, will you?" He shook his head bitterly as he looked at the prone bodies of the guards around us. "We could have used them."

"Used them. Of course, that's what you'd say," I muttered sourly.

"They could have helped us defend the palace," he snapped. "It's what they've been trained to do. Would you call that exploitative, Morgan?"

"All of the Siabra are exploitative. Your sister certainly thought so."

Draven shook his head in frustration. "There's no time for this. We can argue later. Will you help me or not?"

"Help you how? What do you want from me?"

"Your exmoor." He pointed at Nightclaw. "He's an old one, you know. It takes years for their wings to grow in." He met my gaze. "They can do more, you know. Let him show you."

"What do you have in mind?" I said, clenching my jaw.

"You ride, I'll fight. Get on."

"Two fighters on one battlecat? Nightclaw's not trained for this." Neither was I.

A smirk flickered over Draven's face. "You'll hold your own. You always do."

"Fine." I ran for Nightclaw just as a Valtain rider shot a black bolt towards us, then dove upwards again.

We reached the exmoor as below us one of the palace's glass domes crashed inwards. The air echoed with the sound of falling glass and the agonized cries of those caught in the onslaught.

I climbed into the saddle, Draven right behind me.

"You can sit there but don't fucking touch me," I declared, stiffening immediately as he touched a hand to my waist briefly.

"I understand." I felt him shifting, then his back pressed against mine. Suddenly, I understood what he'd had in mind.

"You're going to fall off if you sit like that," I yelled, as Nightclaw raced forward then leaped into the air, his wings beating.

"Don't pretend you care, Morgan." Draven's voice whipped back at me over the sound of the roaring wind.

Below I saw Odessa directing soldiers, setting up archers at prime spots along the parapet. More and more soldiers and guards were appearing all over the walls, stitched there by Ulpheas and others.

For some reason, the sight of the soldiers running into position made my heart swell.

With what? Not pride. No, I could never be proud of these people. They were Draven's people, not mine.

We soared through the air, over the palace.

The Valtain riders, if that's truly what they were, had spread out, covering the palace thinly. By my measure, there were less than fifty of them. But they were on flying raptors while the Siabra were pinned to the ground. They possessed the power to wield lightning bolts, while half the soldiers below were mortal and could shoot nothing more than wood and metal bolts and arrows.

"We'll cover them," Draven yelled. "You shoot from the front, I'll shoot from the back."

"Shoot? Do you see any bows? You talk as if I can control this," I yelled back at him.

"You can. I saw you today."

I scowled to myself. "You were watching? How? From your sickbed?"

"Something like that. Let's just say I had a good view. The gauntlets work. Trust them."

I gripped the reins, feeling Nightclaw's powerful muscles beneath me, strong and reassuring. We soared higher, leaving the crumbling walls of the palace behind as we ascended. The roars and screams of the battle below filled my ears.

A bolt of lightning crackled through the air close to my ears. My grip on the reins tightened, instincts kicking in swiftly as I maneuvered Nightclaw, evading the assault.

"Fuck," I bellowed. "That was too close for comfort."

In response, I heard a sizzling sound from behind me. I turned my head to see Draven crouching forward, his hands extended, unleashing a blazing sphere of flame from the palms of his hand. He hurled them towards the rider on our tail.

The hunter and their mount burst into flames. With a shriek, the menacing figure slipped from the winged raptor's back, catapulting down to the ground below.

"One down," Draven shouted back at me.

"Don't be so smug. One down, forty-nine or so to go," I reminded him.

"Don't be so defeatist," he countered. "We're an unstoppable pair, together like this, and you know it."

"Unstoppable? You mean because you stole my magic, you treacherous motherfucker," I shouted back.

"That was Avriel, need I remind you. And he's dead. Good job, by the way. It was over too quickly, wasn't it?"

Begrudgingly, I knew he was right. Avriel's death had been far too easy. Too swift. He had deserved to suffer. Suffer like he had made Selwyn suffer.

"Yes," I admitted.

"You saved Lyrastra though, that's what matters."

"Speaking of Lyrastra, since when have you and Ulpheas been so fucking close?" I demanded.

"Oh, you know, since I set him straight about his place in all of this and made it clear that if he ever fucked with you again, he was a dead man."

"A dead fae," I corrected.

I felt Draven shrug. "Same thing."

"You told Ulpheas about the bloodwraith. Why?"

Draven was quiet. "It served my purpose."

"Your purpose was to get yourself poisoned? You could have died. Did you remember nothing from Nethervale?"

"I remember that I lived," he responded. "Thanks to you."

"Yes, but..." I stopped. "You knew you'd live. Because of the bond. Your healing abilities. It intensified them."

"Ah, so you admit it's there. The bond."

"The fucking bond," I snarled. "We can find a way to break it. We have to try."

"It's an unbreakable bond, Morgan. How do you think it works exactly? If you die, I die."

I froze in the saddle. 'What?"

"Which is why it's a good thing we both came into this marriage with such exceptional abilities, isn't it? We're much harder to kill."

I growled and heard him laugh.

"What? Marriage? You really hate that word, don't you?"

"I hate the sound of it on your lips. That and 'wife' and also 'husband.'"

It was a lie. The three words hung between us. But deep down, beneath my facade of frustration, a different sensation stirred within me. A spark that ignited at the mere mention of our supposed union.

We had fused before. Merged and became one. Even the memory of our nights together was enough to send heat suffusing my cheeks and racing over my skin.

But not like this. Not in such a final way. Not without my complete and utter lack of consent.

Still, the word "wife" held a secret power over me, eliciting a wellspring of emotions I was struggling to wrap my head around.

I was married. Fucking married to Draven. And the strangest thing of all to me was that he didn't seem the least bit upset. Only vastly amused by it all.

He was right about one thing. Arthur might have married me to anyone he chose. And there would have been little I could have done about it. Was this really so different, a small voice in my head asked? Either way, the marriage had been arranged to solidify a powerful alliance.

An explosion rent the air, unleashing a fiery burst over a section of the palace complex. From our aerial vantage, I looked down to see a scene of pandemonium. Plumes of acrid smoke spiraled upwards, casting an ominous veil over the Court of Umbral Flames.

But I could also see Odessa, strong and firm. Her arms were stretched outwards as she ordered the soldiers around her to release their missiles, again and again. Bolts whizzed from the ramparts, tearing through the wings of the raptor-like mounts and sending some crashing downwards.

"I'd say we're down to a solid forty," Draven called out.

"Odessa's doing you proud," I admitted. "Amazing the incredible people you manage to find who are willing to follow you."

"I'm a born leader. Or so they tell me. But you..." I felt him shift against me. "Daughter of destiny, I believe was the term?"

"Whatever that fucking means. Who even was that? You seemed to... know them."

Draven was quiet. "You wouldn't believe me if I told you."

I scowled to myself. "Probably not. Born leader, did you say? More like a born liar."

Draven chuckled. "You're a force of destiny Morgan Pendragon. Or should I call you Morgan Venator?"

My heart skipped a beat. "Don't you fucking dare."

A rider cloaked in shadow flew towards us from the front.

"Draven..."

I felt him swivel to see. "You know what to do." His voice was quiet but confident.

I swallowed hard. "Right."

Steeling myself for the imminent clash, I fixed my eyes on the approaching adversary.

My senses heightened. The wind whipped against my face, tugging at my braided hair as I leaned forward, feeling power fill my body.

Flames danced and flickered on my fingertips. I focused my eyes on my gauntlets, as if they were an amulet and not simply sigil-covered armor. Flames snaked towards the Valtain hunter like vengeful serpents.

The bolts of searing heat found their mark, colliding with the rider and its steed.

I watched the two figures fall through the air in silence.

"One more down."

"Don't sound so excited," Draven chided. "I might think you're enjoying this."

"You're mighty cheerful for someone whose sister just ran away to join the enemy," I snapped. "Aren't you worried about what they'll do to her?"

Draven was quiet for a moment. "That was... unexpected."

"I'd say so," I muttered.

"But also... not."

"What does that mean?"

"I mean Rychel has never been content. From the moment of her birth, I think." I felt him sigh. "I suppose it's natural, considering how she came into this world."

"After what your father did to her mother, you mean?" I said, my stomach turning. "Lovely man, your father. You take after him more than I thought."

Draven ignored the jibe. "Excalibur is with Orcades. Rychel's taken the grail to the Valtain. The Siabra are exposed. Vulnerable. They need you now more than ever, Morgan."

I couldn't believe my ears. "Are you seriously trying to persuade me to take responsibility for your people right now, Draven? I have my own problems to worry about. My own people to think of."

"Wait."

I heard the crackling sizzle of fire and felt a faint flow of heat as Draven leaned forward.

There was a scream.

I peered down to see a hunter plummeting to the ground, their mount not far behind them.

"I won't be your empress," I started to say, just as Draven shouted, "Duck."

A bolt of lightning flashed over us. I twisted in the saddle, evading the onslaught just in time.

Nightclaw soared downwards without another word, taking us towards a new cluster of dark riders.

"No," I protested sharply. "There are too many of them, Nightclaw. Take us back."

"Not for me," Draven declared. "Fly forward."

Nightclaw responded to the command instantly, leaving me annoyed that Draven could have such an effect on the battlecat not even his own.

Did our bond extend to our exmoors, too, I wondered with a start?

The bond. The fucking bond.

Turning my head, I watched as Draven unleashed a crackling inferno of fire that cascaded out like a sweeping gust of wind.

The group of hunters and mounts ignited, pieces of flesh and burnt wings scattering downwards.

"We've cleaned up the worst of them. We need to get up to the city," Draven announced.

"How do you do that?" I demanded, feeling both furious and envious at once.

"Do what?"

"Wield my own power better than I can!"

Quiet again. Then, "Well, I've been practicing."

"For how fucking long?"

"Since we got back from Meridium."

I clenched and unclenched my fists around the reins. "That long?"

"That long." Draven's voice was soft. "I thought... If I could master this, then I could teach you, too..."

My temper flared to life. "I don't want you to teach me. I don't want you near me. Not ever again. Not after today. Do you understand that? Do you, Draven?"

He was quiet. "I understand that you feel that way now. But I hope, one day, that you might change your mind."

"Well, I won't," I insisted, forcing certainty into my voice.

Down below us there were shouts from the ramparts.

"Odessa is sending soldiers to the surface. They've cleared the other riders. We need to move. Beks and Javer are up there. I don't know who else is with them."

"Sure, I'll just fly you back to the ramparts and drop you off, then Ulpheas can stitch you..."

"Just tell Nightclaw to take us there," Draven interrupted me. "He should be able to do it."

"What?"

"Tell him to try at least. He should be able to go such a short distance."

"How do you know all of this?" I demanded.

I heard him snort. "I'm very, very well-read. Remember?"

"You're a fucking scholar, sure," I muttered.

I touched my hands to Nightclaw's sides and closed my eyes. Can you do this? I asked. Can you do what he's claiming? Do you *want* to?

Instantly I felt Nightclaw's assent.

Our surroundings blurred into a whirlwind of motion, colors merging and warping with dizzying speed. Time seemed to stretch and compress all at once.

And then we were on the surface. Standing amidst the bustling streets of the city of Noctasia.

I glanced down at Nightclaw, silent appreciation passing through me.

In front of us, standing on one of the bridges overlooking the lake, Javer and Beks posed side-by-side at the forefront of a battle raging above them.

High over the city, a tempestuous sky hissed with fury, dark clouds swirling ominously.

Bolts of deadly lightning slashed through the air, illuminating the city below with brief flashes.

Each thunderous strike hammered against the shield that Javer and Beks were so valiantly upholding. I watched as Beks' thin arms trembled under the weight of the magical defense.

I put a hand on Draven's arm. "They can't keep holding it. We have to do something."

The shield would fall and the people of Noctasia would be utterly exposed. The city would be devastated. Did Rychel understand just what she had done today?

Draven nodded. I removed my hand quickly.

"Can Nightclaw fly again?"

I looked at the battlecat. "I... think so." I touched Nightclaw with a wisp of awareness and felt his eagerness to rise once more. "Yes. He says yes."

"Your connection is strong already," Draven observed. "Good. Let's go."

We rose slowly over the city, over the chaos and terror. Below, a frenzy had taken hold. People ran haphazardly through labyrinthine alleys, their eyes wide with fear and desperation. Frantic cries filled the air, mingled with sounds of hurried footsteps and clattering of objects knocked askew. Market stalls lay abandoned, their wares scattered in disarray as merchants and patrons alike sought refuge from the impending attack.

As we ascended into the sky, I glanced back once more to see Beks standing beside his master. His messy black hair fell over his forehead, choppy and uneven. His little face bore the weight of a responsibility far beyond his years, yet there he stood. Steadfast and unswerving. Refusing to yield.

Beside him, Javer briefly laid a hand gently on his apprentice's shoulder. He was standing very close to the boy, murmuring words I prayed were of encouragement.

Human or fae, was Beks not part of this empire, a voice inside me whispered? Was he not worthy?

Javer's thin hands flashed through the air with practice precision, channeling arcane energy as he held the shield. I broke my gaze away from the pair.

And then we were passing through the shield, high above them, and the dark hunters came clearly into view.

"You're not going to like this, Morgan," Draven said from behind me, his voice grim.

Before I could protest, he'd swiveled around in the saddle, positioning himself to face my back.

"I'll try not to touch you," he promised. I glanced down to see his hands gripping the sides of Nightclaw's saddle instead of my waist. "But you might have to touch me."

I scowled even though I knew he couldn't see my face. "What the hell does that mean?"

"It means there are two of us here with the exact same skill. I want you to draw power from me and use it to take these bastards out. All at once."

My heart hammered. Me? Responsible for the safety of the entire city below?

"All at once? Why me? You could do the same thing, probably better. You've been practicing longer."

"No." Draven's voice was hard as glass. "I'm not going to do that. I won't draw power from you. I'm asking you to use me. If you want to save these people, if you want to stop this, then you'll do it."

"How? I don't even know how to do what you're asking." Panic bubbled inside me.

I felt him take a deep breath, his chest pressing against my back, solid and strong. We had been so close before. So very fucking close.

That was then. This was now, I told myself. Things change. My invisible wards were back up, struggling to guard me from Draven in every possible way. But I feared they were not strong enough. My body yearned for him, even now.

"Tell me I can touch you," he commanded.

I gnashed my teeth in frustration. "Is that the only way? Fine. Fucking touch me. Make it..."

His hands were settling on my hips before I could finish the sentence, warm and familiar.

And then energy was flowing between us.

A swell of raw power coursed through my veins as Draven channeled into me.

The feeling was euphoric. As if I had taken a sip of the finest, most exquisite wine, the flavors dancing on my tongue and setting me aglow.

Power flowed through my veins like a heady elixir.

I could feel the surge of power peaking upwards, reaching its zenith. My entire being hummed with purpose, intoxicated with potency.

Anything. I could do anything.

Draven's hands on my hips were the core of it all. I longed to pull them tighter, place them higher on my body. Giddy, I leaned back into him, laughing with excitement.

"Careful now," he warned, keeping his hands exactly where they were. "Focus, Morgan. Remember what we're doing here."

My senses heightened, my spirit aflame, I struggled to focus. I nodded my head. "Right. I'm ready. Let's go."

Nightclaw led us upwards, soaring through the sky over the city.

Straight ahead a row of riders flew towards us at an almost idle speed, as if simply curious to see who and what the hell we were.

Behind them I spotted the main grouping of hunters. They were continuing to unleash their barrage upon the city shields.

I lifted my arms, almost lazily.

An inferno blazed through the sky.

We were close enough for me to see the expressions of shock then terror transform the riders' faces.

They tried to swerve. They weren't fast enough.

For a moment, they wavered, half-turned about, then were overwhelmed by the swell of flames.

Behind them, the main cluster was starting to take notice of what was happening. They scattered, stretching out in all directions.

But it was too late.

I knew what I had to do. No, I knew what I was *capable* of doing with Draven behind me.

Using everything he was feeding into me, I swept energy outwards, guiding a fiery blanket across the sky. With each sweep of my arms, flames charged through the air, clearing every lingering threat.

Below, the city stood witness to my power as I painted the heavens in a display of destruction.

My flames devoured the air with an insatiable hunger. They swallowed the Valtain riders whole, melting their armor into twisted bits of metal and searing their mounts into pieces of bone and ash that fell like rain to the city beneath.

Only when Draven's hands slipped from my hips did I lower my arms.

Slowly, concern penetrated my ecstatic haze. "Draven?"

There was no response.

Nightclaw swooped downwards, taking us back to the city. I gripped Draven's thighs, trying to make sure he stayed in place.

Below, the shimmering shield had vanished. Javer and Beks must have lowered it as soon as they'd realized the threat was gone.

We landed near the bridge.

"Draven?" I turned in the saddle. With relief, I saw he was still upright, his eyes open.

He looked haggard and I was forced to remember just how ill he'd been so recently–no, not had been. Had seemed. Had it even been real?

He smiled faintly. "Told you it would work. Felt good, didn't it?"

I refused to confirm just how fucking good it had felt. "It was fine. Are you... going to be all right?"

"Not that you care, Morgan," he said with a smirk. "But I'll be fine."

Abruptly, I watched his face fall. "Shit."

"What?"

"Morgan, wait..."

But I ignored him, swiveling in the saddle to follow his gaze. "No. No, no, no."

And then I was slipping from Nightclaw's saddle and running across the bridge to where Javer sat, his head hanging low as he cradled Beks' small, limp body in his arms.

CHAPTER 34

There was an altar in the Siabra temple I hadn't paid much attention to the first time Beks had taken me there.

Now I walked towards it with a heavy heart.

A collection of incense sticks lined one side of the altar, waiting patiently to be ignited by devout Siabra. I wondered how often they were used.

The altar seemed to be dedicated to no goddess or god in particular. Perhaps it was meant to provide offerings to all.

Selecting a slender stick of incense, I held it over a candle flame, watching as the fire engulfed the tip, transforming it into a wisp of smoldering smoke.

An earthy, musky fragrance filled the air. Sandalwood and smoke. Draven's scent.

Wincing as smoke scrolls of perfume billowed gently around me, I placed the lit incense stick in one of the holders on the altar then stood back to watch the smoke rise.

How easily a single flame could burn out.

Especially if left unprotected.

"Morgan."

I didn't turn around. The intrusion wasn't unexpected. Somehow, I'd known he'd find me. He always did.

"Javer is devastated, you know." His voice was soft. I sensed him standing a few feet behind me.

"Good. He fucking should be."

"He didn't do this, Morgan."

"He might as well have killed Beks himself, Draven, and you know it. He pushed him too far."

There was silence for a moment. "From what he says, Beks refused to back down. Javer was so wrapped up in what they were doing that he didn't see how drained the boy was becoming."

Withered. That was what they called it when a magic wielder drew too deeply and too quickly and burned themselves out. Beks had withered.

He was just a boy, but he had withered defending a city. While up above him in the sky, I had laughed and enjoyed the feeling of power I had gotten from Draven's magic channeling into me.

I had been drunk on power while below me, Beks had been *dying*.

I might have done the same thing to Draven. Drunk too deeply. Drained him dry. Was that what I had nearly done?

Who was the real monster? Me or Javer?

"You should have let me hit him a few more times," I said calmly. "He deserved it."

"I don't think he'd disagree. But if you're looking to blame someone, it's me you want, Morgan. And you know it." His voice was hollow and bitter. "I sent them both down there. Beks' death is on my head."

I shook my head silently, refusing to take the bait. We each had our own guilt to wrestle with. Neither of us were innocent. It didn't matter anymore.

"Where is he?"

"Javer is with Odessa. If you meant Beks..." Draven cleared his throat. "Hawl and Crescent are seeing to his body."

"Seeing to it? What is there to see?" I demanded, my voice harsh. "He's gone, isn't he? What do the Siabra do with bodies, anyhow? Put them on a pyre? Set them out to sea?" That's what traditionally happened to Pendragon kings and queens. Not that I would ever be one. Not that I was even really a Pendragon.

But it was my name. It was all I'd known. I wasn't about to take Draven's, was I?

Morgan Venator. It didn't sound completely terrible.

Something wet was falling down my cheek. Drops of condensation must have been dripping from the ceiling, I decided, because I certainly wasn't fucking crying right now.

I swiped at my face as stealthily as I could, then heard Draven sigh.

"What? No one asked you to come here. For once, you couldn't have just left me alone? In peace?"

"I... could have. You're right. I just wanted to make sure you were all right. Parts of the palace are unstable. There are reports of cave-ins, flooding. I just thought..." His voice trailed off. For once it lacked its steely quality.

"You looked at me as if you didn't even know me when I came back from the trial."

"I know."

"Why?"

"I needed the court to see I was deadly serious when I announced you were their new empress."

I laughed bitterly. "I'm not their new empress, Draven. For the love of the Three, please stop fucking saying I am."

"I know you hate it. I knew you would hate it. But it's the truth. You are."

"Then I resign. I abdicate. I bestow the honor on you. You're my husband, right? So can't I just... give the throne to you?"

"There might be some precedent for that, but it's a long and complicated legal process. And besides, I wouldn't accept it."

I whirled to face him. "You told me you were doing this because you wanted to become emperor. To rule your people. To change things."

"That was the original plan."

"And then?" My voice was hard. "You decided to set me up instead. To what...? Fake your injury? Pretend to be more impacted by the poison than you really were? Were you conscious in that bed the entire time?"

"I was in a self-induced state of stasis," he said carefully. "A kind of hibernation, if you will. I couldn't see you or hear you. At least, not usually."

My nostrils flared. "Yet you knew just when to wake up."

"I had set a time frame, yes. I told my body when I needed it back."

"How fucking convenient. Meanwhile, I could have *died* down in that arena. Lyrastra lost her arm. And for what? Because you don't want to be emperor after all? Thanks for mentioning it." I threw up my hands and turned away.

"It wasn't like that. I swear." Draven's voice was soft and low. I wasn't used to hearing him this way. But then, he was probably pretending to be contrite. Pretending to care. Everything had been just that. Pretending.

I sniffed.

"Really, Morgan. It wasn't." He hesitated. "I knew you would be safe. Beyond the shadow of a doubt, I *knew*."

I turned back around. "You knew? How?"

His eyes fixed on mine. "I dreamed it."

I stared. "You dreamed it?"

He nodded. "I saw it. All of it. You taking my place. Succeeding in the trial. And I understood why. Of course, I did. It was so simple once I had seen it. So easy to understand why the throne wasn't supposed to be mine in the first place."

"Why?"

"No one who likes power should ever have it, Morgan," he said simply.

My breath caught in my throat. "You set this whole thing up. This dream—when did you have it?"

He looked back at me steadily. "Just before the first trial."

I felt dizzy with shock. "You knew back then. And you didn't tell me. You told me my dreams were false. Meanwhile, you were trusting your own? Do you know how fucked up that is, Draven?"

He winced. "I've always had the true dreaming. I couldn't believe you were receiving it, too. It seemed too cruel to think that was the only power of mine you might have gained. At first, when this dream came, I didn't trust it either. Morgan, I've been blocking them for so long. This gift... It's more a nightmare than a blessing."

"How long have you had them?"

"Since I was a child," he said. "I couldn't control them. Eventually my father found out. He used the dreams however he could, when he could get me to tell him about them. When Tabar... When he did what he did, I had a dream about it. Nodori had just delivered our baby. I was resting in another room. I woke up in a cold sweat, then raced to Nodori's bedchamber. But I was too late."

He looked at me. "Never, not once, have these dreams been a gift before now. I used to think I was cursed. I trained myself to ignore them. For years, I thought I had managed to block them. Then..." He stopped.

"Then?"

"Then they started coming back."

I stared at him. "Just how long have you been dreaming about me for, Draven?"

He glanced away. "I've always known there would be a crown on your head, one way or another, Morgan."

Before now, he had said. They had never been a gift *before now*.

"Is this your plan for peace?" I demanded. "Because I'm no ruler. These aren't my people. You're trying to give your throne to a half-fae girl from another continent and you really think they're going to accept..."

"Not half-fae," Draven cut in.

I shook my head in confusion. "What?"

"You're not half-fae. Not anymore. If you ever were, which I highly doubt."

"What are you talking about?" But I already had an inkling he understood.

"Look at yourself, Morgan. Look at those markings on your arms. What exactly do you think those are?"

I gritted my teeth. "I don't know. But you've always seemed to have some idea. So why don't you tell me?"

He hesitated briefly, then answered. "You're imbued with magic, Morgan. Someone poured everything they had into shaping you this way. Someone powerful."

I gaped at him. "Who?"

"I think you know that better than I."

"You told me not to trust my dreams. But they've all been real, haven't they? What did you do to me, Draven? The dreams, the claws." I raised my hand, feeling a gentle prickling sensation, like a cascade of tiny needles. Slowly, sleek curves extended, glinting in the light. "What am I? You?"

Draven shook his head. "Not me, no. But you're a part of me. Just as I'm a part of you."

"Did you know this was going to happen? When you saved me?"

"I knew there was a chance. There was also a chance you'd simply... die."

"Maybe it would have been better if I had," I said before I could stop myself. "Or you could have leached my powers away, taking them for yourself, leaving me withered like Beks. Was that another possibility? Did you consider it?"

"Never," Draven snapped. "Never. Why would I want that, Morgan? I don't want your powers. I want..." He shook his head.

"What?" I demanded, pushing hard. "What? Say it? You wanted me bound to you forever against my will, is that it?"

"No! I fucking wanted *you*. Just you. Alive. But by my side against your will? No, I didn't fucking want that. Who would want that for anyone they loved?"

Loved. He'd said loved.

"But it was the only way," he went on. "I knew you'd hate me. As I did it, I knew this would be the price. I told myself it was worth it. That I'd pay it, willingly. As long as I could save you. Because I hadn't fucking been able to save them. I'd been useless. Worse than useless." He ran his hands over his face roughly.

"Your wife. Your baby. Your daughter. Did she have a name?" I had never thought to ask him before. Even now the question seemed too intimate. His grief still too fresh.

"Nimue." His voice was very soft.

"Nimue," I repeated. "That's a lovely name."

I watched him, handsome face marred by grief and turmoil. Beks was gone. Rychel was gone.

I thought of what Rychel had said. How she'd only known one other person who'd had the gift of true dreaming. She'd known it was Draven all along. Why hadn't she told me?

And now, he was the only one I could confide in. The only one who might understand.

"I dreamed of my mother," I said abruptly. "A true dream. At least, I think it was."

Draven raised his dark brows. "And? What did you see?"

This was the hard part. "I saw her running through the streets of Numenos. With me in her arms." I met his eyes. "One hundred and fifty years ago. Give or take."

Draven's expression was stunned.

"I guess you're not that much older than me, after all," I said.

"How is that possible?"

"My mother blocked my memories. Orcades suggested something of the sort. She touched me and...undid it somehow." I supposed I should be grateful. "Oh, and... I think she's my sister." The words rushed out. "Orcades, I mean."

Now Draven's expression was almost comical. "What? Orcades? The daughter of the High King of Valtain?"

I nodded. "Right. That Orcades. Is there another one?"

"Why do you think that?"

"Because my mother was the queen. Not just of Pendrath. But of Valtain. She was Gorlois' queen first." I paused. "I suppose she had another name then. Who was the queen one hundred and fifty years ago?"

"Her name was Idrisane," he said slowly.

"In all the chaos of the attack, I'm guessing your people probably lost track of most of the Valtain dynasty?"

He nodded.

"So I'm guessing the Siabra didn't hear about the High King losing a daughter along the way?"

Draven shook his head. "The High King has many children. So you and Arthur..."

"He's a Pendragon. And apparently, I'm... not."

"Morgan Venator is a good name, too," Draven said quietly.

I shook my head slowly.

"Or your true father's name. Gorlois Le Fay."

Morgan Le Fay. It sounded even more wrong than Morgan Venator to me.

"How did your mother do it?" Draven asked suddenly. "You *aren't* one hundred and fifty years old. That much is clear, even if you were born then. So how did she do it?"

I gave a sardonic chuckle. "Stop time? You mean that isn't a common Siabra power?"

Draven's lips turned up in a wry smile. "Not that I've ever heard. Though I'm sure there are many who would envy such an ability."

"I don't know how she did it," I said truthfully. "Not exactly. But I know..." Should I tell him? "I think it involved an arch."

"An arch?" He tilted his head thoughtfully. "Incredible."

"Does the court have more shielders?" I changed the subject abruptly. "Why weren't they up there, with Beks and Javer?"

"Sephone has two in reserve. They manage the wards on the palace. Perhaps they were trying to repair them when..." His voice drifted off.

"Sephone," I said bitterly. "At least she won't be in charge much longer."

"Does that mean..." Draven began.

"No. I'm not doing it, Draven. Dream or no dream. I don't know what crown you saw on my head but no one is placing one there."

"You *are* our empress. With or without the crown, Morgan. Make no mistake."

"No, it's you who has made the mistake. And now you're going to stay here and fix it. You should be ruling this people. You never should have left them in the first place. Someone needs to clean up this mess. All of it. Your palace is in shambles. The people in the city are scared. You've just been attacked by a group of Valtain hunters. Your sister is gone. Rychel gave them the grail. You have a lot of problems to deal with." I stepped forward, jabbing him in the chest with my finger, claw and all. "You. Not me."

I looked up at him. Memorizing every detail, as if it wasn't already embedded in my brain. Then I turned and started walking across the white marbled rotunda.

"We're bonded, Morgan. I know you hate that, but it's a fact."

"What happens if we're separated?"

"Separated?"

"What happens if we're not near one another?"

"You'll still feel the bond. At first, the tether was weak. But you've already glimpsed how strong it can be. Our powers are shared somehow."

"Yes, you took advantage of that nicely with the harpies."

"As did you," he pointed out. "When you climbed that wall. And every time you dream."

"I'm stuck with you. Got it." Stuck with him inside me. Always. And me in him. "So we won't die if we're not together or anything like that?"

"No, we won't, though it could grow... painful. Why do you ask?"

"Because I'm leaving." I paused. "I don't know what this could have been. Whatever this was between us." My eyes locked with his. There was a lump in my throat. I choked it down. "But doing what you did? It ruined it, Draven. We may be bound to one another. And yes, you may have saved my life. Forgive me if I can't say I'm completely grateful. But if you saved my life, you also destroyed my trust. This isn't a marriage. I'm not a Siabra."

"I would never want you to be." He took a step forward. "Morgan, please. Just wait. Just listen. Give me more time."

I held up a hand. "Stop. Please. Just stop."

A whirlwind of emotions was descending upon me. This was harder than I'd thought it would be.

Grief weighed upon my heart. Grief for Beks, yes. But also, grief for the shattered trust between Draven and I.

I fucking *needed* him. I needed him more than I could ever say. It had been so long since we had been apart, I wasn't sure I could be without him.

Yet I couldn't have him. I couldn't let myself be what he wanted me to be.

This bond between us was unnatural. It was suffocating and oppressive.

I couldn't deny our connection. Or that my desire for him threatened to overwhelm me.

And that's why I had to break away.

Because it wasn't real. Whatever we seemed to feel for one another, whatever Draven had nearly just said he felt. It wasn't real. It was the product of this artificial union. Our *marriage*.

The pain that knowing that caused me was almost unbearable.

Knowing this could never, ever be.

And yet beyond the hurt and the anger, the longing was still so strong.

With an involuntary impulse, I felt my feet drawing me back to him.

I looked up at him and the regret I felt was palpable.

Emerald eyes framed with heavy black lashes stared down at me.

"If only," I whispered, touching a hand to an obsidian lock of hair and tucking it gently behind one pointed ear. "If only it didn't have to be this way. You're all I think about. You're all I see. I'm so tied to you I barely know who I am anymore."

"And I to you," he whispered. "Is that such a bad thing?"

I leaned up. Kissing him with everything I had left to give him, my heart aching with longing and resignation.

Our lips met, a collision of fire and silk. Every longing and unfulfilled promise weaving into a tapestry of desire.

His hands tangled in my hair, pulling me closer and drawing a gasp from my lips.

He kissed me the same way he did everything. The way that was his nature. With a ferocity that stunned me, with a forcefulness I couldn't deny.

Perhaps it was the bond. Perhaps it was because I had channeled through him. But I felt it. I felt the current between us. And it left me dizzy.

An indescribable, wonderful heat filled my body, aching and beautiful, as his lips touched mine. I twined my fingers around him, claiming him with my mouth, my lips, marking him with my teeth.

I clawed his back, running my hands through his hair, consumed by the moment, the kiss, this man. My husband.

And then I forced myself to break away.

When I stepped back, I was panting.

The water was trickling down my face again. Fucking Siabra ceiling.

Draven was staring at me, his eyes wild.

"I felt it, yes," I confessed, before he could ask. "I felt it but it's false."

"There's nothing false about it." I had never seen his eyes like this. Desperate and pleading. "Do you want me to say it again? I'll shout it through the palace. I'll never stop. I won't let you go without a fight. Morgan, please. Don't do this. I love you."

I'd been expecting the words and yet still they hit me like a blow.

"Kaye needs me more than you do," I said simply. "And your people don't need me, Draven. They need you."

I glanced over my shoulder.

Behind me lay the ring of paintings. Not of the goddesses and gods, but of the lands.
The lands of Aercanum.

I knew without looking where my favorite one was. Behind me and a little to my left.
The painting showed a lush landscape of rich green forests and rolling hills. And a city in
the far distance that might have been Camelot, if the artist had seen it hundreds of years
ago, before I had ever been born.

I didn't know how to say good-bye.

Maybe there was no good way. But I knew one thing had to be said.

"Don't follow me, Draven. If I make it through, I'll close the portal behind me. You'll
die if you try to follow."

I turned and ran.

Across the rotunda, towards the painting of Pendrath.

I ran towards it, not knowing if my hunch was right. If it was wrong, I would either
look very foolish or would wind up dead.

If I was right, I was leaving Draven behind. Possibly forever.

With a pang I thought of Nightclaw. But I had already considered that. Lancelet's horse
had died days after traveling through an arch. I couldn't take that chance with Nightclaw.
Not when he already meant so much to me.

I hit the painting with full force.

It was like stepping through a curtain. The moment I crossed the threshold, the canvas
shifted and warped around me, pulling me into its depths with a swirl of colors and
shapes.

There was a rush of energy.

And then there was only darkness.

I landed with a gentle thud on a cold stone floor in a dark room.

The air carried a new scent. As if I truly were in a new land. Slivers of light filtered in
from above, as if from under a closed door high above.

Standing up, my eyes adjusted to the light, taking in the worn stone walls and a long
curving staircase leading up to a heavy oak door.

Behind me lay the stone arch I had come through. The counterpart to the one that lay
in the Court of Umbral Flames.

I had only seconds.

I prayed whatever I did to the arch would be clearly reflected in the rotunda where Draven stood, showing him conclusively that the way forward was barred and closed.

With a deep breath, I called the magic from my veins, pulsing and crackling down through my fingertips. Flames flickered up the sides of the stone arch.

Sweeping them together like a curtain of fire, I guided the flames, pulling them together until they encompassed the archway in a blazing embrace.

The fire swirled as the stone began to crumble.

A figure emerged. Hurtling through the flames with reckless abandon.

They landed on the stone floor beside me in a heap, their clothing ablaze.

I swept my hands once more over the arch, watching the stones crumble and fall, then rushed to the figure on the floor. Pulling off my cloak, I beat at the flames.

The smell of burning fabric mingled with the acrid scent of charred flesh, but gradually the flames yielded. As the last vestiges of fire were subdued, I cast my cloak aside and knelt beside the fallen figure.

It wasn't Draven. I had known that from the start.

The smell of singed feathers filled the air.

Javer lifted his head. His black pointed beard was nearly gone. Skin blackened with soot, he looked up at me, dazed.

I swore. Loudly. My voice echoing off the stone walls. "Oh, you stupid, stupid man."

There was a creaking sound.

I whirled around. The door at the top of the stairs was opening.

A figure stood silhouetted in the frame. They stepped forward. The light behind them hit their face.

A ripple of disbelief went through me. Any words I might have said dried up, as my breath caught in my throat.

"Morgan?" Lancelet stepped into the chamber. "Is it really you?"

EPILOGUE

*W*eeks Earlier...

I was lying on a cold stone floor. My body was pressed uncomfortably against its unforgiving surface.

There was a figure hunched over me. A boy.

His face was pale and unsettling. His eyes were a bright inhuman blue.

A question was on my lips, but before I could voice it, the boy opened his mouth and descended upon my flesh, sinking his teeth into the soft surface.

A wave of searing pain.

Anguish engulfed me.

I became aware that the boy was not alone.

Other children surrounded me. Their twisted visages were the stuff of nightmares.

Lifeless eyes betrayed an insatiable hunger.

Gnarled hands clawed and tore at my fragile skin.

The assault was relentless. It elicited a symphony of distorted cries and haunting moans, amplifying my sense of unyielding dread.

I bore witness to my own consumption, piece by piece.

Each bite, each rending of flesh from my fragile bones, registered in my horrified mind with excruciating clarity.

The putrid scent of decay lingered in the air, its origins muddled between the remnants of my own devoured body and the ghastly presence of these macabre children who held me captive within this tormenting hell.

Agony crashed upon me in relentless waves, overwhelming my senses until I could tolerate no more.

With an open mouth, I released a primal scream. The sudden expulsion of air pushed painfully through a ragged hole in my cheek I had not known until then was there.

The echoes of my desperate cries dissipated into the abyss, lost in a realm where pain and terror reigned supreme.

No one was coming for me.

The Temple of the Three, Camelot

"Lancelet!"

The voice was sharp yet tender.

"Lancelet! Wake up!"

Snapping fingers in my ears. I groaned.

A tutting sound. Then the touch of a soft hand on my forehead. "You're drenched in sweat. It's just a dream, my dear." The voice changed to a low mutter, "Only a dream, but your screams are very real and you're waking up the entire dormitory."

The words were not accusing. It was simply a statement. The words of a tired woman who had come to my room many times before.

I struggled to open my eyes.

I struggled to remember.

I didn't want to remember.

My eyes opened. "Where am I?"

"You're in the Temple of the Three in Camelot. I am Merlin. You are Lancelet. You are safe." The last three words were said very slowly and with infinite tenderness. As if they had already been spoken many times before.

"Safe," I echoed. "No."

"Yes," Merlin said firmly, putting a hand on mine and squeezing. "Safe. You are safe."

"They'll come through. They'll come after me. They'll follow." I heard the panic in my own voice. I recognized the irrationality. She had already argued with me many times before.

"You know they won't. They haven't yet and it has been nearly two weeks. If they had found the arch, if they could have used it, they would have done so long before now, Lancelet, believe me. Please, believe me."

She sounded so weary. Had I made her so? I forced myself to look at her. Really look.

When I did, I was aghast.

Merlin, High Priestess of the Temple of the Three Sisters, Keeper of the Sacred Flame, Oracle of the Secret Mysteries, and Guardian of the Celestial Sanctum, gazed upon me wearily. The white strands in her hair had become more prominent, intermingling with her once vibrant ebony hair in a braid that encircled her proud head. Draped in her flowing pure white temple robes, exhaustion permeated her posture. Dark shadows beneath her eyes revealed the weight of countless ordeals.

"Merlin, you look dreadful."

Her lips twisted in a wry smile. "Thank you, my dear."

"I'm sorry," I said immediately. "I only meant..."

She gave my hand another gentle squeeze. "I know how I look, Lancelet. Believe me. It is a price I willingly pay."

I swallowed. "I see."

There was something else here. Something I didn't wish to see. Didn't wish to remember. Merlin was hinting at it.

I pushed the thought away.

"Do you remember now?" she asked softly.

I nodded. "I think so. I came through the arch. I came home. I'm in the temple."

"Good." She hesitated. "You have told me the same thing before."

I stared at her. "Have I?"

She nodded. "You remember. You tell me you remember. Then you push memory away."

I was the reason for her weariness then. I was the cause for those new white hairs. I felt a pulse of guilt.

"No, no," she said quickly, as if able to see my mind. She touched a hand to her face. "This is not from you, my dear."

"Then from what?"

"If I tell you, will you remember anything I have said later on? That is the question. I have tried to tell you the state of things before." She sighed. "The fastest way would be to give you a mirror. But it is also the cruelest."

"The cruelest? I don't understand."

I didn't want to understand. My mind began to scream, to push back into the recesses it had hidden in.

But from those recesses also came the dark nightmares, like the one I had just escaped from. I didn't want to go back to those.

I was here now. I had to make an effort to stay.

There was already a mirror on Merlin's lap, I belatedly realized. A gilded oval, lying face-down. Now she began to raise it slowly, the long white flared sleeves of her gown fluttering like the wings of a bird in flight.

My stomach churned. I wanted to turn my head.

The mirror was lifted into view.

I looked into it.

A stranger gazed back.

I had never considered myself a true beauty, though secretly I was well aware that I was not unpleasant to look upon. Many women had thought me lovely. I had become used to their praise. Even counted upon it.

Well, no one would ever call Lancelet de Troyes "lovely" ever again.

The face that stared back at me from the mirror could barely be described as human.

Matted blonde hair, still sticky in spots with crusted blood. Worse were the places where hair had been ripped from scalp entirely, leaving gaping spots of angry pink flesh.

My face. The jagged hole in my cheek had not been a nightmare. It was there, though it had begun to slowly heal. Already I could touch the inside of my cheek without wincing. But on the outside, the wound was raw and red.

The edges of the gap showed signs of scabbing. Fresh pink flesh around the border suggested the wound would close in time.

But there would always be a scar. A scar edged with the marks of teeth.

As for the rest of me. I lowered the mirror to my neck, then beyond.

The less said about it the better.

I had brought the children back with me after all.

Their marks covered my flesh. They had marred me for all time.

I was no longer beautiful. I was no longer perfect. I was less than human. I was monstrous.

I opened my mouth and began to laugh. A sound horrible and grating.

The harsh noise was cut short as I realized we were no longer alone.

A girl stood in the doorway of the small room, rubbing the sleep from her eyes.

She was short and shaped like a bell. Long lashes brushed gently against the smooth, honey-toned skin of her rosy, plump cheeks.

Curling brown hair reached just below her chin. Hair which had recently been cut–and cut badly. The edges were jagged and I caught sight of longer strands which had been missed, as if the girl had chopped at her own locks ruthlessly and in a hurry. Why would she disfigure herself so?

As if I of all people had any right to ask.

"Did we wake you, Guinevere? I'm sorry." Merlin's voice was rich and soft. Where inside of herself did she find the endless pool to draw from? Giving and then giving still more?

"I heard screaming." The girl's lips were soft and full. She was not dressed like a temple acolyte, I realized. She wore a nightgown of pale blue–while all of the acolytes wore the same dull dove gray. There was lace trim on the edges, and yet while the nightdress was a rich and pretty thing, it looked well-worn, too.

The girl called Guinevere shifted in the door frame. There was a comforting softness to her. Her curves reminded me of a blossoming flower.

"Do you need any help, Merlin?" Her voice was as gentle as she looked.

Suddenly I wondered if the girl had helped Merlin before. How many times had she been forced to see me like this?

To see... me?

"No, we'll be all right," Merlin assured her. "You go back to bed now."

"Very well." Guinevere's lips curved into a soft crescent and I felt an unexpected warmth radiate into the room. "Goodnight."

As soon as the girl's footsteps had faded away, I turned to Merlin. "Who was that?"

"Guinevere," Merlin said, with a hint of amusement.

"Yes, I heard that much," I said, feeling annoyed.

Annoyance was better than self-pity, a bitter voice in my head said.

"And you want to know more?" Merlin tilted her head thoughtfully. "I think you will have to ask Guinevere herself. Perhaps tomorrow, when you leave this room."

The thought frightened me as soon as I heard it.

The chamber I was in was small and windowless, with room only for the bed on which I lay and the chair in which Merlin sat. But the prospect of leaving it? Terrifying.

"Guinevere came to us from the castle," Merlin was saying. "She is from Lyonesse."

"Lyonesse?" That got my attention. "She *escaped* from the castle–is that what you mean?"

Merlin's expression turned sad. "That would be an accurate way of describing it, yes."

"What's been happening? Here in Camelot? What is going on?" My voice was sharp, demanding. I knew nothing. I was blind. What had I missed?

"And Morgan... Where is Morgan? I..." I stopped. In a flash I recalled the last time I had seen her. She had been pulled away by Vesper. She seemed to be struggling.

She couldn't have struggled very hard.

I pushed the thought back. It was unworthy of us both.

But still, she had not come back. No one had come. Not for me.

"You are Lancelet de Troyes," Merlin said. A finger lifted my chin up in the air. Merlin seemed to have no qualms about touching my face–or looking at it for that matter. Guinevere had not screamed in fright either. But then, she must have seen it before. I felt embarrassed to think of what she must have seen. What she must have heard.

"You are a knight of Camelot. Never forget that."

"A knight?" I scoffed, pushing her hand away. "I was never knighted."

"That will be remedied. All in good time. And the time draws near," Merlin said calmly. "You are a warrior of Pendrath. Heed my words."

She spoke not as herself but as the High Priestess, her voice low but commanding. A chill went through me as I heard the power of the goddesses.

"Very well," I managed to say. I was not about to argue with her. Though I knew I was no knight and never would be. Not now.

Merlin smiled slightly. "You think knights bear no scars? That they possess no disfigurements? That they are pure and whole?"

Once again, I felt as if she had grasped my thoughts completely. It was a disarming sensation.

"They are pure," I argued. "As I can never be again. Not now."

Merlin's expression turned shrewd. "We are never pure. Not in the sense you mean, Lancelet. Purity is a virtue best left to the goddesses. It is overrated in mortals. And each of us has our own idea of what it truly means. To some, it is a nightmare to be aspired to all in itself."

"What do you mean?"

"The king demands purity," she said, her face becoming weary once more. "He demands it in his temple. His version of it. Do you remember?"

I racked my mind swiftly. "Galahad..."

"He has returned," Merlin said quietly. "He is in one of the dormitories. He has returned to serve amongst us, if not to take up the priesthood. That path remains forbidden to him."

"Because he dared to love men once?" I cried. "Because he was brave enough to never deny it. Oh, the stupidity."

"Yes." Merin's voice was sardonic. "No women or catamites–" She spoke the foul word with the fullest irony. "–may speak for the gods. So says our noble king. And yet other defilements are freely permitted."

My eyes widened. "No women? But…"

"You forget I am no longer High Priestess, Lancelet. We have told you before. Perhaps this time…" She eyed me carefully. "Well, this time perhaps you will remember tomorrow."

"How many times have you told me?"

She tapped a finger to her chin thoughtfully. "I believe this will be the fifth. But think ahead to the morning. Make the prospect real in your mind. This time in the morning you will not have allowed yourself to forget again. You will rise from your bed and dress. You will go out into the garden. You will sit by the pool. No one will disturb you, I will see to that. You will feel the sun shine upon you. You will listen to the birds." She cast a discerning look. "Perhaps Guinevere might join you for a while. She can share some of her story, if she chooses."

The prospect of seeing the girl again brightened me more than the prospect of hearing birds sing.

Guinevere had reminded me of a bird. Soft and sweet. There had been something innocent about her.

"Perhaps," I said. "But first, tell me more. Tell me everything. I swear, this time I will remember."

"I believe you," Merlin said steadily. And it gave me hope she did.

She smoothed the white samite of her skirt. "Where shall I begin? With Morgan?"

My heart beat faster. "You know where she is? Did she come back? Is she here?"

"No, she is not here. And I cannot say I know with certainty where she is. But I can tell you she is safe."

My heart sank. "Is that all? How can you know?"

"I know. I believe. She is safe. She longs to return."

"And will she?" I demanded.

"Not soon enough. Not as soon as you or I might like," Merlin replied. "We must go on. We must deal with this state of things on our own."

"And what is the state of things?" I asked, my voice already bitter. "What else have women been barred from? I'm surprised they aren't burning us alive yet."

"Not yet. Things have not reached that state," Merlin said diplomatically. She did not deny that they might. "A new temple has been erected. The king makes plans to do away with the worship of the Three. Perun is the god we must all serve now. The High Priest of Perun presides over the new temple, while the High Priest of the Three does the same here."

"You've been usurped by a man?" I shook my head in disbelief. "This is untenable, Merlin. How can you bear it?"

"A man, yes, but at least a good man–in this temple at least," Merlin mused. "And how? We bear what we must because we must bear it."

That cryptic comment made no sense to me.

"You'd be surprised at how much you can bear, Lancelet," Merlin reminded me. "A person can live with just about anything if the desire to go on is strong enough."

"I don't know if I have that desire," I said, and then was shocked by my own admission.

"You're still here," Merlin said simply. "There is nothing you must do but be. You are still with us. That is enough." She sighed and touched her brow briefly. "The High Priest of this temple. A man, yes. But a good man. His name is Tyre. He was already one of my closest counselors." She shrugged. "Not much has changed. You will see. Tyre does what he must to placate the king."

"But you are the true power of the temple?" I guessed.

"We will not say that. Now, the other High Priest. The same cannot be said for him as for Tyre. Cavan is his name. He might have been a good man once, who can say. But like the king, the lust for power has become too strong in him. That nebulous notion of purity? It is in him, too. Let the merciful Three shield us from man's ideals of purity."

Merlin looked more tired than when she had entered. Guiltily, I knew I was putting her through this. This verbal test of her own endurance–and mine. But I could not stop.

"What else?"

"The war continues. The land burns. We prevail."

"We are winning, you mean?"

"Somehow, despite war on three fronts, we have not yet lost. When the people starve and the land burns and the people in other lands starve and burn as well... I cannot call that winning."

"What about the food shortages?" I asked.

"Few complain these days. The king has ensured the capital has more than elsewhere. Who can complain when that is the case? Some praise the king's wisdom in ensuring Camelot would have more than others." Her lips twisted bleakly.

"His wisdom? He set aside food because he knew this would happen," I said. "He took care of himself, nothing more. True foresight would have been preparing without knowing he was staging an invasion. Warmongering, treacherous bastard."

"Most here would agree with you. Though they are prudent enough not to speak such thoughts aloud," Merlin remarked.

Despite myself, I was growing sleepy. I stifled a yawn.

"Any other terrible things you think I should know about?"

"I think you should go to sleep. Your body needs rest right now more than it does knowledge. Especially knowledge that will depress your spirits. There is enough hopelessness in your heart to deal with right now, Lancelet, without my adding to it."

They were wise words and what was more they were true, but would I heed them?

Was my name Lancelet de Troyes?

"Tell me," I said mutinously. "Tell me everything."

Merlin gave me a contemplative look then slowly nodded. "Perhaps knowing there are people faring far worse than you will leave you with something to contemplate besides your own plight."

"I am already aware," I claimed. But was I? Didn't I have it worse than anyone? Part of me wondered how Merlin could deny it. Chunks of my flesh had been ripped away by human mouths. How many in Pendrath could say the same?

And then Merlin spoke and my self-righteousness dissolved.

"Arthur has taken up collecting captives," Merlin began, her voice tight. She did not like to speak of this then. "He keeps the tributes in a special part of the castle. Mostly women, of course." She cleared her throat. "Those who are favored in his court and even some of the soldiers who have stood out in battle may... access the collection."

"Access it?" My belly heaved. "What the fuck does that mean? Is it a library?"

"Use your vivid imagination, Lancelet," Merlin said wearily. "I shan't be elaborating. As long as the captives are returned to the collection in mostly one piece, anything is permitted."

I was revolted. "Prisoners? These people are all prisoners?"

In the past, in times of war, captives were relatively well-treated. There were rules for such things, even in war.

But Arthur had set the rules aside.

"From Tintagel and Lyonesse mostly, yes. Our former allies. Our former friends." Merlin's voice was bitter. "As for his own court, Arthur has not restrained his sensuous evils there either. He has formed a new circle of advisors to serve him. Only men. He demands the wives and daughters of all of the men who wish entrance to this elite group serve him as well. However he pleases."

"Such a man as this does not deserve to live," I growled, feeling the rage building in my heart. I stoked the rage. Let it grow. Let it build. Let it burn. Perhaps I might eventually hate Arthur more than I hated myself. "Let me leave here. Let me kill him."

"We do not even know precisely where he is right now," Merlin said. "I believe he has left Camelot to inspect the troops on one of the frontlines. But I admire your... spirit."

She stood up and stretched. "I think that is enough for now. It is all I can manage for one night. I will see you in the morning, Lancelet. But now do you see? There is something worth living for. Even if it is only a shallow desire for vengeance. We all feel it. Even I."

"I will remember," I promised her. "I will not make you recount this all again. Your words are burned in my mind."

She smiled at me—a smile so full of love it reminded me with a pang of my own mother. Was she still safe in Camelot?

"My family," I choked out quickly before Merlin could leave.

"They are well," she assured me. "Your parents have taken the children to your grandparents in the country." She hesitated. "We have sent a message to them, letting them know you are alive. We will speak more of them in the morning, if you like."

And then she stepped out into the hall, closing the door behind her and leaving me all alone once more.

THE END

Empress of Fae, Book 3 in the Blood of a Fae series, is out now!

Not ready to say goodbye to Morgan, Draven, and the world of Aercanum?

Wishing this book had even more steam?

Head over to my website to sign-up for my newsletter and receive a bonus steamy scene.

This special scene offers a spicy "what if?" moment for Draven and Morgan.

Grab the FREE bonus scene and hear about the latest new releases, giveaways, and other bookish treats:

https://briarboleyn.com

TRIGGER WARNINGS

Abduction

Abuse

Alcohol Consumption

Amputation

Animal Abuse

Animal Death

Cannibalism

Child Abuse

Child Death

Decapitation

Deceased Family Member

Domestic Violence

Drug Use

Homophobia

Infant Loss / Death

Infertility

Murder

Physical Abuse

Poisoning

Slut Shaming

Violence / Gore

ALSO BY BRIAR BOLEYN

Blood of a Fae Series

Queen of Roses

Court of Claws

Empress of Fae

Knight of the Goddess (Coming 2024)

Written as Fenna Edgewood...

The Gardner Girls Series

Masks of Desire (The Gardner Girls' Parents' Story)

Mistakes Not to Make When Avoiding a Rake (Claire's Story)

To All the Earls I've Loved Before (Gwen's Story)

The Seafaring Lady's Guide to Love (Rosalind's Story)

Once Upon a Midwinter's Kiss (Gracie's Story)

The Gardner Girls' Extended Christmas Epilogue (Caroline & John's Story – Available to Newsletter Subscribers)

Must Love Scandal Series

How to Get Away with Marriage (Hugh's Story)

The Duke Report (Cherry's Story)

A Duke for All Seasons (Lance's Story)

The Bluestocking Beds Her Bride (Fleur & Julia's Story)

Blakeley Manor Series

The Countess's Christmas Groom

Lady Briar Weds the Scot

Kiss Me, My Duke

My So-Called Scoundrel

ABOUT THE AUTHOR

Briar Boleyn is the fantasy romance pen name of USA TODAY bestselling author Fenna Edgewood. Briar rules over a kingdom of feral wildling children with a dark fae prince as her consort. When she isn't busy bringing new worlds to life, she can be found playing RPG video games, watching the birds at her bird feeder and pretending she's Snow White, or being sucked into a captivating book. Her favorite stories are the ones full of danger, magic, and true love.

Find Briar around the web at:

https://www.instagram.com/briarboleynauthor/

https://www.bookbub.com/profile/briar-boleyn

https://www.tiktok.com/@authorbriarboleyn

Made in the USA
Las Vegas, NV
02 April 2024

88156193R00236